MARION
LANE

AND THE

MIDNIGHT
MURDER

MARION
LANE

MIDNIGHT
MURDER

T.A.
WILLBERG

ORION

First published in Great Britain in 2021 by Trapeze
This paperback edition published in 2022 by Orion Fiction,
an imprint of The Orion Publishing Group Ltd
Carmelite House, 50 Victoria Embankment
London EC4Y 0DZ

An Hachette UK Company

1 3 5 7 9 10 8 6 4 2

A CIP catalogue record for this book is
available from the British Library.

ISBN (Mass Market Paperback) 9781409196655
ISBN (eBook) 978 1 4091 9666 2

Typeset by Born Group
Printed and bound in Great Britain by Clays Ltd, Elcograf S.p.A.

www.orionbooks.co.uk

For Marion, Werner and Ben

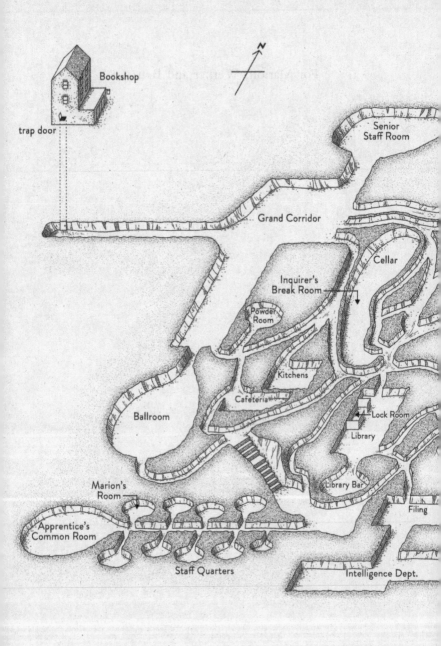

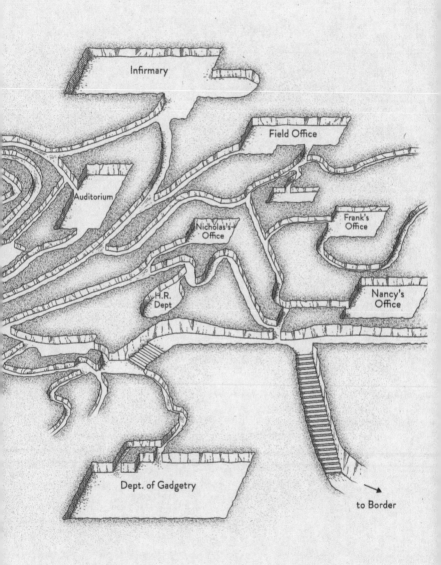

I

The Secret Stealer

Somewhere in London.
Friday 11 April, 1958
11.40 p.m.

Threads of steam rose from the warm tarmac. The alleyway was quiet tonight, the perfect setting for the conveyance of secrets. The woman in the red headscarf checked over her shoulder. No one would have followed her, but she had to be sure.

She stopped three yards from the lamp post and pulled a torch and one sealed envelope from her bag. She knew exactly where the disguised letter case was hidden – on the left, shoulder height, behind the brick that looked a little different from its neighbours – but that wasn't the cause of her indecision. What she planned to do tonight would alter the course of someone's future.

Her grip on the torch handle tightened as she struggled against herself. There were so many reasons to walk away, the potential repercussions of what she planned to do numerous and terrifying. And yet . . . if there was one thing she truly believed in, one thing that mattered more than any of that, it was the truth.

For seven years she'd kept a sickening secret. For seven years she'd held her tongue, bound by the unbreakable oath of those in her trade. But she felt it now more than ever – how much the secret had consumed her, how unbearable its burden had become. If she did not do this tonight, she doubted whether she'd ever forgive herself.

She nodded to herself in the dark, quiet alleyway. Yes, the truth was worth the risk. But with the night pulling swiftly onwards, she knew she had to hurry. She directed the beam of her torch at the wall and there it was – a single grey brick that reflected the light. Metal, not brick. She tapped the thing with the butt of her torch.

Once. Nothing.

Twice (a more confident tap) and the dirty grey block shrunk back into the wall. There was a soft click and, out from where the brick had been, a thin metal plate extended.

Despite the brisk wind now whipping through the alleyway, the woman in the red headscarf began to sweat. She placed the envelope on the metal plate and watched as letter and plate slipped back into the wall and disappeared. She let out a long breath and wiped the perspiration from her brow – the secret was no longer hers alone to bear.

She knew exactly where the envelope would end up, with those people under the ground, those mysterious types who dwelled in the shadows – the Inquirers. They were a band of private detectives who lived beneath the streets of London in a labyrinth of twisted tunnels and ancient hallways, the entrance to which no one had ever found. The Inquirers were something of a myth to the citizens of London, a whispered legend that may or may not exist, depending on whom you asked. But to those who believed, the Inquirers had gained a somewhat ambiguous reputation. They were like ghosts, some said, sleuths who guarded the city. Nameless. Silent. Forever bound to linger in darkness. And while almost everyone had heard about the hundred-and-something secret postboxes (known as letter cases) hidden in concealed locations throughout the city, into which one was encouraged to place suspicions of criminal behaviour, tip-offs and requests, no one was quite sure what happened after that.

Where did the letters go? How did they get there and who was going to read them? Fresh rumours surfaced every few months – *letters are pulled by a string through the wall and into a room just beyond* – was a favourite until someone smashed down a wall in which a letter case was thought to be, and in doing so brought the entire south-facing wall of Mr Silverton's Garage crumbling to the ground. No string, no secret room, just a pile of bricks and a metal pipe that appeared to feed into the ground – a water pipe, most probably.

There were similar concerns about the effectiveness of the Inquirers' investigative skills, since many people who'd claimed to have sent forth a tip-off were yet to see anything come of it. More sensible individuals, however, said that this was simply because the Inquirers did not have the time or resources to bother with concerns of a *personal nature* – cheating husbands, lost pets and the like.

Resources, as it happens, were another topic of hot debate. How did the Inquirers, who never asked for so much as a penny (or a thank you) manage to finance such an elaborate and apparently well-oiled system?

The woman in the red headscarf preferred not to think about any of that, happy to rest in the assurance that the Inquirers were no myth. Having had the very unfortunate experience of meeting a few of them, she knew for certain they were as real as the grimy street beneath her feet. But if anyone asked for her opinion, she'd say they caused more trouble than they claimed to resolve. She'd heard the stories, like everybody else – corrupt businessmen brought to justice, lost children returned to their parents, criminals forced to confess – but had anyone ever asked how? Had anyone cared to dig a little deeper, where bones were buried and lies entombed?

In fact, the woman in the red headscarf would never have considered contacting the Inquirers at all, had the matter not involved one of their own.

She clicked her tongue in disapproval as she walked back up the street, hopeful she was done with the Inquirers and their dubious methods and relieved to be on her way back to her armchair by the fire and a piping hot cup of tea. And maybe a slice of fruitcake.

Envelope encased, the carrier cylinder travelled through miles of pneumatic pipes from its place of origin to the dark, deep dungeon of the Filing Department – falling neatly from the end of the pipe and into the corresponding receiver box, as if delivered by some magical, invisible postman.

A bell chimed as the envelope landed in receiver box fifty-five.

Michelle White's eyes shot open as she lurched back from the edge of sleep. She blinked at the flashing yellow light on the noticeboard above her. It was her job to ensure all letters were sorted the minute they arrived: those that met agency requirements were to be organised by date and slipped into the Inquirers' in-tray for later investigation. Those that did not went straight into the rubbish bin, and those which she was unsure what to do with, into a looming pile on the desk. But crime and crookedness had been on the decline the last few weeks in London and so, assuming the letter would be a lead on something petty, Michelle White staggered across the Filing Department in no particular hurry.

She lifted the lid on receiver box fifty-five, the endpoint of a six-mile pneumatic tube that fed off from a letter case hidden in Passing Alley in Farringdon.

Envelopes and letters pulled from the receiver boxes were

usually addressed to the agency in general: *Dear people under the ground*, or similar.

But tonight was different.

To Miss M. White, Inquirer.

It was odd, yet she couldn't help smile at the thought of it. Michelle had once dreamed of becoming an Inquirer; she had come so close to the reality, too. But she was just not good enough. Not clever enough, not brave or talented enough. Not quite anything enough.

Ten years ago, at the age of twenty-two, she'd been recruited from a textile factory where she'd toiled long hours as a quality control assistant. But like everyone who came to work in the sunless labyrinth, Michelle had swiftly and without much consideration renounced the liberties of her previous, lacklustre life in exchange for the opportunity to begin a new and thrilling vocation as an Inquirer, where she'd hoped to finally make use of her very particular set of skills.

But things had not quite turned out that way, which is why – instead of scouring London's streets for criminals and delinquents – Michelle had ended up here, spending her evenings as the night-duty filing assistant in the establishment's dullest department. In fact, had it not been for her other, far more satisfying role – that of Chief Border Guard, protector of the secret – then perhaps she would have quit years ago.

But now Michelle wondered, as she stared at the envelope in her hand, how whoever had sent it knew where she worked or why they had considered *her* the worthy counsel of their troubles. She ran her thumb over the words – *Miss M White, Inquirer* – as if they might be absorbed through her skin and become true.

For a moment she was reluctant to open the envelope, concerned it might be a joke. One of the young apprentices playing a trick. She clenched her jaw at the thought, breathed, then entered the letter's details into the register file: time and date received, receiver box number and her initials. But when she opened the envelope and read the final detail – the nature of the inquiry – her breath began to quicken.

The letter was short. A name, a time, a place and one simple revelation. And yet it unleashed a torrent of angst.

Several weeks ago, something had gone missing from her handbag – something invaluable, irreplaceable, something that might dredge up a secret long since buried across The Border. At first she'd been so certain of who had taken it, and for countless nights thereafter she'd turned in her sleep, anxious the nasty thief would soon come looking for the paired device she kept locked in her private office, and with that the secret would be uncovered.

But if the letter she'd just received was to be trusted, Michelle's anxieties had been misplaced – the secret had already been discovered. She wasn't sure how, or even why, but if she followed the letter's directions, she might soon find out.

Though sirens of warning blared in her head, Michelle had already made up her mind. Of course she could take the letter to someone more qualified than herself, but it had been addressed to her – whoever had sent it had entrusted her with this, a most precious and urgent secret. And besides, as the letter had said, if only for tonight – Miss White was an Inquirer.

As instructed in the letter, she lit a match and held the paper over the flame. Once it had turned to ash, she packed up her things, grabbed her handbag, locked the office and rushed up the staircase towards the library. She stopped at the Lock Room gate, far on the other side of the grand hall of glorious bookshelves. The gate was ajar, just as she'd expected.

She stepped inside, pausing immediately as a wave of something cool and cutting passed in front of her, a curious thing. She rubbed her eyes and looked around the dully lit room, at the hundreds of steel drawers; safes which held the agency's most hallowed files and documents. The Lock Room, with its thick walls and high ceiling, was always chilly, but tonight it felt particularly so.

CRACK.

Something split from the wall behind her. She turned to the sound but saw only a shadow move across the room and something that looked like a large black box being removed from inside the wall. She hesitated, then moved a little closer. But it came again – a wave of cool air, dancing in front of her. She dabbed her eyes with the cuff of her sleeve – they were now surely playing tricks on her, for everything had turned to a strange blur of nothing. Michelle started to panic, her thoughts as unfocused as her vision. Her head began to spin. Her limbs tingled. This might have been the moment she ran for her life, out of the Lock Room and away from the evil she now knew had been waiting for her there. But terror had immobilised her. There was nothing she could do to get her legs to move, not even when she heard the rush of footsteps, some behind her, some in front. Not even when she felt the brush of air against her neck.

'What's happening,' she asked in a staggered groan. 'I know you're there . . . I know it was you . . .' She trailed off, the words in her head no longer making sense.

She dropped her handbag. Something hard rolled out and across the floor. She was too disorientated to realise what it was.

In a drawn-out moment that seemed to last forever, Michelle's senses grew dull and viscous. She could no longer trust her eyesight or her hearing. She might have seen an amorphous shape crouching in front of her. She might have seen it lift something from the floor. Certainly, however, she felt the sharp burn of a cold, ragged blade as it sunk quickly and easily through the delicate skin across her throat.

Warmth, darkness and nothing more.

2

16 Willow Street

Screwdriver in hand, Marion Lane secured the last steel feather into place, restoring the clockwork sunbird from a pile of metal and springs to its glorious former self. She turned it over, wound up the key hidden beneath the left wing and waited. Just as before, however, nothing happened.

She groaned as she placed the bird on her windowsill, packed away her leather roll of tools and peered down at the street below. As ever, there was little to be seen that bitter morning: a lone cat in search of misadventure, detritus collecting on the pavement, the milkman setting fresh bottles on doorsteps. And of course, the For Sale sign nailed to her front door, as it had been for nearly a year.

It was here, right in the fetid heart of the East End, in a ramshackle two-storey terrace on Willow Street, that Marion had spent her entire existence. For twenty-three years she'd lived within the boundaries of what she knew, not daring to imagine that another life awaited her – one far removed from the mundane and ordinary. Another world, one to which she truly belonged.

And while Marion had discovered this new world four months ago, on the surface it appeared that her life was just the same as ever. She still lived on Willow Street with her grandmother, in a bedroom filled with objects of an exceedingly unremarkable nature, apart from the gilded metal songbird of course.

There was an ordinary single bed in the corner, a partially unpacked briefcase lying on top. There was an ordinary dresser just opposite, stacked with piles of unused parchment, books and two framed photographs: one of the father Marion had barely known, who'd died in the war not long after her fifth birthday, and one of Marion and her mother, Alice. This second photo, taken on Marion's sixteenth birthday, was not particularly flattering for either woman – the lighting dull, the angle awkward and unnatural – and yet for Marion it held the last fond memory she had of her mother, a fleeting moment in which Alice had at least pretended to be happy.

A ray of pale morning sun filtered through her bedroom window, catching just the tip of the bird's tail feather and bringing Marion back to the present. It had been a mistake to offer Bill her assistance in figuring out what was wrong with the thing, though their plan seemed infallible at the time. Marion, mechanically minded as she was, would take the bird home over the weekend and dismantle it. She would check its interior for loose joints, a misaligned anchor, an unsuitable driving weight, making a note of what she found.

Meanwhile, five miles away in a flat nearly as musty and miserable as her own, Bill would bury himself in a hoard of peculiar reference books in the hopes that somewhere, somehow, he'd find a paragraph on what made clockwork birds defective. They'd convene on Monday with all the answers and this, their first project together, would be a successful one. She'd assumed that for her at least, the task would be simple. The sunbird contraption – with its gleaming exterior, yet complicated and delicate core – was one she'd found herself particularly drawn to and whose inner workings she'd become

9

so familiar with. But again, she was reminded that nothing at her new job was quite as simple as it seemed.

For the past four months, Marion and Bill had worked as apprentices at an obscure bookstore that hardly anyone had heard of that stood at the end of a cul-de-sac with no name, just beyond the borders of Eel Brook Common in Fulham: Miss Brickett's Secondhand Books and Curiosities. The shop's only piece of furniture was a butler's desk that served as a reception table, though this was quite unnecessary as Miss Brickett's never had any customers. Of course the desk had another more practical role, but this, much like the existence of the metallic sunbird, was a secret Marion and Bill were forbidden to divulge.

The bedroom door swung open now and Marion's grandmother, Dolores Hacksworth, stepped inside. She eyed the gleaming sunbird suspiciously and looked for a moment as if she might ask what it was. Thankfully, she became distracted by a sight far more alarming.

'Now, darling,' Dolores said with that displeased, twisted frown she wore so frequently, 'what have you done to your hair?'

Marion patted down the nest of short and unruly brown locks that she'd never once paid any attention to. Much like the rest of her appearance. 'I haven't done anything to it, actually. I've just woken up.'

'Well that's just it, isn't it,' Dolores said as she inspected Marion's hair from above with scrupulous attention. 'Dull and lifeless, darling. And you're far too thin. Whatever do you eat at that bookshop?'

Marion considered pointing out that her hair had been just as *dull and lifeless* when she'd been on a diet of Dolores' cooking three meals a day, seven days a week. But she decided against the idea as she still had forty-eight hours of uninterrupted Dolores to endure. She needed to conserve her energy.

'Do run a brush through it at the very least, darling,' Dolores went on, 'and . . .' she turned her eyes to the sealed envelope on Marion's bedside table. 'Oh for goodness sake, you still haven't answered Mr Smithers' letter? It's probably an invitation to his birthday, which might be your last chance to make an impression.' She looked at Marion with her chin tilted to the floor in a way that doubled over the flaps of her neck.

'I've had a busy week.'

Dolores' face flushed with irritation. 'Busy?'

'Yes . . .' Marion hesitated. It wasn't a lie, her week *had* been busy, especially after Wednesday when Marion, Bill and Jessica (another apprentice) had been tasked with sorting through boxes of supplies destined for Miss Brickett's Workshop but which resulted in an unfortunate incident as one of the *supplies* escaped from the box and proved particularly problematic to catch again (and switch off). But Marion couldn't say any of this and so, as usual, she came up with a rather dull alternative: 'One of the bookshelves caved in . . . it took two days to mend and another day to re-stack.'

Dolores gave a nasal, supercilious laugh. 'Two days to mend?'

Marion inhaled and counted to five before answering, having read somewhere in Dolores' recent issue of *Good Housekeeping* that this might stem discomposure, or any such un-ladylike reactions. 'Yes. Two days and a bit.'

Dolores examined her more carefully still. She did not believe the lie, that was clear enough. 'Well, be that as it may,' she said at last and with a little reservation, 'you needn't be so coy with the man. Mr Smithers sent that letter two weeks ago. He was very taken with you, you know.'

'Yes, I can see that. But unfortunately I wasn't taken with him.'

'You do know that he is set to take over the family business? Smithers Furniture and Supplies, do you know how well they've been doing, financially? You would step into a

11

very comfortable life. Not everybody gets a chance like that and I really think—'

'He only met me once,' Marion interrupted, unwilling to engage in yet another lengthy discussion on Mr Smithers' future prospects. 'He wasn't interested in anything I had to say. We talked mostly about the weather. And besides, I'm nearly twenty-four.'

Dolores narrowed her eyes even further so that she was now looking out of mere slits. 'Nearly twenty-four? That is quite the point, dear girl! I was seventeen when I married and your mother was—' she paused. A short, difficult silence. 'I just wish you would give me a chance.'

'You?'

'Yes, me. I have tried so hard to help you, so very hard and all you do is make a joke of things.'

Marion's chest tightened as she rubbed the worn leather watch strap on her wrist, the last gift from her mother. She knew what was coming next – a discussion on how her grandmother had been so kind to move in after Alice had died, how generous she'd been to pay the rent, buy the food and even find Marion the perfect husband. All things she ought to be grateful for. All things Alice would have wanted for her daughter. But it wasn't true. There was only one thing Alice had wanted for Marion and it wasn't marriage, it wasn't a husband or a life governed by societal rules. It was something Alice had never really had herself. Happiness.

Marion got to her feet and turned her attention to the sunbird, the only way she might stall the tears. 'I'm not making a joke. I like my life as it is. I just wish you'd accept that.'

Dolores paused. Perhaps she was counting to five? 'You'd really like to spend the rest of your life working at a bookshop? That is enough for you?'

Marion wanted to say so many things in response, things that were cutting and intelligent, that would make Dolores feel foolish and insignificant, just as Marion now felt herself. Yet as always, the words remained lodged in her throat, fully formed and completely unspoken.

'Well, exactly. That's just what I thought,' Dolores said. Again, she'd won.

It was a brilliant stroke of luck that, just then, right as Dolores looked ready to say something more, the doorbell rang.

Dolores' eyes darted to the window.

The doorbell rang a second time.

'See who that is!' she snapped.

Marion gathered her reserve and peered down at the street outside their front door. Of all the people she'd expected to see standing there, Frank Stone would have been the very last.

'Well?' Dolores said.

Marion pulled herself back inside. 'It's for me, I think.'

'For you?' Dolores walked over to the window.

Dolores had met Frank a few times before, as he'd been an old friend of Marion's mother. Most recently Frank and Dolores had encountered one another when he'd arrived to offer Marion the job at the bookshop four months ago. Unfortunately, that being the second time Marion had rushed to accept a job of unfavourable standards, Frank's offer was met with a considerable amount of reluctance from Dolores.

At eighteen, two years after her mother had died and Dolores had moved in, Marion had been desperate to escape the long and meaningless days at 16 Willow Street. But armed with little education and no talents to speak of, opportunities were scarce. Impossibly so for women.

After many months of trying, however, Marion was offered a clerical position at a dingy auto repair shop. The shop's owner, Felix, was a kind though impractical man who'd refused to close his once thriving workshop in the dull years that followed the war. With rising taxes, food shortages and a people carved hollow with grief, there were few who owned motor vehicles, and even fewer who bothered to have them repaired professionally.

Nonetheless, Felix persisted and although his dreams of bountiful custom never did come true, he found in Marion something more than he'd expected: a skilled and untiring assistant, willing to do whatever work was necessary. Thus, Felix passed onto Marion his passion for all things metal, oil and rubber. For the next five years of her life, she spent her days wrestling with wheel nuts, resurrecting engines, exchanging spark plugs and distributor caps. And amid the chaos and destitution of post-war London, Marion, like Felix before her, found solace in the quiet assurances of gliding gears, rotating screws and coiling springs. The logical assemblage of machinery became her only comfort in an otherwise coarse and bristly existence.

But by the time Marion turned twenty-three, Felix's health had taken a drastic turn for the worse and after so many years of toil and disappointment, his heart finally delivered its closing beat. On 8 July, 1957 the workshop shut down and Marion was left once again unemployed, dejected and alone.

Or so she assumed.

What she didn't know was that the skills Felix had passed on to her had not gone unnoticed. Miles beneath the streets on the other side of London, an arrangement for Marion's future had already been made. Much to Dolores' later despair.

Frank rang the bell a third time, then rapped his knuckles on the door.

'For heaven's sake!' Dolores said. 'What is he doing here?'

'No idea,' Marion said honestly, attempting to keep her voice casual and unsurprised, not at all how she felt. She sped past her grandmother and down the stairs to the front door.

Frank, recruitment officer for the bookshop and head of the apprenticeship programme, stood at the threshold. As he had the day they'd met, he wore a bowler hat and Chester coat.

'What are you doing here?' she asked under her breath.

'Morning, Marion,' he said with a hint of impatience as he removed his hat and peered over her shoulder.

Dolores, who'd managed to tiptoe down the stairs very quickly for her age, pushed Marion aside with a firm hand. She eyed Frank with annoyance. 'Can I help you?'

Frank smiled and, as always, Marion was encompassed by a profound warmth, a feeling of strength and serenity that entered every cell in her body. A feeling she imagined a father should provide.

Frank extended his hand in greeting. 'Good morning, Mrs Hacksworth.'

Dolores pursed her thin red lips and without preamble lurched into an attack. 'Marion received a marriage proposal the day you offered her that job. Mr Smithers of Smithers Furniture and Supplies. They had just had their best year of sales and he even offered Marion a share. Did you know that?'

Frank continued to smile, though a little less brightly. 'I did not. How wonderful!'

Dolores sniffed. 'It *was*.'

'He changed his mind, did he?'

'Of course he changed his mind! What man would be interested in a woman who works twelve hours a day at some ridiculous bookshop? For a pittance, I might add.'

'Oh, yes,' Frank said thoughtfully, 'I can see how that might be a little off-putting, but you know I'm quite sure—'

'I don't care what you know for sure.' She took a deep breath. 'Why are you here?'

Frank slipped his hand into the bag slung over his shoulder.

He pulled forth an envelope. 'As it happens, I came to speak to you, Mrs Hacksworth.'

After a long pause, during which Marion's heart rate doubled, Frank spoke again. This time he looked only at Marion.

'Just a small matter of paperwork,' he said with an attempt at reassurance, 'we need a next-of-kin to sign a few things.'

'Sign a few things? Such as? If you think I'm going to—' Dolores, who Marion was certain was about to launch into a lengthy diatribe about how unlikely it was that she would agree to do anything Frank asked her to, stopped. Marion wasn't sure why, but thought she noticed Dolores' gaze hover over something written on a piece of paper sticking from the end of Frank's envelope. Before Marion could see what it was, he slipped the envelope under his coat.

'Should we have some tea, then?' he asked.

In one swift movement, Dolores both nodded and turned around, leading Frank past Marion and into the kitchen.

'Ah, Marion, I forgot,' Frank said as he and Dolores settled at the table, 'would you fetch the spare keys I gave you last week for the bookshop? I seem to have misplaced mine . . .'

After a moment of horror-induced immobility, Marion made her way up the stairs. Leaving Dolores and Frank alone was terrifying. What if, in the time it took her to fetch the keys and return to the kitchen, Dolores had managed to convince Frank that hiring Marion had been a mistake and that she really would be better off married and unemployed? What if her grandmother was about to destroy the only thing in Marion's life that had ever been worth having? What if, just four months after she'd finally found a world in which she belonged, it was all about to be taken away?

She hurried over to her bed and opened the briefcase she still hadn't unpacked from the night before. Underneath a layer of semi-folded clothes she found a pair of binoculars with oddly curved lenses, a tennis-ball-sized light orb (still glowing a soft white) and a Miss Brickett's Policies and Regulations booklet, dog-eared on page thirty-three: *first-year apprentice general conduct and procedure*.

She paused. There were no spare keys amid the mess and, now that she came to think of it, she didn't remember Frank ever giving her any. She walked over to her bedroom door, partly to check the bunch of keys hanging in the keyhole, partly to eavesdrop on the conversation downstairs.

'. . . you could have saved us all the trouble and not come here in the first place,' said Dolores, her foghorn voice easily reaching the landing.

'I knew what I was doing then. And I don't regret it, but these are . . . unforeseeable circumstances.'

'Unforeseeable?' Dolores' voice was tight with scepticism. 'In that case, perhaps you should consider employing me instead. I predicted this would—'

'Quite impossible, I'm afraid,' Frank interrupted. 'Just let me know by Friday and everything can be arranged.'

'Very well,' Dolores said.

There was a short silence.

'Thank you. And, again, I'm sorry for all this. But I've explained my reasoning as best I can.'

There was the sound of scraping chairs as the two got to their feet.

'Wonderful to see you again, Mrs Hacksworth.'

Marion rushed halfway down the stairs. Frank was already at the front door. 'Frank? I couldn't find the spare. You can have mine though?'

'Oh no, not to worry,' he said hurriedly, placing his bowler hat on his head and opening the door. 'Perhaps it wasn't you I gave them to after all. See you on Monday.' After a curt nod to Dolores, he stepped outside. By the time Marion had reached the threshold, all that could be seen was a flash of Frank's tawny coat as he disappeared around the last bend on Willow Street.

'What did he say to you?' Marion asked as she wandered into the kitchen.

Dolores was standing over the sink, washing the dishes with hands that Marion could see were trembling.

'Papers,' she mumbled almost incoherently, 'papers to sign. Emergency contact, telephone number, that sort of thing.'

'I heard him say something about—'

'What on earth you need an emergency contact for, working at a bookshop, I have no idea . . .' Dolores continued as if she hadn't heard.

Marion didn't answer. There was nothing she could say that wouldn't give away too much. But Dolores was also concealing a truth. Marion had given Frank Dolores' details as her emergency contact the day she started at the bookshop. The same day she'd signed a pile of classified documents all guaranteeing she would never be able to reveal what she saw, or what she did beyond the doors of Miss Brickett's Secondhand Books and Curiosities.

She made her way back upstairs, leaving behind the strange disquiet that now lingered in the kitchen. She sat down on the chair by the windowsill and picked up the sunbird once more, only half aware of what she was doing, her mind caught up in other, darker thoughts. Whatever documents Frank had asked Dolores to sign, it was clear he'd wanted Marion to know nothing of them. But what could Frank possibly tell Dolores that he couldn't tell her? Had she broken some policy at the bookshop she hadn't even known about? Overlooked an administrative detail that would necessitate her dismissal?

Perhaps she'd have lost herself in further uncomfortable thoughts, had the clockwork sunbird in her grasp not suddenly began to convulse. Somehow, she'd managed to bring the

18

contraption to life – exactly what she'd been trying to do all morning. Its metallic wings extended outwards, pushing against Marion's palms. Sharp edges dug into her flesh as the bird struggled against her and eventually she had no choice but to release it. It fluttered up to the ceiling in a purposeful, mechanical motion, coming to rest on the exposed roof beam above her bed. Where, most frustratingly, it stayed all weekend.

3

The Other Miss Brickett's

Marion slipped into her customary uniform – grey and black striped knee-length pencil skirt and white cotton blouse – said a hasty goodbye to Dolores (who had barely made eye contact with her since Frank's visit) and stepped out onto the street. As on every Monday since the start of the year, she slammed the front door of 16 Willow Street behind her in relief.

After a short walk to Upton Park Station, Marion took the District Line towards Wimbledon, coming to a stop at Fulham Broadway. From there she made her way on foot to the western boundary of Eel Brook Common, finally arriving at a decrepit Georgian building, so old that it seemed almost spectral: Miss Brickett's Secondhand Books and Curiosities – the bookshop that had nothing to do with the business of selling books. Though the shop's facade – black-framed bow-fronted windows of frosted glass, dark green paint peeling from the surrounding walls – was meant to deter potential customers, Marion often felt it achieved the opposite. But perhaps it attracted only those who were, like the bookshop itself, *different* – those who didn't quite fit in.

It was here, in a world of dim tunnels concealed below the old shop, that Marion's apprenticeship really took place. For the next three years, she and several other carefully selected recruits were to complete an arduous probationary period after which (if indeed the apprentices had proved themselves capable and worthy) they'd be offered full-time employment (with the option of board and lodging) at Miss Brickett's.

The apprenticeship was designed to prepare recruits for the elusive world of a very particular style of private detection. And while scores of private-eye establishments existed elsewhere in London, charging a fortune for cases the police couldn't be bothered with, Miss Brickett's served the city in a way no other organisation could. Recruits here were trained to track suspects without being seen, listen to conversations without being noticed, enter buildings without invitation. They were expected to conceal the extraordinary behind a facade of mundane and austere, to fade into the backdrop of everyday London and become invisible to all but those who knew how to look. Perhaps more than anything, however, it was Miss Brickett's collection of wondrous gadgets – pioneered and assembled in secret within its walls – that truly set the agency, and all those who trained there, apart.

Marion paused for a moment outside the shop. The frosted-glass windows glimmered like dark jewels in the morning sun, a taste of the mystique that existed behind them. After ensuring she was alone in the cul-de-sac, she slipped a small brass key into the lock at the bottom of the bookshop door, a seemingly impenetrable wrought-iron barrier embossed with strange figures, ghouls, clocks and other indistinguishable designs. The key turned itself 360 degrees clockwise, 90 degrees anti-clockwise and then, as usual, spat itself out of the keyhole. She caught it, only just. Next, extracting a larger silver key from her purse, she opened the second lock located near the handle. She pulled down a lever disguised as a gas lamp and finally the door clicked open.

She squeezed herself into the cramped shop. Even for someone so ungenerously padded, manoeuvring through the tight rows of dusty, precariously stacked bookshelves required a certain amount of finesse. It was dark too, the light switch inconveniently positioned at the other end of the shop. All things considered, it was no wonder she tripped over the body lying next to the reception desk.

'Lord have mercy!' said the body as it sat upright, catching Marion just before her head collided with the sharp corner of the desk. 'Are you all right?'

Marion recovered herself, stood up and switched on the light. 'Mr Nicholas?' she said, her eyes adjusting in disbelief. 'Yes . . . I'm fine. What on earth are you doing here?' It was a silly question, she realised, as she watched Mr Nicholas – head of security at Miss Brickett's, a rotund man with thinning blond hair and an angular scar that cut across his right eyebrow – gather up his sheet and pillow from the floor.

'Very sorry about that,' he said, checking his watch. 'I overslept.'

'Is something the matter?' Marion asked, certain the answer must be yes.

'No no, just a precaution. Just a precaution.' He threw on a thick woollen coat. 'But thank you for waking me. Frightful business going on,' he added, a little more softly. 'Have a good day, Miss Lane.' He grabbed a bunch of keys from behind the butler's desk and disappeared from the shop before Marion had a chance to ask any further questions. Just like Frank, Mr Nicholas had long since mastered the art of swift departures.

'Frightful business,' Marion muttered to herself as she rounded the corner hidden behind the butler's desk. Mr Nicholas had a flair for dramatics, she reminded herself as she pushed the matter from her mind and turned into a short passage, at the end of which was a blank wall and a box of old books. She crouched down and pulled at the fourth floorboard from the right, the only one that had a metal ring secured in its centre. The floorboard reluctantly creaked up, and she stepped down onto the stairs that led into the dark below.

On reaching the bottom, she made her way along another short passage that led to a single steel door. In the dim light, Marion extracted from her bag a silver badge delicately engraved with the letter *A* and pressed it into an indentation in the wall. The door slipped away, she pinned the badge to her chest and stepped inside the lift. She didn't need to choose a floor: it would shudder to a halt only at the very bottom, deep below the bookshop and the streets of London, opening up to the smooth marble-floored entrance of the real Miss Brickett's: Miss Brickett's Investigations and Inquiries.

The Grand Corridor, as it was called, resembled the interior of a Roman basilica. The corridor was vast, both in breadth and length, with vaulted ceilings supported by columns of gleaming pale marble. Standing guard at each column were four-foot-tall brass lamps, carved into the shape of winged men, their hands outstretched, spilling their generous light into the space around them. The statues' eyes followed Marion as she strode past, swivelling cameras that registered the presence of every visitor – of which there were many.

Apart from the apprentices, the establishment was staffed by a legion of permanent, live-in employees: seven high council members, six heads of department, assistants, mechanics and a handful of cleaning and general maintenance staff. Among them all, however, there were none Marion admired as much as the Inquirers – the agency's fully trained private detectives – the only individuals who might one day find their names on the gold-plated exhibit at the end of the Grand Corridor: Cases & Inquirers of Honorary Mention. Marion often paused to admire this gleaming plaque, and more than once she'd imagined her own name immortalised in gold.

Judging from the number of names and dates etched into the display, the early fifties had been the agency's busiest time – a period of London's regrowth and transformation and a time in which Miss Brickett's had secured the respect and admiration of the city.

During the Great Smog of 1952, as London fell into darkness and chaos, the air choked with pollution and fear, the agency was overwhelmed with panicked complaints of looting, vandalism and road rage. And so the Inquirers, long since accustomed to dimness and drudgery, took to the streets: a wave of invisible guardians, armed with glowing orbs and an eye for the untoward.

What impact the Inquirers truly had during the Great Smog was impossible to tell. But for the elderly lady who'd been guided home by a kindly gentleman bearing a curiously bright globe of light, or the family whose jewellery shop had been guarded by a group of cloaked figures, it had been everything.

As the smog dispersed and the air cleared, word swept through the city of a nameless force, bound in shadow. Letter case locations were whispered in passing and all through the streets rumours of the Inquirers' effectiveness stirred.

In the years that followed, the agency had more work than it could cope with. More apprentices were recruited and trained, offices extended, new departments developed and gadgets designed. And as a thank you to their faceless protectors, Londoners painted large murals all around the city depicting the public's emblem for the mysterious band of law enforcers – a half-formed circle encasing the letter *I*.

Today, however, as Marion arrived at the gold-plated plaque, the large noticeboard that hung next to it captured her attention instead. Constantly updated, the noticeboard displayed the apprentices' work rosters and routine announcements. But alongside them today was one unusual message:

Please note that all Herald Stethoscopes are being recalled and will, from today, be classed as a Schedule 3 device. As such, anyone found in possession of a Herald Stethoscope without the required registration warrant will be dismissed without notice.
Thank you,
N. Brickett

'Typical,' said a surly voice over Marion's shoulder. 'More restrictions, more control.'

Marion turned to see David Eston – a fellow first year apprentice – standing behind her. Stocky with short brown hair, narrow eyes and a habit for perennial gloating, David was someone Marion had given up trying to like after the first week of knowing him. He'd been recruited just days before her, apparently from a low-paying job at a metalworks factory. And while Marion could see at least one unique trait, characteristic or talent worthy of recruitment in all her other fellow apprentices, she was yet to detect even the hint of one in David.

'Next they'll be calling in our light orbs for registration warrants,' he grunted, tossing his own glass orb from hand to hand.

Marion turned back to the noticeboard and reread the message. As much as it irked her to admit, she had to agree: the Herald Stethoscope – a long, thin brass tube designed to listen through walls – seemed somewhat out of place on the Schedule 3 list, an index of restricted gadgets and devices labelled with the ominous warning: *potential to inflict serious harm with improper use.*

'I suppose there's been some sort of accident,' she provided, more to herself.

'Accident? Doesn't sound like it.'

Marion turned to the alcove on her left – the entrance to the senior staff office.

'. . . a complete disaster,' said a female voice that almost certainly belonged to Nancy Brickett – director and founder of the agency. 'I can't comprehend the consequences should the police catch wind of this.'

'Let's not jump to conclusions,' said the second voice – Frank's. 'Perhaps someone will come forward.'

'You're expecting a confession?'

There was a brief interlude.

'She was stabbed in the throat, Frank. Right through the larynx, for heaven's sake. If the symbolism doesn't strike you then I don't—' she stopped.

There was another short silence, followed by the sharp snap as the door to the alcove was pulled shut.

Marion turned to David. 'What was that about?' The words cracked as she said them.

A strange look passed across David's face. Fear? Disgust? She wasn't sure. 'Someone's messed up and we're all going to pay for it.' He unpinned his work roster from the noticeboard and was gone without further explanation.

David's vague but ominous warning seeped into Marion's mind, sparking an uncomfortable memory: Frank's unexpected visit to 16 Willow Street. Did Frank's dismissive behaviour that day have anything to do with what she'd just heard? Did it have anything to do with her? She stared at the staff office door, tempted to move a little closer. But no, she was being ridiculous, overly anxious – as usual. She exhaled and unpinned her work roster from the noticeboard.

The work rosters were individually composed for each apprentice, a new one printed every morning, indicating in what departments one was to be stationed throughout the day. That morning, Marion was expected in the Auditorium for the general agency meeting, the Gadgetry Department all the way until lunch and the Intelligence Department the rest of the afternoon, where she was due to give what was certainly the biggest presentation of her career. She slipped the roster into her coat pocket and started the winding journey towards the Auditorium.

The many miles of twisted tunnels and hallways of Miss Brickett's were said to have existed long before the agency opened its doors ten years ago, though much of what the apprentices knew of this history was gleaned through gossip, legend and very little fact. The most commonly accepted theory was that the maze-like tunnels – perhaps built by the Romans originally – were rediscovered in the fourteenth-century by a group of disgraced alchemists, exiled by the church, who'd used the hidden passages to research formulas and strange concoctions that would otherwise have sent them straight to the gallows. But no one seemed to know who had refurbished and modernised the vast subterranean expanse after that – installing ventilation, supports, plumbing and lighting – or what these renovations had been for.

The official story was that the labyrinth had been used in the war as an air raid bunker, though some believed a government command centre, or even a weapons storage facility, was more likely. But whatever the truth, Marion often felt a twinge of unease as she traversed the many quiet passageways, imagining who had roamed them before her.

Which was why she paused as she came to the opening of three dark corridors ahead, contemplating her options. All of them, in some way or another, led to the Auditorium. The right-hand passage, however, followed a meandering course that would take her past the powder room, the library, up a tall staircase and down another. She wouldn't have chosen that way, even if it wasn't now blocked off by a wooden sign hammered across its entrance: **No entry under ANY CIRCUMSTANCES. Use alternate route.**

Without further hesitation, she turned into the left passage, the only other option being the middle corridor; a thin tunnel that splintered off in all sorts of directions, each snaking through miles of confusingly similar-looking rock and brick. She preferred not to recall what had happened when she'd used this way once before but, suffice it to say, she came out the other end only hours later, nowhere near the Auditorium and with a firmly established fear of rats.

True to form, Marion arrived at the Auditorium ahead of time. The room was filled, as it was every Monday morning, with the entire Miss Brickett's staff gathered for the weekly general meeting. But unlike most Mondays, today the atmosphere felt weighted with unease, and Marion wondered if it were not just her and David who'd overheard the alarming conversation between Nancy and Frank.

She moved to a row near the back, alongside Bill Hobb, her partner in the clockwork bird project, and everything really.

'At last, sit.' Bill patted the seat beside him. He looked, as usual, as if he'd spent very little time getting dressed. His black hair was dishevelled, his trousers un-ironed. Thin and tall with delicate features and sickly pale skin, he might've passed more easily as a bank clerk than a private detective. Today, however, he looked a fraction more unkempt than normal.

'Am I late?' Marion checked her watch. It was well before eight. She breathed.

Bill smiled. 'Are you ever? No, I mean *at last you're here* so I don't have to deal with these two. They're at it again.' He gestured to the two women seated in the row ahead.

Maud Finkle – a stout and self-assured twenty-two-year-old from Tottenham who'd been recruited from the streets, where circumstance had honed her skills of cunning and stealth. In accordance with her imperturbable character, Maud was slouched in her seat, legs extended in front of her, looking thoroughly bored with whatever Jessica Meel was explaining to her.

Dissimilar to Maud in almost every way, Jessica was a tall, fair blonde who'd been plucked from a comfortable existence in Oxford where she'd worked at a careers recruitment office. Though Jessica had been selected for her uncanny ability to unpick the intricacies of personality and character, she'd thus far dedicated her apprenticeship to extra shifts filing papers in the Human Resources Department (the department in which one was least likely to suffer an injury).

As was often the case, today the two appeared to be locked in an uncompromising disagreement.

'Dammit Jess, I don't care,' Maud said, boredom transforming into annoyance.

'You can settle this for us, Mari,' Jessica said, turning to face her.

Marion grinned at Bill. She knew what was coming next, but the temptation to encourage the repartee between Maud and Jessica was, as usual, too great to resist. 'I'm sure I can. What's going on?'

'Don't encourage them, for Christ's sake,' urged Preston Dinn, a Ghanian immigrant and first-year apprentice who'd just seated himself next to Jessica.

'Jess thinks Nancy's recalled all the Herald Steths because of our little mishap two weeks ago,' Maud began.

'*Your* mishap,' Jessica noted.

29

'Which was?' Marion asked, fuelling the fire even further.

Preston grunted, lit a cigarette and pulled a copy of the *Daily Telegraph* from his bag – a determined show of indifference.

Maud waved her hand dismissively. 'I broke a steth while adjusting the resonator. No big deal.'

'The abridged version if ever there was,' Jessica retaliated. 'No, I'll tell you what happened: she adjusted the resonator with the improper tools. Tell me, Mari, would you ever use combination pliers on a Herald Steth?'

The answer was definitely no. Combination pliers were for stripping and bending wires, too cumbersome for something as delicate as a Herald Stethoscope. 'It's not the best idea,' she said tentatively. Then, hoping to appease both sides, she added, 'but it depends how you handle them. If you're delicate—'

'Yes, except Maud doesn't handle anything with delicacy,' Jessica interrupted.

Maud grinned. 'Subtle. Actually, that reminds me.' She winked at Preston, who lifted his eyes from the paper, took a moment to catch on, then smiled brilliantly. 'Preston tells me he caught you being rather *indelicate* yourself last week in the library.'

Jessica shifted in her seat. Her cheeks reddened.

'Roger from maintenance ring any bells?' Maud pressed, the pitted skin around her eyes creasing with delight.

This was a development, Marion thought as she turned to Jessica inquisitively.

Preston threw his arm across Jessica's shoulder. 'Ah, Jess, we love you for it! Roger from maintenance,' he whistled, 'even I'd have a—'

'Okay okay, that's enough,' Marion swiftly intervened. Perhaps second only to Bill, Jessica was her closest friend, which is how she knew – from the way Jessica was now rearranging the contents of her purse – that Roger from maintenance was not a topic to be discussed. Not like this, anyway. She changed the subject. 'Back to the note about the recall. I wonder what it means?'

'That's what I was trying to explain,' Jessica said, clearly relieved at the shift in conversation. 'Maud broke a steth two weeks ago and didn't report the incident. She threw it away instead, so now there's one less in the stockpile.' She spoke the last sentence with venom, not that Maud noticed. 'Nancy probably thinks one's been stolen.'

'But they've upgraded it to a Schedule 3 device,' Marion said. 'That can't be because one's gone missing?'

Jessica shrugged. 'No, I suppose not.'

Marion turned to Bill but his focus had drifted across to the Auditorium entrance, where David Eston now stood, leaning against the doorframe. They caught each other's eye. Bill muttered something.

'You all right?' Marion asked. It wasn't the first time Bill and David had done this, stare at one another across a room with contempt, maybe even hatred. Like Maud and Jessica they were polar opposites, natural adversaries. Unlike the women, however, their distaste for one another seemed less in jest. Certainly, over the past weeks, it had grown sour.

Marion had asked Bill about it on numerous occasions, trying to understand the root of their discord and what was exacerbating it. It troubled her, not because she had any desire to seal the rift between the two men (indeed, she fostered her own distaste for David), but because of Bill's uncharacteristic reluctance to confide in Marion on only this particular matter.

Why was it that he'd told her every nuance of his life – where he lived (a dirty two-bedroom near Blackwall), who he lived with (his drug-peddling cousin), how he'd been recruited (from the London Library where he'd worked as an archivist and was known for his *superior general knowledge and unfathomable affinity for books*) – and yet, this one small thing he couldn't tell her?

'I think I figured the Distracter out, by the way,' he said, pulling his briefcase onto his lap and changing the subject. A fitting new topic, she had to admit. 'Might have something to do with the spring on the wind-up mechanism,' he went on, looking down at his copy of the *Basic Workshop Manual,* which he'd extracted from his bag and opened to page eighty-two. 'Apparently it's made of copper and is prone to corrosion, especially down in this damp hellhole. But I'm not entirely sure, depends on the model number. V Three and Four have copper springs but versions Five and Six were made with stainless steel which obviously wouldn't make sense. Marion? What do you think?'

She turned her attention to the diagram on page eighty-two, showing a metallic sunbird, its head turned 180 degrees anticlockwise: the Distracter.

'That's not it,' she said easily, skimming over the page and extracting the sunbird from her briefcase. 'It's the phonograph that's faulty, not the wind-up mechanism.'

'You fixed it then?'

'No, but I got it to fly.' She turned the bird upside down and examined the speaker mesh covering located on its underside. 'I'll see what I can do about the phonograph when I have the parts. It's not just this one though, the entire batch has the same issue.'

She was holding the bird at eye level, inspecting a screw under its wing, when she caught sight of Mr Nicholas, who'd obviously returned from his *frightful business* and taken a seat at the front of the Auditorium.

Bill followed her gaze. 'Did you see him this morning?'

'In the bookshop? Yes.' Marion returned the bird to her briefcase. She watched Nicholas shift in his seat and wondered

32

if she should mention what she overheard near the senior staff office. She didn't much like the idea of being a gossip, but Bill was sure to hear it from someone soon enough.

'I heard Nancy speaking to Frank this morning,' she explained. 'I don't know if I heard correctly, but I think someone was murdered. It sounded as if they were stabbed. In the throat.'

Bill looked uncomfortable, though strangely not surprised. His gaze passed again to David.

'But I don't know,' Marion added to fill the silence, 'maybe it was just a case they're investigating.'

'It's not,' said Preston.

Marion flinched. Somehow she'd forgotten the other three apprentices were in the row ahead, perfectly within hearing range.

'It was a staff member,' Preston explained with an air of nonchalance – a trait he'd likely developed through years of hard labour as a stevedore. There wasn't much he hadn't seen or heard. There wasn't much that disturbed him. 'Murdered.'

'Excuse me?' Jessica asked.

Preston drew on his cigarette. 'What? I can't be the only one who's heard. What do you think they're all talking about this morning?' He gestured to the packed Auditorium.

Several rows ahead, senior Inquirers and staff members were crowded in small groups, chatting furtively between themselves. But it was the expression on Nancy Brickett's face that troubled Marion the most.

It wasn't in any way unusual for Nancy to appear cold and detached. She was built that way. After studying Linguistics at Cambridge, according to rumour, she was recruited by the government during the war and sent to an estate in Buckinghamshire where she worked as a cryptanalyst. She was brilliant at it, Marion had heard, calm under pressure, unreadable. And as she moved on to found Miss Brickett's she had carried with her the same disposition, one of fortitude and stability. It was generally accepted that Nancy's desire to establish a private detective agency of the highest calibre came from her frustration with the rising levels of crime and corruption in post-war London. But Marion suspected it was more to do with the fact that Nancy's ultra-secret war work had instilled in her a sense of importance, of influence. How could a woman who'd played such an integral role in halting the German advance go on to live a life that was anything less than exemplary? Nancy was born to lead, to guide, to protect, and the agency was her platform to do so.

But as Marion watched her now – dull red hair streaked with grey, dark eyes flashing – she appeared to survey the Auditorium with an unfamiliar nuance of agitation. It was as if she were waiting for something to happen, something unpleasant but utterly inevitable.

Marion recalled what she'd heard Nancy say earlier: *I can't comprehend the consequences should the police catch wind of this.* It was the agency's ever-looming fear – that of discovery – which she had alluded to, a fear well grounded in reality.

Though the police must have suspected the existence of Miss Brickett's, and indeed the select few Met officers who liaised with the agency knew of it for certain, it was hard to deny the fact that the Inquirers had crossed nearly every line of conventional law enforcement. Thus, should the secret of their existence and that of the labyrinth itself be exposed, it would mean only one simple thing – Miss Brickett's would be closed down.

And for Marion that would mean the end of everything good in her life. How could she leave this intricate, mysterious world and pretend it never existed? How could she forget the people she'd met and the things she'd learned? Most awfully, how could she ever go back to a *normal* life at 16 Willow Street, back to that lonely, miserable and pointless existence?

34

The sound of Nancy tapping her glass shocked Marion back to the present.

'Good morning,' she said. 'I hope everyone had a restful weekend.' She lifted the corners of her mouth, perhaps an attempt at a smile.

Those gathered in the Auditorium dropped their voices, took their seats and a silence gathered throughout like a storm cloud.

'As I'm sure you are already aware, there has been an incident here over the weekend.' She slipped her fingers into the space between her collar and her neck, shifting the collar downwards in an irritated, possibly desperate attempt to un-strangle herself. 'Unfortunately, it is my duty to inform you that Miss Michelle White, our dear and longstanding filing assistant, passed away on Friday evening inside the library from unnatural causes.'

There was a chorus of nervous chatter.

'. . . Further details will follow in time,' Nancy went on, 'but please note, on account of this incident, the locks to the bookshop door will be changed by the end of the week.'

Something awful then occurred to Marion – no one who was *not* a Miss Brickett's employee had ever set foot inside the agency. No one knew where the entrance was, and even if they did, it would be impossible to get through the bookshop door if you didn't use the right keys in the right order. And then, if somehow you managed to do so, you'd have to find the short passage obscured behind the butler's desk and the trapdoor concealed between the floorboards, then turn on and open the lift without using an employee badge.

There was little doubt, as far as Marion was concerned – the killer was an agency employee.

'Secondly,' Nancy continued, 'I ask that over the next few weeks you maintain an especially low profile. For your own safety, and that of your fellow employees, please refrain from socialising outside the agency and, of course, from mentioning anything about this incident to anyone who does not work at Miss Brickett's. And as always, please be advised that the corridors beyond the Gadgetry Department are strictly off limits. To everyone.'

A sharp silence fell upon the Auditorium.

'Now despite these unpleasant circumstances, we would like to keep things running as normally as possible. Apprentices,' she looked over to Marion and the others in her group, then to the second- and third-year apprentices spread out among the rest of the staff, 'your shifts will continue as usual this week. To that end, third years, your Induction Ceremony will still take place this Friday, the eighteenth of April.' She paused, lifting a piece of paper from the pile in front of her, and pushed her cat's-eye spectacles further up her nose. 'Before we get on with our week, I would like to say a brief congratulations to Verity Gould and Don Shu,' she looked over to a pair of senior Inquirers sitting in the front row, 'for their success on the Jane Holland case. As some of you may recall, six-year-old Miss Holland went missing on her way home from school three months ago. The police investigation ran cold very quickly and Miss Holland's parents turned to us instead.' She smiled at Verity and Don. 'Last Wednesday, Gould and Shu managed to track down Holland and returned her to her parents unharmed. Very good work, thank you both.'

There was a short hesitation from the Auditorium. Marion sensed that they, like her, wanted to celebrate Verity and Don's success and the return of Jane Holland, but it was difficult, in light of the news that had preceded it. Eventually, a round of soft whoops and claps filtered through the crowd, gaining in enthusiasm as they went.

Don Shu turned to face the Auditorium. Like everyone else, he looked exhausted. Unlike most, however, he also looked relieved. 'Might add that we dropped the kidnapper

36

off unharmed, too. At the police station.' There was more raucous clapping, and a few people laughed.

Nancy thanked the two Inquirers again, then signalled the Auditorium to silence. 'Miss Holland's case is the type of work that makes us tick,' she said, 'seeing the look on a parent's face, the relief and delight. Let us hold such images in our minds this week and through the days and hours that challenge our reserve and perseverance.' She took a shallow breath. 'That is all for today. Thank you.'

The audience got to their feet. Inquirers made their way down to Intelligence. Staff and heads to their respective departments, and the apprentices to wherever their work rosters had instructed them.

Bill collected a stack of files from the front of the Auditorium, then followed Marion into the corridor outside as they made their way to the Department of Gadgetry, where they were to spend the morning.

'Why do you think Nancy mentioned that again?' Marion asked as they approached the top of a long stone staircase that led to Gadgetry and the agency's deepest floor.

Bill frowned. 'What?'

'The Border.' She gestured to the dim thread of path that fed off from the base of the staircase. 'She reminded us it's restricted. As if we could forget.'

The Border, as it was often referred to, was the fringe of all that was known to the apprentices. It was where Miss Brickett's Investigations and Inquiries ended and grim rumours began. An expanse of disused corridors and chambers so dark and menacing that Marion imagined no one would dare enter them, even if they weren't strictly out of bounds.

Bill shrugged as he shoved the stack of files he'd collected from the Auditorium into his briefcase. 'I suppose because White's office and bedroom are down there.'

Marion paused. 'What?'

'Yeah. Near the Border.'

'You sure?'

He nodded absently and began to rearrange the contents of his briefcase. He paused. His face had changed, a subtle shift of his features that might have been shock. He crouched down, staring into his briefcase with a look of utter confusion.

'What's wrong? Bill?'

'In the Auditorium,' he answered hurriedly, 'you didn't pick up a piece of paper anywhere, did you?'

'What?'

'A roll of parchment, tied with purple ribbon? Did you see it anywhere?'

'I have no idea what you're talking about.'

'Never mind. Here.' He handed Marion the stack of files. 'The month's order forms. Pass them to Bal for me?'

'Where are you going?'

'To check something. I'll meet you in the Workshop in a moment.'

'Okay but—'

'Won't be a second.' He turned to rush back up the staircase.

If Marion hadn't been so distracted by the clockwork sunbird, which had switched itself on again when she pushed the files Bill had given her into her briefcase, she'd have seen the figure who slipped into the shadows at the top of the staircase the minute Bill was out of sight.

4

In the Department of Gadgetry

While everything above the forty-four step staircase was clearly mapped out, more or less well-lit and ventilated by a vast grid of air ducts, the low-roofed passageways and grime-filled chambers below were mostly abandoned. These miles of stone and grit and strangely shaped rooms formed a network of tributaries beyond the Border that wound ever deeper below the surface of the earth.

Eight years ago, or so the story went, an apprentice by the name of Ned Asbrey, having had a few too many pints at the library bar on a Wednesday night, stumbled down the long stone staircase that led towards the Gadgetry Department in a booze-shrouded haze. But instead of passing through the department's doors, he staggered left and onwards across the Border. Though no official account of Asbrey's fate was ever provided, a general rumour among the apprentices was that he eventually emerged from across the Border days later, oddly withdrawn, his clothes caked with mud, a deep gash across his cheek. He'd been unable (or unwilling) to give an account of what he'd seen and experienced in the tunnels, though shortly after his return and with no explanation, he resigned from Miss Brickett's and was never seen again.

★

Alone and growing more uneasy as the day progressed, Marion made her way to the Gadgetry Department's entrance. She stepped in front of the gargoyle that guarded the main door and pulled its left arm sharply downwards. It shifted, groaned and sunk down into the floor.

The Workshop, as it was called, was a large hall filled with messy workbenches loaded with microscopes, hammers, tweezers, drills and scales of every size. But the hall's most impressive feature was pressed up against the north-facing wall – a large glass cabinet set inside an even larger steel cage. Through the heavy bars and the shiny glass beyond, fifty long wooden shelves were loaded with objects so diverse and peculiar that Marion had often found herself transfixed, staring at the cabinet with admiration and awe. There were pens for recording the temperature of the air, gadgets loaded with poison darts and halothane gas. There were boxes filled with Time Lighters – gas-powered clockwork torches set to ignite at the tick of the hour – and elaborately decorated skeleton keys – the universal lock pick designed to shift and shimmy its way through the wards of any keyhole in existence.

'Morning, Marion,' said Professor Uday Bal, the department's head and principle engineer. Uday was dressed in a long-sleeved tawny shirt, trousers two sizes too big and a beret sitting perilously on top of his thick helmet of hair. He did not wear glasses, although perhaps he should, considering the large magnifying glass he always carried on a chain around his neck. The professor was tall and thin, so thin that at times Marion wondered if he might be ill. But he'd assured her, on the one occasion she'd been so brash as to ask, that he'd never been better and that his physique was a blessing passed down from his mother – a whisper-thin lady from Pakistan.

Marion pulled out the file Bill had given her on the staircase and handed it to the professor. 'Order forms from the Factory, sir.'

40

'Bill is off today?' the professor asked, noting his absence.

'He's just late.'

'Ah . . .' Somewhat out of character, the professor regarded the file with little interest. 'Seems like a lot,' he added, flipping through order forms with a sigh.

'I thought that was a good thing?'

'For our finances, yes . . .'

The Factory was the agency's cover for their covert communication supply sector. Bugs, wire taps, miniature cipher machines and microdot cameras were just some of the items of espionage sold to a range of anonymous buyers from a pseudo-factory in Southend – a miserable building in perpetual disrepair.

Nancy had taken over the Factory in 1947, then a small-scale operation run by Professor Bal that produced and repaired parts for devices of subterfuge used by the War Office. When Nancy opened Miss Brickett's one year later, she moved the professor and the workshop underground, both literally and figuratively, and Uday was given free rein to design what he pleased, no matter how bizarre, intricate, or illegal. The Factory quickly became, and had remained, the agency's primary source of income, and the professor the sovereign of all things clandestine.

Today, however, Uday Bal cast the order forms aside with little consideration. 'Did you find the fault in the Distracter?' he asked instead.

Marion placed a hand on her briefcase. The bird was still rattling inside. 'Not quite. I was hoping I could have a few more days; it might be a problem with the phonograph . . .' she trailed off, the professor's focus had already waned, his gaze resting on a cloth-wrapped object on the workbench before him.

There was an interval of silence, interrupted shortly after as the Workshop door cracked open and Bill rushed inside, out of breath, pale.

'Find it?' Marion asked him.

'What?'

'The thing you left in the Auditorium?'

'Oh. No, no I didn't.'

Marion frowned and turned back to the professor, whose gaze was still vacantly hovering over the cloth-wrapped object. It was news of the murder, she supposed, that had everyone behaving so oddly this morning.

Bill frowned as he, too, cast his attention to the object on the workbench. He craned his neck. 'Is that blood?'

An awkward beat followed. The professor looked torn between wanting to answer and hoping not to. But Bill and Marion's interest had been piqued and neither was now able to dismiss the definite red stains on the cloth.

'You've heard the news? About Michelle?' the professor asked.

'Yes, it's terrible,' Marion said, though somehow it didn't sound quite as compassionate as she'd intended.

The professor removed his beret, bringing it to his chest. His eyes glistened. 'I knew Michelle from the beginning. She was just a little younger than you two are, when she was recruited. I was her mentor. She liked gadgets.' He smiled weakly. 'A bit like you do, Marion.'

Marion was caught a little off guard by the reference. She'd met Michelle White only a few times before. Even through their brief encounters, however, Marion got the impression that she was a snide, solitary and frankly unlikeable woman.

The professor crossed and uncrossed his arms. His unease was blatant. 'I must tell you, though, I saw Michelle on Thursday morning,' he said, his words strained but rapid. 'She came to my office for ten o'clock tea, our tradition every Thursday. But there was something wrong, there had been for a few weeks, actually. I just wish I'd asked her what it was. Maybe

42

I could have helped. Maybe she'd still—' He shook his head. 'I wish I'd comforted her. I don't think she had anyone else, you know. People misunderstood her, I think.'

Odd sounds filled the silence – the occasional clink of a tool or grind of metal as the professor's assistants continued their duties in the shadowy recesses of the hall.

After a time, the professor seemed to pull himself from whatever dark thoughts had consumed him. He spoke quickly and softly. 'It was David, I think.'

Bill flinched at Marion's side. She looked at him. He averted his gaze. She turned back to Uday Bal, contemplating whether to discourage him from whatever he was about to say next. The professor's candour made her uncomfortable – surely such sensitive information should be passed on to Nancy? But before she could voice her apprehension, Bill spoke:

'What do you mean, it was David?'

'The thing that was worrying Michelle,' the professor explained in a low whisper. 'She said there was something bothering her. She didn't say what, exactly, something about *someone looking for it*. And I think she must have been talking about David because he'd—' He stopped again, apparently coming to some private conclusion, perhaps that he'd said too much. He sighed, relaxing somewhat. 'It's strange, isn't it? Unexpected death, it makes us second guess everything, analyse the meaning behind words and actions. What if we missed something? What if we could have prevented it?'

'Jesus!' Bill interrupted, something dawning on him. He pointed at the cloth-covered object. 'That's it, isn't it? The murder weapon!'

The professor hesitated, but only for a second. And Marion's stomach lurched as he unwrapped a bloodied steel pole, about seven inches in length and two in diameter, one end shattered into a spear of broken metal.

43

The professor held the object up to the light – a Herald Stethoscope. And it was then that Marion understood the notice pinned at the end of the Grand Corridor: all Herald Stethoscopes had been upgraded to a Schedule 3: *potential to inflict serious harm with improper use.*

'It was found protruding from her throat,' the professor said carefully, a professional note of detachment to his tone – a coping method, Marion presumed. 'It pierced her voice box, and several blood vessels nearby. I think it killed her instantly.'

A Herald Stethoscope, one of the agency's many intricate gadgets, was designed to pick up sound through almost any barrier – walls, doors, windows and floors. It was a thin pole with a flexible inner lining of rubber and sturdy outer coating of metal. At one end was a powerful bell-shaped resonator for picking up sound, at the other, an ear-piece for hearing it.

While the earpiece remained undamaged, the other end (where the resonator should have been) was broken into jagged extensions of bloodstained metal, turning the once innocent gadget into three ragged yet efficient blades. It was the most unusual murder weapon Marion had ever seen, but it would have had little trouble slicing through flesh, there was no doubt.

'Why is it here?' Marion asked. *And why are you showing it to us?* A cold sweat was building on her skin.

From a drawer nearby, the professor pulled out a bottle of disinfectant and roll of cotton wool. He slipped on a pair of gloves, briefly closed his eyes, as if to mentally prepare himself yet again, then went about wiping the pole clean of blood, taking a break only after he'd extracted a piece of flesh from inside the hollow tube. 'Nancy wants me to tell her how it was broken,' he said solemnly. 'Whether it had been dropped, slammed against the wall, cut with some tool. The problem is, this stethoscope is not like the others.' He shone a pen light into the depth of the tube.

Marion shifted on her feet. 'With respect, professor, I really don't think you should be showing us this.' She felt a spasm of guilt when Uday frowned. 'I just mean . . . it's against protocol. *Surely?*'

The professor looked at her incredulously. 'But you're not going to tell anyone, are you?'

'Well no, of course not, but . . .' She sighed.

The professor nodded, satisfied, then went on. 'I made this one just for Michelle, you see. It was her favourite gadget, right from the first day she arrived as an apprentice. But the brass from which a Herald Stethoscope is usually made is delicate, easily broken if dropped. It shatters. Not like this. She broke three before the end of her first year. So I made her a special one for her twenty-seventh birthday. Much stronger, but if broken, it will not shatter like the others, but break into large shards, like this. I made this one out of stratified steel and I can't believe it, I can't believe this is what ended up killing her . . .' His words trailed off.

'My God,' Marion said. She glanced around the hall. The professor's assistants loitered nearby, some of them focused on tasks, some casting the occasional eye towards the Herald Stethoscope. A knot formed in her stomach. She knew why he'd revealed the murder weapon, and why (as usual) he'd said more than he should. During the countless hours she'd spent working with the professor, she'd come to realise that his most admirable trait was also his greatest flaw – unquestionable faith in the integrity of those he surrounded himself with. But clearly, considering Michelle White's recent demise, not everyone at Miss Brickett's should be trusted.

'Perhaps we should put that away now,' she said hastily, pointing at the weapon.

The professor seemed to arrive at a similar conclusion. He acted swiftly, placing the stethoscope back in the box. 'Well,'

45

he sighed, adding a little awkwardly, 'I suppose we must get on with the day, despite it all.' He lifted a box onto the bench, filled to the brim with mounds of grey steel cords. 'I suspect you know what to do with those. I will be in my office if you need anything.'

'Jesus, what a morning,' Marion said to Bill as the two of them got to work.

Bill grunted. Something about a *bloody mess*. Marion decided not to ask him to elaborate. She didn't want to think about what the professor had showed them, the murder weapon or any of it. 'And now this.' Bill gestured to the box, overflowing with knotted coils of twister rope – cords composed of sections of magnetically charged iron filings that could bind and strangle anything they came into contact with, including themselves, and thus had a habit of becoming tangled into impossibly convoluted clumps. He looked down at his watch. 'That lot's going to take us all day to get through.' He slammed his forearms against a particularly mobile strand of rope, pinning it to the table until, like some dying beast, it settled into stillness. Careful not to recharge the filings (which, according to the *Basic Workshop Manual*, was likely to occur with brisk manoeuvres) he slowly untangled the rope, lifted it into the air, strode across the hall and hung it up in the rubber-lined storage cabinet. 'Great, one down, approximately two hundred to go.'

Marion extracted a length of cord from the box and attempted to unwind it. She watched Bill do the same, his face knotted in concentration, or perhaps it was frustration. After completing several more intricate untying procedures, he sighed and looked up. 'How was your weekend, anyway?'

'The same as ever. I spent most of it preparing for my case presentation in Intelligence today. And Dolores was at me again. Did I tell you about Mr Smithers?'

'Your future husband?' Bill snorted.

'He's still sending me letters. I couldn't really appear any less interested. Will he ever get the message?'

'Mari,' Bill said with a note of levity, 'you do realise it's not Smithers you've got to dissuade?'

Marion frowned.

'It's Dolores,' he explained. 'You told me yourself she selected him for you, which means she's probably coercing him behind the scenes. If he gives up on you, he'll have her to deal with.'

'God help him, then.'

They laughed.

'What about you?' Marion said after a time. 'Anyone on the horizon?' Bill was striking in his own way – tall, clear-skinned, soft featured – and Marion imagined he'd have little trouble in the realm of romantic pursuits. And yet something caught in her chest as she imagined him finding a wife, settling down, moving off. Marion and Bill's relationship had always been platonic, but it was also close and mutually dependent. As selfish as it was to say, if Bill's attention shifted elsewhere, away from Marion and onto someone else, she wasn't sure how she'd cope.

'How exactly am I supposed to meet someone when I spend all my time underground?'

Marion laughed. 'I don't know, but apparently Jess does.'

'Hah, right. Roger from maintenance. Do you even know who that is?'

Marion imagined someone burly and gruff – Jessica's type – though she couldn't say she'd ever met Roger from maintenance. 'Not really.'

Time moved slowly, stiffly, as the two battled in silence with their respective coils of twister rope. But with each passing minute, Bill became more impatient, agitated, cursing and grunting under his breath.

47

'Are you all right?' Marion asked.

He appeared not to have heard. 'Do you know where David is stationed this afternoon?'

'David?' Marion prickled. 'Why would I know that?'

Bill shook his head. No reply.

Here we go again.

Marion watched a rise of unease in his features, the tic that caused a subtle tremor in his hands. She'd seen it only once before, the first time they'd met – the day of Marion's recruitment, when Bill had risked his job in order to cover for her. He'd been anxious then, lying although he'd have preferred not to.

Bill picked up another coil. But he was too distracted now – a dangerous mistake when dealing with twister rope. The strand he'd chosen slipped from his un-ready grip. It uncoiled itself, straightened out, then wrapped itself around his left arm. Before Marion could comprehend what was happening, the other side coiled around his neck. The two oppositely charged ends drew themselves together, forcing Bill's neck into his shoulder, his arm to his neck. 'A little help?' he groaned as the coil swiftly tightened.

Marion grabbed the opposing ends of rope and yanked them apart at the same time, an act which would demagnetise the strands for a split second, thus allowing a moment in which Bill could slip from their grasp. It worked, and only just in time.

'Christ's sake . . .' he spluttered, rubbing the ring of bright ruby bruising on his neck. 'What next . . .'

Marion deposited the offending coil in the rubber-lined wardrobe, careful to hang it up perfectly straight. She then looked up at the clock on the wall. Somehow, it was already fifteen minutes into their lunch hour. 'Come on,' she said, sealing closed the box of rope and pushing it aside. 'We can finish these later.'

But the second they'd left the dank hall, Bill paused. He gripped the strap of his bag and glared up at the long stone staircase. Someone was standing right at the top, the outline of their figure partly visible in the dim light.

'I've got to go,' he said. 'I'll see you at lunch. Or later.'

'Later when? Where are you going?'

'Just need to run through some work for this afternoon.' The tic in his hand was more obvious now. 'See you later.'

As Bill made his way upstairs, the figure at the top of the staircase stepped further into the light. David slipped his right hand into his coat pocket. Words were exchanged and the two disappeared together down the corridor.

Marion felt a resurgence of irritation as she watched Bill and David move off into the dimness. She'd have to confront him properly next time, force him to tell her what all of this was about.

5

The Snitch

In the time it took Marion to reach the cafeteria, just as she'd feared, word of the bloodied and shattered Herald Stethoscope used to murder Michelle White had leaked, and an outbreak of speculation flooded the corridors.

'Clean through. In one side of the head, out the other,' pronounced third-year apprentice Patrick Castle to his friend and fellow third-year Howard Yon as they settled at a table next to Marion.

'Nearly decapitated,' said Howard.

The two looked over. 'You saw it, didn't you, Lane?' asked Patrick.

Marion ignored him and served herself a plate of lunch.

Howard drew his chair over to her table. 'Reckon it was premeditated?' he asked without any reluctance.

Patrick slid over next. 'Come on, Lane,' he urged, his deep brown eyes flashing with excitement. 'You spend all your time down there with Bal. Reckon he had something to do with it?'

Patrick smiled at Howard. 'Stratified steel, nice and sturdy for a weapon don't you think?'

This, Marion could not ignore. 'I'd think twice about making accusations like that. This isn't a joke and I hardly think—'

'Yeah, yeah, we know, Lane,' Patrick interrupted. 'Relax. Just pulling your leg. Never expected a word from you anyway.'

'Hobb, on the other hand . . .' said Howard, grinning. 'He saw it too, didn't he?'

Patrick slapped his knee. 'Dammit! You're bloody right. Why didn't I think of that? Give Hobby a pint or three and he'll sing like a bird in a tree.'

The two laughed, Patrick coming close to tears as they repeated the jibe under their breath: *Give Hobby a pint or three and he'll sing like a bird in a tree.*

'So, where is he then?' Patrick asked.

Marion looked across the cafeteria, preferring to ignore the two.

Howard leaned into Patrick for dramatic effect, though he made no attempt to lower his voice. 'Actually, didn't we see him with Eston just now? They were arguing, weren't they?'

Patrick nodded, his grin growing. 'All looked a bit suspicious, if you're asking me. Wonder what they—' He stopped mid-sentence.

'Yon, Castle,' said a commanding female voice from behind, instantly wiping the smiles off Patrick and Howard's faces.

Marion looked up to see Senior Inquirer and head of the Intelligence Department, Aida Rakes. Though only in her mid-thirties, Rakes was a formidable woman and at six-foot-two the Senegalese-Brit was easily the most revered individual at the agency, second only to Nancy.

'I thought you two were stationed with Simpkins in the library this afternoon?' Rakes asked, her voice smooth and easy, though Marion knew it took little to turn.

'We were just on our way.' Howard gathered his things.

Rakes looked at her watch. 'It's twelve fifty-five. It takes at least ten minutes to get down there and if you're late again Simpkins will make a note of it on your assessment reports.'

Howard and Patrick got to their feet and disappeared without another word.

Rakes turned to Marion. She looked at her untouched plate of lunch. 'You're having a lunch break?'

'Well, yes, I was hoping to.' Marion was confused and slightly annoyed. This was the first moment of peace she'd had all day. With everything else going on, she'd been hoping for just thirty minutes to eat her lunch without any distractions. It wasn't looking likely.

Rakes seemed contemptuous. 'You remember you've got a presentation with me this afternoon?'

Marion checked her watch. It wasn't even one o'clock. 'Yes.' *Of course I remember.* 'At two thirty.'

Rakes didn't reply for a while, which Marion knew was her way of expressing the warning – *You'd better not be late and you'd better be prepared.* 'I'll see you there.'

By the time Rakes had left, Marion had lost her appetite. She pushed her plate away and got to her feet, all hope of having a normal day long since dissipated. There was only one person who could calm her agitation now.

She knocked three times on Frank's office door. It opened a sliver. 'Marion?' He looked disturbed, as if she'd caught him in the middle of something. He didn't invite her in.

'I'm sorry,' she stammered. 'I was just hoping to have a word.'

He hesitated, which brought a flush of red to her cheeks. She cringed at the idea of forcing her company on anyone, even someone she considered family. Sensing this, perhaps, he stepped aside. 'Of course, come in.' His office was untidy – books and files and stacks of paper strewn across the desk and floor. 'Excuse all this,' he said as he caught her staring at the mess. 'Just some rearranging.' He perched himself on the edge of his desk, perhaps because all three chairs in the room were covered in office paraphernalia, or perhaps because he was hoping to hurry the conversation along. 'What is it?'

She decided to get to the point. 'I overheard something outside the staff office this morning. You and Nancy.' She left it there. He'd fill in the blanks.

He looked at the floor. 'It's an awful thing that's happened.'

'Should I be worried? About the agency, I mean. I heard Nancy say she was concerned the police would have to get involved.'

'No, of course not,' he said immediately. 'It's very much under control.' He rubbed his knees, then stood. 'Was there anything else?'

Marion opened her mouth. There was a lot more about the murder she wanted to ask – who he suspected the killer was, or what he thought the motive might've been – but she knew he wouldn't answer those questions, not in the heat of the investigation. Frank wasn't pedantic about rules and policies, but he was nothing if not sensible. Unless there was something about the case she really needed to know, he'd – *sensibly* – refrain from telling her anything about it, unlike Professor Bal. She decided to steer the conservation towards the other thing that had been bothering her. 'Something's going on with Bill and David.'

Frank's expression eased instantly. 'Oh?'

'It's been going on for a while. Some sort of disagreement they've been having. But Bill won't talk to me about it. He changes the subject whenever I bring it up.'

Frank looked genuinely interested. Or perhaps he was just relieved they were no longer talking about the murder. 'And why does that bother you?'

Marion thought for a moment. 'Because we tell each other everything.'

Frank inclined his head. 'Really?'

Marion frowned. What was that supposed to mean? Bill knew everything about her, didn't he? 'Yes, really.'

'Have you told him how Alice died? The truth, I mean.'

A lump formed in her throat. She crossed her arms. No, was the answer. She'd told Bill her mother had died of cancer, the same story she'd told everyone. Except Frank, of course. He knew the truth.

'I'm not suggesting you should've done,' he said kindly. 'We all have our secrets, Marion. Bill has his, you have yours. It doesn't mean you don't trust each other. Some truths are private, and they should remain that way.'

Marion nodded, though she wasn't sure what she was agreeing with. She didn't really know why she found it hard to speak of her mother, and how she'd died. Maybe it was because she despised the pity that came along with such a tragic story – a mother choosing to leave behind her only daughter. Or maybe it was more the scrutiny she hoped to avoid, the probing looks and subtle questions, assessing the damage and resultant character flaws such an event was sure to cause.

Frank waited for her to stir, to emerge from her thoughts. He placed a hand on her shoulder. 'Whatever it is, Bill will tell you when and if he's ready.' He smiled, then guided her towards the door. Once at the threshold, he spoke in a less assured tone: 'I know these are uncertain times. But keep to your work and—' he looked over her shoulder and down the corridor. She turned around, but there was no one there. 'Look after yourself, all right?'

Marion met Aida Rakes in the library half an hour later, just in time for her case presentation.

'It's not just the apprentices talking about the murder weapon,' Rakes said as she and Marion made their way down a small staircase into the library basement. 'Whole bloody agency's gossiping like a bunch of schoolchildren.'

Marion sighed. Her chat with Frank had eased her mood a fraction, but now she was back to thinking about that awful Herald Stethoscope and what it had been used for.

'I know Bal showed you the weapon,' Rakes continued. 'One of the Workshop assistants told me.'

'Yes, I assumed they would,' she said under her breath and then, more loudly, 'I haven't said anything to anyone about it though.'

Rakes seemed to accept this. 'I just hope Nancy doesn't find out, she'll be livid. She's trying to handle the case with discretion. She doesn't need any interferences. Am I clear?'

'Of course.' *Of course.* Despite the fact that Marion found herself – like everyone else – unable to ignore the alarming news of Michelle White's demise, interfering with the investigation was the last thing on her mind. The apprenticeship assessment reports were due the following week so she didn't have much time to regain her focus, but she was going to have to try.

Assessment reports were to be filed by heads of departments and senior staff members for every apprentice every three months. Not only was a collection of favourable reports by the end of the probationary period a sure-fire way to acquire an offer of full-time employment at the agency, but apprentices with gleaming reports were occasionally permitted to select their own shifts and duties – a privilege Marion hoped for as it would allow her to spend even more time in Gadgetry.

'Shirley.' Rakes nodded at a petite blonde who'd been waiting at the base of the stairs – Amanda Shirley, the seventh and oldest first-year apprentice in Marion's group. Amanda's sharp features and pale, deep-set eyes were disconcerting (to put it kindly) and she constantly gave Marion the impression she was teetering on the verge of a rage-induced meltdown.

Amanda handed Rakes a file without returning the greeting and paid no attention to Marion. 'Just three cases for the week. All category two. I suggest you assign them to Barnes, Appleton and Patterson.' Although Amanda was an apprentice just like Marion and the others, in the five months since she'd been recruited she'd somehow managed to claw her way to an additional part-time position of assistant case manager in the Intelligence Department. Frank said she was given the role on account of her organisational skills, sharpened during her time as postmistress for the Royal Mail. Unfortunately for everyone she worked with, the position only served to amplify her already heightened sense of self-importance. At times Marion found her almost unbearable. But she wasn't the only one.

'Thanks for the tip,' Rakes said as the three of them passed under a small arched doorway beyond the stairs.

Amanda quickened her pace to keep up with Rakes' lengthy strides. 'Everyone's struggling to concentrate, you know. After Nancy's announcement in the Auditorium. And they're all saying the killer must be an agency employee. I suggest you have a word with them before the gossip gets out of control.'

'Yes, I've noticed.'

'Actually,' Amanda went on, 'I was going to suggest we freeze operations until the case is solved.'

Rakes stopped. 'Freeze operations? You've clearly no idea what it takes to run this place. If we did that even for a few days we'd be backlogged for months.'

'I don't agree,' Amanda said. 'There's hardly anything coming through the receivers anyway.'

Rakes closed her eyes for a moment. 'And what good would that do? If the killer is one of us – and I do mean *if* – then I believe it's best to let them think they've got away with it. Let them relax, take some risks, make a mistake.'

'A risk like striking again? Killing someone else?' Amanda crossed her arms.

Marion smiled just a fraction as she watched Rakes' mood sour. Amanda was treading on dangerous ground, continuing to be so insubordinate. Rakes didn't mind well-constructed criticism or opposing viewpoints, even if they came from apprentices. But Amanda's incessant disagreements and interruptions often overstepped the line and it was a pleasure to watch Rakes put her in her place.

'If you really have a problem with the way things are being run here, Shirley,' Rakes went on, sharp and quick, 'then I suggest you take it to the highest level. I'm sure Nancy would love to hear your thoughts.' She turned to Marion. 'Something amusing, Lane?'

Marion quickly frowned. 'No, nothing.'

'Good. Shirley, I'll see you in my office at five for the filing report. Lane, let's go.'

Forever stuffy and crammed with lofty towers of paperwork, the drab Filing Department left much to be desired. The same could not be said for the wall that formed its northern boundary. Hundreds of steel receiver boxes hung from a vast concrete panel, fitted directly beneath their numerically corresponding pneumatic pipes. The pipes connected the receiver boxes in the Filing Department to letter cases concealed in a multitude of locations throughout central London – within street walls or tube stations, or even under bridges.

They passed through Filing and stepped into the neighbouring, much larger Intelligence Department – an open hall filled with rows of office desks, low burning lamps and lines of filing cabinets. It was here that all Inquirers (who were not out in the field) would spend their days, pouring through suspect files, evidence and tip-offs that had made it through the Filing Department's first checkpoint.

Marion had worked in the department many times before, though she'd never seen it so crammed with Inquirers. And as Rakes (and Amanda) had recently pointed out, most appeared to be doing more gossiping than work. Rakes shook her head as they passed, a losing battle perhaps. 'Unbelievable,' she snapped. Some of her colleagues shifted uncomfortably, most didn't even notice and Marion was sure she heard the words *throat* and *stethoscope* mumbled several times before they'd reached the other side. 'You'd think they've never come across a murder case before. Right,' she concluded as they reached an office marked 'Special Case Officer'. 'Ready?'

Marion nodded. She'd prepared for her presentation for days and even with Dolores' interruptions and Mr Smithers' delivery of love letters, she'd recited and revised it at least three times over. Admittedly, case presentations were not her strength. But she was ready to prove herself.

She removed a file from her bag marked *SI 0087. The Scorch.*

'Just remember to mention the tracking device we discussed last week,' Rakes said. 'And for God's sake, don't give Swindlehurst any reason to doubt you, or my decision to include you in the investigation. He's already insinuated I'm using apprentices to do my dirty work.' She glowered and rapped her knuckles against the door.

'Come in,' said a low voice from inside.

Edgar Swindlehurst had been recruited nine years ago at the age of thirty-three and was a member of the first group to start at Miss Brickett's. As one of the most brilliant minds at the agency, he quickly rose to the position of department head. But for reasons no one quite knew, Swindlehurst had been ousted from the post just last year, when it was handed over to Rakes instead. Marion wasn't certain why the switch had happened, but it was obvious to everyone at the agency: Swindlehurst and Rakes were swimming in bad blood.

Marion hung back a moment. A flicker of trepidation crossed her mind as she tried to judge the expression on Rakes' face. The Scorch case was the agency's lead investigation. Marion had been assigned to shadow Rakes and record each step as it unfolded. While it had been a matter of luck that she'd been selected for the task, she was well aware that – like everything she did at Miss Brickett's – her future prospects at the agency greatly depended on how she handled it. If Swindlehurst and Rakes were impressed with her she'd score higher on her assess-ment report. But it wasn't as simple as that. Marion knew that everything she reported to Swindlehurst on Rakes' handling of the investigation could ignite a dispute between them, with Marion caught in the middle. If she wanted positive reports from both of them, she'd have to play a cautious game.

'Afternoon, Swindlehurst,' Rakes began, sharp and curt.

Swindlehurst nodded. No reply.

'Lane to present a report on the Scorch case,' Rakes went on in spite of the silence, gesturing for Marion to take over.

Marion greeted Swindlehurst and took a seat at his desk. She was often intimidated by his sheer stature and handsome features, amplified by his unsettling reluctance to speak unless entirely necessary. She cleared her throat and began, opening with a summary of the case.

Two weeks previously, the agency had received a letter from a man by the name of Norman Tucker. Mr Tucker's letter had been short and to the point, unlike the lengthy ramblings that were the norm. The letter, sent with a return address and several alternative contact details, had quite simply stated: *Me wife's been getting it from the Scorch. Follow her, you'll find him.* Normally, a tip-off such as this would be deposited directly in the rubbish bin. Miss Brickett's Investigations and

Inquiries just didn't have the time or the resources to deal with London's ever-growing throng of cheating spouses.

But the Scorch, as he was known to the confused and terrified citizens of London, had been on the agency's radar for nearly two years. A man shrouded in mystery, he stalked the city streets by night, peering up at windows, listening through crossed telephone lines, carefully picking his next victim. Although many people had claimed to have seen him watching them, no one seemed able to describe him, name him, or even note the colour of his hair. It was the fear, of course, that silenced them, for the Scorch was ruthless in his attacks – nearly every fortnight he would strike, launching petrol-laden torches through his chosen window. The attacks would come in the early hours, and with his victims sound asleep, the blaze would ravage their homes before they had a chance to escape. To date, twelve young men had been killed or severely disfigured.

Up until last year, no one had understood the Scorch's motivation. But several survivors had eventually come forth to expound a theory that the agency now knew to be true: the Scorch was a violent, merciless homophobe and his only goal was to rid London of what he saw as a dreadful plague.

'. . . we placed a tracking device in Tucker's wife's handbag last week,' Marion said, coming to the end of her report. 'Unfortunately, she hasn't left the house all week so it's not been of much use.'

Swindlehurst looked annoyed. It made Marion anxious. Had she said something she shouldn't have? He glanced at the file before him, a draft of Marion's report, then seemed to struggle with himself for a moment, almost as if he were trying to calm himself down. 'And what do you suggest next?'

She looked tentatively at Rakes. 'I discussed this with Rakes on Friday,' she went on, 'and I believe this is a case that warrants cooperation from the Met Police Force.'

Rakes said nothing, though Marion knew her opinion on the matter. Interacting with law enforcement was risky. Even the few external relationships the agency fostered had to be approached with caution. As ever, risk of exposure was a major concern and the greater the number of individuals on the outside who knew of the agency's existence, the more likely it was that one day one of them might turn against Miss Brickett's. Since the agency's establishment, only six members of the force – four detective inspectors, one constable and one chief officer – had ever been entrusted with the secret. And while these individuals were provided with only the most essential facts – the agency is privately run from a concealed location somewhere in London, specialised surveillance equipment is occasionally used in investigations – most eventually became too curious to be kept in the dark and were recruited as Inquirers. Most notably Frank Stone, previously a DI for the Dorset Police.

'They might have some information we're missing,' Marion added. 'Perhaps Frank could advise us on whom to speak to?'

Swindlehurst leaned back in his chair with an air of superiority. He glowered at Rakes. 'I suppose I'm expected to ask your opinion on this?'

'I don't like it,' Rakes said categorically, ignoring whatever subtext Swindlehurst had been hinting at. 'And they've got nothing, I'm sure of it. No one on the outside is getting anywhere with this case. I actually overheard that idiot Constable Redding say, "At least he's given himself a good name." For Christ's sake . . .'

Swindlehurst considered his notes. 'All right, then I suppose the best option is to continue to keep an eye on Tucker's wife. She's bound to make a move soon enough, even if she thinks she's being watched.'

Rakes nodded, exhaling with relief.

'In the meantime, Lane,' Swindlehurst went on, 'I'd like you to write up a full character profile on both Tucker and his wife. To be delivered to me by Wednesday the twenty-third.'

'*Wednesday*. Next week?' Marion said with alarm. She looked at Rakes pleadingly. Character profiles were arduous to complete, requiring hours of research, note taking, typing. She did a mental calculation in her head: two character profiles in just over a week, was that even possible?

'Do you have something more important to be doing?' Rakes asked. It was a challenge, not a question. But the answer was *yes*. She still had mountains of work to complete with Professor Bal in Gadgetry, including fixing the Distracter – which the professor was sure to follow up on once he'd recovered from the shock of Michelle White's murder.

Swindlehurst had grown impatient. 'I'm very happy to hand the case over to Shirley if you're not up to it.'

'No,' Marion said quickly. The only thing worse than being overworked was giving Amanda another reason to feel superior. 'I'll manage it.'

Rakes nodded. 'She'll have the report to you by two p.m. next Wednesday. You have my word.'

Swindlehurst looked as if this assurance meant very little. 'That'll be all, Lane.' He gestured to the door. 'Rakes, if you can spare a moment, there's something I'd like to discuss.'

'Regarding?'

Swindlehurst breathed, again it seemed as though he were trying to calm himself down. 'The state of the department.'

Rakes looked at Marion. 'Take over from Perry in filing for the afternoon. I'll meet you there later.'

Marion started for the door, glad to leave the tense atmosphere. Swindlehurst and Rakes had already engaged in some hushed debate by the time she'd closed the door, though she was sure she caught the phrase *pause of operations*.

Was Swindlehurst about to suggest what Amanda had earlier? A halting of internal operations as a result of White's murder? Perhaps Amanda had a point, as painful as it was to admit. It was all very well keeping everyone busy with paperwork and distractions, but no matter the extent of the Scorch's evil, surely the Inquirers really did have a more pressing problem on their hands. And as Marion crossed the Intelligence Department, she was convinced of a single chilling truth: the most urgent and deadly threat now no longer wandered the dirty streets of London – it lived down here, locked in this twisted, sunless labyrinth.

She arrived at the Filing Department and stepped up to the first of two tiny, miserable looking cubicles. One had been for Michelle White and now stood vacant, the other was for her colleague, John Perry.

'Afternoon.' She nodded at Perry. 'Rakes said to take over from you for the afternoon.'

John Perry stared at her for three long seconds before seemingly comprehending what she'd said. 'And you know what you're doing, Miss . . .?'

'Lane. And yes. Anything that comes through the receivers gets sorted and filed accordingly. I've been on duty before.' She knew she sounded terse, but she was reaching the end of her tether with everything.

Perry blinked. He looked exhausted and Marion knew why. The receiver boxes had to be monitored all hours of the day and night, so the task had been split between Michelle White and Perry, with White taking all shifts from 6 p.m. to midnight and Perry or the apprentices all those in between. Now, of course, Perry was forced to double up and by the looks of it, he'd not slept in days.

'Right then, all yours,' he said hastily, perhaps before Marion could change her mind.

63

Moments after he'd left, a bell chimed from across the office, indicating that a letter had come through one of the receiver boxes. A light flashed on the dashboard above.

Marion located receiver box 101, flipped it open and removed the letter inside.

Don't know if you care, but there's someone suspicious like living in the Clapham Common. Sleeps under that big birch tree (you know the one). Seen him steal a handbag once, almost took mine the other day. Also has two street dogs, very nasty rabid things and one of them killed me cat. Can't go to police, don't ask why. And don't come looking for me, neither.
 Thanks, Harriet

Harriet's handbag thief could surely be handled by the most inexperienced of Inquirers – a few days of surveillance at Clapham Common, a couple of photographs of the criminal in action and, finally, an anonymous package sent to the local police station: the handbag thief himself, bound and unconscious along with an envelope containing the photographs.

She flipped open the register file and began to fill in the details. She noticed that the last entry had been made on Friday 11 April at 11.45 p.m. The entry appeared to be incomplete. The time, date and the receiver box number had been recorded, but the category listing had been left blank. As was customary, the entry had also been initialed by the staff member who'd collected it. This one was initialed in hurried script: *M.W.*

'Shirley's bloody gone and done it, spoken to Nancy about pausing operations,' Rakes said to Marion as she met her in the Filing Department nearly an hour later. 'Can you believe that? She actually went behind my back. And worst of all, she

must have done it this morning before she even spoke to me.'
She pulled a cigarette from her handbag, slumped her boots on
Perry's desk and lit up. 'Now Swindlehurst's in a rage because
Nancy thought the idea came from him. Jesus Christ, what a
mess. I'll tell you what, Lane, you'd better get those character
profiles to him on time or he might explode . . .'

She went on but Marion was hardly listening, distracted
by what she'd seen in the register file – Michelle White's
initials – made the very night she was murdered. Had Perry
noticed it? Surely someone would have checked the file by
now, all things considered.

'. . . and at this rate we might as well all go home, since
nothing's getting done around here anyway,' Rakes went on
in the background. She stopped to glare at Marion. 'Say it.'

'I'm sorry?'

'Something's on your mind. Spit it out.'

Marion hesitated, but the look on Rakes' face was one of severe
impatience. 'It's just that I saw White's signature in the register,
it looks as if a letter came through a receiver box the night she
was murdered. I wondered if Perry had reported it to anyone?'

'You're as distracted as the rest of them.' She shook her
head. Instead of irritated, however, she now looked defeated,
resigned. 'Nancy checked the register first thing after the
murder. Of course she knows about the signature.'

'Right, obviously.' She dared not ask what the letter said.

Rakes sighed, her expression softening somewhat. 'But no,
it wasn't Perry who reported it. God knows he wouldn't lift
a finger to help the investigation.'

'Why's that?'

Rakes shrugged. 'He just doesn't care.'

'You mean he and White didn't get along?'

'Of course not. White was Perry's superior. She was also
younger than him. He hated taking orders from her.' She

grinned. 'I know what you're thinking: Perry sounds like the perfect suspect, eh? Thing is, if you're going on personality clashes, you'd have to suspect the whole agency.'

'What do you mean?'

Rakes blew a trail of smoke into Marion's face. It was unintentional, she hoped.

'There were very few people who *did* actually like Michelle. I was one of them. Professor Bal and Nicholas were just about the only others.'

Marion looked around. She was probably imagining it, but it seemed that the chatter of the Inquirers next door had paused. Were they listening in?

'As I say,' Rakes went on, 'I liked her guts. She didn't give a damn what people thought of her and she got right up in everyone's business whenever she felt like it. But that was the thing, you see. That was what got on Perry's nerves. His and nearly everyone else's.' A small smile played on her lips. 'You must have figured it out by now, the reason everyone's so interested in this news of the murder weapon. Tell me, Lane, what's the old name for a Herald Stethoscope?'

'I didn't know it had an old name.'

'*The Snitch*,' Rakes said. 'Same as White's nickname when she was an apprentice. Ironic, isn't it? If anyone ever had something to hide in this place, Michelle was the one who'd know about it. Whatever she found out this time, well, I reckon it cost her her life.'

6

The Memory

It was a clear and concise memory. In light of Aida Rakes' and Uday Bal's recent revelations, an incident that had once seemed barely significant now carried a more chilling implication.

It had rained all day, that cold Friday in February. A torrent of icy rain pelted down relentlessly, rattling the bookshop windows, flooding the gutters in the street outside and turning the cul-de-sac into a grimy river. And so it was no particular surprise that at five o'clock most of the apprentices were still at the agency, either taking their time to complete their duties, or lounging over a game of cards. Anything to delay their journey home until the weather improved.

But for Marion, who'd been stationed in the Gadgetry Department that afternoon, delaying the daily rush home had nothing to do with the weather. Through trial and error, she'd discovered the trick was simply to appear busy. Every afternoon without exception, she'd hang around the agency, offering her assistance wherever it was needed for as long as reasonably possible.

Fortunately, that Friday, despite the relative calm throughout the rest of the agency, the apprentices stationed in Gadgetry were burdened with such a plethora of tasks that by lunch-time Marion didn't have to offer extra help, Professor Bal had begged for it.

Marion's task was relatively simple – place five test wires on the workbench in front of her, turn them on, say something, then retrieve the recording for analysis. Perfectly easy, except for the fact that Professor Bal had forgotten where he'd left the defective batch of button microphones and Marion had therefore spent the first half of the afternoon scouring the Gadgetry Department for twelve wonderfully undetectable tiny black discs.

Then she was set the chore of cleaning and refilling Professor Bal's ever-increasing stock of halothane emitting hip flasks. This was fiddly, tedious work – five small mesh-covered halothane-filled balls having to be cleaned, then squeezed through the hip flask's narrow aperture, which almost always resulted in an accidental rupture or two and a swift trip to the infirmary for all those close enough to inhale the gas.

At six thirty that evening, after depositing the last flask, filled and ready for use, on Professor Bal's workbench, Marion left the department and made her way up to the cafeteria. She'd planned to slip in an early dinner before the inevitable return to 16 Willow Street. Dolores would surely be waiting for her, probably with a pot of cold vegetable stew and a list of questions related to her lateness. She wouldn't have to eat the stew, at least.

Her evening would take a strange turn, however, for on her way to the cafeteria Marion was forced to take a detour.

The shortest route from Gadgetry went past Mr Nicholas's office, merging with the corridor that ran past the main library entrance and eventually down towards the cafeteria.

But as Marion neared the bend in the corridor outside Nicholas's office, she'd heard something that made her pause. At first it sounded like an argument between Frank and Nancy. She couldn't see them, as they were standing just on the other side of the bend, but she recognised their voices.

'. . . you can hardly blame the boy,' said Frank. 'He's only—'

'I don't care what he is, Frank,' Nancy said. 'And your sympathy for his situation changes nothing. What was he doing there out of office hours? And what was he doing with a skeleton key?' She paused. There was the sound of shuffling feet, then nothing.

Frank sighed. 'You can't fire him. Please, Nancy. I'm sure Rupert has the situation under control and if not, I will speak to him myself.'

Marion heard Nicholas's office door swing open and two sets of boots rush out. She took a step forward and peered round the corner.

Mr Nicholas, Nancy and Frank were standing cross-armed in front of David Eston, who looked furious.

Nicholas smiled warily. 'Not to worry,' he said, rather out of breath, 'everything is well and sorted. I was just assuring Mr Eston that he will soon come to realise everything we've done has been in the best interest of . . . well, everyone. Now, have you two come to a decision?'

Nancy looked sternly in Frank's direction. There was a long hesitation and eventually she spoke. 'Yes. I have decided to take Mr Stone's advice in the matter. You may remain at Miss Brickett's, Mr Eston, so long as you assure us that we will not have a repeat of this situation.'

David's cold expression did not change.

'An assurance is needed, Mr Eston,' Nancy repeated, holding out a sheet of paper.

David didn't take it from her. 'What's that supposed to be?'

'The assurance, in writing. You will not go down there or anywhere near the Gadgetry Department out of office hours or unaccompanied. Sign it,' Nancy demanded.

David sneered. 'You can't be serious?'

'I will explain this to you one last time, Mr Eston.' Nancy had turned on her coldest, most severe voice, one she reserved for occasions such as this. As she spoke, her words were clear and sharp, so much so that even David, even then in his most brutish state, did not dare interrupt. 'I have run this agency for ten years on inflexible principles, implemented to protect all those for whom I am responsible. You were not forced to join us, and you are free to leave should you wish to do so. But as long as you are under my care, so long as you work within these walls, you will abide by each and every policy and regulation I have put in place. Or you will suffer the consequences without question. Now, sign it.'

It must have been at least a full minute that David stood there, staring at the document in Nancy's hand. Nobody spoke, nobody even seemed to breathe. Eventually and with great hostility, David received the piece of paper (and a pen swiftly provided by Nicholas) and scratched a signature at the bottom.

The party began to disperse and Marion to panic. She could not risk being seen, as it would have been quite plain that she'd been eavesdropping. Fortunately, and just in time, she noticed a crevice in the wall behind where she was standing. She dashed towards it and wedged herself into the tight space. As she edged further inside she realised that the space was larger than she'd expected – a decent-sized oblong room whose north facing wall was also the outer boundary of Nicholas's office.

She waited in the darkness and quiet until certain the party outside was long gone. The incident she'd inadvertently witnessed had left her uneasy, though David was just the sort of person she'd expect to end up in Nicholas's office within the first two months of his apprenticeship. He'd obviously been found trying to steal something from the Gadgetry Department, and had been rightfully threatened with dismissal should he be caught doing so again.

She heard a shuffle of movement behind her, from further within the crevice. She turned around to find Michelle White standing in the shadows.

Michelle smiled curiously as they locked eyes. 'I see . . .' she said softly, taking a step forward.

Marion froze. She'd been so sure the crevice was empty. 'Miss White, I was just—'

Michelle nodded knowingly. 'Don't worry, my dear, a little eavesdropping never harmed anyone.' She looked down at the leather handbag hanging over her shoulder. And there, poking out from the centre compartment, as if rapidly shoved inside, was her trusty Herald Stethoscope. Michelle caressed the exposed end of the stethoscope as if it were a beloved pet, then pushed past Marion, her stride confident, triumphant even. There was no doubt in Marion's mind that Miss White was very happy with what she'd just overheard.

7

A Note of Desperation

Tuesday morning, Marion left for work earlier than usual. Dolores had not yet woken, nor had Marion seen her the evening before. Thank heavens. After the Monday she'd just had, the last thing she felt like doing was concocting a plausible excuse for her exhaustion that had nothing to do with murder, stethoscopes or agency gossip.

She pulled on a brown swing coat and stepped into the biting spring air, nearly colliding with the rag and bone man who'd deposited himself on the pavement outside her front door. He grunted and cursed as she passed, but Marion hardly noticed. As with the rest of her journey to the bookshop that morning, something else was occupying her thoughts.

As much as she tried not to, over and over she found herself replaying the memory of David's rebuke. Whatever he'd been reprimanded for, Michelle White had known about it. Marion realised now that as a known snitch, Michelle likely harboured a number of agency secrets, but perhaps David's in particular interested her more than usual.

She thought back to what Professor Bal had said the day before – Michelle had seemed disturbed, worried. Something about *someone looking for it*. Something about David. So was the thing Michelle said someone was *looking for* the same thing

David had been trying to steal in February? Had Michelle caught David looking for it, or trying to steal it, again? Had she got in his way?

A vile yet credible thought naturally followed – was David Eston then capable of murder? But perhaps this was foolish to ask. Marion had known David just four months, a minute space of time, surely not long enough to unravel the layers and intricacies of another's character. Of course, if she hadn't known David long enough to decide whether or not he were capable of murder, was the same not true for everyone she'd crossed paths with at Miss Brickett's?

Despite her early start, Marion arrived at the bookshop just before eight – the tube ride towards Fulham Broadway had been a mess of bodies and soot, taking longer than expected.

She unlocked the bookshop door, stumbled through the darkness, through the trapdoor and down the staircase to the lift. She pressed her silver apprentice badge against the wall and waited.

The trapdoor creaked open above her. Someone was coming down the stairs.

'Hold the lift.' David appeared on the staircase. He paused, appearing almost as surprised to see Marion as she was to see him.

They stared at one another in the dim light. Neither greeted the other.

The lift arrived, groaned, shuddered and slid open. They stepped inside. Marion pressed herself into the corner, unnerved by his presence, the residue of the memory fresh in her mind. The doors rattled shut and the lift began to move. Tension choked the cramped space as the silence between the two occupants continued.

Marion examined David's features, noticing how hard and worn he appeared: the deep hollows beneath his eyes, the sharp angle of his nose, the roughness of his skin. She'd heard rumours of his upbringing, of how regularly he'd been involved in brawls and family disputes, one of which was said to have left his stepbrother with two black eyes and temporary hearing loss. Indeed, she'd experienced his unchecked temper firsthand during a shared afternoon in the Gadgetry Department where he'd lost his patience while assembling a microdot camera. She remembered watching the rage build behind his eyes as he fumbled with the delicate parts. Eventually it culminated in an outburst that destroyed both the camera and one of Professor Bal's magnifying glasses.

She wondered now, as she had many times before, what Frank and Nancy had ever seen in David worthy of recruitment, what skills he'd gained at a metalworks valuable enough to be considered for the apprenticeship.

She wondered what made him tick. What might make him snap.

She lowered her gaze to focus instead on the thing in his hand. At first she thought it was just a roll of parchment. But the longer she stared at it, the more details she took in. It was old and while apparently devoid of any script it appeared to be etched with lines of strange, silvery furrows that criss-crossed its surface at random. It was also tied by a thin strip of purple ribbon.

The lift rocked and swayed as it slipped deeper below ground and despite the cooling air, a film of perspiration formed on David's forehead, reflected in the lift's fluorescent light.

He noticed her staring at the parchment and pushed it into his pocket. Out of sight. 'I heard a rumour yesterday,' he said. His voice was fractured, blunt – just like his features.

Marion's throat tightened. She took a moment to answer. 'Concerning?'

'Word is, you've caused some trouble with Perry in the Filing Department.'

'What's that supposed to mean?'

'He's been called in for questioning regarding White's murder.' He raised an eyebrow. 'Didn't think that was your style, Lane. Thought you preferred to stay out of trouble, out of official agency business.'

Marion moved further into the corner. He must be lying, pushing her buttons.

Relax. Don't rise to it.

'I don't know what you're talking about.'

'Apparently he might get the sack now, which I suppose means he's innocent. Doubt they'd fire a murderer. Bunch of imbeciles. You'd think they'd have figured it out by now, wouldn't you?'

'Figured what out?' Marion asked, the words escaping her with little consideration. She wanted the lift to stop. She wanted to be out in the open, away from him.

'Who the killer is, of course.' He cast his eyes around the lift. The brakes were screeching. It was coming to a stop at last.

'And have you? Figured it out?'

He didn't reply, though his eyes glinted, the reflection of some dark thought perhaps. He fiddled with the thing in his pocket.

'What is that?'

David's features changed almost instantly. Gone was the sneer he'd worn moments ago. In its place was a flash of anger.

The lift jerked to a stop and the doors slid open.

It was clear David was trying to control himself, to hold back the wave of fury inside him. 'As if you don't know.' He pushed past her and into the corridor but paused a few yards on. He turned back. 'This is between me and Hobb. So you mind your own business, you hear me?'

Marion held back a shudder. 'You're threatening me?'

'I'm *warning* you. Just stay the hell out of our business.'

★

75

Marion arrived at the cafeteria and waited. The room slowly filled with staff members and apprentices but Bill was nowhere to be seen. Once the buffet had been set, she served herself an egg sandwich and cup of coffee and settled at a table by the fireplace. It was only the second time since her recruitment that she'd eaten a meal without Bill.

Our business.

She flinched at the memory. What had David meant by it? He'd been trying to scare her off, of course. But from what? Something he believed she already knew, it sounded like. Something to do with the thing in his pocket. But why did he think she knew anything about it?

Our business. David and Bill. He must have assumed Bill had filled her in. Except he hadn't.

She looked at her watch. Eight thirty rolled by, then eight forty-five. Bill wasn't coming to breakfast, just as he hadn't arrived for lunch the day before. She picked at her food, then at her nails. The buffet table was cleared away and the cafeteria began to empty.

She knew she was overreacting, that Bill's absence over the past twenty-four hours surely meant nothing. He was just busy, or preoccupied. But still she felt ill at ease. Was it because she feared something was wrong, or because she felt slighted, left out?

Since the very first day they'd met, she and Bill had been inseparable. They'd found comfort in each other's oddities, the way neither quite fit in. They'd laughed at Maud and Jessica's bickering, groaned at David's snide remarks. They'd listened to the same programmes on the wireless during their breaks and joked about the similarities between their awful relatives. They weren't just friends. They were each other's family at Miss Brickett's. So why would Bill keep a secret from her? Why would he suddenly not trust her? Despite what

Frank had said – that everyone had their secrets and should be allowed to keep them – she knew this was different. She knew Bill well enough to sense that this wasn't a secret he *wanted* to keep.

She pulled her work roster from her pocket and unfolded it on the table. It was a busy day, as usual, but she had two free slots before lunch, which she'd spend in the library working on the character profiles for the Scorch case.

She inhaled three times.

Relax. David was just being his usual self. Bill is fine, he's probably just busy with a project. Everything is fine. You have work to do. Concentrate on that.

'Miss Lane, did you hear what I said?' Marion flinched, ripped from her reverie. She looked up. Edgar Swindlehurst was towering over her.

'I'm sorry?'

Swindlehurst's stark, handsome features were already twisted with impatience. 'I asked you how the character profiles are coming along?'

Marion coloured. She didn't dare admit she hadn't even started. 'Very well, actually. I'm almost done.'

'Good, because I now need them to be submitted by the twenty-first.'

'That's Monday,' Marion said in disbelief. Finishing the profiles by the following Wednesday, as originally expected, was bad enough. Finishing them in six days when she hadn't even started was quite impossible.

'Yes. And?'

She opened her mouth. She was really in for it now.

'Would you like to know why?' Swindlehurst pulled a file from under his coat and threw it unceremoniously onto the table. Marion started to sweat. The file was stamped: Human Resources, Employee Complaint Form. She stared at it but didn't move. 'Your colleague, Miss Shirley, has registered a complaint about the running of Intelligence.'

Swindlehurst's tone was searing. So much so that Marion actually shuffled backwards in her seat. 'She thinks Intelligence should free up some of its resources and time to concentrate on White's case. Nancy agrees, which means I'm expected to present case progress reports on all our investigations to Rakes on Wednesday, so I'll need the profiles before then.' His voice was low and rasping when he spoke again. 'I'm reporting to Rakes now, can you believe that?'

A rhetorical question, Marion realised. She waited for Swindlehurst's mood to settle before she spoke, though there really wasn't much she could say. 'I'll have the reports to you by Monday.' *God knows how*, she added to herself as he nodded and left.

Later that morning, Marion arrived at the library. She found an empty cubicle in the reading corner and immediately began the Tucker character profiles. It was tedious, intricate work but Marion pushed through, driven by the sheer terror of imagining herself arriving at Swindlehurst's office on Monday empty-handed.

She worked furiously for two hours before her thoughts started to drift, almost as if her mind was trying to work something else out in the background.

At twelve forty, she relented. She wasn't anywhere near to finished with the profiles, but she'd got a start on them at least. She closed the file and pressed her thumbs into her eyes. They stung with exhaustion and frustration. She surveyed the forest of shelves surrounding her, long shadows cast on the marble floor like towering oaks in the afternoon sun. The only person who loved the library more than her was Bill, and often she'd found him cross-legged on the floor, his back resting against a shelf, a book on his lap. But of course he wasn't here today.

She stared vacantly ahead. Why was her recent encounter with David nagging her so, now especially, as she thought of Bill?

Finally, she realised.

It was the thing she'd seen in David's hand. That strange looking parchment. It had struck a flame of recognition in her mind the minute she'd seen it, though she couldn't place why or from where. But she remembered now. It wasn't that she'd ever seen it before. She'd heard of it.

A roll of parchment, tied with a purple ribbon.

Bill had spoken about it yesterday morning on their way to the Gadgetry Department. He'd asked her if she'd seen it anywhere.

Someone was looking for it.

She rubbed her forehead. Her thoughts were chaotic, unclear and yet she felt close to it – the thing she had to understand.

Voices drifted towards her from the southern wing of the library, where the bar was located. One of them was Preston's, the others were muffled and unrecognisable. Maybe Bill's was among them.

She crossed the library and entered the bar. The space was small and cosy with dark wooden furnishings, dim lighting and air that smelled of stale beer. Other than the common room and the cafeteria, this was the place you'd be most likely to find the apprentices during their breaks. The bar was run by a man the apprentices referred to as Harry Nobody (on account of the fact that no one knew his surname), an elderly, gaunt man who doubled as the agency's head cook.

Jessica, Maud and Preston were seated at the counter. No Bill. No David.

'Wine?' Maud asked as she approached.

'It's the middle of the day,' Marion said, taking a seat.

'My point exactly.' Maud smiled. 'Harry? Two whites please.' Harry groaned but poured the glasses all the same. 'On me,' Maud said as Marion pulled out her purse.

'Thanks.' She examined the dark room once more. Bill was definitely not there. But someone else was, someone she didn't recognise. Seated alone several tables away was a tall, broad-shouldered man with light olive skin and a thicket of sandy blond hair. He was wearing a ridiculously bright electric-blue shirt and white trousers. This brazen attire – coupled with body language that suggested he was surveying the room, watching, waiting – caused Marion to feel instantly unnerved, or perhaps intrigued. The man paused when his gaze settled on her. He tapped a forefinger to his head in salute. Was she supposed to know who he was? The stranger cast his attention elsewhere, but she felt the heat of his attention linger. 'Who *is* that?'

Jessica chewed her lip. 'Gorgeous, isn't he?'

Yes, she thought. 'Odd, more like,' she said. 'What's he doing here?'

'Apparently he's just been hired, from New York I think.'

'He's American?' Marion said, examining him again. 'I suppose those clothes are fashionable over there?'

Maud snorted. 'Brilliant. Anyway, we were just talking about the murder.'

'Oh good,' Marion said sarcastically. She took a large sip of wine. It was awful stuff, cheap and acidic. Even so it seeped into her blood, dulling her thoughts. She took another sip.

'Jessica reckons Nancy's in on it. Covering something up,' Maud went on, her eyes shining. This was obviously not her first drink of the day.

'Don't be ridiculous,' Jessica said hurriedly. She looked at Marion. 'That's not what I said. I just said that I think it's strange we've heard nothing more about it. We should be kept in the loop. At the very least, we should be told if they know who did it.'

'If I were a betting man,' Preston intervened, now grinning almost as broadly as Maud. 'I'd say it was Amanda.'

Maud laughed, a thunderclap of delight that rattled through the otherwise still, stiff atmosphere.

'I don't see what's funny about any of this,' Jessica said reproachfully. 'And Amanda's had a hard day. If any of you paid attention—'

'A hard day?' Preston was unconvinced. He ordered a beer from Harry. 'What's happened? Her driver quit and she's had to take the tube to work like the rest of us?'

'She has a driver?' Maud's voice rose several octaves.

'Yeah, I've seen some bloke drop her off at least five times.'

'Huh . . .' Maud finished her wine and gestured to Harry for another. He refused. She didn't seem bothered. 'Reckon he's a lover?'

Preston shook his head. 'Impossible. Only a mother could love—'

'Okay, come on,' Jessica cut in. 'I'm serious. Something happened in Intelligence and I think she's at risk of losing her position there. Just a miscommunication I think. Apparently, Amanda went to Nancy with a few things she thinks Rakes and Swindlehurst could improve upon on the administrative side—'

'Oh Jesus,' Maud said.

'Amanda thought she could do a better job than someone? Doesn't sound like her,' Preston chided.

Jessica ignored them. 'The whole thing seems to have caused another feud between Swindlehurst and Rakes, and now Nancy's reconsidering Amanda's position.'

'Good,' Marion said, unable to stop herself. 'It's thanks to her I'll have to work overtime every night this week.'

Jessica frowned but didn't ask for details. 'Anyway, my point is, I think we should go easy on her.'

'Poor lass,' Maud said, thick with sarcasm. She looked at Preston. They raised their (empty) glasses. '*To Amanda.*'

Jessica sighed and turned to Marion, seeming to read her thoughts. It was unnerving, as usual. 'You seem agitated?'

'I'm fine.' Marion averted her eyes. She was not in the mood for Jessica's frustratingly accurate observations. She looked over her shoulder. The stranger in the corner had left.

'You don't look it. Someone's upset you?'

'No. Really, I'm fine.'

Jessica was unrelenting. 'I'm finding it difficult, too. I'm sure everyone is. We're expected to just carry on as if nothing's changed.' She waited. Her eyes flickered and shone, it was impossible not to feel that, under their watch, you could say anything.

'I'm just tired. And stressed,' Marion finally admitted. 'And I think there's something going on with Bill, but he won't tell me what—'

Jessica drew in a breath. Marion's attention was momentarily diverted to Amanda, who'd just entered the bar.

'Wine?' Maud asked again, this time directing the question at Amanda. Unlike Marion, she didn't resist in the slightest.

'You all right, Mands?' Preston asked without much sincerity.

Amanda turned to Marion. She looked at her with contempt. 'Would've been if we weren't short-staffed for the morning shift.'

It took Marion a while to realise Amanda was talking to her specifically. 'What are you looking at me for? I was stationed in HR this morning.'

'I'm talking about your friend, Hobb. He was supposed to be on duty with me and Jessica but conveniently he had to run off.'

Marion's pulse quickened. She waited for Amanda to elaborate.

'. . . tell him to try a better excuse next time.'

Marion put down her glass. 'What are you talking about?'

Amanda frowned, something between confusion and irritation. She looked briefly at Jessica. '*Urgent meeting with Marion. Ring any bells?*'

Marion opened her mouth. Her throat was dry, her mind firing a mile a minute.

'Crap . . .' Jessica opened her purse and pulled out a folded note. 'So sorry. Bill said to give this to you.'

'When did you see him?' Marion's voice wavered.

'This morning, on my way to Intelligence. Would have passed it on sooner but I forgot . . .' Jessica began to explain how she'd been so busy in Intelligence and so distracted with everything she'd been tasked with.

Marion heard none of it. She unfolded the note.

Mari,
Sorry I missed you at lunch and breakfast. I've been caught up in something and I need your help. I should have said so sooner but things are complicated – it's about David. I'm really worried. Meet me in the common room at eleven and I'll explain. Please don't be late.

'Jesus, Jess!' Marion looked at her watch. It was nearly one.

'I'm sorry. Mari . . . what's wrong?'

Marion jumped up, addressing the group. 'Does anyone know where David is?'

Everyone stared at her.

'He took leave for the day as well apparently,' Amanda said.

'No he didn't,' said Preston. 'I saw David after breakfast. Said he had a meeting with Bal at one.'

'Hang on . . .' Jessica said after some time. She frowned at Preston. 'David's meeting Bal?'

Preston shrugged. 'Yeah.'

'Meeting him in the Workshop? Today?'

'Maybe. I don't know where.'

Marion looked anxiously at Jessica. 'What?'

'Well, Bal's not here, is he? He left last night for Edinburgh to visit his family. Coming back tomorrow.'

'You're sure?'

'Definitely,' Jessica said.

The knot in Marion's stomach tightened.

Maud, who had been observing the disjointed conversation with a look of mild interest, spoke: 'I feel like I'm missing something here.'

Marion picked up her handbag and slung it over her shoulder.

'Where are you going?' Maud asked.

'I need to find them.'

'Who?'

'Bill and David!'

'Right . . .' Maud said. 'And why's that?'

She hesitated. Maud, Preston and Jessica were looking at her – Jessica anxiously, Maud curiously, Preston casually. Amanda, however, avoided her eye. 'It's a long story,' she said quickly, leaving the bar without elaborating.

8

The Spy in the Corridor

There were several things Marion now understood.

David had been called into Nicholas's office that Friday afternoon in February for something he'd been attempting to steal – the same thing Bill had lost yesterday morning on his way to the Gadgetry Department, a roll of parchment tied with a purple ribbon. And now David and Bill had disappeared, one in possession of the parchment in question, the other perhaps hoping to get it back.

But more disturbingly, Marion feared the parchment was also linked to Michelle White, and to her murder.

She came to a halt at the top of the stone staircase. In the dim flicker of the tunnel lights and in the cool, thin air, Marion could hardly breathe. She ran her fingers through her sweat-damp hair, trying to decide whether to trust her suspicions. She'd already searched the common room, although she'd been sure Bill wouldn't still be there. He was surely with David now, but if David's Workshop meeting with Bal had been a ruse, where had they gone?

'You're right to be worried,' said a voice from behind her, as if in reply. Amanda was standing in the corridor, a thick scarf around her neck. 'About Bill, I mean. He looked pale when he ran off. Afraid. David was hovering around, too.' She came further into the light.

Marion's heart rapped against her chest, but Amanda seemed in no rush to elaborate. 'Do you know where they are?'

Amanda took a step closer. It was only then that Marion noticed how tense and weary she looked. Her face was stiff and cold at the best of times – her pale eyes piercing, her thin lips tight and emotionless. Today she looked more distant and removed than ever. 'They were staring at this piece of parchment,' she said, not answering the question Marion had asked. 'Looked very old, strange. When they saw me coming, David shoved it into his pocket.'

'Do you know what it is?'

'Of course not.' Amanda put her hands in her pockets. 'Funny Bill hadn't told you already. I thought you two were friends.'

Marion took a breath, in place of saying something she might regret. She turned to the staircase to think.

Amanda watched her as an entomologist might observe an interesting new species of insect. 'I think they've gone down there.' She pointed to the foot of the staircase.

'The Workshop?'

'No,' Amanda hesitated. 'White's office.'

Marion's breath quickened. 'What?'

'I told you. I saw them together after Bill handed Jessica the note. I tried to ask David where they were going because I was so fed up with Bill's excuse for leaving. I followed them for a bit, but only heard them say something about White *having one* . . .' She paused, then: 'I don't know what they meant by that.'

Marion looked again to the foot of the staircase and the narrow path that threaded off into the greyness, beyond the Gadgetry Department, beyond the fringe of the agency, over the Border and into the unknown. If she travelled that way looking for Bill, she might get lost and never return. And if she did return, she might wish she hadn't – being fired from the agency was a fate as awful as nearly any she could imagine. But if Bill truly was in danger, then could she forgive herself for doing nothing?

She turned back to Amanda with the vague hope that maybe she'd know what to do. She'd always seemed so sure of herself, so frustratingly knowledgable. But Amanda had already disappeared. Marion checked her watch – one fifteen – then pulled her coat tighter about her shoulders and made her way down the staircase.

At first the path towards Michelle White's office seemed brighter and wider than it'd looked from the staircase, lit by a number of softly glowing lamps. But the further she travelled, the darker, danker and narrower it became. She trod carefully and noiselessly, fearful of whom she might bump into along the way. With every step towards the Border she questioned herself. Would Bill and David really have come down here? Had Amanda been lying? Was she about to be apprehended by Nicholas? Nancy? Michelle White's killer?

A few yards further on, she rounded a gentle bend and allowed herself a moment of relief as what must have been White's office came into view. A sign hung over the door, which stood ajar: *Miss M. White, Border Guard.*

She hesitated as she reread the sign – *Border Guard* – and regarded the dark tunnel that wound past White's office. It sent a chill down her spine as she was reminded of the old rumours, of what Miss Brickett's had been before – air raid bunker, command centre, a refuge for defamed alchemists. Was any of it true?

'Hello?' she called, placing her hand on the doorknob. 'Bill? David?'

No one answered.

The office was bare, cleaned out, packed away. It smelled of must and the air tasted like chalk. What Bill and David had come here for, she couldn't understand.

She stepped back into the corridor and glanced to the right. The corridor beyond was completely black, no lamps, no light – the path that led over the Border. No part of her wanted to carry on that way. She was already far too deep below the streets and sunshine than any human should be.

A voice. A groan, echoing off the walls, impossible to pinpoint.

'Bill?' Her voice was high and strained. Panic rose inside her, slow at first but gaining ground until every breath was weak and shallow.

Another groan, more urgent this time.

She followed it into the blackness, over the Border. Onwards she went, following the groans and the sound of an underground stream that was probably a minor tributary of the Thames as it flowed through the tunnel gutter, deeper and further into the earth. She had no idea where she was going, or even if the tunnel would lead her towards Bill or something else.

She took her time and counted her turns, pausing after each to listen for signs of movement, of life. But the silence was disturbed only by a low babble of water and the odd scuttle of tiny legs, cockroaches, rats or some other creature of the dark and cold.

She must have travelled less than half a mile (though it felt like more) by the time she came to the tunnel's first fork. The stream, now three times as wide and overflowing its gutter with murky, foul water, curved to the left. To the right was a dry but narrower tunnel.

'Bill? Where are you? Please answer me.' She hesitated. The babble of the stream was almost deafening now in the relative silence of the labyrinth.

Something moved behind her.

She turned, catching sight of a low shadow that darted across the tunnel floor. She took a shallow breath, shoved her hands further into her coat pockets and took another step forward.

Then it came.

Muffled, breathless voices drifted up from the dark to her right. Or had she imagined them? The walls here appeared to be of a different kind of material, ancient and brittle limestone, so porous that even her footsteps might be heard for miles.

She waited. Nothing.

Footsteps. Coming from the corridor before her, in fact, they sounded almost as if they were coming from *inside* the limestone wall. She unclipped a small latch on the side of her light orb, then pulled out the long cord attached. With the entirety of the cord slung over her forearm and the end wound tightly through her fingers, she tossed the orb a good distance down the tunnel.

Whatever she'd expected to see as the burning orb bumped its way along the uneven stone floor, it was not what she found herself looking at: two bright orange eyes attached to a long, thick, scaled metal creature.

Her body was dancing with adrenaline as the eyes grew brighter, bigger. She attempted to reel in the orb, but the cord slipped through her sweaty fingers and fell to the floor.

A bizarre sound crept through the silence. It was coming from the floor, from the thing with the orange eyes.

Clink – schlik, schlik – clink – schlik, schlik.

Long and thin, hardly visible save the glint from its metal scales, a six-foot long metal snake slithered towards her. Of all the brilliant and bizarre gadgets she'd seen in the Workshop, never had she come across something so real. Its movement was frictionless, effortless, as if each scale was a slip of perfectly polished steel, oiled twice over. More flesh and bone than metal and screws, it seemed to have a will of its own.

It slithered closer.

Though every part of her was twitching to move, Marion found herself unable to do anything but stare. The snake slithered over her feet. Even through the leather of her boots she felt the chill of the steel, the pull and twist of its clockwork muscles. Blood drained from her head and the ground began to sway. The last inch of tapered tail finally slipped over her. The tension in her limbs receded, the hot breath in her lungs released.

Clink – schlik, schlik – clink.

The creature slid into the darkness and was gone.

She bent over her knees and caught her breath. She heard the snake stop up ahead. The faded yellow light of a faraway tunnel lamp caught the edge of the snake's head. It had turned around. She lifted herself upright, which seemed to excite the dreadful creature. Much faster than it had moved before, it raced towards her. Its arrow-shaped head turned to face her. The creature reared into the air so that the top half of its shiny body was now just inches from her face.

Marion wished to close her eyes, but dared not risk it. The creature opened its mouth, a dark grey metal tongue tasted the air, rotating left and right, up and down. It hissed. For a moment that felt like a decade, the serpent hovered in front of Marion's face. Its long tongue slid in and out of its mouth as if trying to detect a flicker of movement, a wisp of air. Marion kept utterly still. Then, just as the snake's split tongue looked as if it might actually touch Marion's cheek, she heard the sound of someone running down the corridor. The snake immediately lowered its head to the ground and shot off after the noise like some bloodthirsty beast.

It was at that moment that Marion realised the end of the orb light's cord was moving away from her. Someone was pulling it forward, but because the orb itself now lay around a bend and out of sight, she could not see who. Or what.

Against all her better judgement, she followed the cord as it slid erratically, slowly away from her. It was only once she'd rounded the bend and was again cast into the orb's brilliant white illumination that she was able to see the body splayed out in the centre of the tunnel, one hand gripping the orb, the other appearing mangled and unnaturally thin.

Her heart thumped uncontrollably. She strained her eyes, pausing for just a moment, fear and cowardice threatening to take over.

'David?' She held the orb light over his body. Her stomach turned. His left leg was so blood-soaked and mangled, it was hard to make out in what direction it lay. His knee seemed to be turned nearly ninety degrees and his ankle the other way.

'Oh god! What happened?'

Her hands came to somewhere near the top of one of his legs. The skin was wet and sticky, just warm enough to be blood.

He pointed behind him. She turned the orb light to the wall.

In all the confusion and fear, Marion hadn't even noticed the gaping round hole in the limestone. It was like some odd door and appeared to lead into a tunnel so narrow it would've had to be entered on all fours. Marion crawled over and stuck her head into the hole.

David pulled her back. 'No, don't. It closes . . . whenever it likes.' He pointed at his leg and then she knew. 'Please, just get me out of here.'

Footsteps again. This time coming straight down the centre of the tunnel, and at a run.

A torch was switched on and its beam dazzled her eyes. The bearer galloped towards her.

'Marion. Jesus!' Bill lowered his torch and crouched down beside her. He directed the beam at David. 'Did you see the snake?'

David groaned and tried to move.

'David!' Bill repeated more viciously. 'Did the snake come past here. Did you see it?'

'No . . .' David eventually moaned.

'You saw it too?' Marion asked Bill.

He nodded. 'It belongs to Nicholas, I think. It's a spy, patrolling the tunnels.'

'What?' Marion said stupidly, her mouth so arid it came out as just a croak.

'Its eyes are motion-detecting cameras. They switch on only when they detect movement.'

Marion had a million questions – *Where did the tunnel in the wall lead to? Why was David crawling around inside it? Where had Bill come from? Where had the snake come from and why did Bill care whether David had seen it?* – but instead she looked down at David, his chest now barely rising. They had a more pressing problem.

She and Bill lifted David to his feet, a monumental effort with the bulky dead weight of his large frame. They carried him along the corridor, past White's office and onwards for what felt like miles until they reached the bottom of the long stone staircase.

'There's no way we'll get him to the top without doing more damage to that leg,' Bill panted. 'Wait here with him. I'll go find us some help.'

Marion's nerves felt as if they were on fire. She opened her mouth, yet nothing came out.

Bill gazed at her, his eyes were wide and terror-filled, his cheeks bruised, his bottom lip sliced open. 'He fell down the stairs.'

'Excuse me?'

'We have to tell everyone that David fell down the stairs. No mention that we were across the Border. No mention of the snake.'

'Bill . . .'

'I'll explain everything later. Just trust me, Marion. Please.'

9

Bill's Secret

It was five minutes to ten on Tuesday night. Marion stood inside the common room by the fire waiting for Bill, her legs a little weaker than they'd been all day, which was surprising in itself.

Several hours earlier, Bill had returned to the bottom of the stone staircase with Nancy and Professor Henry Gillroth – the agency's oldest employee, Head of Human Resources and High Council member. Marion flinched at Gillroth's arrival, simply because she knew his presence at the scene meant that Nancy suspected the accident required investigation. It was fortuitous, then, that by the time Nancy and Gillroth arrived, David had slipped into shock and had to be rushed to hospital for emergency surgery. There was no time for a thorough inquisition. And as planned, Bill told Nancy and Gillroth the bare minimum – David had slipped down the stairs and broken his leg. Admittedly, this was quite believable – the staircase and its forty-four smooth stone steps was just about as treacherous as anything else in the agency. Just about.

Marion was far too anxious to notice whether Nancy believed the lie, or to think about whether the snake, *the spy*, had recorded their presence in the tunnels. But Bill shot her a few meaningful glances, blatant warnings to keep her mouth shut. He promised he'd explain everything to her that evening when they planned to meet in the common room, late enough to ensure they'd be alone.

The door edged open and Bill stepped inside and joined her on the couch by the fireplace.

The apprentices' common room, located in the south-west wing of the agency, was a circular space fitted with mismatched chairs and couches, two fireplaces and a central oak table. Occasionally an overworked or intoxicated apprentice would spend the night curled up on one of the couches, though this seemed less desirous of late, considering a murderer was on the loose.

Bill poured them each a glass of water and lit himself a cigarette. It was only the second time Marion had seen him smoke. 'David's going to be fine. He did break his leg but it looked worse than it was. He'll stay in hospital for about a week, then spend the rest of his recovery here in the infirmary.' A trail of smoke wafted up to the ceiling and disappeared.

'And what about that snake? Did it see us?'

Bill looked uncertain. 'I think if it did, Nancy or Nicholas would have fired us by now.'

A suffocating tension filled the room. Marion was on edge, her nerves jittery. The four months she and Bill had been friends had felt like a lifetime at the start of the week. But now it seemed like an impossibly short fraction of time. She trusted him, though probably more than she should. She hoped whatever he'd been doing in the tunnels beyond the Border was innocent and dismissible. More than anything, she hoped her trust in him hadn't been misplaced.

She picked her nails under the cover of her coat pocket and waited.

Bill put out his cigarette and finished his water. 'I take it you didn't get my letter, then?'

'I did. Two hours late. If I hadn't, I would never have found you.'

Bill nodded. He looked off into the distance. Marion didn't rush him. She looked at his hand, the subtle tremor was back and now accompanied by a new tic, one she'd never seen before. 'A few weeks ago, I stole something,' he began, tapping his thumb against his middle finger. 'I'd been on duty in Filing for nearly five hours. Perry was away and White had been asked to fill in for him. She was in a horrible mood, I suppose because she'd been on duty the whole of the previous night as well. Anyway, there wasn't much to do, so White asked if I'd mind watching the receivers while she went up to the library bar for a drink. I agreed, not that I had a choice. You remember how she was?'

Marion nodded.

'Anyway, only one envelope came through the receivers while she was away and it was when I was filling in the letter's details in the register that I found something on her desk. I never intended to keep it, really. I just wanted to see what it was because it looked so odd. But I had it in my hand when she returned and it was just too awkward for me to give it back to her then so I slipped it into my bag.'

'What was it?' Marion asked, though she was certain she knew. The parchment.

He got his briefcase from the floor and pulled out what appeared to be a plain roll of parchment. He handed it to Marion. She unfolded it, noting its frayed edges, its surface mottled and yellowed with age. She held it to the light, tilting it at various angles. Although it did indeed appear to be plain, nearly imperceptible furrows of silvery thread criss-crossed its surface. Some were thicker than others, some appeared to connect to their neighbours and others to run in circles. Depending on how the light caught them, the furrows shifted position. Some even disappeared altogether.

She put it on her lap. Though the parchment and its silvery furrows were certainly unusual, she'd seen something similar once before. And so had Bill. So had everyone who worked at Miss Brickett's. 'Grey Ink?'

'Invisible ink. Yes. Similar to the stuff our recruitment letters were written in.'

Marion recalled the bizarre and seemingly plain letter Frank had presented her with the day of her recruitment. As she'd done then, she now held the parchment under the coffee table lamp, right against the bulb, until the paper was so hot it could burst into flame. But unlike with her recruitment letter, nothing happened.

'It won't work,' Bill said. 'It's definitely Grey Ink, just a different kind.' Again he opened his briefcase, and this time he removed a rather peculiar contraption: a copper eyeglass fitted with four lenses of varying size and thickness. 'This is a Grey Ink Monocle and the only way you can read that particular type of invisible ink.' He handed Marion the monocle and nodded at the parchment. 'Try it.'

Marion placed the parchment on Bill's lap and brought the first of the four lenses to her eye. Immediately it was as if she were looking into a pool of murky water. She tried the next lens. In an instant, the parchment was transformed. Hundreds of lines of greyish-blue ink emerged from their papery graves, some long and narrow, some thick and circular, an intricate mass of contorted pathways at last illuminated.

'My God . . .' she traced her finger across the centre of the page, then down to the left-hand corner. It was a complete map of the agency, every passageway, every room, every slipway. Including, it seemed, the tunnels beyond the Border – all far too complex and detailed to take in at once. And then something peculiar happened. The tunnel she had been staring at – one on the bottom edge of the map, beyond

Miss White's office and the Border – disappeared. When it reappeared seconds later, it had halved in length, intersecting with another that hadn't been there before. 'They move!' she added, a little too loudly. 'There, it happened again . . .'

'Right. And that's what happened to David. The walls down there . . . they shift, blocking off corridors, forcing you into alternative passages. I think they're on tracks or something but one minute you think you know where you're going, the next there's a wall blocking you in.' He breathed deeply as if recalling the ordeal. 'David and I, we were trying to find our way through a door that had just appeared in the wall in front of us. He was almost through it when it closed again. Right on his leg.'

The air in the common room was stuffy and hot. She laid the map and monocle on the coffee table and for a while said nothing. It wasn't that she didn't have anything to say, quite the contrary. Her head was heavy, overfilled and swelling with questions. She just wasn't sure which to ask first. 'But I don't understand. What were the two of you doing down there in the first place?'

He inhaled again, as if filling himself with the courage to continue. 'Ever heard of Ned Asbrey?'

Marion frowned, recalling the rumour she'd heard countless times. 'The apprentice who got lost in the tunnels eight years ago? I thought that was just a story.'

'Well, it's not. Ned was an apprentice with a drinking problem, just as the rumour goes, and one day he wandered into the tunnels. Thing is, Asbrey didn't quit the agency after coming back like everyone believes, because he never made it out of the tunnels. And Asbrey is David's stepbrother. He was quite a lot older than David, thirty-two when he disappeared. At the time, he and David lived together without any other family. When Ned was recruited, David didn't know anything about the agency. He just thought his stepbrother worked ridiculously long hours at a bookshop somewhere in London.

'But eight years ago, Ned didn't come home from work for five days. So David went to the bookshop for answers. I think he encountered Nicholas there but nothing much came of it. David went back the next day and tried again. This time he threatened to get the police involved if he wasn't provided with an explanation as to where his stepbrother had disappeared to. Problem was, Nancy couldn't allow the police to get involved, as you know. So she decided she had to tell him something. She said Ned had stayed at the bookshop later than usual the day of his disappearance, he'd been drinking and possibly wandered into the street and that was the last anyone saw of him. But David wasn't satisfied, or maybe he just sensed an opportunity. However it played out, in the end Nancy had no choice but to pay him off.'

'To keep quiet?'

'That's what he told me. And apparently it worked for seven years. The agency paid David's rent – it wasn't much but he got to live an easier life than he'd ever been able to before Ned's disappearance. And that was that. For a while at least.'

'Nancy paid him off for *seven years*?' Marion felt sick at the thought. Both because David had accepted the money and because Nancy had offered it.

'After a while, though, David got greedy. I'm sure you're not surprised by that . . .'

'Not at all.' David was exactly the type she'd imagine would strive to make a living off a family member's misfortune.

'Right. Neither was I when he told me. Anyway, he started asking for more money, more benefits,' Bill went on, 'but eventually Nancy had enough. She decided to change her approach. She probably realised she needed leverage, something that would prevent him from going to the police, which would in turn put an end to the bribes. So she offered him a job.'

Marion nodded. Finally, the reason behind David's recruitment made sense. Of course he hadn't been hired because of some hidden talent only Frank and Nancy had been aware of. He'd been hired because Nancy had been backed into a corner. She had no other choice.

Bill went on: 'Nancy probably knew she could convince him to join the agency quite easily, since the prospect was a lot more interesting than life at a metalworks factory, and he didn't tell me this, but I'm pretty sure he was offered a much better salary and benefits than the rest of us.' He seethed as he said this. Marion felt similarly. 'Anyway, once he joined, he had to sign those non-disclosure, culpability and consent documents we all had to sign upon recruitment. And then Nancy had him trapped, didn't she? He couldn't really go to the police after that, nor could he demand any more money. Not after he'd put his name on a piece of paper stating he knew everything he did at the agency was technically in breach of about fifty privacy laws.'

A constricting sensation was building around Marion's chest, a vice that tightened with every breath. She knew the documents Bill was referring to. The ones Nancy and Nicholas had made her sign upon recruitment – papers that listed her full name, her home address, stapled together with copies of her birth certificate and statements of consent and culpability. At the time, she'd been so overwhelmed with delight at being selected, she'd paid little attention to the fine print. But yes, she knew that if law enforcement were to discover the agency, it wouldn't just be Nancy or the High Council who'd be held accountable for Miss Brickett's covert operations – their illegal use of lock picks, tracking devices, spy cameras – it would be everyone who'd signed those documents.

Someone opened and closed a door in the corridor outside. Marion and Bill both twitched.

'You still haven't explained what any of this has to do with that thing,' she gestured at the map, 'or what the two of you were doing across the Border.'

Bill took a while to answer. 'When David started at the agency this year, I think some part of him realised he'd been manipulated and maybe he decided he did actually want to know what happened to his stepbrother after all. By then he must have heard the rumours, that Ned had entered the tunnels beyond the Border and disappeared. He became convinced there was more to the story. He started investigating, asking people questions: when they'd last seen Ned; had he been acting oddly the day he'd disappeared. After all, it didn't really make sense that someone would go down there for no reason. Even if they were drunk. What had he been looking for?

'Not many people had anything to say, but those who did all seemed to agree that Ned's disappearance probably had something to do with a strange piece of parchment that had been floating around the agency since the beginning, changing hands over the years.'

'The map?'

Bill nodded. 'The only map of the agency that shows *everything*. First it was said to belong to someone on the High Council. Then it passed to Ned, and after his disappearance it was seen in Michelle White's possession. People weren't sure how White got the thing, but it was generally assumed that Ned had seen something on it that had prompted him to go across the Border the night he disappeared. A few days later, Ned's backpack was discovered in the tunnels outside White's office. White handed the backpack to Nancy and that's how the rumour about him disappearing started.'

'So White stole the map and monocle from Ned's bag before she handed it over to Nancy?' Marion guessed.

Bill shrugged. 'David seems pretty certain that White would have had a rummage through Ned's things before she handed them over, and that the map and monocle were just too interesting not to keep. Anyway, when David was asking around, no one seemed completely certain what the parchment was, but most assumed it was a classified agency document of some sort – otherwise why would everyone have been so interested in it? And so I guess David decided he had to find the thing and see for himself. Sometime in February, he attempted to break into White's office to look for it, unsuccessfully, I'm told. White caught him hanging around her office and reported him to Nancy and Nicholas. Which is really how this whole mess started. You see, the day I took the map from White's desk, I was working alone in Filing, but David was just next door in Intelligence. White didn't realise the map was missing until the following morning, but as soon as she did, she confronted David.'

Marion nodded. 'Of course. Because of the incident in February. She must have known, even then, that he was looking for the map, since Ned was his stepbrother and the map's previous owner. Which explains what Professor Bal said yesterday, about his last meeting with White. *Someone was looking for it*,' she repeated the phrase the professor had used. 'I suppose, if she assumed David already had the map, she must have been talking about the monocle?'

'Yes, I think so.' Bill wrung his hands together. 'She knew he couldn't really use the map without the monocle, which she always kept in a separate location, but I suppose it worried her because she suspected he'd come looking for the monocle too. David denied everything, of course. And while White didn't want to let him off the hook, she couldn't really go to Nancy or Nicholas with the suspicion because then she'd have to tell them what he'd taken. Something she was never supposed to have in the first place.'

'Does Nancy know about the map?' Marion asked.

'I'm not sure. Seems likely though. Nancy knows everything. Anyway, the point is that David knew if he hadn't taken the map and it had gone missing when I was in Filing, then I was the only viable suspect. He confronted me. I should have just handed the bloody thing over right then but the truth was . . . the longer I had it, the more interested in it I became. I wanted to know what it was and how to read it, almost as much as David did. But then he began to threaten me. Every time we passed each other in a corridor or were stationed together for a shift, he'd say how he was going to expose me for stealing the thing from White.'

Marion then realised that this, at last, was the answer to the question that had been on her mind for weeks – the cause of Bill and David's ever deepening disdain for one another. She was relieved to have an answer. Mostly, however, she was frustrated with Bill for causing so much unnecessary tension between them.

'Why didn't you tell me any of this at the time?'

'I considered it. But then I wondered if it was fair for me to involve you. Technically, I'd stolen something from a senior employee. If I told you, you'd be an accessory to that.' He paused to refill his water glass. 'Obviously I realise now you'd rather have known,' he added when Marion shook her head. He sighed, then continued. 'Things came to a head on Monday morning after Nancy announced White's death. Somehow, David knew about it before the rest of us did and he followed me to the gent's before the meeting in the Auditorium. Somewhere along the line he stole the map from my briefcase, though I only realised it was missing on our way to Gadgetry.

102

'I knew it was David who'd taken it. It was the only thing that made sense. But when I confronted him, he told me that he'd figured out the parchment can only be read with a Grey Ink Monocle and if White had the parchment, she must have had the monocle too. He said that now that White was dead and her office empty, we had a proper chance to go looking for it. Of course I told him I wanted nothing to do with any of that, but—'

'But in the end you agreed to help him?'

'Not so much agreed as was forced. He said that if I didn't help him get into White's office today, he'd expose what I'd done. And considering I'd stolen the parchment from a woman who'd just been murdered . . . well, let's just say it wouldn't have cast me in a great light.'

The tremor in his hand was growing more rapid now and the frustration Marion had felt towards him earlier was swiftly transforming into compassion. She could sense his agitation as if it were her own. She felt his guilt and annoyance. David had a knack for getting his way and she doubted whether Bill, with his timid disposition, ever stood a chance against him.

'That's when I sent you the note,' he added. 'I wanted advice. I hoped you'd have some clever idea of how I could separate myself from the mess, from David . . . but when you didn't show in the common room, I had no choice.' He inhaled with difficulty. 'We found the monocle easily, lying in White's desk drawer. But when we tried to go back the way we'd come, a wall blocked our path and we were forced to cross the Border to find an alternative exit. I tried to use the map, but it was so dark down there and since the walls move so often, it wasn't much use anyway . . .' He trailed off, casting his eyes to the floor.

Marion was silent as she attempted to process everything Bill had told her. She glanced at the map on the coffee table.

'I'm sorry you're involved in all this,' Bill said. 'But we need to be careful. If Nancy finds out David and I broke into White's office or that any of us were across the Border, we'll be fired at the very best. That's why I told you to lie about David falling down the stairs. No one can know about the map, or what we were doing down there. No one.'

'David knows, about the map I mean. You think he's just going to forget you have it?'

'I'll tell him I lost it in the tunnels or something. We don't have to worry about him for a while anyway, not until he comes back from hospital.'

'Do you think he did it though? Do you think David killed White?'

Bill tensed. 'I don't know. He had motive, I suppose. To get White out of the way so he could find the monocle. Or maybe White decided to go to Nancy after all, about him stealing the map.'

For a long while, Marion and Bill just sat there. Neither said anything, nor even moved. Eventually Bill got to his feet and strolled closer to the fireplace. He crouched down and warmed his hands by the flames, which were beginning to die. Marion was weary, exhausted and overwhelmed. At some point she was going to have to make her way back to Willow Street and get some sleep, though the idea seemed incredibly unlikely now.

'I suppose David still doesn't know what his stepbrother went looking for in those tunnels?' she asked, staring again at the map. She picked it up and brought the monocle to her eye.

Bill shrugged. 'Maybe he just saw the shifting lines on the map and wanted to see what they were. Bad idea, obviously.'

Marion didn't say so, but that seemed improbable. Everyone who'd ever owned the parchment seemed to have been obsessed with it, willing to risk life and career to hold onto it. Why? What secrets did it reveal? She inspected it once more, noting rooms and passageways she hadn't known existed. Among the lines and passageways before her, she noticed something that chilled her blood – a line of labelled squares somewhere near the eastern edge of the agency. She removed the monocle and looked at Bill. 'What are the Holding Chambers?'

Bill said nothing. He looked at the common room door, as if waiting to ensure no one was crossing the corridor outside.

'I've heard of them,' he said eventually, lowering his voice. 'Just a rumour but—' He hesitated for a moment, then went on. 'Have you ever wondered what the agency does with Inquirers gone rogue? Or staff members who've committed a crime worthy of a jail sentence?'

Marion didn't answer, but of course she'd wondered. Most recently she'd thought about it in relation to Michelle White's death, for whoever had committed the crime could not be handed over to the police, nor could they be set free. There had to be a third option.

'Anyone who's committed a class three or higher transgression is sent to the Holding Chambers, or so I've heard,' Bill explained. 'No one is supposed to speak about them. Most staff members and apprentices don't even know they exist because they've never been used, apparently.'

'Maybe that's what Asbrey was looking for?'

Bill looked as if he'd rather not consider the possibility. 'Empty holding cells? Don't think so.'

Again Marion was aware of a tightening across her chest. The Holding Chambers might be empty now, but they'd certainly be put to use when Michelle White's killer was caught.

Bill moved back over to the couch and settled beside her. He placed an arm over her shoulder. 'Listen, Mari. It's a lot to take in but maybe we should just try to forget. Forget we ever heard of this bloody map. Or Ned Asbrey. Or the Holding Chambers. We're here to train as private detectives. Let's just focus on that.'

'And David? You don't think we should tell Nancy—'

'No,' he said gravely. 'I told you. We can't say anything about the map or what we were doing over the Border. Please. If David's guilty, Nancy will figure it out.'

'Yes, I suppose.' She squeezed his hand. 'But can we agree, no more secrets? You can tell me anything, really.'

He smiled for the first time that evening. 'I know. And I knew it then, too. I was just an idiot.'

She took his hand. His tremor had ceased. The atmosphere in the common room – and between Marion and Bill – had eased. The once crackling fire died down to glowing embers but the smell of woodsmoke lingered in the air. It reminded Marion of an evening in January when she and Bill had stayed up all night in the common room, lounging on the hearthrug in front of the fire, a chessboard and a bottle of wine between them. It was the first time they'd really talked, about their families, their lives outside Miss Brickett's. And as dawn broke and they'd staggered from the bookshop and to their respective homes across London, despite the icy weather, Marion had felt – perhaps for the first time in her life – the warmth that comes with camaraderie, friendship.

'There's something I want to tell you,' she said to Bill now.

He looked at her curiously. 'Yeah?'

She took a breath and explained the truth about her mother's death. It was easier to do than she'd expected and she realised, when she'd finished, how silly she'd been to assume that Bill's reaction would be probing or piteous. He looked surprised, though not as much as she'd imagined. Perhaps he'd already guessed the truth, as best friends often can. He dropped his head onto her shoulder. 'Thanks for telling me.'

10

The Induction Ceremony

The next two days passed without incident. David had not yet returned from the hospital, though apparently his surgery had gone well and he was expected to be transferred to the infirmary by the end of the following week – more than enough time for Marion and Bill to figure out what to do with the map.

The apprentices' duties and training went on as usual, though Marion was finding it increasingly difficult to keep up with the workload. She and Bill were required to complete several extra shifts in the Gadgetry Department that week to make up for the box of knotted Twister Rope they'd failed to get back to on Monday evening, and the Distracter they were yet to fix. All this had to be completed before the end of the week, when the long-awaited third year Induction Ceremony was to take place. In addition, Marion hadn't come close to finalising the Tucker character profiles and with Amanda desperate to prove she still deserved her position as assistant case file manager, shifts alongside her in Intelligence and Filing were now more unbearable than ever.

All the while, the atmosphere in Miss Brickett's shifted from acute fear to guarded, chronic unease. Life for the Inquirers and apprentices had certainly changed since Michelle White's murder – gossip and hearsay still shrouded the hallways – and yet the cogs of the agency still seemed to turn, if somewhat more stiffly than before.

But that was the thing about death, as Marion knew so well. No matter how much the deceased were loved, life does not wait for the grieving. Though on the inside everything will change and what used to matter falls away, the routine and ordinary remain unchallenged.

She could remember the feeling so well. She'd found her mother hanging from the ceiling of her bedroom at twelve twenty-one on a Thursday afternoon seven years ago. But life didn't care. The sun still set that dreaded day and the rain came down just as it had the night before. There were dirty dishes in the sink from Alice's last meal. They would have to be washed and stacked away. The bucket on the staircase, positioned perfectly beneath two large leaks in the roof, was full again, and it would have to be emptied. And as much as she resisted it, eventually Marion would have to bathe and wash her hair. She'd have to be Marion again. At least on the outside.

Now, as the days ticked on after Michelle White's death and the incident with Bill and David beyond the Border, Marion found herself falling back into a rhythm.

And then the whispers began.

'What do you mean they know who did it?' she asked Maud as she, Bill, Amanda, Jessica and Preston sat down for lunch that Friday afternoon. Marion was eager for a change of subject – even one as grim as this – because, just minutes before, they'd been discussing David's injury, Amanda questioning Bill and Marion on exactly how it had happened, and looking as if she didn't believe a word of it. Overall, the conversation was beginning to feel awkward. It was obvious the group realised Marion and Bill were hiding something, and thus Maud's revelation was a welcome relief, instantly wiping the previous topic from everyone's mind.

Maud nodded earnestly as she served herself a plate of ham salad from the canteen. 'They figured it out this morning, heard Nicholas and Gillroth talking about it over breakfast.'

'Well who is it then?' Marion snapped, irritated that she even had to ask this question. She looked at Bill, he raised an eyebrow. *David?*

Preston grinned irreverently at Amanda. It was extraordinary how he managed to breeze through life untroubled by almost everything. Marion would have to ask him for tips one day. 'Come on, Mands,' he teased. 'Confess.'

Not even Maud laughed this time and Amanda shot him a stern glance. 'They're not going to tell anyone, including the accused, until the council's deliberated. That's how it works,' she added, filling the silence that followed. 'You'd all know that if you bothered going through the Regulations and Policies Booklet they gave us in January.'

Marion had read it. Every last word, multiple times. She decided not to mention this, however.

'The what?' said Preston, holding a coffee inches from his lips.

'Hold on,' Jessica said, cutting Amanda off before she could repeat herself, 'you're saying that the council knows who murdered Michelle and they're just letting that person roam free until they've deliberated? Surely not?'

'I didn't say they know who did it, that was Maud,' Amanda said. 'But yes, if they do know, they can't do anything until the council's held a formal deliberation.'

'How do you know they haven't already had a deliberation?' Maud asked, seemingly unmoved by the news.

'Because you just said they only identified the suspect this morning. Jesus, Maud. Do you ever—'

'And then what happens?' Jessica cut in once more. 'Once they've deliberated. What happens to the accused?'

Silence followed. No one in the group seemed to want to answer.

The Holding Chambers.

Maud got up after a long pause. 'Well thanks for the lovely chat, everyone. See you at the ceremony.'

Marion and Bill rose next and together made their way into the foyer outside the cafeteria.

'Do you think it's true?' she asked once they were alone. 'That they now know who did it?'

He sighed. 'I'd hope so. It's been a week.'

Marion looked past him, her attention drifting to the cafeteria entrance. The broad shouldered, bright-clothed stranger – the one she'd seen in the library bar the other day – stood, arms crossed, leaning against the doorframe. He was staring at them.

Bill turned around, frowned. 'Him again.'

'You've seen him too?'

'*Everywhere,*' Bill said with rancour. 'Why's he looking at you like that?' He moved a step to the left, blocking the stranger from Marion's sight, or vice versa.

She retuned her focus to Bill. 'Are you going tonight? To the Induction Ceremony?'

'I thought it was compulsory.'

'Right, yes. It's just with a killer on the loose—'

'Or still in hospital.' He inclined his head knowingly. 'Look, Mari. Remember what we said about moving on, forgetting? Don't think about it. It's not our problem.'

She nodded. He was right. *Not our problem*, she repeated to herself.

Marion stood in front of the ladies' bathroom mirror as she fixed her silver badge, with its engraved 'A', to her chest. She'd polished it that afternoon, as she had every other Friday, but it gleamed now more than ever and she was reminded of her first day at the agency, how Frank had pinned the badge to her chest for the very first time, how proud and elated she'd been.

Jessica appeared behind her in the mirror. She rested her chin on Marion's shoulder. 'Two years and we'll be pinning an *I* to our chests instead.' She came to Marion's side, tapped her own badge and smiled, a glint of silver reflected in her deep green eyes.

'Hopefully,' Marion said, making it sound like a joke though that wasn't exactly how she felt. Even if life at the agency was slowly returning to normal, it was difficult to forget that just three days ago she'd crossed the Border, entered a deceased staff member's office without permission and helped Bill and David cover up a host of further transgressions.

Hopefully was the right word.

She fixed a thread of brown hair behind her ear, applied a line of red lipstick, attempted to curl her lashes and even gave herself winged eyeliner. Usually she wouldn't have bothered with all the effort, but somehow she needed the distraction now.

'You look lovely,' Jessica said, as she fastened a crystal-studded bobby pin into her perfectly rolled golden hair. 'But that watch strap . . .' she eyed Marion's old leather watch strap, frayed, faded. 'I can lend you one of my bracelets, it might go better with your earrings—'

'That's all right, thanks,' Marion said quickly. She pulled her sleeve down over the strap, an easier thing than explaining how the old leather, its familiar roughness and encompassing strength, was the only way she could still feel her mother with her. And lately she was finding she needed that comfort more than usual.

Jessica smiled. No doubt she registered the sensitivity behind Marion's words and knew better than to demand an explanation, which made Marion regret her reaction. Jessica really was a rare class of friend. 'Of course, but if you change your mind . . .' She jangled a black silk pouch in the air then slipped it into her purse.

Amanda and Maud emerged from the stalls behind them, Amanda eyeing Maud's outfit of grey slacks and white blouse with obvious distaste. 'You can't wear that,' she snarled.

'It's our uniform,' Maud said, admiring herself in the mirror. She always knew how to hit a nerve, and while Jessica was her primary target – mostly because she guaranteed a reaction – Amanda and the others were fair game, too.

'No, that's the men's uniform. We wear skirts.' She pointed at Marion, Jessica and herself. 'Skirts, not trousers.'

'Been promoted to assistant wardrobe regulation officer or something?'

'It's just common sense,' Amanda chided.

'You really are a git,' Marion said, then turned to face Maud. 'You look lovely, by the way.'

'I agree,' Jessica said. 'Trousers are the fashionable thing for women, anyway. Everyone's wearing them.'

Maud struck a theatrical pose in the mirror: hands on her hips, her right leg splayed to the side. 'That's right, ladies. I'm a trendsetter.'

Marion and Jessica roared with laughter. They each took Maud by the arm and pranced from the bathroom, leaving Amanda – now twice as irate as before – to primp her hair and apply her make-up alone.

The wide circular ballroom, with its vaulted ceiling and copper coloured Corinthian-styled columns, was by far the most opulent room in the agency. Tonight it was filled with white-clothed tables and a long purple carpet that extended from the entrance to a small stage that had been erected on the other side.

Above the stage hung a purple and silver silk banner with the words 'Miss Brickett's Investigations and Inquiries. Induction Ceremony of 1958' stitched in an elegant arch. Silver ribbons were draped from the ceiling and hundreds of soft white, diamond-shaped lights filled the room with a creamy glow.

While Maud and Jessica collected drinks, and Amanda stalked off to sit with a group of second years, Marion settled at a table near the stage. Bill joined a little while later, just as the lights dimmed and Nancy stepped on stage.

She was dressed in her most formal trouser suit, black silk, her cat's eye spectacles and a roll of parchment in hand. Marion watched her carefully as she surveyed and studied the rows of tables and chairs before her. Her eyes then passed to the ballroom entrance. She nodded and looked away.

Standing just outside the doorway was Mr Nicholas, twirling something that might have been his pocket watch between his fingers. Something large and scaled slithered behind him into the shadows. She hoped it wasn't what she thought it was.

She shuddered and turned quickly back to the stage.

'Good evening and welcome to the Induction Ceremony of 1958,' Nancy said, unfurling the roll of parchment. 'The five apprentices here tonight have worked incredibly hard over the last two and a half years to learn the particular and intricate craft of what I like to refer to as Shadow Inquiry. I started Miss Brickett's ten years ago with the intention of creating an agency that would serve the public in a way that was not violent, politically motivated or biased. I could never have dreamed of how large and industrious we would become. I have tried to hire individuals who I believe best represent my vision. And I'd like to say thank you, for all of you have lived up to this standard, if not surpassed it.' She drew a breath.

'As you know, though tonight marks the end of your two-and-a-half-year training course, the next six months may well be the greatest test of all. You will be expected to work tirelessly in your selected departments, proving to us that you are capable of a long and fulfilling career here at Miss Brickett's. I do hope that you keep this in mind.' She looked back down at her notes. 'There is just one other quick announcement I'd like to make before we begin,' she said, her voice the tiniest fraction less assured than usual. 'Among the third years graduating from apprentices to Inquirers tonight, I will be handing out an honorary Inquirer badge to someone who will be joining us from New York to assist with some of our more complex investigations. It is my honour to introduce to Miss Brickett's former private investigator at Hilton and Associates, Mr Kenny Hugo.' She motioned to the front row.

There was a clamour of mutterings around the room. Marion looked over to where everyone else was looking, a table right next to the stage where Frank and Professor Gillroth were sitting. It was the stranger from earlier. He got to his feet and made his way on stage. Dressed in a bright yellow shirt, grey trousers and slick white leather shoes, he waltzed onto the stage as if he'd done it a thousand times before. He smiled at the perplexed crowd, displaying a row of perfectly aligned, bright white teeth.

Nancy shook his hand and pinned to his chest an Inquirer badge.

'Congratulations, Mr Hugo,' she said, 'and welcome to Miss Brickett's Investigations and Inquiries. I hope your time with us will be long, productive and enjoyable.'

Mr Hugo smiled again, then gave the silent crowd a short bow before climbing back down to his table.

Marion turned to Bill. He shrugged.

'Right, Professor Gillroth, will you assist with the others?' Nancy said. 'Apprentices, when I call your name, please step onto the stage to receive your badge.' Nancy looked up. 'Allan, Marcel.'

The room, which was only then beginning to recover from Nancy's unexpected announcement, clapped unenthusiastically as Marcel made his way towards the stage.

'Armstrong, Dora.'

More applause.

'Baxter, Heather.'

'Castle, Patrick.'

The cheers and excitement eventually grew louder as the room forgot about Mr Hugo and by the time the final name was called – Yon, Howard – the applause was positively deafening. Marion looked over to the third-year table and watched as Howard opened the small purple velvet jewellery box and admired his gleaming Inquirer badge, before pinning it to his chest. A solid silver square with rounded edges and four small five-pointed stars, one in each corner. Inside the square lay an unfinished black circle that wrapped itself around an elegantly scripted *I*. The date was carved into the silver at the bottom of the badge, as was the name of the wearer.

Though it felt like she'd been at the agency for ages already, Marion was now forced to remind herself that she still had two years left to prove herself. Would she one day be up there on that stage, receiving her own badge? She knew that's what she wanted more than anything. Would Bill? Would David?

As Nancy announced that a quick dinner service would soon commence, and most of the apprentices dispersed throughout the room, Marion made her way to the drinks table and poured herself a glass of wine, observing the crowd before her.

Mostly people were gathered in groups chatting, some dancing, laughing. She spotted Maud and Jessica standing together near the buffet table talking to Dora Armstrong and a hulking young man with a rough face who Marion vaguely recognised as Roger from maintenance – Jessica's 'friend'. At the other end of the room, Edgar Swindlehurst was weaving aimlessly through the crowd, as if searching for someone. He paused near the stage. Aida Rakes emerged from a door that led into the staff bathroom. She approached Swindlehurst and immediately the two commenced an obviously heated conversation. Swindlehurst gesticulated madly. Rakes looked ready to knock his lights out. Marion was pretty certain their argument had to do with Amanda's complaint form and the consequent case presentation Swindlehurst was expected to perform in front of Rakes.

She felt a twinge of compassion for Swindlehurst and the situation he'd found himself in the past year, with Rakes taking over his position as Head of Intelligence. Rakes was sharp, efficient, confident – an obvious leader. But as far as Marion had heard, Swindlehurst had always been a dependable, untiring employee and with his experience as an operations manager for the British Army, it seemed strange that Nancy had decided – after allowing Swindlehurst five years at the helm – that Rakes was suddenly more suited to the job. But then, Nancy had made many seemingly bizarre decisions at Miss Brickett's that turned out to be well considered, once you knew the full story – such as the reasoning behind David's recruitment.

Marion leaned up against the ballroom wall, her eyes unfocused as her mind eventually wandered from the scene in front of her. For reasons she couldn't quite explain, it was as if she were standing on a shifting sheet of ice, everything unstable, breakable. She thought about David and Bill and about all the odd things that had happened since White had been murdered. For the first time since the week began, Marion thought of Frank and his unannounced visit to 16 Willow Street. Something she'd forgotten to ask him about during their last conversation.

She scanned the ballroom and there, seated at one of the only remaining tables, were Professor Bal and Frank. Their eyes met. Frank nodded in acknowledgement, whispered something to the professor and started towards her.

'Enjoying yourself?' he asked as he arrived at her side and poured himself a whisky from the drinks table.

Marion examined his soft features. His sallow complexion, pale grey eyes creased at the edges. 'I've been trying to. Though it's rather conflicting, a celebration like this less than a week after what happened to White.'

He smiled weakly. 'Yes, I agree. Though the show must go on, as they say.'

Marion twisted the cuff of her blouse. 'I heard the news, of course. About the murderer.'

Frank's face remained unmoved. 'Just a rumour.'

'So you don't know who did it?'

'My dear, *I* don't know a thing. Though I believe Nancy has her theories.'

Despite the disconcerting subject of their conversation, Marion found comfort in the familiar rhythm of Frank's voice – slow and deliberate. He placed a hand on her forearm. She looked at his left hand and noticed – strangely for the first time – a gold ring on his fourth finger. She didn't think he'd ever been married, but then again, Frank rarely talked about his private life.

'My father's,' Frank said, glancing at his ring. 'He died last year. Silly to wear it, I know, but I suppose it keeps him close.' He glanced at her watch. He'd been there when Alice had given it to her. Did he know she wore it for the same reason he claimed to wear his father's wedding ring? 'It's odd to think everyone down here has another life up there, other people they interact with.' He pointed to the ceiling. 'Away from the dark and unnatural. Isn't it?'

117

'Yes, in a way I suppose it is.' She finished her wine and considered Frank's words more closely. She thought of the people she knew above ground: her grandmother, a few other distant relatives, Mr Smithers. She wasn't sure they constituted *another life*. At least not one she wished to associate with. 'But there isn't really anything else, not for me.'

Frank nodded. 'I used to feel that way too when I started here.' He paused, his eyes drifting to the distance, slipping into an old memory or some lost part of himself. He shifted back into the present. 'But I've come to see how unhealthy that can be.'

'How do you mean?'

'We all need a bit of normality now and then. Some sunlight, someone to talk to who doesn't know what goes on down here.'

'Someone like Dolores?' Marion laughed but it wasn't with joy. More like pity. 'Do you still have anyone on the outside? Or did you, other than your father?' She was coaxing him as usual, hoping he might speak of Alice, of what they'd meant to one another, or whether he missed her as much as Marion did. But as always, he didn't budge.

'Only my sister, Mae, and her family. They live in Amsterdam,' he said instead. 'I visit every few months. It's never enough of course.'

Marion nodded. She rubbed the band of her watch as a familiar heaviness descended on her chest. She'd have to change the subject before the feeling overwhelmed her. 'I've been meaning to ask you something actually, about the day you visited Dolores—'

Something cool brushed the back of Marion's neck. She turned around, only to see Mr Nicholas just a few yards away.

Frank followed her gaze. 'What about it?' he asked. He placed his glass on the drinks table. Mr Nicholas was now staring directly at them.

'Well, what were you doing there?'

'I already told you, didn't I?'

'Yes but . . . I . . .' Her skin prickled. She wanted to say she didn't believe he'd come all that way for Dolores to sign some arbitrary next-of-kin forms, as he'd told her. But somehow, the idea of suggesting Frank was lying seemed wrong.

'Listen, Marion,' he spoke quickly now, 'we can discuss that another time. But there is something I need to tell you. Something more urgent.'

'What?'

'Not here. Not now.' He gripped her wrist. Mr Nicholas was striding towards them. 'I'd like you to go home to Dolores as soon as possible tonight. Will you do that?'

She frowned.

'If you come back on Monday, meet me in my office at ten to eight that night. I will explain everything then.'

Marion took a minute to process what she'd heard. 'What . . . what do you mean, *if*?' she stammered.

Frank was no longer paying attention to the conversation, but rather to Mr Nicholas, who was now trailed by his vile clockwork serpent.

'Frank,' Marion said urgently, 'I don't understand—'

'Ten to eight,' Frank said. 'Not a minute later.'

'Mr Stone,' Mr Nicholas said, reaching their side. He placed his right hand on Frank's shoulder, then turned a dial on his pocket watch. Marion backed away as the snake slithered to Frank's side. 'Shall we?'

119

I I

Dolores' Ultimatum

On Saturday morning, Marion awoke in her bedroom at 16 Willow Street. As Frank had insisted, she'd left the agency the evening before as soon as she'd been able, slipping away from the ceremony almost as quietly as Frank and Nicholas had done before her.

But she'd had a troubled sleep, unnerving dreams of shadows and faded memories that lingered even after she woke. She wanted so desperately to do as Bill had suggested. To forget. But her journey into the corridors beyond the Border, her encounter with Mr Nicholas's snake, the ominous darkness and disorienting passageways from which it had slithered and everything she'd learned since then had triggered something she could now not seem to repel. And while she'd hoped that the lightness and festivities of the Induction Ceremony would finally extinguish this feeling, really it had done nothing but amplify it.

Whatever Frank needed to speak to her about on Monday, she hoped it would finally do something to settle her mind and allow her to focus on work instead.

'Marion, darling,' called Dolores from the kitchen. 'Come in and help me, will you.'

Marion made her way downstairs, noting that the cobwebs had been cleared from the hallway ceiling and the mirrors wiped spotless. Even the threadbare carpet at the base of the stairs looked on its way to being free of dust and the thousands of mites who called it home.

The kitchen, however, was another story.

Dolores stood over the stove, three pots steaming under her frizzy hair. The kitchen table was covered in crockery, clearly taken out from the cupboard to be washed. The sink was piled to the brim with dirty pans and pots and the air smelled of burned bread.

Dolores looked round, her right hand stirring one pot, her left the other. 'Don't just stand there! The bread! Quickly, take it out of the oven!'

Marion wandered over to the oven in something of a daze. Despite the six hours of sleep she'd just had, she was exhausted. Her only plan for the weekend was to do anything and everything other than think about the previous week.

She opened the oven and a wave of heat and a cloud of smoke hit her in the face. 'Think it's a bit overdone.'

Dolores shrieked as she caught sight of the blackened loaf, waved Marion over to the stove and hurried to take her place at the oven.

'What's all this, then?' Marion asked once Dolores had removed the bread from its tin and cut away the charcoal edges.

'Your cousins are coming over for tea.'

'Reginald and Erin? What's the occasion?'

Dolores turned to the sink and busied herself with scrubbing the bread tin. No answer was given, which made Marion nervous. Dolores eventually scuttled back over to the stove. 'I'll do the rest while you go upstairs and change. You look awful.'

Marion looked down at the brown checkered shift dress she'd thrown on in a hurry, creased and ill-fitting. She took a calming breath and hauled herself upstairs. Her bedroom was a mess, clothes strewn across the bed, notes and files from the agency thrown onto the armchair by the window. She picked out a yellow cotton shirtwaist dress from her wardrobe that surely even Dolores would approve of.

The front door opened and slammed shut downstairs. Dolores' anxious voice welcomed her guests inside. Marion wanted nothing more than to crawl under her duvet and fall asleep, to wake up on Monday morning feeling refreshed and finding that everything at the agency was back to normal. She had no idea why Dolores would have invited Reginald and Erin over for tea since, as far as she knew, Dolores didn't like either of them. She also wondered why she'd gone to such great lengths to clean the house for the occasion. She didn't care to find out the answers to such questions, although she knew she was about to.

'Oh, much better,' Dolores beamed as Marion sat down in the lounge, facing her third cousin twice removed, Reginald Grunstone, a well-cushioned man with an aristocratic face, and Erin Grunstone, who looked almost exactly like her husband, only slightly smaller and with more hair.

A tray of tea and biscuits had been laid out on the table. Erin and Reginald helped themselves.

Dolores smiled at Marion. 'Some tea, darling?'

'I don't drink tea, you know that.'

Dolores ignored her and handed over the tray of biscuits instead. Together, Dolores, Reginald and Erin picked up their cups and took a sip, the silence now disturbed only by their low, polite slurps.

Marion leaned back in her chair and watched as Reginald and Erin turned to Dolores as if expecting her to get started with whatever it was they'd been invited for.

Eventually, Dolores realised this and began. 'I invited your family here tonight,' she said, addressing Marion, 'as I thought it would be easier,' she paused, turning from Reginald to Erin and back to Marion, 'if we told you together, all of us who love you most in the world.'

Marion surveyed the three faces in front of her: a grandmother whom she'd hardly known before Alice had died, a third cousin twice removed who had once thought Marion's name was Mary, and his wife, a woman who had never said a word in Marion's presence. If these were the people who loved her most in the world, she felt very sorry for herself. 'Tell me what?' Marion asked, picking her nails under the pillow she'd placed on her lap.

Dolores and the others, in perfect unison, smiled at Marion. A pitiful smile, one you might give to someone who looks not altogether well. Dolores cleared her throat and brought together her veiny hands, resting them on her lap. 'I am moving to Ohio,' she said, holding her smile.

'America?'

'Yes of course America.' Dolores' face was so stiffly stuck in the act of smiling that it was starting to make Marion uneasy. Was she having a stroke?

A spark of panic ignited in Marion's chest. 'Do you mean you've sold the house?'

'Yes.'

'When?' Marion's voice was rising, quickening. The house had been for sale for so long – nearly eighteen months now – that she'd almost forgotten it still was.

'Recently.'

'I don't understand what—' She breathed and tried again. 'You're moving to America because you sold the house. What am I supposed to do?'

Dolores was doing something odd with her lips, turning them in as if sipping from a straw. 'Well, I was hoping you'd consider joining me. Reginald and Erin moved there last year and have a lovely set-up.' She gestured to Reginald. 'Reginald has opened a small motor repairs company there and they're looking for a reception girl, rather similar to the work you did with Felix at the garage. Clerical and all that.'

Marion clenched her jaw and inhaled through her nose as she held back from correcting her grandmother. The work she'd done at Felix's garage had been anything but clerical. 'Well I'm not just going to pack up and move, if that's actually what you're suggesting.'

'It's all quite simple, really,' Dolores went on, 'you can come with me, we'll find a lovely place to live close to Reginald and the motor store and everything will be just perfect.'

Marion's mouth was dry, her cheeks burned with shock. 'Who did you sell it to?'

Dolores placed her teacup on the table beside her. 'Does it matter?'

'Yes, it does matter. It's my house too. Whoever it is, you'll just have to tell them you've made a mistake.'

'Don't be ridiculous, that's impossible. The papers are already signed.' She picked up her teacup again. There was a low clink as the cup and saucer rattled against each other. 'I'm afraid the facts of the matter are simple and plain. You must come with me to America or you'll have to find another place to live here in London, which I know you can't do. Rent is far too high these days, most certainly with that pittance of a salary you earn at the bookshop.'

Marion almost didn't want to ask the next question on her mind. She braced herself. 'And the money from the sale?'

Dolores' eyes flashed swiftly to Reginald. 'No.'

'No what?'

'There isn't any,' Dolores said. 'The house sold for very little and I've had to use every last penny for the move. But as I've already explained, you may live with me in America. Free of charge until you find your feet.'

124

Marion was trying her very best to keep her voice from trembling, and her fingers from wrapping around Dolores' scrawny neck. 'You can't actually think I'm just going to leave everything in London and relocate to America at the drop of a hat?'

'Everything? What exactly is this *everything* you will be leaving?' Dolores made some horrible snorting sound. 'Oh, dear darling . . .'

'Stop calling me darling!'

Dolores' face twitched. 'The movers are arriving on Monday. Everything must be sorted by then. That's all there is to it.'

'Excuse me?'

'You heard me quite well. We must be all packed and ready to leave by Monday.'

'You can't be—' Marion tried to calm herself down. 'How could you do this without even asking me? Mother said the house was to be put in my name.'

'Your mother had no clue what she was saying, or to whom. Which is why, as you well know, I was left in charge of her estate.'

Marion felt as if she would either explode or do some permanent damage to Dolores' face. Fortunately, Reginald picked up on this and grabbed Marion's hand, gently patting it as he spoke.

'Marion, your grandmother and I are only looking out for you, please understand,' he said. 'This will be a good thing, in the long run. You will get a chance at a nice career and—'

'*And*,' said Erin, whom Marion had forgotten was even there, 'you just wait until you see the men in that motor store!' Her face was red with excitement. She turned to Reginald, perhaps to check whether she had gone too far, before continuing. Reginald didn't seem bothered. 'Oh my! Just you wait and see.'

'There you go,' Dolores said, opening her hands to the good news. 'It will all be wonderful. So, what do you say?'

After taking a while to filter through the many things she would have liked to say and boiling them down to the bare essentials, Marion spoke. 'No, is what I say.'

Dolores tried to smile again but this time, even for her, it seemed impossible. Her face hardened into a carving of stone. It was a frightful sight, all taut and cold as if it belonged to a corpse. 'You are the most ungrateful girl I have ever known,' she snapped. 'All we are trying to do is help and you just toss it away. It's no wonder your mother—' she stopped herself, almost too late.

Marion glared at her, she was sure her eyes had turned black with rage.

'And don't forget,' Dolores pressed on, 'I have had a hard life too . . . it hasn't been easy, you know. Looking after you all these years. I didn't have to. But I did, out of the goodness of my heart. I've never asked for a thing in return, not a thing.' She stopped. Reginald and Erin looked awfully uncomfortable. Dolores looked embarrassed. 'You think you're special, don't you?' she continued. 'You think you deserve *more*? Well, let me tell you something – you're just like the rest of us, bound to the very same fate – hardship and toil.'

Rage was beating inside Marion but she held it there. She nodded a polite goodbye to Erin and Reginald and gave Dolores a ten-second stare before leaving. Without giving herself a chance to think twice about it, she pulled a suitcase from under her bed and began to fill it with the few belongings she had left. Dolores' voice drifted up from downstairs, Reginald's too. They were talking about her, about how ungrateful she was, how rude she was.

She slammed her suitcase shut, gave her room one last look and dragged herself downstairs.

'Where do you think you're—' Dolores said, screeching from the kitchen the minute she caught sight of Marion. 'Don't you dare walk out of that door. I won't be here when you come back.'

Marion whipped round. Hot fury bubbled up inside of her. 'Good. I hope I never see you again. Goodbye.'

Reginald had now pushed his way past Dolores and was trying to follow Marion into the street. 'Please, Marion. Just hold on,' he said gently as he caught up with her. 'It's difficult for your grandmother, she's only—'

'Only what? Trying to help? Please don't say it again.' Reginald's face had lost all its colour. Dolores looked pained. But Marion didn't care. For too long she'd respected boundaries. Held her tongue. Compromised. And for what? Dolores had done nothing for her, just as she'd done nothing for Alice.

She looked at her grandmother. Long and hard. When she spoke, her voice was even and low. 'I'm leaving now. And I won't be back. Don't ever try to contact me again.' Her eyes stung but no tears fell.

Dolores stood in the doorway looking out, arms crossed. Erin stood just behind her, cowering in her shadow. Marion had nothing left to say to any of them. She pulled her suitcase off the ground, and up to her side. It was light; there hadn't been much to pack. Without saying goodbye, or even a second look at Dolores Hacksworth, Marion walked away. And then the tears came.

She stood outside Miss Brickett's. The gentle rain that had started halfway through her journey from 16 Willow Street was now bucketing down in veritable waterfalls. Her hands shook. Her eyes were blurred with tears.

But in her haste to leave Dolores and the others behind, Marion hadn't quite had time to think her next step through.

127

It was all very well to come to the bookshop, but what then? Rooms were provided at the agency only for Inquirers and senior staff members. Nancy might be willing to make an exception, but for Marion, admitting she was homeless, completely alone and desperate for help – especially to someone as self-assured as Nancy – was an acknowledgement of vulnerability, something she'd worked her whole life to conceal.

When her mother died, Marion had cried and screamed and cursed only in private. When she lost her job at Felix's auto repair shop, she'd told everyone she was bored of the work and needed a change anyway. And since Frank had stepped into her life, she'd gone to lengths to disguise how desperately she needed him – his approval, his acceptance, his protection.

But she remembered what Alice had always proclaimed: that vulnerability demonstrated courage, not weakness. And despite the turmoil and fear and uncertainty, Marion knew something had shifted inside her the moment she'd left Dolores and 16 Willow Street behind. She was proud of herself for walking away, for finally confronting her grandmother. And maybe that spark of courage could now be coaxed into a flame.

She took a breath, pulled out the new set of keys Nicholas had given her and the rest of the agency the day before and unlocked the bookshop door.

As she rounded the last bend in the corridor that led to Nancy's office, she paused.

Kenny Hugo, the newly inducted private detective from New York, emerged from a room to her right. He nodded, as if he'd been expecting her. They stared at one another for a moment, then Kenny began to smile.

'What are you doing here?' Marion blurted out, pushing her hands into her pockets.

Kenny looked offended. He came closer. His eyes were deep brown and alluring. Marion made a point of focusing on his forehead instead. 'That's a stupid question, Lane. I work here.'

Marion opened her mouth. How did he know her name? She was going to ask but the words lodged in her throat. What was it about this peculiar man that both enticed and infuriated her?

Kenny looked at her handbag. Then at the suitcase at her feet. 'Going somewhere?'

'You've been following me,' she said, thinking out loud. The library bar, the cafeteria. Why was he always watching her so intently?

Kenny grinned more broadly and ran his fingers through his hair. 'Not you in particular.'

Marion raised an eyebrow. 'So everyone?'

Kenny shrugged. 'You seem agitated.' He stepped closer. His aftershave enshrouded her: cinnamon and musk and sandalwood. 'Am I making you uncomfortable?'

Yes. She pulled her handbag tighter across her shoulder. 'You're making me late.' She picked up her suitcase. 'Now, if you'd excuse me—'

'It's the weekend. You're an apprentice. Shouldn't you be at home?'

Marion clenched her jaw – Kenny Hugo could do with a lesson in etiquette. She decided not to answer. 'Have a good day, Mr Hugo. I suppose I'll see you around.' She pushed past, feeling his eyes bore into the back of her head as she marched off towards Nancy's office door. She looked over her shoulder as she arrived. The tunnel was dim and empty.

'Miss Lane?' Nancy said as Marion entered. 'This is a surprise.' Her eyes surveyed Marion's suitcase. 'What can I do for you?'

Marion hesitated, breathed, then began to explain her situation – Dolores had sold her house without her knowledge and without compensation, she had nowhere to live and no money to afford rent. 'I was hoping there is some way I could stay at the agency for the time being?'

Nancy's face wasn't exactly soft or comforting but she seemed to be doing her best not to look irritated at least. 'Is there really no other option? We're rather overwhelmed with . . . other things at the moment.'

Marion's cheeks burned a little. 'Well, no, I'm afraid not.' A lump formed in her throat. 'I really don't know what else to do.'

Nancy pulled a file from the drawer behind her and began to page through it silently. 'We could provide you with a room in the staff quarters, though the cost will come off your salary. A thirty per cent deduction.'

'Fine, that's fine,' Marion said quickly, not that a thirty per cent deduction was a good thing, but she'd take what she could get.

'Very well. There's a small office in the staff quarters that's vacant. Number twenty-six. I'll have Harry show you the way.' She closed the file. 'Is that all?'

Marion stood up. 'I was wondering about that new Inquirer, Mr Hugo?'

Nancy already looked impatient. 'Yes?'

Marion shifted on her feet. She wasn't sure how to phrase the question: *Why is he always loitering around? Was he watching her, or everyone?* 'What exactly is his role here?' was the best she could manage.

'He's an Inquirer, Miss Lane. He's here to solve cases. As I explained at the Induction Ceremony.' Nancy stared at her without flinching, without giving anything away. It was hopeless.

Marion nodded. 'Right, of course.' She'd have to ask someone more forthcoming. 'Is Frank in his office, by the way?'

Nancy's eyes flashed with alarm. 'Frank is not available. He's very busy. And no,' she added, 'he's not in his office. Now please, if that's all?' Her tone implied the conversation was over and, from experience, Marion knew it was pointless to argue.

Marion followed Harry to the staff quarters and a small room on the second floor. It was cramped and cold, furnished with a single bed, a side table, two armchairs and a wash basin.

She waited for Harry to leave, then unpacked her things, finishing with the framed photograph of her mother that she placed on her bedside table. She'd have liked to visit Frank before the evening. Not really to talk about Kenny Hugo, though that would've been her excuse. She wanted to talk about Dolores and the house and how the whole thing made her feel. Frank knew what her grandmother was like. He'd know what to say.

But instead she was here, alone in a cold room that felt so unfamiliar. With the adrenaline of the day slowly receding, a wave of exhaustion returned. She rubbed her watch strap absently as she considered her current reality. Miss Brickett's had always been a refuge, the one place to which she truly belonged. But now, with 16 Willow Street sold, the agency really was all she had left. If anything went awry with Michelle White's case and Miss Brickett's had to be closed down, Marion's destitution would reach a new low.

She closed her eyes and, for the first time in her life, prayed.

I2

The Smoking Clock

'Well at least you'll save yourself the tube ride every morning,' Bill remarked in response to Marion's tale of Dolores' ultimatum and her newly appointed room as they sat down together in the Gadgetry Department the following Monday morning.

Marion smiled, but it didn't feel natural. Since her relocation to the staff quarters, she'd been overwhelmed with claustrophobia and uncertainty. The memories of 16 Willow Street still haunted her – the last tangible link to her old life now ripped away.

'Mari?' Bill was staring at her, a copy of the *Basic Workshop Manual* open in front of him, a dismantled Distracter to his left. 'You all right?'

Marion breathed deeply and picked up the Distracter. She wasn't all right, far from it. 'Have you heard anything more about White's case?'

Bill looked confused. 'No . . . have you?'

She said nothing as she adjusted the Distracter's pendulum. She hadn't heard anything more and that was the problem. What was going on? Who had the agency found guilty and why hadn't they told anyone about it?

'Mari?'

132

She sighed. 'I was just thinking, what will happen if the police really do have to get involved? What if we're shut down?'

'That's not going to happen, come on.'

'You don't know that. White has a family, doesn't she? A life outside the agency. What if people start asking questions?'

'Then they'll do what they did with Asbrey. Lie, say it was an accident and if that doesn't work they'll pay them off. Don't worry, I'm sure Nancy has more at stake than you do. She'll handle it.'

Marion reassembled the clockwork bird in silence. She wasn't quite sure Bill was right this time. She closed her eyes for a brief moment, forcing her mind to quieten, driving the unease into the shadows and focusing instead on the task before her.

The malfunctioning batch of Distracters Professor Bal had tasked her with fixing had turned out to be even more challenging than she'd initially imagined. It seemed that no matter how many parts were rearranged and replaced, the bird never did anything other than fly a few feet into the air and peter out. She'd dismantled and reassembled the device countless times, while Bill scoured the library for further resources. Nothing seemed to be working. And over the past four days, whenever she asked Professor Bal or his assistant for advice, she was met with the same response: 'Sorry, we're too busy. You're on your own this time.'

What they were *too busy* with, she later came to understand, was *an exciting but highly classified assignment*, something to raise agency morale after Michelle White's murder. Marion might've pressed the professor for assistance anyway, but she realised quickly enough that this assignment – whatever it turned out to be – was the only thing keeping Uday Bal from falling apart after the trauma of his friend's passing. Thus the task of the malfunctioning metal sunbird had fallen to Marion and Bill alone.

But now, despite her utter exhaustion and frustration, as she studied the bird's innards for the hundredth time, she realised she'd finally figured it out.

'It's a sizing issue,' she blurted out, suddenly excited.

Bill looked down at the manual. He began to thumb through, bewildered. 'Sizing of what?'

'The phonograph. There, pass me that one. The smallest.' She pointed hurriedly at the box of parts, then replaced the bird's old phonograph with a new, much smaller version. She tightened the wings and screwed the head in place. 'Right, hold thumbs.' She wound up the key under the bird's wing and released it from her grip. Immediately it fluttered upwards and came to rest on the top of the glass display cabinet.

Bill glanced at her in apprehension. He looked at his watch. If the new phonograph was going to work, they'd know about it in exactly fifteen seconds. 'Five, four, three, two, one . . .'

An enormous bang thundered through the Workshop as the Distracter went off.

'Bloody brilliant!' Bill slapped Marion on the back. 'You think the fault is the same for the entire batch?'

Marion beamed. 'Yes, yes definitely. So long as we keep the parameters the same.'

Bill smiled as they packed up their tools. 'You're really good at this stuff, you know. You should apply for a position here at the end of the year. Assistant mechanic or something. Pull an Amanda.'

Marion shrugged. The end of the year seemed an impossibly long way off. She'd have to get through the next week first.

'What's he doing here?' Bill asked, gesturing to the workshop entrance. Edgar Swindlehurst was standing at the door, a large satchel slung over his shoulder. He started towards them.

'Oh . . . *Christ*,' Marion's heart thumped. How could she have forgotten? With everything that had happened lately – her trip across the Border, Dolores and the house – the matter of completing the Tucker character profiles (which were due that afternoon) had slipped her mind.

'What? Mari?'

'Is he coming over here?' she asked urgently, not daring to look across the hall.

'Er, yeah.'

'Miss Lane, Mr Hobb.' Swindlehurst reached the workbench seconds later.

'Afternoon, sir,' Marion and Bill said together. Marion forced herself to make eye contact, expecting Swindlehurst's full wrath to come down upon her at any minute. She inhaled, preparing an excuse in her head – she'd been so busy, so distracted, she was sorry, she'd explain it all to Nancy herself.

But Swindlehurst spoke first. 'Where is the professor?'

Marion swallowed, confused. 'I'm sorry?'

Swindlehurst looked over her shoulder, to the back of the workshop, to Professor Bal's office. 'Is he in his office? It's urgent. I need to speak with him.'

Bill glanced at Marion. Then, realising she wasn't going to answer, he said: 'Bal's taken the afternoon off. He'll be back in the morning.'

Swindlehurst clenched his jaw. Once again, Marion was reminded of just how handsome, almost disturbingly so, his features were. 'He's on leave? For Christ's sake, at a time like this?' He rubbed his neck and breathed. His eyes then focused on Marion, they flickered as if he were trying to remember something. She stiffened. Was there a chance he'd actually forgotten about the character profiles too? 'Right,' he said, turning to leave. 'Well, if he comes back unexpectedly, tell him to meet me in my office.' He didn't wait for an acknowledgement.

Bill turned to Marion as soon as Swindlehurst had left the department. 'What was all that about?'

'Just something I forgot to do for him.' She threw her tools into her suitcase and slammed the lid shut. 'He seems to have forgotten about it though, which will buy me some time. Thank God.'

Bill frowned. 'Right, but I meant what do you think Swindlehurst wants with Bal? He looked pretty riled about something.'

True, she thought. Swindlehurst never seemed to be in a good mood, not least when dealing with apparent delays and perceived inadequacies. He was obviously a perfectionist, which made Marion shudder, considering the very imperfect character profiles she was going to have to present to him that afternoon. 'He always is.'

'But why's the professor taken leave anyway? I thought he was supposed to be swamped with work.'

'He is. And he's not on leave. He's gone off to fetch some parts from Berlin.'

'Huh.' Bill looked intrigued, but not enough to continue the topic. 'Any plans for tonight? I was thinking we could have a drink somewhere outside after work. Get out a bit. Maybe some dinner too?'

'Sorry, I can't. I've a meeting with Frank.'

'Tonight? What about?'

Marion felt a chill run through her as she recalled Frank's odd behaviour the night of the Induction Ceremony, the urgency with which he'd told her about the meeting, the way he'd phrased it all. She shrugged, hoping she appeared less anxious than she felt. 'He didn't say.'

That evening, at exactly quarter to eight, Marion slipped from her room, past the common room and onwards to Frank's office. She'd only just managed to complete the Tucker character profiles – albeit haphazardly – earlier that afternoon, though thankfully Swindlehurst hadn't been in his office when she delivered them. In fact, since five p.m., it seemed the entire agency had vanished from the corridors, which now throbbed with a sickening silence.

She arrived at Frank's office and knocked three times. There was no reply. It was just past ten to eight, but surely this would make no difference. She gave the triangular doorknob a tug, the way she'd seen Frank do many times before, but nothing happened. She knocked again and began to pace, mumbling to herself. Then, another thirty seconds later, there was a tiny click and scrape from the wall to the right of the door. A metal post tray – similar to those located throughout the city, though not attached to any pneumatic tubes – emerged from the solid facade and on it, a handwritten note appeared: *Two tugs down while standing on lever.*

Admittedly, it took her a minute to realise what the note was getting at, but once she did, the rest was simple. She placed her boot on a pedal to the left of the door and tugged at the handle two times.

It swung open.

The usually bare wooden floor was scattered with open boxes packed with belongings. The large mahogany desk was covered in folded clothes, paper-wrapped breakables and stacks of files. The only thing that remained untouched, it seemed, were the bookshelves – vast and covering the walls on either side, they stretched nearly to the ceiling, laden with leather-bounds and paperbacks. But between the books there were other things. Things that could have been just what they looked like – a black and gold painted goblet, a wooden spear, a jewel-coloured spinning globe – or perhaps something more.

The goblet looked as if it had been buried in a pharaoh's tomb. It was old, ancient, lined with a railroad of hairline

137

fractures that threatened to turn it into a pile of dust at any moment. The spear's tip was stained, dark red or black – poison or blood. She strolled along the length of the bookshelf, transfixed and distracted by the aura of the ancient and forgotten.

As she contemplated the questions now brewing in her mind – *Where was Frank? Why had he told her to meet him here if he wasn't planning on coming?* – an unpleasant smell drifted across the room towards her. She did her best to ignore it at first, but this was soon impossible. The pungent odour filled the air, something akin to burning rubber or singed hair.

She spun around, trying to locate the source of the smell. With a start, she noticed a plume of black smoke rising from the corner of a large square clock held within a wooden case on the bookshelf opposite her. Urged on by the fear that she had somehow set fire to Frank's office, she lurched for the clock. She hesitated before touching it, holding her hand near its surface until she was certain it was cool. She attempted to pick it up but it was secured to the bookcase. She stood back, examining the expensive-looking antique with confusion. It did not appear to be working (unsurprisingly, considering the smoke), the time stopped at two twenty. She opened the clock's glass covering, realising as she did so that instead of a covering, the door was the clock face itself. Intricately painted onto the glass was the perfect replica of hands, numbers and an opal background. Behind this facade, however, deep within the belly of the hoax timepiece, lay a fuzzy monitor screen.

She brought her face closer to the screen as a moving image appeared from the haze and showed a bird's eye view of Nancy's office. Seated around an oval desk were the seven members of the Miss Brickett's High Council: Nancy,

Edgar Swindlehurst, Rupert Nicholas, Delia Spragg, Professor Gillroth, Barbara Simpkins and Frank.

Marion adjusted a dial on the side of the screen, causing the smoke to billow some more. There was a loud crackle, followed by voices, strangled and distorted.

'Delia, will you take the minutes?' Nancy said to Mrs Spragg – an elderly, dour woman who doubled as agency tailor and council secretary. 'Very good,' Nancy went on, 'let's get started. Council meeting, three-ten-two, Monday, April twenty-first, 1958. Case review of Mr Frank Stone in the murder of Miss Michelle White.'

Marion's stomach turned, her heart rate quickened. She stood for a moment unmoving, unaware of her surroundings, trying to process what she'd just heard. But there was no time for hysterics. She pulled herself back from the verge of unchecked panic and turned up the volume.

Nancy listed all those present at the meeting and then gestured to Mr Nicholas. 'Rupert, you may proceed.'

Mr Nicholas stood up. He looked particularly satisfied with himself, as if this were a moment he'd long awaited. 'Thank you, Nancy. I will begin with a brief summary of what we know thus far, as requested. According to his testimony, Mr Stone was having a drink alone in the library bar on Friday night, eleventh April. At about eleven fifty-two, Mr Stone claims to have heard footsteps coming from inside the library proper. He looked through the door that adjoins the bar to the library and saw Michelle White, running, apparently,' he added with an air of disbelief, 'from the staircase that leads up from the Filing Department and north-west through the library. Mr Stone has stated that Miss White appeared to be "ashen-faced and sweaty" . . .' He cleared his throat, again as if he were not convinced.

Marion noticed Frank shift in his seat. Nancy passed him a brief glance. 'Please continue, Rupert.'

Mr Nicholas nodded. 'Mr Stone claims that from where he was sitting, he was able to see exactly where Miss White went. Which, as we know, was the Lock Room.'

Marion took a moment to recall what the Lock Room was – attached to the library, a medium-sized storage room that contained lines of locked and encrypted drawers for the safekeeping of precious or dangerous intelligence, personal effects and the like.

'After finishing his drink at around five minutes past midnight,' Mr Nicholas went on, 'Mr Stone realised that Miss White had still not emerged from the Lock Room and thus he decided he should see what was going on. When he entered, however, he claims to have found White already close to dead, bleeding profusely from a deep gash in her throat, inflicted by the broken edge of a Herald Stethoscope, which was still protruding from her neck.'

Everyone shuffled in their seats. A cold shudder rippled through Marion's body as she pictured the scene Mr Nicholas had described.

'After we'd examined the . . . er, weapon, for fingerprints and found none, I took the thing down to Professor Bal at the Workshop for thorough examination. Since the weapon was such a bizarre choice, I thought it was essential to learn whether the crime was premeditated.' He looked uncomfortable for a moment. 'I'm sure the significance of Michelle's cause of death has struck you all. A snitch, stabbed with a snitch.' Mr Nicholas let his words ferment in the air before he continued. He then removed a piece of paper from his coat pocket. 'The professor cleaned and inspected the weapon and he has thus assured us that the weapon did indeed belong to Michelle. He also said, although I remind you this is just an opinion, that the stethoscope had not been sharpened or fashioned into a weapon, but had simply been broken haphazardly in two. Nancy, do you have it?'

Nancy slowly, perhaps reluctantly, removed the cleaned, stratified steel Herald Stethoscope from a cupboard behind her desk. She laid it on the table for everyone to see.

'Yes, there we are,' Mr Nicholas added unnecessarily, pointing at the gadget.

'Can we then assume the object was taken from White and broken at the scene of the crime?' Mrs Spragg asked.

'I suppose, yes. Make of that what you will.' He paused for effect. 'But perhaps we should leave this matter aside for the moment. I'm afraid you will all realise that it is somewhat inconsequential when I reveal the—'

'Yes, thank you, Rupert,' Nancy interrupted, 'but I would first like the council to hear what evidence you managed to collect from Michelle's person, the night of her murder. Anything of interest?'

'Of course.' He cleared his throat and lifted a large black cloth bag onto the table. 'Not much of anything, I'm afraid,' he said, emptying the bag's contents – a pile of crumpled papers and personal effects – onto the table. He presented each item to the council in turn. 'A notebook, filled with names of agency employees. It appears this was some sort of marking system. Each name has a number of ticks next to it. Er . . . Nancy's name, for example, has three ticks, Delia's has two, Frank's, I might just note, has ten.'

'Go on,' Nancy said.

'David Eston's has eight, Edgar's has two—'

'Not with the marking system, Rupert!' Nancy snapped. 'What does it *mean*?'

'Well, I'll tell you, it's a very interesting matter in fact—'

'She used it to check on us,' Miss Simpkins said, her voice scratchy and shrill. Everyone turned to her. Miss Simpkins was a peculiar-looking woman at the best of times – tall and narrow with gaunt features and an air of perpetual bewilderment (a consequence of her strong affiliation with wine, Marion had heard). But tonight she seemed even more unsettled, unsure of where she was and what she was doing there. 'I was an apprentice with Michelle, if any of you remember. She kept a notebook like that for as long as I can remember. That and a few other things.' She leaned over the collection of Michelle's possessions as if looking for something. She then leaned back, apparently satisfied that whatever she was looking for wasn't there. She gestured to the notebook. 'She made one tick for every time she noticed someone doing something against the rules. It was a habit, more than anything else. A highly annoying habit, I might add.'

'So,' Mr Nicholas said triumphantly, 'there we have it. Isn't that fascinating? Frank Stone had the most marks against his name.'

Frank rubbed the back of his neck. 'Michelle and I crossed swords occasionally but never over anything of consequence.' He gestured irately at White's notebook. 'What about Eston, then? Everyone here surely knows what happened between the two of them?'

'I don't,' Miss Simpkins said.

'Mr Eston was reprimanded in February for a suspected break-in at Michelle's office,' Mr Nicholas explained.

Miss Simpkins' eyes widened. 'Well, how interesting. And?' She glanced around at her colleagues. 'Does anyone know the meaning of this?'

Professor Gillroth muttered something inaudible, to Marion at least.

'We aren't certain what Mr Eston was doing that day, or why he was doing it,' Nancy said. 'Michelle found him outside her office, not trying to break in exactly, although that is what it looked like considering we found a skeleton key in his pocket.' She looked at Gillroth and he shook his head. 'But make no mistake, Mr Eston is on my radar. As soon as he's well enough, I will have another word with him about the incident in February.' She turned back to Mr Nicholas. 'Now, was there anything else of interest you discovered in Michelle's possessions?'

Mr Nicholas shook his head. 'Lipstick, perfume, a pair of satin gloves, a few pencils and some scraps of paper . . .' he trailed off, examining each item with mild interest.

After some time, Nancy spoke again. 'I'm not quite sure of the significance of this information, but I was made aware of the fact that Michelle appears to have received a letter from receiver box fifty-five just moments before she would have left the Lock Room the night of her murder.'

Heat rose to Marion's face as she recalled the signature she'd pointed out to Aida Rakes in the register file.

'I called Perry in for questioning on the matter but I'm afraid he was rather unhelpful and said that he's seen no trace of this letter anywhere, if indeed there was one.' She sighed. 'It seems the letter would hold the key to what Michelle was doing in the Lock Room. Unfortunately, as it stands, we will just have to speculate.'

The council deliberated for a moment. Marion couldn't make out everything that was said, but the general consensus seemed to be that the sender of the letter must have played a part in Michelle's death – intentionally or otherwise. Somehow, the letter had prompted Michelle to leave the Filing Department for the Lock Room where she was murdered by someone who, more than likely, was in cahoots with whoever had sent the letter.

The problem was, Michelle seemed to have destroyed the letter before leaving the Filing Department. And because receiver box fifty-five was attached to one of the agency's most well-used letter cases – located in Passing Alley – there was simply no chance of ever being able to trace who had sent the letter, or what it might have said.

143

'I think that perhaps we should proceed with another, far more significant piece of information?' Mr Nicholas said, glancing at Nancy for permission.

'Go on.'

After rummaging around in his suitcase for some time, Mr Nicholas placed a small grey object, something that looked a bit like a large ladybird, in the centre of the desk.

Mr Nicholas took a dramatic and exaggerated breath. 'This, ladies and gentlemen, is a spy camera. It was placed above the Lock Room gate five years ago by Nancy herself, as a precaution against theft, I'm told. The camera was hidden in the owl gargoyle above the gate and turns on only when it detects human presence. If anyone entered the Lock Room, they would have passed right under the sensor, causing the camera to switch on and record the moment on film. Of course this recording would have been taped over within one month . . . thankfully, I discovered the existence of the camera before this happened.'

The council members were squirming in their seats even more and Mr Nicholas appeared to be enjoying it very much.

'I was rather surprised by my discovery,' he went on, 'after my third examination of the Lock Room and its surroundings. It baffled me, you see, because I expected the camera's existence to have already been brought to my attention, as its tape would surely be very useful in our investigation.' He didn't dare to look directly at Nancy as he said this, in fact he was obviously avoiding her gaze, yet his voice remained commanding, confident. 'Unfortunately, Nancy had apparently forgotten that the thing existed until then.'

'Nancy,' Mr Swindlehurst said, 'is this true?'

'Perfectly,' Nancy said.

'So you're admitting that you knew the camera was there all along and yet you failed to mention it?' Mr Swindlehurst asked, his voice wavering a fraction.

'Of course I knew it was there, Edgar. I installed it. However, I did not remember it was there until Rupert brought it to my attention.'

Marion felt as Mr Nicholas looked – unconvinced. It was rare, if not unheard of, for Nancy to forget anything. Let alone something as important as the placement of a security camera.

'Did anyone else know you'd placed it there?' Mrs Spragg asked.

'Not that I'm aware of,' Nancy said.

'And has anything been removed from the Lock Room drawers?'

Nancy shook her head. 'Each drawer is fitted with an alarm that only I know how to disarm. No alarms went off that night so we can assume no drawers were opened.'

Mr Nicholas cleared his throat impatiently. He was beginning to look flustered. 'Never mind all that, the point is I've analysed the camera footage from Friday, eleventh April.' He drew six reels of film from his suitcase and handed them around. 'You are welcome to go through the footage yourselves, or I can just tell you what it shows right now?'

Nancy sighed, glanced quickly and sympathetically at Frank, then said: 'Go on, Rupert.'

Mr Nicholas smiled broadly and without a moment's pause, began. 'Very well, the footage clearly shows Miss White entering the Lock Room at eleven fifty-five, followed ten minutes later by Frank Stone. I might add that I analysed the entire reel of film, a month's worth, just to be sure that no one entered the Lock Room without leaving it within that period. We can therefore dismiss any suspicion that there was anyone else in the Lock Room that night. Michelle and Frank were the only ones to enter in the last two weeks. Both on the night of Friday the eleventh of April, and only Frank is seen leaving. In a panicked hurry, I might add.'

'Of course I was in a panicked hurry!' Frank said, dropping his head into his hands. 'Michelle was dead! Jesus Christ, Rupert . . .' he looked up at the council and then, so briefly that Marion wasn't sure it happened at all, his eyes darted to the camera. To Marion.

His face was contorted, twisted with desperation, fragility. The look caused all the breath to be sucked from Marion's lungs.

'Please . . . you know me, all of you,' Frank said, now addressing the council at large. His voice was split and gaunt, awful. 'I know what the footage shows. I've watched it. I know you'll do the same, and you'll find it impossible to believe any alternative to the one Nicholas is providing. But please, I'm begging you to just ask yourselves. Do you really believe I did this? Any of you? Do you really believe I'm capable of murder? For what?' His breathing was now so shallow and laboured it sounded as if he might choke. 'Jesus Christ . . . please.'

Marion felt sick with desperation. She pressed her fingers into her temples so hard that her head ached. She allowed the pain to flood through her, distract her from the look on Frank's face.

Mr Nicholas snorted. His face plastered with disinterest, not a hint of sympathy.

The rest of the council, however, remained still. Nancy looked down at her notes – it was only the second time Marion had seen her look frightened. 'I'm afraid that in light of such evidence,' she said slowly and clearly, almost as if she wanted to be sure everyone in the room understood, 'we have no choice but to hold Frank under suspicion of murder, for the time being. Although,' she added, 'it is my opinion that simply placing someone at the scene of the crime does not automatically ensure their guilt.'

'It most certainly does if there was no one else around,' Mr Swindlehurst said. 'What other explanation is there? Are you suggesting White died of her own accord? I'm sorry, Frank. I don't see how you can expect us to believe you.'

There was another long pause, this time broken by Mrs Spragg.

'Are we absolutely certain the camera was not tampered with? Don't we have some gadget that can—'

Nicholas looked impatient as he interrupted. 'Professor Bal has assured me that he has never produced a device that would interfere with a security camera, therefore, if a gadget was used for such purposes it was not produced here. In addition and as I already mentioned, the professor is quite confident that neither the lens nor the recording device was tampered with.'

'Then it's a matter of logic,' Mrs Spragg said conclusively. 'I must agree with Edgar. I simply can't see what other explanation there is.'

There was a low murmur from the council members.

Frank shifted in his seat. 'What type of camera is it, Nicholas?'

Nicholas appeared put out by the question. But it was Nancy who answered. 'A passive infrared intrusion sensor.' She paused. 'In other words, it detects body heat and when it does, it turns on.'

Again, though perhaps more certainly this time, Frank's gaze shifted upwards to Marion. Then he spoke. 'And is there no means by which someone might override such a camera?'

Mr Nicholas was fiddling with the piece of paper in his hand, the report from Professor Bal. He was reluctant to answer. 'Not that I'm aware of.'

Nancy interrupted. 'There is a way.'

The council looked at her, confused.

She explained. 'It's not impossible, just highly improbable, as one would have to find a way of disrupting the infrared emission from their body.'

Mr Nicholas's eyebrows all but reached his hairline.

'Oh yes,' chimed in Miss Simpkins, 'I heard a story about something like that once. A thief covered themselves in foam boards and managed to get past—'

'Please, dear Lord!' Mr Nicholas groaned. 'I think if someone had waltzed through the agency covered in foam boards, we'd have noticed.'

Miss Simpkins looked offended.

Nancy quickly intervened. 'Yes, thank you, Barbara. I think the council gets the idea. As I said, there is a possibility someone found a way to override the camera's sensor and we should keep that in mind.'

'But it's beside the point,' Mr Nicholas urged. 'Because no one knew the camera was there. And certainly not what type of camera it was. Am I correct?' He looked at Nancy.

'I can't answer that for certain. As I said, I put the camera there many years ago. I never told anyone about it but if someone searched hard enough – as you've done, Rupert – they would have found it.' She breathed. 'And as it stands, I'm afraid that the only thing we are able to prove is that Frank was the only other person in the Lock Room that night. It is now up to us, the High Council, to decide if this is enough to convict him of murder.' She phrased it as a question, though Marion wondered if perhaps she meant it more as a statement.

'Before you answer that,' Frank intervened, his voice having regained some of its strength, 'I have something I'd like to mention. When I entered the Lock Room that night, it was dark. I could hardly see Michelle, not until I was standing right above her. But it was not just the lack of light that affected my vision. There was something *off* that night. I don't know what it was but . . . it was as if there was something in the air, something cold.' He paused to survey the council's reaction. They looked severely sceptical.

148

At last Mr Nicholas spoke. 'Oh for Christ's sake, what utter nonsense!' He stood up.

'Please, Rupert,' Nancy said. 'Everyone is permitted to have their say. And I think it's safe to say that, as longtime members of Miss Brickett's, we've all experienced happenings down here that seem to bend reality and logic.' She turned to Frank. 'Is there anything else you can tell us about that night, about the atmosphere?'

'I just felt disorientated. I couldn't see anything clearly.'

Mr Nicholas looked as if he had something to say to this but changed his mind.

Nancy looked defeated. 'In that case, Frank, I'm afraid there's nothing more I can do.' Her words were soft, as if meant only for him. 'According to our official policy booklet, if a crime is committed on Miss Brickett's property, it falls to the High Council to identify those responsible and punish them accordingly. This code was put into place not only to protect our staff and members but also our secrecy. The enforcement of this, our very own system of justice and punishment, is imperative if we are to continue to evade the ever-prying eyes of the outside world.

'Now, according to official decree number thirteen,' Nancy went on, her voice having regained its sharpness and volume, 'the crime of murder is classed as a category five transgression and comes with two additional notes. The first is that the accused must be given a fair trial in front of the High Council, and a chance to oppose their conviction. Which, I believe, we have now done. The second states that should the head of the council, that is to say me, believe there is reasonable doubt of the accused's guilt, a ten-day extension period may be implemented before the final sentencing. This extension serves to provide the council with a chance to examine the possibility of a secondary suspect.' She adjusted her spectacles. Marion's heart thumped with the smallest flicker of hope. 'Should this happen, and another suspect is brought before the council, a new trial will be undertaken, the outcome of which will determine the final verdict. However, should no new suspect be brought forward, sentencing of the first accused will go ahead as planned.'

Mr Nicholas looked as if he might explode with indignation. 'Outrageous! Another ten days? You might as well set him free!'

Mr Swindlehurst and Mrs Spragg nodded vehemently.

Nancy closed her file and the seven council members sat in silence. The room was so still, all Marion could hear was her own breathing.

Nancy spoke at last. 'This trial is hereby on hold for ten days, or until such time as a new suspect is brought forward.'

Mr Nicholas shook his head. 'Outrageous!' He said again and no less aggressively.

'I have made my final decision, Rupert,' Nancy said. 'The council will meet again on the first of May where, if Frank is indeed found guilty of this crime –' she took a deep breath – 'he will be transferred to the Holding Chambers for life.'

Marion didn't realise it until then, but she had been holding her breath. She exhaled, just as she felt she was about to faint.

Mr Nicholas cleared his throat and stood up. 'Nancy, I think you have overlooked something,' he said, holding up the policy document and pointing to a sentence he had underlined. 'It says here that the accused must be kept in complete isolation during this extension period to ensure any new evidence brought forward will not be tainted by his influence.'

Nancy, it was clear, had hoped this small detail would have been overlooked. 'Indeed,' she said uncertainly, 'I'm just not sure where we can keep Frank.'

'Lock him in his office,' Miss Simpkins suggested coldly.

Mr Swindlehurst laughed. 'How comfortable and convenient.' He stood up in a hurry. 'I've had enough of all this nonsense. Quite unbelievable that after all these years, after all we've worked so hard to achieve at Miss Brickett's, one of our very own turns into a cold-blooded killer and we're now perfectly happy to let him wander around as a free man!'

Professor Gillroth raised his hand. 'I have an idea . . . what about chamber number forty-eight? Far away from everyone, isolated, quite safe and sound.'

'That will do, thank you, Professor,' Nancy said quickly. 'Meeting adjourned.' Without giving anyone the chance to contend, she stood up and strode away to the other end of the office where she busied herself with loudly opening and slamming shut a line of filing cabinets.

'Well then,' said Mr Nicholas, 'I suppose we're done.' He got up, followed by a highly disgruntled looking Mr Swindlehurst.

Marion turned down the volume on the clock and sunk to the floor. She wrapped her arms around herself. She couldn't move, she couldn't think. All she felt was a sickening cold. When eventually she managed to stand, she glanced again at the clock.

Though the council had adjourned, Nancy and Professor Gillroth remained behind. They stood together directly below the camera's eye. Gillroth looked withdrawn, perhaps even frightened. Nancy looked furious. They appeared to be having an argument.

Marion adjusted the volume.

'. . . to have known it then, what a fool,' Nancy said.

'The position was redundant,' Gillroth said. 'But she liked it. It gave her a sense of purpose, I suppose.'

'Purpose?' Nancy seethed. 'She's dead because of it.'

'Are you suggesting Michelle's death and her role as Border Guard are connected?'

'She was afraid, Henry. Before she died, she came to me.'

Gillroth shifted on his walking stick. 'And did she say why she was afraid?'

Nancy dropped her voice to barely more than a whisper. 'She feared someone would find it. That is why she wanted extra protection, and why I sent Rupert's snake into the tunnels.'

'Michelle thought a lot of wild and ridiculous things. But that is beside the point. You did as she asked. Rupert's snake found nothing.'

'There was movement recorded on Tuesday.'

Gillroth waved the suggestion off. He spoke nonchalantly. 'Probably just an animal, a rat most likely.'

Marion stiffened at the memory of Mr Nicholas's spy. So it *had* seen something of them, after all.

'For goodness sake,' Nancy lowered her voice even further.

Marion adjusted the volume as high as it would go, but already she'd missed a part of the conversation.

'. . . Lock Room was the site of the crime, that's all. Perhaps the letter Michelle received that night was a warning, or a trap.' She sighed. 'Someone was looking for it, Henry.'

Gillroth's eyes flickered with something akin to disbelief. 'Nonsense. Why would they? No one even knows it exists.'

Nancy hesitated for a moment. 'What about the map?'

Gillroth looked surprised. 'The map?'

'You told me once that there was a map that showed everything, the original layout of the labyrinth. Perhaps it reveals—'

'It doesn't,' Gillroth cut in. 'And besides, the map is gone. I haven't seen it in years.' He nodded, as if the conversation were over. He turned to leave, pausing halfway to the door. He seemed to consider what he was about to say, then spoke with a deep, almost threatening tone. 'I do hope, Nancy, that you won't take this too far. We have our killer. There is no need for further investigation, leading to further questions that I needn't remind you we cannot answer.'

Nancy's face was still and cold. 'Of course, Henry. I agree.' It was impossible for Marion to tell if this were a lie.

13

Professor Gillroth's Warning

Marion stumbled back to her room in a daze, everything she'd heard slowly sinking in. She lay on her bed and stared at the cracked ceiling. The gas lamp beside her flickered and hissed, casting strange shadows across the room, now so cramped and suffocating. She took a breath and attempted to arrange her thoughts, to piece together what she understood: Michelle White received a letter from receiver box fifty-five the night of her murder. No one knows what the letter said, or who'd sent it, but it prompted her to leave the Filing Department for the Lock Room, where she was murdered minutes later. Frank was the only other person recorded entering the Lock Room that night, though according to his testament, Michelle was dead by the time he got there.

Marion believed him, of course she did. And so the killer – and really this could be anyone, White had myriad enemies – must have found a way to slip past the camera. But how? Or maybe more importantly, why?

She watched the shadows on the ceiling dance as her thoughts unravelled. Somehow she knew that the conversation Nancy and Gillroth had at the end (and in private) was more significant than anything that had been said by the council. The pair knew something about the case the others didn't, something they were trying to hide.

Marion sat up. Sleep was going to be impossible now. She waited for morning, counting the hours, so filled with angst it made her nauseous.

After what seemed a lifetime, her alarm rang. Seven thirty.

She washed her face with icy water in the wash basin opposite her bed. The cold shocked her senses to life but did nothing to quieten the clamour of thoughts in her head. She needed a release, someone to untangle it all with. She rushed down to the cafeteria.

'Thank God.' She pulled Bill from the canteen before he'd even picked up a tray.

'Blimey, you look awful. Rough night?'

They sat down at their usual table by the fireplace. It was unlit, though last night's coals still glowed in the grate.

'What's going on?' Bill asked more anxiously now as Marion waited in silence, to be certain no one was close enough to eavesdrop.

'I know who they've accused of White's murder,' she whispered. Her voice sounded unfamiliar, even to herself. Thin and worn, like her nerves.

Bill's face turned from confused to terrified as Marion recounted the tale of what she'd witnessed through Frank's office camera. She tried to include every detail, every nuance of the High Council's meeting.

'Bloody hell . . .' Bill stared at the floor, aghast. 'And you really think it was intentional? Frank wanted you to see all that?'

Marion didn't answer, though she had no doubt Frank had planned the whole thing: the exact timing of her arrival, the letter tray emerging at just the right moment (set by a timer, no doubt) with instructions on how to open the door, the plumes of smoke from the clock guiding her towards the screen.

Bill's new tic was back. He tapped his thumb and finger together, a rapid, anxious beat. 'You know, if everything is as Nicholas explained – the camera above the Lock Room gate, the timing of White's death, it really sounds like Frank is, well, the most likely—'

'Frank is innocent,' Marion cut him off. She could not let Bill say the words, lest they distract her. 'I can't explain how, or what any of this means. But I know that at least.'

He sighed. 'I know you don't want to believe he's capable of anything that awful, Mari, but maybe everybody is. People make mistakes, they snap.' He trailed off and tilted his head to the floor. 'This place.' He stared vacantly at the cafeteria. 'I've always wondered if it's something in the air, or maybe the lack of daylight. People down here aren't the same as they are above ground, you've noticed that?'

Marion said nothing. But Bill was right. The stifling atmosphere, the dim and silent corridors, now felt more deviant than ever. She'd sensed it most strongly the day she'd crossed the Border and entered the wet and winding tunnels beyond. A seething, visceral darkness lurked there. Clawing, scratching, spreading.

Bill looked afraid now. He gripped Marion's hand and pulled it towards him. 'I'm sorry, Mari. I know this is difficult but sometimes, maybe we just have to accept the facts—'

Marion pulled herself free. 'And by that you mean accept Frank is a murderer?' She almost choked on the word. It was like acid in her throat. She stiffened as she realised there was only one course of action she could now take. 'I have to do something.'

'Something like?'

She was tiring of Bill's lack of encouragement. 'I don't know yet.' She got up.

'Wait, Mari.' He pulled her back down. 'Okay, okay.' He sighed. 'Let's go over what we know.' He waited until Aida Rakes collected a newspaper from the table opposite

155

and moved off to the other side of the cafeteria. 'Okay, so White was killed in the Lock Room with her own Herald Stethoscope. Sounds quite vindictive to me.'

'Right, I know. Problem is, nearly everyone at the agency had something against White.'

Bill looked thoughtful. 'Okay . . . and what about the letter she received? It motivated her to leave the Filing Department for the Lock Room. Why?' He paused again to think. 'Maybe the letter suggested something was going to be stolen from the Lock Room and White went there to investigate?'

Marion shook her head. 'No, I don't think that's it. Nancy said none of the drawers had been opened.'

'Right.' Bill looked across the cafeteria again. 'White was dead when Frank found her. What type of camera did you say—'

'Passive infrared intrusion sensor,' Marion supplied. She was unbearably restless. Every second they sat there talking, however necessary the conversation, was another second Frank was closer to being wrongfully imprisoned.

'A motion detector?'

'No. It detects body heat.'

'Okay . . . but no one knew the camera was there except for Nancy and if they did, wouldn't they rather remove the camera than try to get past it undetected?'

Again, Marion shook her head. 'We're getting off track, looking at it from the wrong angle. We can figure the *how* out later. We need to understand the *why* first, which will lead us to the *who*. Why would someone have killed White?'

'But we've discussed this already, it's a dead end. She was a snitch. She could've had something worth killing for on just about everyone.'

'I know, but—' Marion lowered her voice, afraid that if someone were listening this would be the part of the tale most dangerous for them to hear. 'Remember what I told you about the conversation Nancy and Gillroth had at the end?'

Bill strained his forehead. 'That White used to guard the tunnels? Yeah, I saw the sign outside her office – Border Guard. I thought it was a joke.'

'Nancy seems to think that White's murder had to do with her role as Border Guard, which probably means she was killed by someone she thought was planning to uncover something from those restricted tunnels, right?'

'Maybe.'

'No, not maybe. Nancy said White came to her a few days before the murder. She was nervous because *someone was looking for it*. Professor Bal told us the same thing.'

'But we already know what that means. White thought David was going to break into her office to look for the monocle.'

'That's what we've been assuming, and maybe what Professor Bal was assuming too. But—' She paused, refocusing. She was more exhausted than she ever remembered feeling and the dissection of information she'd gained from Frank's office was unfolding sluggishly. 'I don't think that's what White meant, not exactly.'

'I don't understand.'

'White was the Border Guard, right? So what was she guarding?'

'The restricted tunnels, obviously.'

'Why?'

'Because they're dangerous?'

'No. Because there's something down there, Bill. Something only White, Nancy and Gillroth know about. Something the map reveals. I think that's what she meant when she told Bal and Nancy that *someone was looking for it*. She was worried that if someone stole her map, and then the monocle, they'd

157

find it. That's why Nancy sent that awful snake down there to patrol the tunnels, and whatever it is they're hiding. I bet Ned knew about it too, all those years ago.' She waited. 'Well? Any ideas what it could be?'

'You're asking *me*?' Bill looked incredulous. 'How would I know?'

'You're always in the library. You've studied the agency's history, haven't you?'

'Mari, come on. If it's some massive secret that Nancy and Gillroth are trying to hide, I don't think we're going to find it in a book lying around in the library.' He sighed. 'All I know is what they told us when we were recruited. What everybody else knows,' he added as if this should include her. 'The tunnels were originally discovered by someone who worked for the Underground Electric Railways Company. They were then used as bunkers in the war, or command centres, and later handed over to Nancy, who opened the agency in 1948. That's all they ever told us, probably for good reason,' he muttered.

Marion nodded. She remembered all that. But there was something else, a part of the history that hadn't come from Nancy, but from rumour instead. And as Marion was beginning to realise, rumours at Miss Brickett's often turned out to be true. 'What about the alchemists?'

Bill looked dubious, and a little frightened. 'Come on—'

'I'm serious. What do you know about them?'

'Again, probably nothing more than you do. A group of alchemists was exiled by the church in the fourteenth century for practising necromancy or something along those lines. Then supposedly they came down here and continued their work underground.' He frowned. 'The thirteen hundreds, Mari. That's a bloody long time ago, far too long for a secret to stay hidden.' He looked at his watch. 'Listen, I'd really like to help more with all this but it's nearly eight, and I'm due in Gadgetry this morning. Bal's got thirty new orders from the Factory to complete by next month and if I don't show up—'

'It's fine. Go. We can talk about it more later.' She got up.

'Where're you stationed this morning?'

'I don't know. I haven't checked the roster.'

Bill opened his mouth but Marion shot him a look. She knew how off-colour it must seem, her not having checked her roster, having no idea where she was stationed or what duties were lined up for her that day. But things were different now. Her priorities had shifted.

'It doesn't matter, Bill. I'll put in for leave, for Christ's sake.' She stopped. 'I can't just carry on like everything's fine. I can't complete my shifts. I can't even sleep. This extension period is Frank's last chance. Either someone else is brought forward as a suspect or—'

'I'm just trying to be rational here. Think about it. Do you really believe Frank wants you to get involved? Why you? You're an apprentice. You're a *first-year apprentice*. Do you really think he wouldn't ask someone with more experience to help?' Bill was staring at her, his eyes filled with concern. 'I'm just trying to make you think. I don't know why Frank wanted you to witness the trial, it's strange, but maybe it wasn't because he wanted you to help. Maybe he just wanted you to know the truth. Maybe he was just saying goodbye.'

'No. No, I don't believe that,' Marion said immediately. She wouldn't allow herself to consider the possibility that he was right. She couldn't suffer another loss – not after losing her father, her mother, the house. Frank and the agency were all she had left. She was invested now, whether Frank had wanted her to be or not.

Bill sighed, defeated. 'All right, so what's our plan?'

'I need to see it.'

Bill's face paled.

'Please, Bill. I need to see it. Now.'

'*Now?*' He surveyed the room. Marion did the same. The cafeteria was mostly empty, though a group of apprentices and Inquirers were still gathered near the canteen. Marion shuffled over to obscure their view as Bill opened his briefcase and pulled out the parchment, along with the monocle – now wrapped in several layers of cloth. He hesitated before he handed them over. 'We already looked at it though.'

'Yes, but we must have missed something.'

'Just promise me you're not going to go down there, across the Border?'

'Of course I'm not.'

'Promise me, Mari.'

She sighed. 'I promise. I just want to look at the map.'

Bill had never looked so unconvinced. 'I'll come to your room as soon as I can get off. We'll figure it out together.'

Marion kissed his cheek. 'Thank you.' She slipped the cloth-covered map and monocle into her handbag and turned to leave. She knew Bill was right to be concerned – not just by the fact that she was now embroiled in an internal agency matter, but because she was allowing it to take precedence over her apprenticeship duties.

A sure sign her world was in turmoil.

Marion spread the old map open on her bedside table and brought the monocle to her right eye.

A web of silvery, shifting lines materialised. Hundreds of them: long and convoluted, short and segmented. Most of what the map detailed above the level of the Gadgetry Department and before the Border was familiar – the ballroom, kitchens, cafeteria, staff quarters, library – though indeed she noted a number of connecting tunnels, hidden doors and rooms she was yet to explore. But, as it had been the first time she'd looked through the monocle, the maze below the Gadgetry Department, beyond Michelle White's office and over the Border, was the most fascinating. Or perhaps fascinating wasn't the word. Disconcerting.

Occasionally a minuscule label would appear on the parchment's surface – *chamber eight, chamber ninety, top hall* – but whenever Marion attempted to trace the lines that led to it, she failed. For the paths beyond the Border bisected and converged everywhere, until eventually their origins and termini seemed to disappear altogether. She searched every crevice, though she wasn't quite sure what she was looking for. Would anything of particular importance really be labelled?

She removed the monocle and threw it onto her bed. Her neck ached, her eyes itched with exhaustion. Two hours had passed and the only thing she'd been able to learn from the map was something she already knew: the tunnels beyond the Border were a confounding death trap. If there was something down there Nancy and Gillroth were trying to keep a secret, no one would ever have been able to find it, even if they knew where it was.

She turned her attention back to the map and noticed something she hadn't taken an interest in before. A faded mark, not made with invisible ink but with a normal pen, a long and wavy line drawn from near the bottom of the map to the middle. She'd seen it the first time Bill showed her the parchment but had thought it nothing but an unintentional scribble.

She held the map under her bedside lamp. The mark was not a line. It was an arrow.

She attached the monocle to her head and adjusted the straps. The arrow, faded and nearly indecipherable, appeared to connect two points: one in the maze beyond the Border, one in the very heart of Miss Brickett's. The problem was that under the monocle's lens, the line of normal ink was pale, almost bleached, and Marion couldn't quite make out where it led. Without the monocle, the line became clearer, yet it was impossible to tell what it connected. She studied the arrow further, noticing a line of thin script written in Grey Ink just beneath, so small it was nearly impossible to read: *To the Border. To the truth.*

There was a tap on her bedroom door. She ignored it, hoping whoever was there might leave.

Tap tap tap. Louder this time.

'Who is it?'

'Ah, Miss Lane. You're in.' The voice was frail, old. Professor Gillroth.

Marion threw the map and monocle under her bed and pulled open the door.

The professor smiled, his rheumy eyes sweeping over her shoulder as if to check she was alone. His face was so wrinkled and worn that Marion thought he looked even older than his eighty-eight years. 'I was hoping to have a word. Would you mind?'

'Actually, I was just about to leave for . . .' She paused. She didn't know what shift she was late for, or had missed. It might even have been one with Gillroth himself. 'The infirmary,' she lied. 'I'm feeling a bit off today.'

Gillroth appeared not to have heard; he turned on his walking stick and began to move. 'Follow me, my dear. We can have a word in my office.'

Marion was tempted to protest, to lock herself in her room. But if she hoped to continue her investigation to clear Frank's name, appearances were of the utmost importance now. She could not allow the professor to grow suspicious of her, if he was not already.

162

Though the professor was nearing ninety, Marion found it difficult to keep up as they wound their way through tiny corridor after tiny corridor, past the common room and the staff quarters, down a short marble staircase and into a narrow passageway that threaded through an enormously thick section of stone wall. Out the other side they came to another, somewhat taller staircase, at the very top of which was a wide wooden door.

Professor Gillroth stretched his right arm around the doorframe and yanked at a tiny metal lever near the light switch. There was a click, as if a bolt had slid out of place. He gestured for Marion to enter. 'Welcome, make yourself at home, dear. It's quite the walk, but I like my little office, all the way over here, away from all the noise.'

The round room smelled of candle wax and soap. The walls were rustically painted and covered in portraits of old men and women Marion didn't recognise. The floor space was scattered with tables of various sizes, each completely covered with books, papers, pens, and odd pieces of crockery.

Gillroth lowered himself into a cushioned chair that stood under the largest portrait – of a long-bearded man in oversized spectacles and a scarlet blazer, smoking a cigar – and pointed Marion to the chair opposite. She had decided to follow his lead, although she hadn't a clue what was happening.

He groaned as he shifted himself into a more comfortable position. 'Sit, please.' He waited for Marion to settle, then continued. 'I hear that your grandmother has left the country?'

Marion had always thought of the professor as wise and a bit odd, but frail and unthreatening. Today, however, as she sat opposite him in the stifling office, something changed. The old man's eyes seemed hollow and cold and she realised, as she'd come to see with everyone at the agency, that she really knew nothing about him. Sweat leaked though her blouse, dripping down her back. She could taste the air, thick with candle smoke. She wanted to leave. 'You said you wanted a word?' she prompted, unwilling to engage in small talk.

The professor shook his head. 'I have been here since the very beginning, did you know that?'

Yes, Marion thought but did not say. She knew Gillroth – a civil engineer with an additional degree in sociology – had been around since Miss Brickett's opened its doors ten years ago. He and Nancy had met during the war, when Gillroth worked as a consultant to a team of engineers and mathematicians responsible for what Marion understood to be a highly classified government operation. The two stayed in contact after the war, reuniting in 1948 as the agency opened. Nancy had put Gillroth in charge of Human Resources, where he spent the majority of his time, though unofficially he was also responsible for overseeing the maintenance and repair of Miss Brickett's endless network of tunnels and corridors – another reason Marion now suspected the professor may know more of the labyrinth's secrets.

'I've seen so many of you before,' he went on, 'young and ambitious apprentices. You're all the same in the beginning, curious and afraid. I . . .' he paused to breathe, a horrible dry crackle like sandpaper drawn against glass.

Marion twisted the cuff of her blouse as the professor's words carried sluggishly across the smoky office.

'There are secrets here,' he continued. 'I'm sure you are aware of that. I'm sure you're eager to know everything, but let me tell you something I have said to all those who came before you, Miss Lane. You are here to learn the craft of detection. You are here to serve the city of London. Keep yourself busy with this work and do not stray from your purpose.' He straightened somewhat in his chair. 'For your own good.'

Marion looked at her watch, attempting to appear casual and hold back the fear in her voice. 'Thank you, sir. But that is what I'm doing and why I should really be getting along.'

164

'Mr Eston is recovering well, by the way,' the professor went on, unruffled by her attempt to end the conversation. 'Though the hospital staff do seem most perplexed by the circumstance of his injuries.' He stopped to inspect Marion's reaction and in turn blood flushed to her cheeks. She'd never had much of a poker face. 'They simply do not believe it is possible that he sustained such injuries from falling down a flight of stairs. Seems to be more of a crush injury, I'm told. But I suppose you know that already.' He twirled his fingers around his walking stick.

Marion's blouse clung to her back, her hair to her forehead. Whatever she said now could seal her fate, Bill's and even David's. She chose silence instead.

The professor nodded. With the aid of his walking stick, he stood and wandered over to his desk and opened a drawer. From inside he produced a yellow file. Marion's heart thumped in her throat as she realised what it was – her quarterly assessment report.

'I suppose you forgot about this,' he said, holding out the file.

Marion opened the file to the first page. A summary of her performance since recruitment. It was clear, without much analysis, that since the fourteenth of April (the day Nancy announced Michelle White's death) her work ethic had taken a drastic dive. She turned to page two: *Performance Report, Intelligence Department*. She felt the professor's gaze upon her; he knew what she was reading. Her eyes flicked over the report written by Edgar Swindlehurst: *failed to produce Tucker character profiles of adequate quality resulting in dismissal from the Scorch case*.

She closed the file, her cheeks burning with embarrassment, with frustration, with anger. She wanted to pound her fists against the wall. She was furious with herself. Her inadequacy had led to her dismissal from the agency's biggest case, which in turn meant she'd have to work three times harder to stand a chance of making it to the end of her apprenticeship without being fired. Mostly, however, she was frustrated because Gillroth could have left her report where everyone's was sure to be – in a tray at the end of the Grand Corridor. But instead he had given it to her now, in his office, in front of him, isolated, cornered. She felt he was manipulating her, coercing her.

But why?

She wondered if it were possible he knew she'd witnessed Frank's trial, that she'd heard what he and Nancy had said to one another at the end. Maybe, by forcing her to confront her dismal assessment report, he hoped she might reconsider getting involved in White's case. Well, he was wrong.

'As protocol suggests, I'll have to pass the report on to the head of the apprenticeship programme,' Gillroth went on, 'unfortunately, Mr Stone is somewhat incapacitated at the moment.' Again, he paused to assess her reaction. She must have given something away – fear or dejection – because what he said next suggested he understood more of her predicament than he originally let on: 'I understand, Miss Lane. Truly I do, but as I said, please try to remember why you're here. You have been given an opportunity to be an Inquirer. To complete your apprenticeship. That is all that is expected of you.' He looked off into the distance, into a memory perhaps, and a shadow passed over his face. 'I am sorry things are the way they are,' he added, so softly it was almost inaudible, 'but you must be careful. You must forget everything you've heard.'

14

The Before

The day Marion was recruited as a Miss Brickett's apprentice was a Sunday, four days after Christmas, four months ago. It was a particularly cold morning, the skies thick with grey and the ground outside 16 Willow Street wet from sleet.

Dolores was downstairs decorating the lounge with streamers and newly dusted plastic flowers, drawn out from storage for this most special of occasions. A tray of scones was brought from the oven and a fresh bowl of cream beaten to a perfect peak. It would be an afternoon like no other – Mr Smithers, proprietor of Smithers Furniture and Supplies, was on his way. As arranged, he would propose, offering Marion not only an escape from her lacklustre existence but a purpose, too. She would be a wife, a mother, a useful human being at last – or so Dolores assured her. Not a single piece of Marion wanted what Mr Smithers was offering, yet it was safe to assume that the life she was about to step into would not be any worse than the one she was leaving behind.

But from somewhere deep beneath the grimy streets of London, miles below the world of the ordinary and the mundane, another life, another chance was about to arrive.

Marion watched from her window as a man in a bowler hat and Chester coat wandered down Willow Street, something that appeared to be a pocket watch in his right hand. She knew immediately who it was and the sight lit a spark of hope inside her. Somehow, Frank Stone always seemed to materialise when she needed him most.

'You're home. How wonderful,' he said as Marion opened the door. He smiled and tipped his hat, his grey eyes gleaming at her.

She stared at him in silence, assembling the series of memories in her mind: the first time they'd met – a cold and smoggy night in February, 1948, when Frank had walked Alice home from the factory she worked at fourteen hours a day, six days a week. Alice had introduced him as a friend, someone she'd known since childhood. But Marion could tell from the glow in her mother's eyes that perhaps once before, if not still, they'd been more than friends. Then again at Marion's fifteenth and sixteenth birthdays, and shortly after at Alice's funeral. He'd placed a hand on Marion's shoulder then and promised that one day things would get better. He promised her she wasn't alone and that whenever she needed him, he'd be there.

She thought of him frequently after that, and every time she did she was overwhelmed with a sense of longing, one she could not quite make sense of. She wondered if it were because he was the closest thing she'd ever had to a father, or rather because seeing him reminded her of happier times, of the days when Alice had seemed full of life, hopeful.

True to his word and for the next seven years of Marion's life, Frank appeared at 16 Willow Street whenever things became difficult or desperate, a welcome interruption to her troubles. And so, when he arrived at her front door that day in December, Marion couldn't help but feel the visit had to do with Mr Smithers' imminent proposal, and the sense of dread she felt along with it.

'Excuse the intrusion,' Frank said, peering over her shoulder at the vase of plastic flowers in the hallway. 'But I have something I thought you might like to see.' He handed her a crisp white envelope. He went on to explain that the envelope contained an offer of employment at a local London bookshop, a position Marion had been highly recommended for, though by whom he did not say. Further details of the offer were scarce, though Frank assured her more would be explained in the letter and at an interview, which would take place at the bookshop that very afternoon, one thirty exactly. 'Ah, and Marion,' he added just before he left, 'do bring your tools, just in case.'

'Tools?' Marion frowned.

'Yes, my dear. The leather roll Felix gave you.' He smiled, tipped his hat and was gone.

Despite their short and perplexing encounter, Marion was unable to think of anything else and she'd waited only until Frank had disappeared into the gathering fog before slipping a butter knife through the envelope's paper sheath. But the letter inside was blank.

For nearly an hour she examined the bare piece of paper, confused and anxious. She knew Frank had a flair for the mysterious. But never without meaning or purpose. Even if the letter appeared to be blank, it couldn't be. Not completely.

She studied the letter more closely, more intensely. And then she saw it – a tiny line of script on the letter's bottom right corner: *A little heat will do the trick.*

Marion read the line several times over, trying to understand. And then it hit her. She swept clear her bedside table and switched on the old reading lamp nearby. She held the letter directly beneath the bulb and waited.

Nothing happened.

The heat of the lamp's rays penetrated the parchment, warming the blood pounding through her fingertips. One

169

minute passed. Two. The parchment was now so hot it might very well burst into flame. Five minutes elapsed before the edges of a nearly invisible layer of translucent film wrinkled inwards. She plucked and scraped at the edges until she had some purchase, then, like dead skin from a blister, peeled it free from the parchment beneath.

She cast the peculiar material aside. Just as she'd hoped, beneath it was a letter:

Dear Miss Lane,

Congratulations on your selection.

Please follow the directions to your interview at Miss Brickett's Secondhand Books & Curiosities (as listed below).

We will meet you inside the bookshop at exactly 1.30 p.m.

Late arrivals will not be rescheduled.

Without hesitation, Marion threw the letter inside her handbag, along with the leather roll Frank had suggested she bring. She tidied her hair, pulled on a coat and slipped down the staircase to the front door.

Dolores would be in hysterics once she realised Marion had left just before Mr Smithers arrived, but something inside her knew without doubt or reason that this was the opportunity she'd been waiting for. One she could not miss.

She arrived at the bookshop well ahead of time. It was a curious building – somewhat dilapidated, black paint peeling from the window frames – yet alluring at the same time. She tried to peer through the windows, but their frosted glass gave nothing away. She knocked several times on the wrought-iron door. No one answered. She then tried the doorknob and as she did, noticed its ostentatious (and certainly out of place) brass padlock. According to the letter, she was to enter the bookshop at one thirty exactly, or forfeit the interview altogether. She looked again at the padlock, more closely this time. It was more like a puzzle, really, a collection of symbols and buttons that could be rearranged in a multitude of sequences, one of which would obviously unlatch the lock and allow her to open the bookshop door.

She drew a wavering breath. Time was slipping away. She was missing something, clearly. There must be a way to figure out the sequence, but she was hopeless at puzzles. And what if she got it wrong? Would she get another chance? She considered her only other option – the one Frank had, in a sense, suggested.

She threw her handbag on the pavement, then flipped the padlock over in her hand, tilting it sideways, studying its structure in the thin winter light. And there it was. A crease, a near invisible joint on the back of the padlock. She traced her finger along its edge until she felt what she'd been hoping for. A divot. And secured inside, a pentagon head bolt, one on each end of the joint line. Designed to be tamper-proof, the bolts were exceptionally challenging to remove. Unless, of course, you had the right tool.

She kneeled down on the cobblestone street and extracted from the rubble of lipstick, hair pins, handkerchiefs and coins, a small leather roll containing an arrangement of compact tools. She removed a spanner fit for the job and, as quickly as she could despite the unsteadiness of her hands, coerced the bolt from its moorings. She repeated the process with the second bolt and the brass padlock was reduced to the sum of its parts.

Something moved inside the bookshop. She ignored the prickling on the back of her neck and removed the key that had fallen from the padlock to the pavement and finally opened the bookshop door. A soft bell chimed as she stepped inside.

'What the—' A tall, reed-like figure appeared from the darkest back corner of the bookshop. He couldn't have been any older than Marion herself, though several heads taller and barely any wider. 'Who are you?'

'I'm . . . here for an interview,' she stammered, realising how strange this might sound. 'Frank Stone sent me.' Her heart thumped unsteadily, the beat palpable in her throat. Had it all been a mistake? Was she about to be arrested for breaking and entering? Oh, what Dolores would say about that!

The reedy man stirred. Someone else was approaching from the depths of the shop.

'Bloody hell,' he said with a spark of recognition. 'You're the new recruit, aren't you?'

'Well, I suppose so,' Marion said uncertainly. *Recruit* was an unusual term for a bookshop assistant.

The reedy man looked at his watch, then at the door now swinging open in the wind. His hands began to tremble. 'Oh Christ! You broke it!'

Marion frowned, then peered at the disassembled padlock in her hand. 'The lock? No, I didn't. I just dismantled it.'

The sound of a third presence was now clearer than ever. It seemed they were just feet away, behind the butler's desk, perhaps.

'Listen,' the reedy man said with a note of urgency, 'you'd better put that lock back together before he comes up here or you won't be hired and God knows, I'll probably be fired—'

'Who? Comes up from where?'

'*Just do it!*' he pleaded. 'You're supposed to figure out the code, not break the lock. They won't hire you if they see it's broken.' The reedy man turned to the back of the shop. 'Christ, he's here. Hurry!'

172

All at once, he dashed to the back of the shop and disappeared into the shadows behind the butler's desk. A muffled voice called angrily from beyond – *Hobb? Is that you? What's going on? Open up!* There was a rattle of wood and the crashing of something falling to the floor and, at last delivered from her trance, Marion began to fumble with the padlock, her sweaty, trembling fingers desperately attempting to reassemble the dismantled device.

She'd not quite tightened the last bolt into place when an almighty crash and some muted protests came from the back of the shop, followed by the reappearance of the reedy man and another, more rotund, flustered middle-aged man in a thick checkered waistcoat and corduroy trousers.

He absorbed the scene before him: the bookshop door swinging in the wind, Marion on the threshold, the brass padlock open in her hand and a spillage of feminine effects strewn across the pavement outside. 'I see . . .' he said after some time. 'Miss Lane, is it?' He took several steps forward. 'You're just in time.'

'Afternoon, sir,' Marion said, the only words she could manage.

'You deciphered the puzzle?' he asked.

'Yes, quite simple,' Marion lied. She handed the rotund man the padlock, inwardly hoping he wouldn't notice the second bolt, the one she'd only half managed to secure.

He inspected it in silence, then turned again to the reedy man behind him, who smiled unconvincingly and confirmed: 'She was very quick. Brilliant, actually.'

To this, the rotund man's inquisitive expression at last dissolved. 'Very good. Well then,' he said, his tone now a fraction brighter, 'Welcome, Miss Lane.' He extended his hand. 'Rupert Nicholas, Head of Security. And this,' the rotund man ushered the pale, reedy figure to his side, 'is

173

William Hobb, first year apprentice.' He gave Hobb one last cautionary glance. 'I expect you two will get on rather well. Now, collect your things, Miss Lane, your interview will take place in my office. Follow me,' he concluded, disappearing into the dim back corner of the bookshop once more.

Marion beamed. Her heart rapped steadily against her chest, though no longer with anxiety and fear but with excitement. As she followed Rupert Nicholas and William Hobb around the butler's desk and through the trapdoor, she realised that at last the tide was turning on her tedious, mundane existence. Her entire body tingled with anticipation as she entered the Grand Corridor, taking in her glistening new surroundings – the towering columns of marble, the vast library and its gilded shelves, the Workshop teeming with wondrous inventions – all hidden right here, beneath the grey and cold of ordinary London. She couldn't believe how she, someone who'd never considered herself unique or special in any sense, could be chosen to be a part of such an extraordinary new reality. It was like a dream, only one she hoped would never end.

And of course she knew it was no coincidence that Frank had handed her the recruitment letter the very same day Mr Smithers was to propose. Indeed, Frank had kept the promise he'd made at Alice's funeral and been there for Marion whenever she'd needed him. Now it was time for Marion to return the favour.

15

Beneath the Break Room

Marion left Gillroth's office and rushed back to her room in the staff quarters. She still felt shame pulse through her body thinking about how her performance had suffered these past few weeks. Yet as desperately as she wanted to be an Inquirer, what would that position mean if Frank, the person who'd opened her eyes to this secret organisation, was no longer around? Whether Gillroth's warning was meant to protect or discourage her, really it suggested the same thing: he knew she was close to uncovering the secret.

And while she realised that any further steps she took to uncover the truth behind Michelle White's murder might set in motion a series of consequences she'd have no way of stopping, she was too deeply indebted to Frank to even for a moment consider turning back.

She arrived at her room to find Bill pacing the corridor outside.

'Bloody hell, where've you been? I've been waiting here for nearly thirty minutes.'

Marion pressed a finger to her lips. 'Come,' she whispered, unlocking her door and pulling him inside.

'Listen, I've got to tell you something,' Bill began, but Marion interrupted.

'I found it.' She pulled the parchment and monocle from under her bed and laid them on the side table. 'Put it on.' She gestured to the monocle. Bill looked uncertain, as if there was something more important they should be doing. Even so, he applied the monocle and studied the map. 'There's a line here,' Marion explained, trailing her finger along the pen-drawn arrow she'd examined earlier, 'but because it's written in normal ink, it's nearly impossible to see when you're looking through the monocle.'

Bill nodded. 'Yeah, I mean . . . I can sort of see it. And what's this . . . *To The Border. To the Truth*,' he repeated the line of script beneath.

'Follow my finger,' Marion said, tracing the line from one end to the next. 'Where does it lead? What does it connect?'

'Looks like it's an arrow. It starts from somewhere beyond the Border and . . . cuts right through to . . . is that the break room?'

'Yes. That's what I thought, too.' Marion hadn't been sure, but she'd suspected the arrow pointed to the Inquirers' break room, south-east of the Grand Corridor.

'Hold on.' Bill brought the map closer to the monocle lens. 'No, it's not the break room, it's beneath it.' He removed the monocle and turned to Marion. 'Do we know of anything that's down there?'

'A cellar maybe?'

Bill said nothing. The gas lamp between them hissed. The echo of distant voices filled the silence, Inquirers and apprentices continuing their day as normal. Concerning themselves with assignments, malfunctioning Distracters, devious knots of Twister Rope, and outside cases. How far away it all seemed now.

'I think the arrow is showing a passage that connects the two areas,' Marion went on. '*To The Border. To the truth.*'

'Do you think White drew it, or someone else before her?'

It was a question Marion had been trying to answer herself, though of course there was no way of knowing. But certainly the arrow seemed to provide an alternative route from Miss Brickett's to whatever lay in the tunnels beyond the Border, thus bypassing the passageway that ran past White's office and all the dangerous tunnels thereafter. 'I don't think it matters, really. The point is, this must have been what White was worried about. What she thought anyone who had the map would discover. So not exactly the secret itself, but the path to it.'

Bill seemed to consider this but said nothing. He pushed the map aside.

'What's wrong? You don't think I'm right?'

'No, it's not that.' He inhaled. 'Where were you just now?'

'Gillroth's office,' Marion said impatiently, unsure what this had to do with anything. 'Why?'

Bill's eyes widened. 'Don't tell me you broke in—'

'Of course not. He wanted to speak with me. Turns out he doesn't believe our story of David's tumble down the stairs.'

'Christ. Are you serious?' Bill began his tapping again, thumb to finger, finger to thumb. 'What else did he say?'

'That I performed horribly on my assessment report. Did you get yours, by the way?'

He nodded. 'I did okay. Nothing that's going to get me a promotion though.'

'What?' Marion said to the look of bewilderment growing on Bill's face.

'You're just, I've never seen this side of you. I'd almost encourage it if it wasn't about to get us fired, or worse.'

'What are you talking about?'

Bill got to his feet. 'While I was working with Jessica in Gadgetry this morning, we had a visitor. Nicholas. He started asking a lot of questions about you.'

'Such as?' Her heart was rapping now, almost too fast to feel.

'Where you were. Why you hadn't shown up to your shift in Intelligence this morning. Did you even know you had a shift in Intelligence?'

'I haven't checked my roster today.' Her voice shook. As much as Bill didn't recognise this side of her, neither did she. It was liberating and disorienting at the same time.

'Anyway,' he went on, 'he said you're on his watch, and I should tell you so. He said to remind you that an apprenticeship at Miss Brickett's doesn't guarantee a position here. Mari, I think,' his face was strained, desperate, 'I think Nicholas suspects we've been involving ourselves in the investigation.'

'How would he know that?'

'He's head of security, Mari. It's his job to know these things – David's injury, you missing your shifts, your connection to Frank. He just needs a little proof and we're fired, or you are at least.'

Marion was silent.

'That doesn't worry you at all?'

'Of course it worries me, Bill. We've had this conversation already. I wish there was another way. I wish I didn't have to be involved in any of this. But I can't just sit around and do nothing. You realise what will happen to Frank if he's convicted of the murder?' She didn't wait for an answer, she didn't want to linger on the thought. 'I need to find that tunnel beneath the break room and see where it goes. If I can find out what Gillroth and Nancy are hiding down there, maybe I'll understand what it has to do with White's murder.'

To the truth.

Bill ran his fingers through his hair. He was conflicted, that much was obvious. He cared about Frank and the investigation, and of course he cared about Marion. But she suspected Nicholas's threats made him fear for his own future at the agency, and what might become of him should he involve himself in the matter any further.

At last, he seemed to come to a decision. He gathered himself and straightened up. 'If we're going to continue with all this, we can't be reckless about it. You're no good to Frank if you're fired, and God knows if you get the sack, so will I.'

Despite the terror ripping through her, the exhaustion and guilt, Marion was relieved. Of course she'd have understood if Bill chose to turn away now, but without him and his calm logic, she'd soon fall apart. As always, she needed him more than he realised. She hugged him. 'Okay, yes. I agree.'

Bill opened his briefcase with an air of impatience. 'Good. Because you're due in the Filing Department in half an hour.' He handed her a roster, her own. 'I took the liberty of collecting it for you from the noticeboard this morning. If we're going beneath the break room, now's definitely not the time.'

They entered into a lengthy debate. They knew that if they had any chance of entering the break room – a place apprentices were not permitted – without being seen or causing suspicion, they were going to have to do it during a time they could be certain no Inquirers would be there.

Bill pulled out his own work roster. 'You can't miss any more shifts today but there's no point doing this during lunch, the break room will be crawling with Inquirers.'

'Tonight then?'

Bill grunted. 'No. The break room is like our common room, the Inquirers hang around there whenever they're off duty.'

'So when, then?' Marion rubbed her temples. A headache was brewing, making it hard to think.

Bill consulted his and Marion's rosters side by side, then looked up to the ceiling in thought. 'The Inquirers' weekly Intelligence briefing in the Auditorium. Thursday morning.'

'Thursday morning? But we're due at the field office then. Both of us.'

Every second Thursday at eight, the apprentices were expected at the field office for three hours of training with Frank — a session designed to test their skills with gadgets, their stealth and agility. Marion wasn't sure who'd be supervising the sessions now that Frank was being held, but she was certain it wouldn't be cancelled.

'Yeah,' Bill said thoughtfully, 'unless we can be in two places at once.'

Early on Thursday morning, after a seemingly interminable and frustrating day, Marion and Bill spoke of their newly developed plan over breakfast in the cafeteria.

'You're going to have one hour at the most,' Bill said, handing Marion a coffee. 'Whoever's taking us for the sessions will get suspicious after that.'

'Right, okay. And what about Nicholas? He won't be at the Inquirers' briefing and since he's on my tail . . .'

'No, you're right.' Bill thought for a moment. 'But I have an idea for that. Just trust me,' he added as Marion opened her mouth to protest. 'I've a knack for deceiving Nicholas, if you remember?'

Marion smiled and squeezed his hand. 'Couldn't forget it.'

The field office, despite the banality of its name, was an elaborate emporium of trickery, a two-storey construction that resembled the frame of a large house. Beyond the 'house's' foyer was a line of ten doors and beyond them a series of rooms, corridors and hallways fitted with an arrangement of traps — shifting floorboards, invisible tripwires, cameras, microphones — all put in place to hinder the apprentices as they attempted to move through the building.

Field office training had always been more enjoyable than

challenging for Marion. She was light-footed and observant with an eye for detecting snares and hidden cameras. Today, however, things would be a little more complicated. Already her nerves were firing.

Bill checked his watch as he and Marion paused outside the foyer. 'We're ten minutes late, that should do it.'

Marion nodded. She probably looked more certain than she felt. 'Good luck.'

Bill smiled. 'It'll work. Trust me.'

They crossed the foyer and went up to a line of doors where Aida Rakes and the other first year apprentices (barring David, who was yet to return from the hospital) had already gathered.

Bill grunted. 'Rakes is taking us, couldn't be worse . . .'

Marion felt a surge of unease. Rakes had been a fiercely brilliant apprentice in her day and apart from being revered for her strong will and sharp tongue, she had gained a reputation as a keen observer, too – a skill Marion assumed had only improved with age and experience. There wasn't much they'd be able to get past her. But Marion was nervous for another reason as well. 'Do you think that means she's going to miss the briefing, or that it's been rescheduled?' Since Rakes was head of the Intelligence Department, it seemed odd that she should be the one to take the field training in place of the Inquirers' briefing.

Bill didn't have time to answer.

'Lane, Hobb,' Rakes said, eyeing them contemptuously, 'good of you to join us at last.' She consulted her watch and then the clipboard in her hand. 'I suppose you two will have to be paired together, since I've already paired the others.'

Marion and Bill exchanged a glance; an essential part of their plan was to make sure this happened – thus the reasoning behind their late arrival.

Rakes addressed the group at large. 'Right. Let's get on with things. Each of you will be sent through a different

181

door.' She pointed to the line of doors behind her. 'As you know, the point of this exercise is to get yourselves through to the other side without setting off any alarms, or as few as possible. And without requiring a trip to the infirmary.'

At this, Jessica's breathing became audible – field training was not her forte. 'Will there be any poison darts this time?' she asked, reminding Marion of an incident four weeks ago where she and Jessica had been paired together for a session, and which resulted in Jessica receiving several darts to the leg when she set off a tripwire.

Rakes grinned but didn't answer.

'So yes, then,' Jessica said. She looked at Preston, her partner for the session. 'God help me.'

Rakes opened a black box on the bench next to her. 'Everyone will be allowed to choose one gadget from this box for the session. Pick carefully.' She called the apprentices forward.

Marion selected the skeleton key, Bill a light orb and the apprentices took their places in front of their assigned doors while Rakes disappeared around the back of the emporium and out of sight.

'You've got the map?' Bill asked under his breath. 'You might need it.'

Marion patted her breast pocket.

'Okay. And just remember,' he added, looking down at the skeleton key in her hand, 'it's not going to be as simple as lock-picking a door. If there really is something beneath the break room and you find the entrance, it'll be snared.'

Snared. Of course it would be. She was reminded of Gillroth's office and the latch he'd had to pull down before entering. And of Frank's office, the lever on which she'd had to step to open the door.

'Tripwires, trapdoors, I don't know,' he went on. 'It's pretty easy for anyone to get their hands on a skeleton key around here. I doubt a locked door will be your only obstacle. You ready?'

A loud bell rang from the ceiling. The lights in the foyer dimmed and three doors creaked open. The teams stepped over their respective thresholds. Bill and Marion waited behind.

'Okay,' he said, 'Remember, an hour at most.'

Marion nodded. Her legs were heavy, unwilling to move.

'I'll clear everything for you as best I can,' he went on, 'and wait for you before I exit.'

Marion hesitated. Suddenly, the whole thing didn't seem like such a great idea.

'Mari! Hurry up!' Bill panted, already halfway through disarming the tripwire one foot beyond the door.

She sped from the field office, down the corridor that led towards the western wing of the agency.

She dived right and into a storage room as she heard a racket of voices coming down the passage towards her.

'. . . don't be absurd, how could it be on fire? That's impossible,' said Nancy, out of breath as she marched past.

'Saw it with my own eyes, I'm afraid,' said Nicholas as he followed in her wake.

Marion waited until they were out of earshot, catching just the last thread of the conversation: something about a Time Lighter having gone off in the common room.

She reached the end of the Grand Corridor, then took a right into one of its smallest tributaries. She came to a halt outside a plain wooden door – the entrance to the break room. She paused, listening for movement, for anyone who might not be at the briefing.

When satisfied, she turned the handle. It was unlocked.

The break room was larger than the apprentices' common room and more lavishly furnished. Chairs and couches were scattered around a fireplace, three large oak desks and a small kitchenette. It was empty and quiet. She made her way around the room, examining each floorboard, each section of the wall, but nowhere could she see any hint of something that might be a door.

She checked her watch. Fifteen minutes had already passed.

She walked the perimeter of the room again, gliding her hand along the wall as she went, feeling for joints, disturbances, notches. She realised that if a concealed door was hidden here, it would be very difficult to find. This was the place the Inquirers spent most of their free time and if none of them – detectives trained to see what others missed – had noticed anything untoward, it must be exceptionally well disguised.

Unless you knew where to look.

She pulled the map from her coat pocket, unfurled it on her knee and traced the course of the indistinct arrow drawn in normal ink. Then, marking the origin of the arrow with her finger, she applied the monocle to her eye and examined the break room perimeter under the lens. The arrow seemed to start somewhere near the south-eastern wall. She removed the monocle and surveyed the room once more.

She paused for a moment, trying to orientate herself.

South-east.

She muttered to herself: *The Grand Corridor is north-west from here so . . .* she turned to her right, to the fireplace. And there it was, subtle evidence of a joint line. She scrutinised the wall more closely, touching it with her fingertip, feeling the subtle giveaway of a joint. She applied a gentle pressure and although it felt as though the wall might soon give way, it didn't move.

She tried again. Still nothing.

She got up and ran over to the kitchenette, retrieved a sturdy butter knife and repositioned herself at the wall. She slipped the knife's blade into what she assumed was a concealed joint. There was a scratching, turning sound as she jimmied the blade further into the wall.

At last she felt it, a catch deep within the crease. She jabbed it with the blade, feeling it release almost instantly.

There was a round of soft clicks, like the turning of a wheel. Marion took a step back. Slowly, the wall split in two, parting to reveal a man-sized hole and a ladder that led down through the floor. She got on her knees and peered into the blackness. A musty smell wafted up from unseen depths.

She got up and scoured the room until she found something suitable – a pile of books sitting on one of the side tables. She grabbed the top three books and ran back over to the hole in the floor. Moving quickly, she positioned herself just to the side and, choosing the heaviest of the three books, dropped it into the hole.

The book landed with a thump. Nothing. She waited another ten seconds and then she heard it – a chorus of whistles beneath her. She did not need to peer into the hole to know what they were: darts, a lot of them, whistling through the air below. Eventually the noise stopped and she dropped the second book into the hole. She waited again, this time, however, nothing came.

Half satisfied with her efforts, but with no more time to waste, she climbed down the ladder and into the secret lair.

The ladder was much shorter than she'd expected. She landed on the two-book pile directly below the last rung then, careful not to step anywhere else, reached to the wall behind her, where she found the light switch. The floor and space around her illuminated – a small and cramped basement. It was cold, damp and lined with cobwebs and dust.

A chill settled in the air.

She shuddered and moved towards the furthest, darkest corner of the room. Here the walls were bare and formed of grimy, jagged stone. As she'd expected, part of the wall had split apart to expose a winding passageway, a gaping throat of black that snaked its way into the shadows, into the depths – a slipway across the Border.

She tried several light switches, eventually finding the one that turned on a series of low glowing lamps dotted along the tunnel walls. She stood for a moment at the mouth of the passageway, imagining the many miles of rock that lay ahead. She took a step forward. A soft breeze touched her face, a foul smell, as if from something long dead and forgotten.

A chill rippled down her spine, but she entered the tunnel anyway.

She felt the walls press in around her. Despite the lamps, the way forward was barely visible. She moved quickly, knowing that if she didn't discover something soon, she'd have to turn back and try again another time.

But several yards further on, she saw it. The tunnel petered out at a fork, one way leading onwards into the dark, the other to a rusted metal gate, standing ajar and beyond, a large rectangular room. She stepped inside. Lining the walls were shelf upon shelf of jars and vials and containers of every shape and size. Some were empty, most were filled with swirling gases and unusually shaped stones, some that looked like glass orbs, others like precious metals. In one corner of the basement was a workbench on which sat a row of Bunsen burners, pots, trays and an assortment of unfamiliar instruments.

On another workbench, perched just on the edge, was a glittering grey eagle. It wasn't moving, though Marion guessed from the tiny hairline joints on its legs, wings, neck and beak, that it could. She touched its wing – cold and solid. Then its beak – sharp and delicate. While the bird's solid white and pupil-less eyes stared fixedly across the room, it still gave the unnerving impression it was watching her.

On second inspection of the workbenches, Marion found a glass box filled with hundreds of tiny crystal vials. Next to the box were a stack of old papers, some so weathered their script could not be made out. But among the ancient and illegible papers she found something that turned her blood cold.

It was a hand-drawn diagram depicting the several constituents of what could only have been a bomb. The diagram and script below was dated December 1943 – *Operation Grey Eagle*.

Marion's breath quickened as she attempted to make sense of the diagram: a shell casing, a timepiece, a chamber, a detonator. Some of it she was able to decipher, most was far too complex. Below the diagram were a few paragraphs. She scanned through them with haste, picking out what she could: *Operation Grey Eagle . . . production and testing commenced in underground bunkers, location classified . . . clockwork bomb . . . top secret chemical weaponry project . . . privately funded enterprise . . . in preparation for German invasion . . . effects of concealment gas (known as Grey Eagle) similar to mustard gas with additional components to act on neurological system including disorientation, confusion, lethargy, diffuse neuromuscular symptoms, ocular irritation . . . alchemic explosive fifteen times more powerful than dynamite.*

She paused, breathed, then read the final line of the document: *Experiment failed due to numerous casualties during testing phase.*

She turned back to the diagram of the clockwork bomb, her brain firing, trying to understand. Her hands started to shake. Sweat trickled down the back of her neck. She picked up one of the tiny crystal vials and studied its contents in relation to the diagram: it held a type of translucent mist, scattered with specks of silvery light. It was labelled Grey Eagle and, according to the diagram, was to be inserted into the bomb before deployment.

She uncorked the vial and tipped just a drop of the strange substance onto the work bench. It smelled like sulphur and a

187

whitish near-translucent mist rose, cooling the space around it. In less than the time it took for her brain to take in what she was seeing, the mist had caused her eyes to water and sting, her head to spin. The longer she stood there, transfixed, the more her eyes burned and the colder and more disoriented she became.

Her mind was fogged. Sluggish. She knew that what she was looking at and experiencing was significant and yet she couldn't piece together why. She'd lost track of time and purpose. Her muscles twitched but failed to move.

She shook her head, reawakening her senses. She resealed the vial and slipped it into her pocket. The effects of the mist faded, slowly but certainly. She checked her watch. Time to go.

She stumbled back through the tunnel and into the lair beneath the break room in what felt like a daze. She gripped the sides of the ladder and pulled herself up, then slipped through the gap in the wall and flipped the same catch she had used to open it. The wall slid closed behind her.

But it was too late.

'Well, well. Isn't this interesting?'

16

The Grey Eagle

Marion turned to face Kenny Hugo, dressed as usual in bright, dazzling attire, his aftershave a cloud hovering around him.

He gripped her by the shoulders, his eyes focused on the wall through which she'd just emerged.

'Let go!' She pulled from his grip and stepped back, hugging her handbag to her chest.

Kenny's eyes darted from the wall, now seemingly solid, to Marion and back again. She watched as his bewilderment transformed into understanding. He settled his gaze on the bag in Marion's clutches. 'I think you'd better come with me.'

Marion sidestepped him and made for the door. 'Actually, I have somewhere else to be, if you don't mind.'

'I do mind, as it happens.' He gripped her again by the shoulders, forcing her to a halt. 'You're not going anywhere until you tell me what you're doing here and,' he glanced again at the wall from which she'd appeared, 'where you came from.'

She tried again to escape his grasp but this only made him grip her tighter.

'Where did you come from?' he repeated, now through gritted teeth.

There were footsteps and voices outside, in the corridor. Marion could have sworn one of them belonged to Mr Nicholas.

She began to scramble and squirm, a blind panic rising inside her. It was bad enough that this fool had seen her here, but things would get desperately worse if Nancy or Nicholas stepped through the door. 'Goddammit, let me go!'

'Listen here, missy. I'm giving you one last chance. Tell me what you're doing here or I'm delivering you straight to Nancy.'

Marion would very much have liked to kick Kenny Hugo in the shins and be on her way, but she was running out of time. She didn't know if she could trust this strange man, in fact she was sure she couldn't. But it was useless trying to escape, or pretend he hadn't just seen her stepping out from a hole in the wall.

'I was looking for something,' she said quickly, 'I'll tell you what,' she took a breath, the first in a while, 'but not now. I need to get back to my training session before anyone notices I'm not there.'

He laughed. She wasn't sure why. 'And where's this training session taking place?'

'The field office. Now please, I really have to get going.'

'Fine,' he said. 'But I'll be waiting for you outside and I'm warning you, if you try to get away I'll—'

'Yes, I heard you the first time. Now out of the damn way!' She shoved past him, and this time he let her. She shot back up the tributary and into the Grand Corridor, thankfully bumping into no one and reaching the field office less than fifteen minutes later.

She collected herself before stepping into the foyer and through the door she and Bill were supposed to have entered together. Hopefully Bill had done as promised and disarmed the traps beyond because she didn't have time to check. She dashed through and up a small staircase, along a corridor and into a bedroom without pausing.

'Finally!' Bill panted, stepping out from behind the bedroom wardrobe. 'I've had to disarm the corridor tripwires five times!'

'Sorry,' Marion puffed. 'Bit of a delay. The Time Lighter in the common room, was that you?'

Bill smiled.

'You're brilliant, you know that?'

He smiled again as he adjusted a dial on a small clock that hung above the exit. 'Did you find anything?'

'Yes. A lot.' She showed him the crystal vial and the strange fluid inside, filled with dots of silvery light.

'What the hell is that?'

But Marion couldn't answer just then. She waited for the dial to click three times. She and Bill both knew exactly how this particular trap worked and as the third click came, they stepped quickly to the left. A long metal pole shot out from the centre of the exit door.

'I'll explain later. Someone saw me, by the way.'

'What?' Bill's panic was evident.

'Don't worry. I'll sort it out.' She handed him the vial. 'I think this is the answer to everything, so look after it. Keep it on you in case he searches me. And . . . don't open it.'

'He? Who's he?'

'The person who saw me!'

Bill looked irritated but he obliged. He and Marion opened the exit door and stepped through at last.

'Good evening,' Rakes said as they exited. 'What took you so long?'

'Sorry,' Marion said, 'we took a few wrong turns.'

They followed Rakes back around to the front of the house. 'Zero marks for that dismal performance, Lane, Hobb,' she said, noting it down on her clipboard. 'It's really not that hard, you know. And haven't you both been through that door before? I frankly expected more from you two.'

191

Marion and Bill apologised and blamed their delay on nerves. Rakes didn't look at all convinced but continued the training without further interrogation.

When the session was over and Marion and the others stepped into the corridor outside the foyer, Kenny appeared around the corner.

Marion leaned into Bill. 'Don't show anyone the vial and meet me at my room tonight after dinner.'

'All right, missy,' Kenny said as he caught sight of Marion. 'Time you and I had a little chat.'

Reluctantly, Marion followed Kenny to the staff quarters, room thirty-one. He unlocked the door and ushered her inside. The room looked as if it'd been ransacked by an intruder. Clothes and books were strewn across the floor, gadgets across the bed, cigarette butts and a half empty whisky glass lay on the bedside table. The only thing that had any order was a shelf above the wash basin, where a vast collection of male grooming supplies were assembled in a neat row – oils, waxes, creams, cologne.

'Sit,' he said, gesturing to an armchair while he ripped off his shirt, threw it on the floor and bent over the basin to wash his face.

Marion watched him, his back bent over the basin, taut muscles rippling beneath his skin. He straightened, dried his face, ran some wax through his hair, then turned around. She looked away as he picked a new shirt and pulled it on.

He settled on the edge of the bed, lit the oil lamp on his side table, then a cigarette. His eyes blazed with intensity. 'Okay, Lane. I'll go first.' He drew on his cigarette. 'As you must know, Nancy hired me just under two weeks ago. She said she needed an outsider to have a look at an investigation they were struggling with at the agency. I know Frank, too, by the way. He and I met when he came to New York to help our agency with a case that involved a British citizen. It was a few years back and the details are unimportant. When I arrived here, Nancy said that while she'd "induct" me, as it were, she wasn't going to be able to provide me with full disclosure on the case, just the essential details. All she said was that there'd been a murder, one of her employees, and that the circumstances surrounding the case had become complicated. She gave me a summary of what had happened and said that Frank had been framed for the murder—'

'Framed?' A cold sweat formed on Marion's forehead.

Kenny smiled. 'So you do know, I thought so.'

Marion gritted her teeth. She'd been so shocked by Kenny Hugo's choice of words, she'd forgotten to pretend that she, like the rest of the agency, didn't know Frank was the one the High Council had recently accused of White's murder.

'I've heard a rumour,' she lied. A plausible explanation, at least.

'And do you think he did it?'

'Of course I don't.'

Kenny nodded, apparently satisfied. 'Good. Neither does Nancy, which is why she hired me to find an alternative suspect. Thing is, it hasn't been the kind of investigation I'm used to. I haven't been given free rein, haven't really been given much of anything.' He exhaled. 'It's been all very hush-hush. I think she's afraid that if anyone knows what I'm really here for, it'll hinder the investigation.'

Marion didn't say so, but she had a different theory as to why Nancy wasn't flooding Kenny with case details. It wasn't that she was protecting the fragility of the case, she was protecting the agency itself. If Kenny Hugo turned over one too many stones in his quest to find an alternative suspect, Nancy and the agency might find themselves in more trouble than they were already.

'And what has any of this got to do with me?'

Kenny exhaled a plume of smoke and threw back the entirety of his whisky. 'Please, Lane. It's obvious you know more than you should. I won't ask how. Frankly, I'm not interested in office politics.' He paused for a moment, perhaps considering if it were a good idea for him to say anything further.

Marion was tense. It was obvious now that if she wanted to continue with the investigation, she would need Kenny to trust her. And to some degree, she was going to have to trust him. She nodded, then began to explain about the camera in Frank's office and how she'd witnessed the High Council trial.

Kenny looked less shocked than she'd expected him to be at the revelation. Perhaps out of everything he'd seen and heard at the agency since his arrival, this was the least surprising. He played with the cigarette between his lips as he absorbed this new information. The muscles in Marion's face began to twitch as she waited for him to speak.

Eventually he seemed to arrive at a decision. 'All right,' he said, more to himself. He stubbed out his cigarette. 'So where is it, then? The map, Lane. I know you have it.' He got up and took a step towards her.

Her stomach lurched. Her heart thumped. 'I have no idea what—'

'Bullshit! I've been watching everyone. I know you and your little friend Hobb are in on this together, and I know you have the map.'

She said nothing.

'Let me put it to you like this. Either you give me the map and I'll forget what I saw in the break room, and all the other things you've just told me, or you don't and I take you straight to Nancy while we search your room.'

'You have no idea what you're getting involved in,' Marion snapped. 'It's more complicated than Nancy will have you believe.'

194

Kenny sighed, pushing his fingers through his perfectly coiffed locks. 'What's the problem here? You don't trust me? You don't trust Nancy? Don't be a fool, Lane. Nancy is on Frank's side.'

'How do you know that?'

'She hired me to clear his name!'

'It sounds more like she hired you to be her courier. You said it yourself, you have no idea what you're doing in this investigation. Or why.'

'Nancy knew about the camera.'

'Excuse me?'

Kenny inhaled impatiently. 'In the Lock Room. Nancy knew right away when White was murdered that she'd be able to know who did it just by analysing the footage from the camera above the Lock Room gate. She removed the footage just hours after the murder and had a look. Alone.

'Of course, what she saw wasn't what she expected. She confronted Frank in private. They were both in a panic. Nancy never believed Frank was guilty, not for a second, but there he was entering the Lock Room after White and running out just minutes later. Blood literally on his hands. That's when she called me. She explained the situation and we discussed all the possibilities. I asked if there was any way the camera could have been manipulated, or someone could have slipped past without it registering. She said there was a possibility of the latter, though she thought it unlikely.

'Anyway, we weren't getting anywhere with that line of thinking, so Nancy decided to focus her attention somewhere else. *Motives*. Why would someone want White dead? Yeah, White was a snitch, but she'd been that way for nearly nine years and it hadn't got her killed. So what changed? That's when Nancy brought up the idea of the map. She said she suspected there was a connection between a previous employee's disappearance and the map and somehow, both are linked

195

to the murder. You see, Nancy believes the employee who disappeared had gone looking for something he never should have known about. She didn't tell me all the details, only that she'd recently come to suspect this employee had found out about a highly guarded agency secret from an old map she'd once thought only existed in myth.' He paused, as if waiting for confirmation.

Marion tried to keep her body language neutral.

Maybe it worked, because Kenny went on regardless. 'As I said, she didn't go into the details, but she seemed pretty certain White's killer was likely to have had the map at some point. So of course I was tasked with tracking it down. But we were running out of time. Nancy knew that Nicholas was determined to solve the case. He'd been scouring the Lock Room for clues, every day for hours at a time. Nancy couldn't stop him, or remove the camera because it would seem too suspicious. But she knew he'd find it eventually. And, as you now know,' he added with an air of exhaustion, 'that's exactly what happened. Nancy's only choice was to hold a trial, though she knew the evidence against Frank was insurmountable. Her last option was to make use of the only loophole she had left and provide Frank with an extension period. Like I said, Nancy is on Frank's side. And so am I.'

Marion considered this. Certainly, she believed that Nancy thought Frank was innocent, but did that necessarily mean she'd go to any lengths to clear his name? She wondered what Nancy would do if, by revealing the real killer's identity, she'd be forced to reveal the fact that something sinister – something that appeared to be a hand in chemical warfare – existed right beneath their feet.

'Fine,' she said, at last coming to the realisation that as much as she'd have preferred to, she couldn't clear Frank's name on her own.

'Fine, you'll give me the map?'

'I told you, I don't know anything about a map.' A lie, of course. The map was still in her breast pocket. 'I do have something more interesting, however. And I'll show you what it is.' It was a gamble. If Kenny couldn't be trusted, she was about to destroy Frank's last chance at retribution.

'Well go on, then,' Kenny said as he smoothed a flick of wayward hair back into place.

Marion got up. 'I don't have it with me now.'

'Blazes, Lane. Are you serious?'

'Meet me in my room tonight and I'll show you. And don't tell anyone anything yet.'

'You've got to be kidding me—'

'If what I show you reaches the wrong people,' she went on, unperturbed, 'it'll either get us killed or fired. You included. And then there'll be no one to clear Frank's name.'

Kenny lit a second cigarette and began to pace. 'Listen here, Lane. You're not the one calling the shots. I saw you crawling from that gap in the wall, and I'm pretty sure I can go and see what's down there myself.'

'Oh really? I'd like to see you try. It's snared. Do you know how to disarm tripwires? Do you know how to use any of the gadgets we use here? You need me.'

Kenny contemplated this, examining her. Marion was the one with everything to lose. Did he really need her? Could she really play that card? She looked around the room properly for the first time, and noticed a pile of Professor Bal's gadgets strewn haphazardly over the small single bed in the corner. A coil of Twister Rope had wrapped itself around a pillow and a pile of screws and springs – the innards of a microdot camera – lay beside it. Two workshop manuals were spread open on the side table, several pens and notepads accompanying them.

Marion sat on the edge of the bed and, in silence, began to reassemble the camera.

'What are you doing with that?' Kenny asked, somewhat unnerved.

'Demonstrating my point.' She slipped a reel of film into place and secured the camera's backing. She handed it to him, now fully functional. 'As I said. You need me.'

Kenny smiled. He looked genuinely impressed and, just for a moment and by just a fraction, the tightness in Marion's chest eased.

'How do you know all this stuff? Haven't you just been working here for three months?'

'Four,' she corrected him. 'And most of it I've spent with Professor Bal in Gadgetry.'

'Okay, listen, Lane. I'll play it your way for now. Lucky for you, Nancy is away at the moment—'

'What?' The churning ache in her stomach was back. 'What do you mean she's away?'

'Just for a few days. She had to consult with a colleague or something. My point is, I'm going to have to tell her when she returns . . .' He trailed off, something about his responsibilities as a detective. Marion had stopped listening. What could Nancy possibly have to do that was more important, more pressing than finding the real murderer?

'Hey, Lane.' Kenny snapped his fingers in her face. 'Did you hear what I said?'

She gazed at him absently.

'I'm going to tell Nancy whatever I need to as soon as she's back. You understand?'

Marion didn't reply. She looked at her watch. She was due in the library in five minutes and if she didn't show up and behave as if everything was normal, she'd blow it all. 'I have to go.'

Kenny opened his mouth to protest. Marion spoke before he had a chance.

'Meet me in my room, number twenty-six. Tonight after dinner. Come alone and for Christ's sake, don't tell anyone where you're going.'

Kenny considered this. The muscles in his jaw seemed to twitch with indecision, perhaps frustration too. 'I'll see you there.' He began to pack away the array of gadgets on his bed, with some difficulty as a spool of Twister Rope had now caught him around the waist, pinning his right arm firmly behind his back.

'Tug the ends in opposite directions,' Marion said as she turned to leave. 'It'll demagnetise them. I'll see you tonight.' She left without pausing to check he'd heard, or whether the Twister Rope had overpowered him yet.

'Bill, this is Kenny. Kenny, Bill.' Marion made quick introductions as the two men arrived at her room later that evening. A part of her had hoped Kenny wouldn't show, that he was still entangled in a spool of Twister Rope. She hadn't truly accepted the fact that Frank's fate now lay partially in Kenny's hands. And while she knew she had no choice but to trust him, the notion disturbed her.

Bill looked similarly unnerved by the new addition to their investigation.

Kenny seemed nothing less than outraged. 'You can't be serious?' he snapped, eyeing Bill. 'You told me I shouldn't tell anyone about this meeting.'

Marion closed and locked the bedroom door. 'Bill knows everything I know. I'm not shutting him out now.'

The two men sized each other up. Bill, just as tall as Kenny but half his width, shook his head. Kenny rolled his eyes. Marion ignored them both.

'Right.' She held out her hand to Bill. 'The vial?'

He scowled at Kenny with obvious distrust.

'We don't have a choice, Bill. Just hand it over.'

He passed her the vial and slunk off to sit on the edge of the bed.

'This is what I discovered beneath the break room,' Marion began, uncorking the vial and handing it first to Bill, then to Kenny. She poured a droplet onto the desk in front of her. The droplet shimmered and vibrated as soon as it came into contact with the table. The silvery particles, now awoken from their liquid state, were quickly shifting into a wall of gas. As the substance rose into the air, Marion's eyes began to sting and water.

'What the blazes?' Kenny lowered his face into the mist.

Marion pushed him away. 'Careful how much you inhale. I'm not sure how it works yet. More than a drop and you'll be disorientated, almost blind.' She waited for the effects of the substance to fade before continuing. 'There seems to be some sort of laboratory down there, in the tunnels beyond the Border, and the cellar beneath the break room leads right to it.' She glanced at Kenny, hoping he wouldn't ask how she'd discovered this tunnel. He said nothing, so she continued: 'I didn't have time to go through everything, but I found enough evidence to suggest—' She paused, doubting herself. It was as if the past few hours had been a dream, some strange half reality. But no, there could be no mistaking what she saw in that grim, dank pit. She looked at Bill, then Kenny. 'It looked as if it were the recreation of some failed chemical weaponry experiment from the war. Some sort of bomb they were trying to make with an explosive that, well, that I've never seen or heard of before.'

'Jesus.' Bill rubbed his forehead. 'And this is part of it?' He pointed at the vial.

'Yes, definitely.' She ripped a piece of paper from the notepad in her bag and began to sketch a simplified version of the diagram she'd seen in the laboratory. 'I recognised the mechanism's design only because it's almost identical to that of a Time Lighter, which is really just a safer version of a simple clockwork bomb.' She went on, despite the confusion on Kenny and Bill's faces. 'Clockwork bombs have been used for ages, throughout history. They've been used for political sabotage, terrorism. Most recently on United Airlines Flight 629.' She looked at Kenny to elaborate.

He hesitated before answering. 'It was placed in the luggage compartment, killed forty-four people mid-flight.'

'Right,' Marion said. 'And that's just one of many examples. Delayed action clockwork bombs were also used in the war, both by the British and Germans. They're simple and devastating. Explosives detonated by a timer, even a simple wristwatch.' She pointed at her diagram. 'But this . . . this is different.'

'Different how?' Bill asked.

'Well, in two ways. First, the type of explosive used. Most clockwork bombs use dynamite, or some variation. This bomb was designed to be loaded with something I've never heard of before.' She closed her eyes for a moment, trying to recall the exact phrasing. 'An alchemical explosive, fifteen times more powerful than dynamite and laced with something acidic, corrosive.'

'Alchemical,' Bill murmured. He stared into the distance for a while. 'Christ . . . you were right. The group of alchemists who were exiled by the church?'

'Well not exactly. I mean, it might have started with them but . . . I did a bit of research this afternoon in between my shifts. Apparently, there was a group of chemists who worked at Porton Down in Salisbury—'

Bill frowned. 'The government facility?'

Marion nodded. 'Right, where scientists have been testing chemical and biological weapons for decades. But in the late thirties, there was a group of chemists who became interested in more "fringe experiments", substances and concoctions produced by the ancient and mostly forgotten methods of alchemy. Obviously, there wasn't much I could find in the archives about this group. All I know is that they left Porton Down soon after the war began; apparently they were fired for "non-adherence to general protocol". Whatever that means.'

'Left and went where?' Kenny asked.

'No one seems to know. The group vanished from society, every last member. No record of where they went or even if they're still alive. Almost as if the earth swallowed them up.'

'They came here,' Bill said.

Kenny was glancing from Marion to Bill with a look that suggested he understood what Marion had explained, he just wasn't certain he believed it. 'And the other difference? You said there were two differences between the diagram's design and a normal clockwork bomb.'

Marion turned again to the tiny crystal vial. 'Well, this. It seems to be part of the mechanism, part of the bomb's design.' She held up the simplified sketch. 'You see here' – she pointed at a small depression in the rear of the bomb's outer casing – 'there was an arrow that pointed to this, indicating the insertion point of something they referred to as the Grey Eagle. According to the diagram's instructions, the Grey Eagle is also attached to the timer, but set to be released just moments before the explosive is ignited by the fuse.'

'What the hell is a Grey Eagle?' Kenny asked.

'*This*, Kenny.' She held up the vial.

'Bloody hell.' Bill looked up. He hesitated for a moment, perhaps as he pieced together what Marion had said. 'The perfect weapon, isn't it? The stuff in the vial is released moments before the explosive detonates. It'll disorientate, maybe even blind everyone in range. Then boom. Before you know what's going on, you're turned to ash.'

The room fell silent. Even though Marion already understood, the realisation of what she'd uncovered was only now truly sinking in.

Kenny was the first to speak again. 'Shit.' He snubbed out his cigarette. 'You think this has anything to do with White's murder?'

'I know it does.'

'Yeah?' Kenny prompted.

Marion turned to Bill instead. 'Remember I told you the camera above the Lock Room gate was an infrared sensor?'

Bill nodded. 'Turns on when it detects body heat.' He was beginning to understand. 'In order to bypass the camera, you'd have to lower your body temperature just a few degrees and—' he picked up the crystal vial once more.

'Exactly,' Marion said. 'It was something I'd been trying to understand for a while. How could anyone other than Frank have murdered Michelle White? How did anyone get past the camera without it picking them up? Now I realise they didn't. It wasn't that the camera didn't see them, it's just that it didn't switch on.'

Bill held the vial tight in his palm. 'It's cold.' He looked at Marion, then spoke more hastily. 'You think someone could have used it on themselves?'

'I don't see why not. You could apply just a few drops to your clothes, then make sure your nose and mouth are covered to prevent inhalation. You'd block enough infrared emissions to trick the camera and if even if you bumped into anyone along the way, they'd be so disorientated they wouldn't realise what they'd seen.' She paused to take a breath. 'Frank said that when he was in the Lock Room the night of the murder, he sensed something odd in the air. His eyesight was blurred, he felt disorientated. Whoever the real killer was, there's no doubt they were using the Grey Eagle as a disguise.'

Bill looked only half convinced. 'But what was the killer, and White for that matter, doing in the Lock Room in the first place? You said nothing was removed from the drawers. The letter she received that night? We still don't know what that said, or who sent it.'

'No. But it has to be connected to all this.' It was the final piece of the puzzle and one that Marion hadn't had time to consider just yet. 'We can still assume the killer didn't know about the camera above the Lock Room gate, but considering they were using the disguise anyway, it means they must have been doing something in there they didn't want anyone to see.'

Again, the trio went silent and Marion was sure that Bill and Kenny were considering, as she had done all day, the implications of what this meant.

It was Kenny who broke the silence. 'So, we're certain that whoever's been producing these bombs is also the one who killed White?'

Marion nodded. 'It's the only thing that makes sense.'

'And any ideas on who it could be?'

'Not yet.' Marion turned to Bill, who passed her a cautionary glance. 'I'm uncertain of who to trust, of who we can tell without risking the investigation.'

'We have to tell Nancy,' Bill interjected. 'I mean, she can't be involved, surely not?'

Marion looked at Kenny. 'Is there any way we can contact Frank? Ask him what to do?'

'Of course not. He's locked up and under twenty-four-hour surveillance. You pass information like this to him, you're passing it to Nicholas and the council. No, Hobb is right.' He gestured at Bill. 'We tell Nancy. There's no other option.'

Marion considered arguing but really, she didn't know what else to do.

'Listen, Lane,' Kenny went on. 'You've done well. Nancy will be grateful and I'm sure she'll know where to take this next. She's supposed to be back tomorrow morning anyway.'

'And we're just supposed to wait around until then? Do nothing?'

'For now, yes.' Kenny offered Marion a cigarette. She refused. 'How about this. I'll speak to Nancy as soon as she's back. I'll even leave you and Hobb out of it. It'll make me look better anyway.' He smirked. Marion bit her tongue. 'I'll meet you back here tomorrow at lunch with an update. Okay?'

She grunted a non-committal reply. It wasn't really okay. No matter what Bill or Kenny believed, she still wasn't convinced Nancy or the High Council could be trusted. If her assumptions about what she'd uncovered were accurate, it meant that the agency had been used as a chemical weaponry laboratory before Nancy had converted it into a private detective agency after the war. It was obvious Nancy knew about the weaponry project, so why had she not figured out that the substance in the crystal vial was how someone had got past the camera?

A scraping sound pulled Marion from her thoughts. She turned to the wall beside her bedroom door. A post tray she hadn't even known existed emerged from the stone facade, bearing a crisp piece of white card with silvery-green ink.

Marion read it out loud.

You are cordially invited to the first annual Miss
Brickett's Circus Ball!

Join us for a night of extravagance and excitement with
a special performance from Thomson & Thorpe (ex-
Inquirers and trained acrobats) as well as acts from a
range of Professor Bal's clockwork masterpieces!

Drinks and food will be provided.

Date: Friday 25 April
Time: 7 p.m.
Location: The ballroom.
Dress: formal/black tie.
We hope to see you there!

'What the hell is a circus ball?' Kenny asked.

Marion didn't answer, though the cogs of her frazzled mind began to turn. This must have been Professor Bal's 'classified assignment', the thing he'd been so busy with the past few days. But was it a coincidence it was happening now, just as Nancy had mysteriously disappeared? She read the invitation again. Maybe it was exhaustion, or the remnants of angst from her trip into the cellar beneath the break room, but something about the event troubled her.

17

The Lie and the High Wire

Friday morning, still weary from the events of the night before, Marion made her way down to the cafeteria for breakfast. It was immediately obvious that news of the upcoming Circus Ball had caused a mix of excitement and confusion throughout the agency. It was also obvious, from the notice hanging at the end of the Grand Corridor, that preparation for the event would take precedence over everything else that day – all training, work sessions and general goings-on had been cancelled for the morning and afternoon, and anyone who planned to attend the ball was encouraged to remain in their offices, the cafeteria or the common room until seven o'clock.

Nearly every staff member and head of department could be seen charging through the corridors towards the ballroom or the kitchens in a panicked hurry to get everything done before the end of the day. By the time Marion had reached the common room, she'd passed at least ten staff members all with the same frazzled look on their faces, boxes of lights, silk banners, crockery, cutlery, tablecloths and all manner of curious decorations clutched to their chests. Harry and the kitchen staff were similarly occupied, and all through the day a cacophony of aromas – charred meat, mixed spice, fresh bread – filled the upper-level corridors and chambers.

Yet the charged, almost dizzying atmosphere only added to Marion's swiftly growing unease. She paced her room as she counted the hours to lunchtime when, if Kenny kept his word, they were due to meet.

But lunch came and went without any sign of him and Marion was left anxious, alone, frustrated. She crossed the corridor to the common room. The fire had been lit and the central oak table – designed for general meetings and discussions, but mostly used for playing cards and board games – was littered with half-drunk bottles of liquor and dying cigarette butts, evidence of a lazy afternoon off. But where had everyone gone?

She lingered by the fire, her thoughts stagnant, unable to move past the vile discovery she'd made in the tunnels beyond the Border, and what it all meant. Why was a wartime chemical weaponry experiment being brought back to life here at Miss Brickett's?

A sound filled the silence. A low and rattling hiss.

A fractured shadow, long and twisted, was cast across the room. And then she knew.

Clink – schlik, schlik – clink.

The room's chandelier, a tear-drop crystal that hung from the ceiling, flickered as a line of silver scales moved across the threshold. The snake she'd seen in the corridors beyond the Border, now more difficult to see than ever, glimmered only when it fell directly under the ceiling light – right at the foot of the couch.

Clink – schlik, schlik – clink.

'His name is Toby,' Mr Nicholas said menacingly as he appeared in the doorway. He took a few steps forward and the snake slithered to his feet.

A cold sweat beaded on Marion's upper lip.

'Brilliant, isn't it? Professor Bal, such a genius but sometimes he needs a little push.' He settled down at the table.

'His designs have been somewhat bland of late. But I had a word with him, you see.' He grinned, looking down at the sleeping serpent then up at Marion.

Marion sat quite still, trying to calm the thundering in her chest, slow her rapid breath.

'Nancy has put me in charge while she's away, to be on the lookout for suspicious behaviour.'

Marion finally managed to thaw herself from the clutches of whatever icy terror had come over her. 'Then I suggest you look elsewhere.'

The grin on Mr Nicholas's face grew more twisted. He flicked open his pocket watch.

Toby stirred.

'Toby has been patrolling the tunnels beyond the Border for some time, just as an extra precaution. His tongue is designed to detect and record human movement. As soon as it does, cameras in his eyes switch on and I am alerted.' He paused. 'But perhaps you already knew that?'

'How could I?'

Nicholas shook his head. 'Now, now, Miss Lane. Please don't lie.' He straightened up. 'There was someone down in those tunnels on Tuesday last week, just before Mr Eston's apparent tumble down the stairs. Toby sensed it, only it was too dark for the cameras to make out who it was.'

Marion felt a wave of nausea come over her. The common room was hardly ever empty during the day for longer than five minutes. Where, now, was everyone?

'I know it was one or all three of you, Miss Lane. You, Mr Eston and Mr Hobb,' he said, flicking a notch on his pocket watch.

Toby, now completely solid and clearly visible, shivered – a lightning-fast ripple travelled up from his tail to his head. He shifted, then reared up. But Marion stood her ground. She knew, from Nancy and Gillroth's conversation after Frank's trial, that Nicholas was bluffing. His snake had detected movement, but it hadn't picked up anything that looked like a human being. Nicholas might have his assumptions, but he had no proof.

'One more mistake, from any of you. One more and you're out. I hope we,' he gestured to Toby, then himself, 'make ourselves clear.' He grinned, nodded and turned to leave. Toby slinked out after him.

Marion stared blankly through the bookshop window as the last rays of pale, weak sunlight set beyond a milky sky. After her encounter with Toby and Mr Nicholas, she'd felt desperate to remove herself from the oppressive, suffocating atmosphere of Miss Brickett's and had made her way to the lift and through the trapdoor, where she planned to remain until the Circus Ball commenced.

She realised now, as she strolled around the cramped shop, how much she'd missed the comfort of its untidy shelves, its snug lighting, the familiar scent of old paper that saturated the air. There was something about the ordinariness of the place that she craved: the misplaced books, the un-filed stacks of paper, so acutely contrasting to the world for which it was a porthole, a bridge.

When she'd first set foot inside the bookshop, that evening late in December, she'd felt somewhat let down by its lacklustre appearance. Now she realised how significant this unpretentious facade was; not just as a defence against public intrusion and curiosity, but as a reminder that sometimes the extraordinary existed just below the surface of the ordinary. The bookshop was a link to the outside world, to stability and normality and a portal into the mysterious and intoxicating world of Inquiry.

She picked a book from the shelves – *Little Women*, her childhood favourite – and sunk to the floor, resting her head against the butler's desk, overcome by that familiar deep and hollow ache of loneliness. The past two weeks had been a blur of happenings, of dread and fear but also of purpose. She'd been so consumed with uncovering first the root of Bill and David's discord, then the truth behind Michelle White's murder. But now that she'd been forced to take a break from the investigation, the loneliness returned. Perhaps worse than ever.

She pressed her knuckles into her temples and breathed. Long and deep. Slow and deliberate.

The trapdoor creaked open behind her.

'Thought I'd find you here.' Jessica clambered through the hole, ungainly and out of breath. 'The girls and I are getting ready in Rakes' room. For the ball,' she added when Marion failed to reply. 'She's arranged everything for us, wine, music. Rather out-of-character for her but I suppose she's just trying to get into the spirit, raise morale as everyone's been saying. Thought you might like to join?'

'Oh, I don't know.' She hesitated.

Jessica looked at the book in Marion's hand. She would be making some analysis about the choice. And it would probably be accurate. 'I love that one, too.'

'Mum and I used to read it together. Always at Christmas.' She held back the burn in her chest. She didn't want to cry.

'I did the same, though not with my mother. I believe she thought it might give me the wrong sort of aspirations.' She sighed as if remembering something. 'One might argue she was right.' Marion was struck with a spasm of guilt. Jessica was an observer, a listener. And she was always there to provide comfort, if not advice. She didn't expect much in return, though that was no excuse. Even listeners liked to be heard. But Marion had been so consumed with her own troubles lately, she wondered how much of Jessica's life she'd missed. She'd have to dive right in. 'How's Roger? Anything happening there?'

Jessica chewed her lip. 'Oh . . . he's, we've seen each other again.'

'And? What's he like?'

'*Delicious*,' she laughed. 'But that's all. Really, he's quite dull. I'll have to put an end to it.'

'Probably for the best. Work and love seldom go together.' She wasn't ever going to admit it, but she thought of Kenny Hugo as she said this.

Jessica looked around the shop in contemplation. 'You know, I've always thought we should hold a book club up here. Just for employees of course. Once a month or something. What do you think?'

'I'd love that. Might have to sit on the street though, it's a bit compact in here.'

They laughed.

Jessica offered her hand and pulled Marion to her feet. 'I've seen how distracted you've been lately.' She looked at her, through her. 'I don't know what's going on, Mari, and you don't have to tell me. Just know that I, *us* . . . even Amanda, believe it or not, we've noticed. And we're here for you.' She squeezed Marion's hand. 'Now come on, I think tonight is just what everyone needs.'

Marion's eyes welled with tears, not from sadness but gratitude. She watched as Jessica studied her face, looking at what lay behind her silence, and for a moment she wished she could say more, explain her reticence, the reason she'd been so distant and distracted.

'As I said,' Jessica added, 'you don't need to explain.'

They hugged and the tension in Marion's chest eased. 'Thank you, Jess. Really. And you're right. I think tonight will be fun.'

They arrived at Aida Rakes' room in the staff quarters to a clamouring of excited voices as Amanda and several second and third years gathered around the only mirror, admiring their silks and pearls. All furniture had been shoved to the perimeter of the room, creating a large open centre in which one dressing table stood, now layered with petticoats and an assortment of makeup, brushes and bottles of hairspray.

After collecting her things from her room, Marion changed into the only gown she owned and one she hoped no one would remember she'd worn before – a light grey chiffon sheath dress dripping in worn and cracked glass beads. With Jessica's help, she fixed her hair into a cascade of tight curls, applied lavish amounts of cream foundation, blush and blazing red lipstick.

'All right ladies,' Maud said, dressed in a bright blue rayon suit (much to Amanda's distaste) and carrying a large black satchel, 'let's get a bloody groove going.' She opened the satchel and pulled out a collection of liquor – wine, whisky, sherry and an arrangement of ciders. 'Courtesy of Harry and the library bar. No need to mention it to Rakes . . .' she surveyed the room. 'Where is she, by the way?'

'He gave you all that?' Jessica asked sceptically, ignoring the question.

'Not exactly, but what he doesn't know . . .' Her face was illuminated, delighted perhaps more at the horror on Jessica's than the bounty she'd plundered from the bar. 'Relax, Jess. We're here to celebrate.' She slung an arm over Marion. 'Right, Mari?'

'Exactly right,' Marion said, grinning. She poured them each a glass of wine, turned on the gramophone and relaxed, just for a moment forgetting the dread churning her insides – Frank's fate, the agency's, her own.

Once dressed, coiffed and well-liquored, the women made their way across the corridor to the common room where

213

the rest of the apprentices had gathered, dressed in varying degrees of formality, trailed by clouds of perfume, cologne, hairspray and excitement.

Bill – dressed in an ill-fitting tuxedo and sky-blue bowtie – lowered himself awkwardly into a chair next to Marion at the central table. He regarded her outfit with something of a bemused expression. 'You look . . . nice.'

Marion smiled, smoothing her gown across her thighs. 'Thanks. You too.' He really did, despite the oversized tuxedo. Though tousled and certainly in need of a trim, his black hair gleamed against his milk-pale skin and he exuded a ruffled, unintentional charm.

'Any news on the bomb factory?'

'Bill! Keep your voice down!' She checked they hadn't been overheard, but thanks to the gramophone blaring Johnny Cash, no one appeared to have noticed. 'And no,' she said. 'I was supposed to meet with Kenny this afternoon but he didn't show.'

Bill poured them each a glass of wine. 'On that note, I've been thinking. You're convinced White's killer is the person who's been recreating the,' he lowered his voice, '*bomb*.'

'Yes. Definitely.'

'Okay, but doesn't that mean the killer must have had the map at some point? I mean, that's why White was worried in the first place, right?'

'Yes. And I know what you're going to say. Only you, David, Ned and a High Council member ever had the map, according to rumour at least. So the killer must be one of them. But it's obviously not you, and David never had the map and monocle at the same time so it seems unlikely it was him. Ned is long gone. Which leaves—'

Bill took a sip of wine. 'The High Council member? Gillroth?'

'Thing is,' Marion said, 'it's not a watertight theory, is it? First, we don't know if the rumours about who had the map and who didn't are true, or comprehensive. And second, two or more people could have been working together. Like we are. I mean, you wouldn't need the map to find the laboratory if I showed you where the break room entrance was.'

'So that doesn't help us at all then.' He lapsed into contemplation for a few moments. 'Oh, and by the way. I've some bad news.' He angled his chin towards the door.

'Can it wait? I really just need a few hours . . .' she trailed off, following Bill's gaze to the common room entrance and David Eston, who'd appeared at the threshold in a wheelchair.

'He was discharged last night,' Bill whispered. 'We've had a little catch-up, don't worry. I explained that the map went missing in the tunnels and if he wants to go looking for it again, he'll have to do so alone.'

'And? He bought it?'

Bill shrugged. 'Probably not but he seems frightened, to be honest. I think what happened to him down there was a big shock. I don't think he wants anything more to do with the map or the tunnels. At least for the time being.'

Marion watched as David wheeled himself towards the table, a look of cold detachment on his face. She wasn't quite as convinced as Bill that David was the type of person to let anything go, especially something he'd pursued so fervently, something so personal. Even so, she pushed the notion to the back of her mind. Tonight, she was determined to enjoy herself.

'Everyone going tonight?' Jessica asked the group at large, as she set up a game of Miss Brickett's Cluedo – Professor Bal's frivolous invention, created as an in-house joke with tailored weapons (agency gadgets) and murder suspects (apparently picked from the professor's wide array of relatives and acquaintances).

Preston ground out his cigarette. 'I'm definitely going. Bound to be some drama that won't be worth missing.'

'I think it's a good idea. Raise morale a bit,' Jessica contested, with a slightly more forced smile.

'A pay rise would raise my morale, not a damn circus,' Amanda said.

'Come now,' Maud slurred (by Marion's count, she was on drink number four). 'Let's just relax. It's like Jess said,' she paused to finish her drink, 'we all need some fun. Can't hurt to forget what's been going on lately and . . . get a little boozed.'

'That's not exactly what I—' Jessica began, interrupted by David who smirked and raised his glass in a toast.

'I agree. Waste of money but, hey, to raising morale.' His eyes drifted to Bill and Marion. 'And to *forgetting*.'

The group raised their glasses in unison.

'To morale,' Maud offered.

'*To morale*,' the group chimed.

Jessica handed out the Cluedo tokens and cards. 'Amanda, you're Archibald Horrib, Bill, you're Master Spike, Preston, you're Porter Lynn, David, you're Madame Mey, Maud, you're Doctor Evans and Mari and I will be Professor Govender.'

In the centre of the board, which was intricately painted with a map of the agency, there was a simple black square and inside the square, a scrawled message in silver ink: *Who killed Lady Mill?*

Preston leaned across the board, placing a tiny wooden figurine in the ballroom. 'Horrib in the ballroom with a—' he looked at Jessica. 'Where're the weapons?'

'Ah, sorry.' Jessica placed a pile of tiny clockwork murder weapons in the centre of the board. A Time Lighter which emitted tiny clouds of hot steam, a fierce-looking gargoyle that resembled the one on the workshop door, a cigar case filled with poison darts, a writhing reel of Twister Rope, a halothane ball and a silver dagger.

'Horrib in the ballroom,' Preston repeated, 'with the Twister Rope.' He placed the tiny reel of rope on the board, where it immediately turned itself into a firm knot. 'What a bloody awful way to go.'

'Not as bad as this,' Maud said, examining the gargoyle at eye level.

Preston shook his head. 'I've never understood how that's supposed to kill anyone.'

'It could fall on you. Cracked skull?' Maud provided.

'Nah,' Preston said, 'heart attack I reckon. It'll scare you to death . . .'

Thus a debate on the particular mechanics of death-by-gargoyle ensued. Taking his chance at the otherwise distracted table, Bill leaned into Marion and whispered: 'Mari, I think we need to discuss this Kenny Hugo character.'

Marion flipped her cards through her fingers. 'Discuss?' Frustration stirred inside her. She was put out by Kenny's absence through the day. And now she was annoyed Bill had anything to say about it.

'I'm not sure we should trust him.'

'We've been through this, Bill. We have no choice.'

'He's keeping something from us. I mean, where's he been all day?'

Marion shrugged, but said nothing.

'I'm just saying,' he went on, speaking more delicately, 'don't believe everything he says just because he's got great hair.'

Marion glared at him. 'What is that supposed to mean?'

Fortunately for Bill, he didn't have to answer as his turn came up next. He rolled the dice. 'Madame Mey in the Workshop with a poison dart.'

The game moved swiftly from there, ending as Maud called the correct combination of Master Pike in the library with a Time Lighter and Marion and Bill's discussion on Kenny Hugo was forced to a close. At ten minutes to seven, the group packed up, finished their drinks and left the common room together.

Every inch of the ballroom's pale marble walls and ceiling had been covered with black silk banners, embellished with thousands of white crystal studs, creating an illusion of a clear and star-filled sky. The air was a cauldron of incense, butter, caramel and humidity, illuminated only by the glow of five tall lanterns and their soft grey light. A circular stage had been erected in the centre, encapsulating a tented ring. Inside the ring, an array of black and silver boxes lay scattered across the floor. Two tall poles stood at opposing sides and held up a tight wire that hung six feet from the floor.

When Marion looked closer, she noticed Professor Bal and his assistant crouched behind the stage, apparently wrestling with something long and of gleaming silver. A coil of Twister Rope, she suspected, though what purpose it might have at a circus she had no idea. Tentatively, she traversed the perimeter of the ballroom, surveying the expressions of the staff members and employees she passed, subtle looks of bewilderment as they too examined the illustriously adorned room.

She arrived at a line of chairs erected near the buffet table, covered with silver platters layered with steaming cuts of beef and pork, roast vegetables, mounds of bread and jugs of gravy.

'Blimey,' Bill said, joining her. 'Harry's outdone himself tonight. Reckon we can help ourselves?'

She ignored him.

Bill sighed. 'Look, I'm sorry for what I said about Hugo. Rude, I know. I was just trying to . . .' He inhaled deeply. 'I think we should be cautious.' He held up his hand as Marion opened her mouth to protest. 'But please, let's leave it for now. Okay? Let's enjoy ourselves tonight.' He smiled pleadingly, raising the gravy boat, as if making a toast. 'To morale?'

Bill's comment had stung. She didn't trust Kenny because she wanted to, and certainly not because he had good hair, for heaven's sake. But she didn't have the energy to argue, or explain (again) exactly why they had no choice but to believe he was on their side. Tonight was a time for celebration. A time to forget. She smiled. '*To morale.*'

Satisfied with their reconciliation, Bill served himself a plate of roast meat, an assortment of vegetables and a few slices of bread, all smothered in gravy. 'I overheard some of the senior Inquirers talking this afternoon,' he said, as he popped a potato into his mouth, 'apparently the High Council planned this as a surprise for the staff but now the Inquirers think there's something fishy about it all.'

'The circus?'

Bill nodded, his mouth stuffed. He swallowed, then went on. 'I didn't catch why, just that they think it's odd.'

'Well, so do I. Nancy's away and all of a sudden we're having the most extravagant event of the year. Do you know whose idea it was?'

'I just told you, the High Council.'

'But who's at the helm, who's organising it?'

Bill shrugged, not seeming to care.

And while something about the event still tapped away at Marion's subconscious, as the ballroom filled with guests, the lights dimmed even more, and the air swelled – luxurious, thick, warm – she felt her nerves unravel. Tension slipped from her muscles like water, worries from her mind like silk and soon she'd melted into her chair, lost in the collective and feverish enthusiasm until, just like everybody else, she could hardly wait for the show to begin.

'They're handing these out at the entrance, got us one each,' Bill said as he finished his meal. He was holding two brass squares that Marion immediately recognised as Trick

Locks, similar to the gadget she'd encountered latched to the bookshop door the day of her recruitment. 'No cheating this time, okay?' he chided, passing her one.

'God, I'm useless at these things.' She examined the device. Carved into its superior surface was a line of four symbols: a key, a feather, an arrow pointing skywards and two horizontal lines so close to one another that at first glance they appeared to be connected.

Bill handed her a slip of paper. 'Came with this, a riddle I presume. Apparently Amanda's already opened hers. Surprised?'

Marion laughed. 'She's probably hoping it'll get her another promotion.' She read the riddle out loud: *When darkness falls, the lock will open.* She frowned. 'Any ideas?'

'Well, it's a sequence. I suppose we're to press the symbols in the correct order and the lock will open. *When darkness falls, the lock will open.* A key, a feather, an arrow, two lines . . .' He trailed off and Marion's attention wandered from the Trick Lock and back to the stage, where Professor Bal was now conversing with Gillroth and several other senior staff members. Occasionally Professor Bal would turn to survey the crowd, and although Marion couldn't be sure, his expression now seemed more tentative than excited.

'Opposites!' Bill called out.

'What?'

'The answer to the riddle,' he explained. 'Opposites in order. What's the opposite of darkness?'

'Light?' She stared at the symbols again. There was nothing that resembled a light but . . . 'Feather! The opposite of darkness is light, *light as a feather.*'

Bill nodded and pressed the corresponding symbol. 'Okay . . . and the opposite of falls?'

'Wait, I've got it,' Marion said, jumping several steps ahead. She pressed the symbols in the order she'd just worked out:

a feather, the upward facing arrow (*up*, the opposite of falls), the key (*unlock,* the opposite of lock) and finally the two lines that were so close together they almost touched (*close* . . . the opposite of open).

She was right.

The Trick Lock clicked open, revealing three tokens. She passed them to Bill. 'And these are?'

'Blimey,' he said, repeating the sequence and opening his own. 'Beer tokens. Might have been easier to get my wallet out.' He collected the tokens and made his way to the drinks table, returning shortly after with a tray of six pints.

'I'm not drinking all that,' Marion said.

Bill frowned. 'It's free, and it's all they're serving.' He pushed a pint into her hand and took a sip from his own. 'Huh . . . that's odd.'

'What?'

He held his pint at eye level, examining it. 'Tastes off.'

Marion took a sip. She had no idea what off beer tasted like, though the liquid in her mouth was bitter and flat. 'I suppose.'

Bill opened his mouth, perhaps to discuss the matter further, but stopped when the ballroom lights flickered off and everything went black.

The starlit walls and ceiling gleamed. A drone of murmurs came from the crowd and then, all at once, silence. The air buzzed, whirled, hissed and finally began to rattle with the slow drum of a circus march. A red-tinged cloud of smoke rose from the centre of the ring and as it lifted, Professor Bal appeared, dressed all in white.

'Welcome to the first annual Circus Ball,' the professor announced to the crowd, his voice wavering. There was slow applause. Then, from somewhere in the shadows behind the stage, Edgar Swindlehurst appeared. He stepped slowly into the light and as he did, Marion noticed a glistening grey eagle perched on his arm. The professor and he looked at one another, an exchange of words was had and the eagle took flight, swooping across the room, pouring a rain of silver sparks from its wings that drifted down through the air, dying out just before they collided with the heads of the now completely enthralled crowd.

'That thing,' Marion said to Bill, taking another sip of beer, 'that . . .'

'What?'

Marion rubbed her lips. They had begun to tingle. 'That eagle. It's grey.'

Bill looked confused. He cast his eyes upwards, at the thing swooping above his head. 'Yeah . . . yeah it is.'

Marion opened her mouth, though whatever point she'd been trying to make left her as swiftly as it had arrived. She looked at the stage, behind it and into the darkness of the alcove from which the eagle had appeared. Swindlehurst moved back into the shadows, his outline now barely visible. Marion's insides twisted and pulled, her head swirled, her breath grew thick and hot.

Professor Bal drew a loudspeaker to his mouth. 'Let the show begin!' he roared, prompting the crowd to break into thunderous applause.

Marion felt her vision cloud over, not so that she couldn't see, but as if a soft mist had surrounded her. Bill, too, looked as if he were lost in some pleasant dream, his mouth slightly open and his eyes fixed, unmoving, on the show before him.

Two blond men stepped into the ring next, removing a white silk covering from the large wooden cart they pushed in front of them. Each man took one step backwards so that they came to stand on either side of the cart. In absolute unison they reached one arm into the cart and pulled out a red sheet of silk. Together they twirled around themselves and behind the sheet, appearing again moments later many feet taller. The men in stilts, their heads dusting the ceiling, then began to juggle. Marion fumbled for Bill's hand as she realised the things the two men were juggling with were not balls but rather five light orbs each. This time, for a reason Marion was too tired or drunk to understand, the crowd clapped a little less enthusiastically.

Bill slumped in his seat, apparently on the verge of sleep as the two men (still on stilts) clapped their hands. Instantly, something from inside the cart began to sizzle, followed by a high whistle. From deep within the cart, red and green sparks burst into the air, hit the ceiling then floated down and onto the crowd. Marion caught one between her fingers, it burned her skin for a fraction of a second, then turned to green-red dust.

It hadn't occurred to Marion that the spectacular display unfolding in front of her was having the very effect it had been designed to. The lights and sounds – the shimmering eagle, the acrobatics, the fireworks – had mesmerised her. There was nothing she, or anyone else in the room could do to tear their eyes from the dazzling extravaganza. Except for, it turned out, a man who was already quite used to bright colours and flashy things.

18

The Room on Fire

'Lane! Get up!' Kenny pulled Marion from her seat as an enormous blaze of bright blue fireworks spilled from the centre of the stage.

She stumbled to her feet as the fireworks contorted themselves into something that looked like a raincloud, looming just a foot below the ceiling. Kenny hauled Marion through the crowd and out of the ballroom, just moments before the illusionary cloud burst, dispatching a swarm of glossy sparks that fell to the floor as a fiery rain.

Marion steadied herself as they came to a halt, realising for the first time that not just her lips, but her entire body was lingering between a state of numbness and hot prickling. She grabbed Kenny's shoulder. 'What's happening?'

Kenny picked her up. She would have liked to elbow him in the stomach for it, but could not gather the energy to do so. He carried her to the powder room and laid her down on the chair by the mirror. 'The beer was laced with something. And I think there was something in those fireworks, too. A hallucinogenic maybe. Here, take this.' He handed her two white tablets and a glass of water.

'What — are those?'

'Just take them. You really need to be more alert if you want to be a good detective.'

Again, Marion couldn't find the energy to retaliate.

'Now show me how to use this darn thing,' he said, holding out something round and shiny.

Marion stared at him, unable to move, to think, to understand.

'Blazes, Lane! Swindlehurst is on the move and we can't let him get out of range.'

She was trying to listen, she really was, but her head was spinning uncontrollably. Kenny's dazzling form slipped in and out of focus, she was unable to speak and the only thing she could bring herself to think about was whether the Circus Ball had actually happened or whether she'd just imagined it. She threw the two tablets down her throat and curled up in the chair until her head had cleared.

She dragged herself to her feet once more. Though she now had a thumping headache, her logical, rational brain was making a slow comeback. Kenny stood by the door, still staring at the shiny device in his hand. 'Where were you all day?' she asked.

'Busy.'

'With?'

'We've had a little development. I'll explain later.' He handed her the shiny round object which, at last, she realised was a Vagor Compass. 'Planted a tracker on him around lunchtime but it's damn impossible to read, so I've had to resort to following the blasted man around all day long. Surprised he hasn't caught on yet.' He wiped a trail of sweat from his forehead. 'How are you feeling?'

'What are you going on about? Following who?'

'Goddammit, Lane. Swindlehurst! He laced the kegs with God knows what. The whole agency is staggering around like half-conscious idiots. He's up to something tonight, something big.'

A gnawing ache formed in her stomach, nothing to do with whatever drugs were coursing through her veins. 'The eagle . . .' she stammered. 'The eagle . . . I saw it.'

'What? What eagle?'

She took a sip of water and several long breaths. 'There was a mechanical eagle used in the circus, I recognised it but couldn't remember where from at the time. Now I do. It was in the laboratory. A grey eagle. My God, it's Swindlehurst, isn't it? He's the murderer.'

Kenny unclipped the topmost button of his shirt and loosened his collar. 'Bingo. When I woke up this morning, I received a note from Professor Bal. He said Nancy and the High Council approved the ball a few days ago, though it had been primarily Swindlehurst's initiative. Already a bit bizarre since apparently Swindlehurst's not the type for extravagance and frivolity. But the professor really started to get uncomfortable when Nancy left on her trip. He said Swindlehurst started pestering him at the Gadgetry Department, wanting to make sure everything was perfect, obsessed that the ball went ahead exactly as planned. He seemed especially interested in the fireworks, too, which now makes sense. Anyway, the professor suggested I keep an eye on Swindlehurst until Nancy gets back. Just in case.' He pointed to the Vagor Compass. 'Hence the tracking device.' He paused. 'How are you feeling now?'

'Same as I was two minutes ago.'

'Well, that'll have to do.' He pushed the compass into her hand. 'You're going to have to read it for me.' He smiled. 'It's as you said, Lane. I need your help.'

Marion turned the gleaming device over in her hand. 'Let's go.' She followed Kenny from the powder room and into the foyer outside the ballroom. Lights still spilled from inside. Sharp cracks and ear-splitting hisses resonated across the hall and through the dazzling smoke and sparkling mist emitted by the relentless fireworks, Marion could just make out the last rows of chairs, the audience slumped in their seats, staring blankly in front of them.

She flipped the compass lid open. Beneath its glass face was a thin needle attached to a central pivot. Where north would be on a regular compass was instead a brilliant emerald light (the indicator) that glowed brighter the closer the compass was brought to its paired Vagor Stone. Just below the central pivot was a direction board, a rectangular metal plate on which appeared a simplified guiding map. So long as the compass' needle was pointing at the emerald indicator, you could be sure you were going in the right direction.

Marion watched the emerald indicator as it glowed dimly, barely at all. The paired Vagor Stone had to be right on the edge of the compass's range – approximately half a mile. She adjusted her stance until the needle pointed at the indicator, then looked up. In front of her and slightly to the right was the entrance to the corridor that led past the library. On her left was one that wound upwards and towards Nancy's office.

'I was certain he'd be hanging out in the break room,' Kenny explained, 'considering your little discovery. But I waited there all day and he didn't show. Eventually, I found him in the ballroom where he fussed around for a bit, all for appearances no doubt. But then when the show was in full swing, I lost him completely. I tried to use the compass but it just went dead; maybe he was out of range but—'

'Please, Kenny. I'm trying to concentrate.' She took a step forward. 'It just requires a little practise. And patience.' The guiding map flashed on, something that only happened when the compass sensed its user was lost. A delicate line of glowing green light appeared, connecting two points. One was black, this belonged to Marion, the other green – the Vagor Stone. 'He's not in the break room or anywhere near it – actually

. . . it looks like he's in the Intelligence Department, moving north-west. Come on. This way.'

It was a reasonably calculated guess, and the compass guided them through the tunnels and chambers that wound towards Intelligence. Normally busy and brightly lit, even this well-used part of the agency now seemed deserted. They continued past the cafeteria, past the kitchens, turning left or right according to the compass's tiny needle and flickering green light.

As Marion had guessed, the needle guided them towards the short staircase that led from the library's ground floor to the Filing and Intelligence Departments beneath. She flipped the compass closed, the light now at full burn. She nodded. 'He's definitely down there—' She was cut off by a loud clang as the door at the bottom of the staircase burst open. 'He's coming!'

'This way,' Kenny pulled Marion behind a bookshelf to the left side of the staircase.

They waited. Their eyes began to burn. The air around them started to ferment, to thicken.

Marion ripped two long strips from the hem of her chiffon gown. She handed one to Kenny. 'Wrap it around your nose and mouth.'

'What?'

'Just do it. Quickly!'

The effects of the haze did not disappear altogether, the air still thick and clouded, but when Marion peered around the corner of their hiding place and squinted into the darkness, she saw a shape that vaguely resembled Swindlehurst's tall, wide frame drifting up the staircase. He too was protected from the effects of the mist, a gas mask covering his nose and mouth.

'Check the compass,' Kenny whispered.

She flipped it open. The needle quivered as it attempted to realign itself and the green light of the indicator dimmed. Swindlehurst had moved past them.

Keeping a safe distance behind, far away enough to minimise the effects of the translucent mist but close enough to keep Swindlehurst within the compass's range, Marion and Kenny traced Swindlehurst across the library.

With adrenaline flowing through her veins and the effect of the drugs now completely worn off, she was starting to feel sickeningly nervous. Whatever was going to happen next, whatever Swindlehurst had planned that required a distraction as gargantuan as the Circus Ball, Marion could feel the threat of it gnawing on her nerves.

Swindlehurst's form filtered in and out of view. At times, especially when he passed through an area of minimal light, he vanished nearly completely.

'Where'd he go?' Kenny asked, as Swindlehurst's outline faded behind a bookshelf.

Marion caught sight of him again. 'He's heading for the Lock Room.'

But it was difficult to be sure. The library's perimeter lights, small bell-shaped bulbs, had been switched off and the main ceiling light lowered to just a flicker.

Marion and Kenny slipped from behind one bookshelf to the next as Swindlehurst edged towards the Lock Room.

'He's coming towards us.' Marion elbowed Kenny in the ribs and gestured to what might have been Swindlehurst in a dark corner just a few feet from where they hid. Neither of them moved, for it was now nearly impossible to make out where he was.

Marion's breath caught in her throat.

'*Don't move . . .*' Kenny whispered.

The sound of footsteps clipped against the marble floor. A speck of light flickered into view, then faded into the greyness. The footsteps came again, then stopped. The gate to the Lock Room opened and after a short hesitation, Marion and Kenny stepped through.

But inside the long, rectangular room, darker still than even the library, there was simply no chance of making out where Swindlehurst had gone. The room was lined on either side by rows of steel sliding drawers, labelled numerically from 1 to 114. And Marion finally understood why the council had little choice but to believe Frank guilty – there really was no way in or out of the caged room other than passing through the camera-guarded gate.

Kenny gripped her arm.

Footsteps on the stone floor. A shadow moved on the other side of the room. There was the sound of a zip being undone and a scraping, as if something was being removed from the wall – a large box, or so it appeared.

'I think it's wearing off,' Marion whispered, as the air around her started to clear.

Swindlehurst began to hurry. He turned a dial on the black box and pried it open. The moment the lid was unhitched, a ticking started from inside. He looked at his watch, then removed a single glass vial from the box.

Unlike the crystal vials Marion had seen in the laboratory, those filled with the silvery mist, the vial Swindlehurst now held contained something very different. A solidly black substance that seemed to hiss and sizzle.

He slipped it into his coat pocket.

A new sound, like steam pushing its way through the narrow aperture of a tiny pipe.

Footsteps hurtled across the room and towards the gate. It opened and shut in a hurry.

'Kenny,' Marion said, her heart in her throat. An unusual smell, of rot and burning rubber, had filled the air. Ribbons of black smoke poured from the box lid, so pungent that it was becoming difficult to breathe.

He nodded and pulled her back towards the gate. 'Time to move!'

They reached the gate. Marion yanked at the hinges. 'It's locked! Oh God.'

She turned around. A soft grey veil had enveloped the room. The hissing and ticking ceased, only to be followed by a final plume of dark smoke. The air was hot and short of oxygen.

There was a rush of footsteps as someone crossed the library floor beyond the gate, though Marion was now too delirious with fear to comprehend what it meant or who it was. She sunk to the floor, her eyesight tunnelling, her limbs weak.

A sharp crack split the air and everything went black.

19

The Seven-Year Safe

Saturday morning. Marion's pupils adjusted to the bright light of the infirmary. The inside of her elbow stung where a drip had been plunged into her vein. Her head throbbed, as if someone had drilled a bolt through her skull and was twisting it around just for fun. She turned to her left. Kenny was lying in the next bed, apparently asleep. Several beds away (which were occupied by a number of disgruntled-looking apprentices and staff) was Bill.

She disentangled herself from the drip and attempted to get to her feet.

'Miss Lane, what are you doing?' Dr Fitzpatrick, Head of Medical, raced to her side.

'I'm fine.' She steadied herself with Fitzpatrick's assistance.

'You're not fine. Sit down.' She pressed Marion back onto the bed.

'Bill . . .' she stammered. The words burned in her throat. 'What happened to him?'

'He's fine, though we've sedated him for the time being.'

'Sedated?'

'He was injured in the blast, Miss Lane.'

'The blast?' She stared at Fitzpatrick absently, trying to remember the last moment before everything went black.

Someone had opened the Lock Room gate or was at least standing there just outside, she was almost sure of that. But what happened next, she had no idea.

Fitzpatrick provided no elaboration.

'Is it serious?' Marion pressed, craning her neck to get a better look at Bill. He seemed to be attached to a multitude of tubes and wires, though no injuries were immediately obvious.

'He'll be absolutely fine.'

'How long will he be sedated for?'

'For a few hours. Please relax, Miss Lane. He just needs some rest.'

'And Hugo?' She looked at Kenny. His eyes flickered.

'Mild intoxication, just like you. Everyone's fine.' She adjusted a dial on the drip, then moved off to the dispensary next door.

Kenny stirred and opened his eyes. He turned to Marion, extended his left arm, reaching for the small brass compass on his bedside table. Her heart thumped. For those first few precious moments of consciousness, she'd happily forgotten the entire point of last night's expedition – to keep an eye on Swindlehurst, to make sure he didn't disappear. Even if the tracking device was still on him, the compass would only detect the Vagor Stone's pull if he was within a half-mile range.

Kenny flipped open the compass.

'And?' Marion asked eagerly.

Kenny heaved a sigh. He showed her the face of the compass, devoid of even the slightest green glow.

Marion sunk down into her pillow. Kenny looked defeated. His usually perfectly slicked blond hair was now dishevelled and dull, his face edged with disappointment and angst. Strangely, however, she sensed this rawness was perhaps the first glimpse she'd had of the real Kenny Hugo – not all hair wax, cologne and confidence after all. 'How are you feeling, by the way?'

He rubbed his forehead. 'Certainly been better.' His eyes traced her limbs, her face. He winced as he noticed a large bruise on her elbow. He reached out to touch her hand. 'I'm sorry. I should have left you in the ballroom. I should have followed Swindlehurst on my own.'

'No. I want to help. You must know that by now.'

Kenny nodded and pulled himself upright. 'Frankly, I'm surprised either of us are alive. Least we know why Swindlehurst wanted a distraction.'

The infirmary door opened once again, this time Professor Gillroth stepped inside. Marion recoiled at the sight of him. It was an involuntary reaction, instinctual. Gillroth's warnings to retract herself from the investigation and cease her meddling ways now seemed well founded. She still didn't know if that meant he'd been trying to protect her, or himself.

The professor lowered himself into a chair between Marion and Kenny's beds, placing his walking stick on the floor. He looked worn and pale, older than before.

'Miss Lane, Mr Hugo. How are you feeling?' His rheumy eyes swept over them with concern.

Marion opened her mouth, her throat dry and cracked. 'We're fine, I think.'

Gillroth nodded. For a moment he looked uncertain whom to address. 'Fitzpatrick informed me that the two of you witnessed some sort of gas leak. Near the Lock Room, I'm told?'

Marion and Kenny stirred as they eyed one another. They hadn't yet discussed what their cover story would be, nor had they discussed what had really happened in the Lock Room. Fitzpatrick had mentioned an explosion and now Gillroth was talking about a gas leak, neither of which sounded quite right.

Kenny's expression was one of caution, as Marion herself felt. The less said the better, they seemed to agree without words.

'Yes,' Marion said at last. 'We were in the library. I'm not sure what it was. There was a lot of smoke.'

'I see.' The professor pulled a handkerchief from his breast pocket and dabbed the corner of his eyes. Not tears of sadness but old age. 'And what were you doing in the library? The circus bored you, did it?' He smiled, or perhaps it was more a grimace.

'We'd like to speak to Nancy,' Kenny interjected after a note of silence. 'Could you send word for her to contact us?'

Gillroth breathed, coarse, strained, shallow. 'I'd be most happy to, Mr Hugo, however I'm afraid that since yesterday, no one's heard from her.' He turned to Marion. 'The beer kegs were laced with a peculiar substance, something alchemical I'm told. I'm also told that Professor Bal is conducting an examination of a rather interesting black box found at the site of the, eh, gas leak. And one other thing. Edgar has disappeared. His office has been cleared out.' He waited. He watched. The aged and atrophied muscles of his face twitched with distress, agitation.

Marion and Kenny held their silence until the professor gave in.

'Very well, Miss Lane, Mr Hugo.' He struggled to his feet, the walking stick creaking with the strain of his weight. 'I'm very sorry for what happened, to both of you and to Mr Hobb. I do hope your recovery is swift.' He nodded, as if confirming a thought. 'Please know, as ever, that I have your best interests at heart.' He paused, lowered his voice and continued. 'Whatever Edgar has done, whatever he plans to do, I have had no part in it. Please know that.'

'I think we've got to tell him,' Kenny said as soon as Gillroth had left. 'About what you found in the tunnels, I mean. It's the only link between Swindlehurst and the murder and since Nancy is MIA . . .'

Marion ripped the drip from her arm. 'You can, if you like. But Gillroth knows more than he's letting on, I'm sure of that. I doubt whatever you tell him will be a surprise.'

'Okay, so what then?'

'Keep an eye on the compass and leave a message at my room if it lights up.' She collected her purse from the drawer beside the bed and groaned as a lightning-sharp stab of pain caught her in the back.

'Where are you going?' He gripped her arm, gently. It made her catch her breath. 'We're in this together now.'

'Swindlehurst is gone, Kenny. And I guarantee he took all evidence of Operation Grey Eagle with him. No one's going to believe what I discovered down there unless we can find him.' Her voice was sharp, strained.

'Yes, I agree. But how are we going to do that? The compass is out of range.'

'By understanding what happened last night. If we know what he removed from the Lock Room, maybe we can figure out where he's gone. I have to visit Professor Bal.'

Marion made her way down to the Gadgetry Department with Kenny in tow.

Along the way, they didn't encounter a single Miss Brickett's employee, and Marion wondered what everyone who'd been affected by the mass drugging the night before might be thinking. Had they awoken sometime after midnight to find themselves slumped uncomfortably in their seats in the ballroom with no recollection of what they'd been doing there? Had they stumbled off to their rooms or back home, waking the next day from what must have been a very bright, unusual dream?

For Marion, it was all starting to feel like a nightmare. Frank's sentencing would take place in just five days and

236

although she now knew how Swindlehurst had slipped past the camera and into the Lock Room the night of the murder, she wasn't quite sure the vial of silvery mist she'd uncovered from his lair was enough to clear Frank's name. She needed to know his motive.

She side stepped the gargoyle outside the Workshop door and entered. Professor Bal emerged from his office.

'You're okay!' he gushed at Marion, glancing only briefly at Kenny. He guided them towards a workbench nearby covered in a pile of broken steel. 'I'm so sorry,' he added, shaking his head. 'The circus – we wanted it to be a surprise but . . . I thought there was something off about it towards the end. I'm so sorry.'

'It's hardly your fault, Professor,' Marion said. She placed a hand on his shoulder, then steered the conversation towards the purpose of her visit. 'We were hoping you might be able to explain what happened in the Lock Room?'

The professor looked uncertain. 'Rupert has said not to speak to anyone about it for the time being.' He contemplated the pile of collapsed steel before him. Through the mess of springs, screws and bolts, Marion could make out something that looked remotely like the large black box she'd seen Swindlehurst remove from the Lock Room wall. It was really just the frame of the box that remained, and part of the door – a flap of black steel, in the centre of which was the small dial of a combination lock, completely intact.

'Yes, I know,' Marion said, attempting to keep the impatience from her voice, 'but Kenny was hired by Nancy to solve White's murder. Nancy would approve of any information you pass to him. And thus to me,' she added quickly. 'Please, Professor. We're in a hurry. We need to know.'

Bal removed his beret with an air of acceptance. He turned his focus to the workbench rubble. 'It's called a clockwork

237

safe,' he began. 'I made all the drawers in the Lock Room myself. There are one hundred and fourteen of them down there. All are safes that can be opened with a key or a combination. They're very simple, with minimal security features and if you know a thing or two about codes, they're easy to open. But this one I did not make.' He pointed to the pile of metal and springs. 'It's a very rare version of what we have in the Lock Room. Very difficult to make. I'm afraid that if I had known it was there—'

'You didn't?' Marion asked, glancing at Kenny.

'I don't think anyone but Edgar did. He must have had it installed without our knowledge.'

'What's so special about it then?' Kenny asked.

'Well . . . you see,' the professor said, lifting from the rubble a mangled face of what appeared to be an ordinary clock, 'clockwork safes are special because they are designed to hold the most secret of secrets. Things you would rather have destroyed than discovered. They were very popular in the early thirties and forties – I suppose there were a lot of dangerous secrets in those days.' He trailed off, as if remembering something, perhaps a secret of his own. 'MI5 found them quite useful, as you can imagine. Mostly for classified documents, papers they'd prefer never saw the light of day.'

'Did you sell them at the Factory?' Marion asked.

'Oh no, Marion. Not me. There is only one person in the whole of Britain who knows how to make one.'

'Yes, and? Who is he?' Kenny asked impatiently.

The professor glanced nervously around the workshop. '*She* . . .' he hissed, low and cautious. 'Not a very nice lady.' He shook his head to emphasise the fact. 'No no, but very clever, very skilled.'

With a pounding head and aching body, Marion was in no mood for riddles. She felt as if she hadn't slept properly in days. 'Right, so Swindlehurst went and bought this clockwork safe from this . . . unpleasant woman?'

'Yes, Marion, he must have had a very dangerous secret to keep.' He bent back over the pile of broken metal on the workbench and removed what looked like some sort of key. 'You see this, it's used to set the timer on the safe. The timer is attached to the safe's locking mechanism and is used to set the date and time on which the lock can be opened. With every turn of the key, the clock winds up another twenty-four hours.' He demonstrated, turning the key in mid-air: 'One day,' he turned it once, 'two days,' he turned it a second time, 'three days . . .'

'Yes yes, we get the point,' Kenny snapped.

Marion glowered at him. 'Go on, Professor.'

Bal smiled gingerly and continued. 'It is believed that the longer the timer is set for, the more dreadful the secret locked within. I'm told a member of the British Secret Service bought one in 1946 to store highly classified wartime papers. As the rumour goes, he asked for the timer to be set for an indefinite period. It was set for 876,000 hours, or a hundred years.'

'That's all very interesting but—' Kenny began, but Marion cut him off.

'Can you tell us how long this one was set for, Professor?'

The professor brought his magnifying glass to his right eye. He picked up the heart of the tiny clock and turned it over, examining the miniature cog that sat in the centre. 'Two thousand, five hundred and fifty-five days. Or, seven years exactly.'

Marion frowned. 'Seven years.'

'But why did the whole thing go off like that?' Kenny asked. 'Is that supposed to happen?'

'No. And yes. You were not listening. I told you, clockwork safes are very secure because you're only able to open them when the timer expires. And only the person who sets the timer can know when this is.' He drew a long breath. 'You see, if you set one today' – he looked at his watch – 'Saturday, twenty-sixth of April, to open in one year, then you must open it on the twenty-sixth of April, 1959 at exactly ten minutes and one second past ten a.m. If anyone tries to open it before the timer expires, a trigger is set that ignites a flame inside the box. Everything inside would then be destroyed within seconds.'

'So, the safe's contents will be destroyed if the safe is opened *before* the timer expires. But what if it's opened afterwards?' Marion asked.

'Then you'll get what happened in the Lock Room. A series of deterrents is released, chosen by the original owner.' He pulled the magnifying glass from his neck and laid it on the table next to him. 'You see, there is a good chance the owner could forget to open the safe at the exactly right date and time, or be unable to for some reason. Therefore, there must be a way the safe can be opened post-expiration. And so they are loaded with deterrents, different for every safe and avoidable if you know what they are.'

'Swindlehurst knew what the deterrents were,' Marion said as she leaned over the rubble of broken springs and screws. 'He knew there was going to be an explosion and he probably knew exactly how much time he had to remove the safe's contents before it went off. I remember him checking his watch, rushing from the Lock Room as the detonator began.'

The professor looked confused. 'Detonator? Explosion? There was no explosion, Marion. You'd both be dead if there had been. The deterrents were only meant to look and sound like one. It was just an alarm, preceded by a trail of gas, something similar to sleeping gas.'

'Makes sense,' Kenny said. 'We blacked out, didn't we?'

Marion thought for a moment. 'I suppose, and anyway, it doesn't matter. The point is, Swindlehurst knew what the deterrents were and he was prepared for them. Unlike the rest of us. That must be why he planned the Circus Ball, all the lights, the fireworks. It was a distraction. But it couldn't have been his original plan. There must have been a reason he didn't open the safe when it was supposed to be opened. Professor,' she said, going out on a limb, 'can you tell us exactly when the safe was meant to be opened. The date and time?'

'I can try.' He picked up the tiny clock and tweaked something set in the back with a screwdriver. 'I've never made a safe like this before, as I told you, but . . . maybe . . .' He fiddled with a series of tiny clockwork parts for what felt like ages. 'Ah, here we are.'

Marion's heart began to race. She was fairly certain of what his answer would be, and the thought of it made her blood run cold.

The professor frowned and grumbled to himself, again twisting and jabbing at the clock's heart until at last: 'It was set seven years ago, as I said . . . April twelfth, 1951 at twelve midnight.'

'So, the night of April eleventh.' She turned to Kenny, his face as pale as her own must have been. 'Nineteen-fifty-one plus seven.'

'The night White was murdered . . .'

A vague and indistinct memory loomed in the back of Marion's mind, an additional significance of the date – April eleventh, 1958 – one she couldn't quite grasp.

'Did White know it was going to happen?' Kenny asked, disrupting her train of thought.

'Yes, I think so,' Marion said. Even though the pieces of the puzzle were now beginning to fit together, it wasn't making her feel any better. If anything, she was more terrified than ever. 'Swindlehurst intended to open the safe the night

241

of April eleventh and White somehow knew it,' she began, now voicing her theory. 'Maybe White wanted to stop him from removing whatever was inside the safe, or maybe she just wanted to see what it was. Either way, she must have known the exact time he was going to be in the Lock Room.' She looked at Professor Bal, whose dark skin was now ashen. As he busied himself with something on the neighbouring work-bench, Marion turned to Kenny and spoke in a low whisper.

'It all makes sense now. Swindlehurst enters the Lock Room at around eleven-fifty. He wouldn't have needed longer, under the disguise of the Grey Eagle. The camera doesn't pick him up, even though he probably didn't know it was there. He gets to work removing the safe from the wall but must wait until exactly midnight before he unlocks it, or the contents will be destroyed.

'White leaves for the Lock Room around the same time. Frank sees her run past the library bar. The camera above the gate records White entering the Lock Room at eleven fifty-five. Swindlehurst is there, perhaps the safe had been removed from the wall already but he couldn't have opened it yet. White sees it, she's intrigued, or frightened. She knows Swindlehurst must be there but she wouldn't have seen much of him under the disguise of the Grey Eagle. Maybe White tries to open the safe and Swindlehurst has to stop her, or else whatever's inside will be destroyed. Or maybe White knew it was Swindlehurst, even if she couldn't see him. She confronts him. It's the last thing she does. Swindlehurst and White's confrontation takes them past midnight. He can no longer open the safe without a lot of noise, so he places it back in the wall. By this time the Grey Eagle is wearing off and he knows he has to make a run for it, he has to escape past anyone nearby or any cameras before he's seen near the Lock Room. He manages to escape just before Frank enters.

White has already been stabbed in the throat and has bled to death. There's apparently no one else around.'

Professor Bal returned, even paler than before. Perhaps he'd overheard.

'I guess the only remaining questions are,' Kenny said, 'what was in the safe that Swindlehurst was desperate to keep a secret, enough to kill for? And how did White know about it?'

It was this that brought the memory back to life.

11 April 1958 – the date Marion had seen entered into the register, the last entry Michelle White had made.

'What is it?' Kenny asked, he and the professor now staring at her with interest.

'The letter White received the night of her murder. I saw her signature in the register file. I can't remember the exact time recorded but it was definitely around eleven.'

'You think it was a tip-off?' Kenny asked uncertainly.

'How else would White have known the exact time the safe was to be opened?'

Professor Bal said nothing. Solemnly he got to his feet and staggered out of the Workshop through a door in the back wall. He returned shortly after.

'There is only one other person in the world who should have known,' he said, turning a piece of paper over in his hand. 'When you buy a clockwork safe, you cannot set the timer yourself, it's too complicated. At the very least, you'd need some experience in working with clocks. But even then . . . the maker would have set this one, I'm almost sure. She would have seen what went inside.' He handed Marion the piece of paper, upon which he'd written a name and address:

Helena Jansen
12 Holly Grove
Peckham

'As I said, she is the only person in Britain who can make a clockwork safe. She is a Safe Keeper, as they like to call themselves. If someone told Michelle about the safe, it had to be Helena. But if she did, she'd have broken the Safe Keepers' oath. I can only imagine she had very good cause to do so.'

The professor's words hung in the air, a thunderous cloud threatening to burst. Marion slipped the note Bal had given her into her pocket. It would be risky, tracking down Helena Jansen with Swindlehurst on the loose – if he'd been willing to murder a colleague to protect his secret, he'd surely have no trouble doing the same to a woman who'd betrayed him. That is, of course, if he hadn't already.

Kenny flipped open the compass. 'Nothing,' he said before Marion could ask. 'I'll keep an eye on it. And try to get hold of Nancy again, in the meantime.'

Marion nodded, but didn't speak. Once Kenny had left and she was certain Professor Bal was otherwise occupied in his office, she made her way across the Workshop to the storage cabinet, extracted two small black buttons, the wires and batteries attached, and slipped them into her purse.

Following her trip to the Workshop, Marion visited the infirmary. She settled on the edge of Bill's bed. He was still asleep, or sedated. But his eyes flickered; he knew she was there. Though Fitzpatrick insisted he would make a full recovery, Marion was stricken by the sight of his fragile state and she felt a pulsating regret that their investigation, *her* investigation, had come to this.

She stayed with Bill until he came to. Though groggy and only mildly aware of his surroundings, his face sallow and grey, his memory seemed intact. And through a series of disconnected sentences he described the events of the night before: how he'd dragged himself from the ballroom after realising

Marion was no longer sitting beside him. How at some point along his journey from the ballroom to the bathroom (where he planned to douse himself in water) he'd caught sight of Marion and Kenny disappearing down the corridor that led to the library.

'I knew something was wrong,' he recalled. 'I suppose that was obvious enough, from the state of things in the ballroom. But as you know, I wasn't convinced I trusted Kenny. I wanted to see where he was taking you. So I followed you to the library and waited in the reading corner. It was a bit of a blur after that. I didn't know where you were for a while, then I heard Kenny calling for help and followed his voice to the Lock Room.' He paused to breathe. 'I saw him, Mari. Swindlehurst. He was visible, but only just. I tried to apprehend him as he left the Lock Room but he got me in the ribs. Apparently one fractured, nothing serious though. I told Fitzpatrick my injuries were from an explosion in the Lock Room. Don't know if she believed it.'

'God, I'm so sorry.'

Bill raised a hand. 'I'm fine, really.' He smiled. 'I'm just glad I managed to reach the Lock Room gate and get you out before Nicholas saw you were inside there.'

'How did you open it?'

He grinned proudly. 'Got the keys from Swindlehurst's pocket during our little exchange.'

'Thought pick-pocketing was more Maud's style?'

Bill tried to laugh, but winced instead. 'What happened in there anyway?'

Marion looked at him, his eyelids flickering with exhaustion. His head lolled to one side. 'I'll tell you all that later,' she said, pressing his fingers into her palm. She kissed his cheek and left.

Back in her room in the staff quarters, she placed the note from Professor Bal on her side table and fell into bed fully clothed. She closed her eyes to the play of strange shadows as the gas lamp's flame danced in the darkness. She knew without even thinking it over that Nancy would not approve of Professor Bal's handover of Helena's address, or of anything Marion was planning to do with it. But she didn't care. Nancy had disappeared when Frank and the agency needed her most.

20

The Safe Keeper's Tale

Without intending to, Marion slept straight through the afternoon. In fact, had someone not set off a volley of fireworks in the Grand Corridor (presumably stolen left-overs from the Friday night Circus Ball), which echoed through the staff quarters, rattling the doors, she might have slept all through the night, too.

She sat on the edge of her bed and examined the array of newly blossomed bruises formed on her limbs. Her head throbbed with exquisite ferocity, as did the rest of her body. She stumbled to the wash basin and splashed her face and neck with icy water while examining the gaunt reflection staring back at her. Her eyes were dull and grey circles like pits of ash encircled them. Her lips were dried and cracked and stung with dehydration and her skin was etched with streaks of smeared mascara, or perhaps they were bruises too. She'd never looked so destitute or weak, or felt more agitated. She feared she'd slept too long. She had to hurry.

She pulled on a change of clothes, then removed the two small black buttons she'd pilfered from the Gadgetry Department. She checked their wiring and connections, then placed one in the most obvious position she could think of – just below her blouse collar. She threaded its wire down her front and attached it to a minuscule battery on the belt of her skirt. With the second device, however, she was more creative. She fit the microphone button to the underside of her bra and attached it – via a short line of wiring – to a separate battery beneath her arm. She checked each bug's placement in the mirror and once satisfied, pulled on a coat and made her way down to the cafeteria.

Though she wasn't hungry, she forced an egg sandwich down her throat, followed by a cup of coffee. Neither did anything but make her nauseous, awakening the lurching dread that had been lingering in the pit of her stomach. She left the cafeteria, just as a group of Inquirers appeared for dinner service. She didn't have time for greetings. She slipped into the passageway outside and followed it until it met the Grand Corridor, then made her way up in the lift, through the bookshop and into the street.

It was a warm evening, though the sun had already sunk behind a blanket of cloud and smog. Marion had an idea of where Holly Grove was, having visited Peckham on numerous occasions while on expeditions to find particular shades of cotton yarn for Dolores's never-ending knitting projects. The memory felt heavy on her chest, an old and familiar pressure neither pleasant nor uncomfortable, and for a fleeting moment she thought of Dolores and of 16 Willow Street. Had her grandmother made it to America by now? Did she ever think about what she'd left behind, about the house, about Marion?

She kept a brisk pace as she marched down the narrow, quiet streets that surrounded the bookshop until she found a taxi. She hopped inside and handed over the clockmaker's address.

After a half-hour drive, she found herself in a particularly run-down neighbourhood. While most of the buildings here were nondescript red-brick blocks in disrepair, 12 Holly Grove seemed out of place. The shop was small and square with a low wooden door and two stained-glass windows on either side, through which a stream of light filtered – a kaleidoscope of colour that glowed like a jewel amid its otherwise grim, battered surroundings.

Marion knocked on the highly polished wooden door. It opened immediately, though apparently by no one.

'We're closed,' said a woman's voice from the shadows.

Marion made her way to the counter. All around her antique clocks hung precariously on the walls, rested dismantled on workbenches or sat proudly in glass display cabinets. The air hummed with their unsynchronised ticking and somewhere deep within the back of the shop, a boiling kettle whistled incessantly.

In perfect unison, the kettle lid began to rattle and a woman shuffled into view. She was short with a fossil-like face – crusted in dirt and older than Marion had expected. Her eyes were dark grey, her hair too, which fell to her shoulders in oily wisps.

'Hello, ma'am,' Marion said above the rattling kettle. 'I'm not here to buy anything,' she added quickly. 'I'm looking for Helena.'

The woman, far plumper than Marion had pictured, a large belly protruding from under her dirty apron, rested her hands on her hips. 'That's me. What d'you want?'

Marion extended a hand in greeting but removed it when the woman did not reciprocate. 'I was wondering if you could help me with something.'

The woman's left eye twitched. 'Who are you?'

Marion thought it best not to lie, there'd be no point if she hoped to extract what she needed from Helena. 'Marion Lane. I'm an apprentice at Miss Brickett's and a friend of Professor Uday Bal.'

The woman's face went from static discontent to liquid fury. Her eyes narrowed, her lips quivered, her forehead furrowed.

Marion took an automatic step backwards.

'That man!' she spat. 'Any friend of his is an enemy of mine! Get out! OUT!'

Marion brought her hands in front of her in defence. 'Sorry, I just—' she stumbled backwards, crashing into the glass display cabinet.

The old woman picked up a rag attached to her apron and flung it about in the air as if swatting away a pesky fly. 'OUT!' she repeated, shooing Marion towards the door.

Marion placed her hand on the doorknob but paused. 'Someone came here to buy a clockwork safe seven years ago,' she said in a nervous hurry. 'Edgar Swindlehurst. I know you sold it to him.'

The woman paused mid-swat and lowered the rag to her side. Though her face still looked like it could melt steel, her body language gave Marion the impression that whatever she despised about Professor Bal (a person Marion couldn't believe anyone could truly hate) she had to put it aside for this more important matter. 'Seven years ago, you say?'

'April eleventh, nineteen fifty-one. You set it to open at midnight on April twelfth of this year.'

The woman secured her rag back under her apron. 'And what of it?'

'Well, it's just that someone other than Mr Swindlehurst found out when the safe was going to be opened, and I can only presume you were the one who told them.'

Helena sunk her hands into her apron pockets. Her face, again, had changed. Now she was awash with anguish.

'I'd really like to know why you did that,' Marion went on when Helena said nothing. 'And I need to know what was inside the safe.'

Helena's chest began to heave and a bulbous vein on her forehead to pulsate. For a long moment she appeared to hover between two decisions: to whack Marion over the head with her rag or to give into a mess of confessions.

Fortunately, she chose the latter.

'Do you know how the professor and I knew each other? Did he tell you?' she began on an unrelated note. Though the professor had made it plain he and Helena did not get along, he'd been vague on why. The history between them would've interested Marion at another time, but right now she felt it would only delay her.

'No,' she said impatiently. 'But I'm afraid I don't have time—'

Helena cut in. 'You want to know about Edgar or not?'

Marion sighed. 'Go on, please.'

Helena nodded. 'Like I was saying, Bal and I used to work together. You've heard of the Factory, I'm sure. I'm sure you've heard how clever all the things the professor designed there are? Yes, but did he tell you they were my ideas? All of them.' She smirked. 'Didn't think so. The professor and I worked there together during the war, you see. We made and sold all types of brilliant things. Bugs, wire taps, spy cameras. You wouldn't believe how much business we got. Not just from the British, either.' She raised an eyebrow. 'I'll leave it to your imagination as to who else was in need of those types of devices in those days.

'Anyway, Bal was good with the making and fixing of the things, I'll give him that. But I was better at the designing, the *ideas*. And clockwork safes? My idea, of course.' She spat the words out, a vicious show of dislike, distrust.

'The Factory closed down after the war. Not to say there was no business, there were plenty of spies around then, maybe even more than during the war. It was just that London had been brought to its knees, no one had any money, rent was

251

more expensive than ever and Bal and I just couldn't afford to run the place no more.' She sighed, her hard face creased with the memory. 'So we had to close down and that's why we were without a job when that Nancy woman came sniffing around. She said she'd like to reopen the Factory, that she could pay the rent and give us back our jobs. She said there was just one change she'd like to make. One change. What a joke . . .' She trailed off, muttering to herself.

Again, Marion felt agitated, impatient. She decided not to show it this time, however, as Helena did not seem like the sort of person who took kindly to interruptions.

'Anyway,' the old woman went on, 'when I heard what this change was, what Nancy wanted to do, I wasn't impressed at all. She wanted to move the whole production underground, away from intrusion and restrictions. Away from the law, too. The professor jumped at the opportunity, course he did,' she added with a sneer. 'But not me. I didn't like the sound of it one bit. Living down there in a dark hole, never seeing the light of day, hidden from everyone. I smelled a rat, I did.' She paused to lumber over to a Morris chair. A wooden clock stood next to it, carved into the shape of a rather aggressive looking female face. The clock had only a second hand, which rotated around its centre in an anti-clockwise direction and at least three times faster than it should.

'Eventually I realised I didn't have the luxury of turning down the opportunity and I decided to work for the agency on a contract basis. It was a strange situation, now I think of it. Me sitting up here, the only person on the outside who knew so much about the agency, about what they did down there and how they did it.' She looked up at Marion, disgust evident on her face.

'In the beginning I kept my distance, just did what I was told and carried on. It was easy, really. All I did was design parts for the gadgets. Not just the stuff sold through the Factory, but the stranger stuff too. The stuff you only use down there.' She stamped the ground with her shoe. 'Vagor Compasses, Distracters, the lot. But things changed when Nancy hired the first apprentices. She used to send them up here to spend the afternoon with me. I'd show them how to fix the gadgets, how to clean them. I, well, I s'pose I liked it.' She looked up at Marion, her eyes now softer. 'Never had children of my own, you see. And that was the problem, really, because I became attached to them, *involved* with them. And I think they realised I was the only one on the outside they could talk to about their problems.'

Marion felt a twinge of warmth for the woman, imagining how it must have been to have someone like her to speak to, someone who knew the agency's secrets and yet was unencumbered by the weight of them herself. Helena would have been an outlet for the apprentices, no doubt.

'They were all very different, that first group,' she went on. 'There was young Edgar – the leader of the pack, I s'pose you could say. He was brilliant. Really, he was. But also . . .' She thought about it for a moment. 'Superior, I think's the right word. He thought he was smarter than everyone. Which was probably true, he just liked to make sure you knew it. Then there was Barbara Simpkins' – she smiled – 'liked her. Yeah, I liked her a lot, almost as much as she liked her wine.' She chuckled to herself. 'There was also—' She seemed to check herself.

Marion waited, but when Helena did not continue she prompted. 'Also?'

'Well his name was Ned Asbrey, very good friend of Edgar's. Two of them thick as thieves. Came to a bad end though, the poor lad.' She looked up. 'You heard of him?'

Marion's stomach churned. 'Only rumours.'

Helena nodded but said nothing further on the matter. 'And finally, there was Michelle – dull as a plank and bitter. The odd one out, you might say. She never did well on her assessment reports, maybe because no one liked her, maybe because she botched everything. Either way, by the end of her first year, Nancy told her she was never going to make it as an Inquirer. She gave her a choice: either she had to leave, get the sack, or she could stay on as night duty filing assistant. Michelle chose the latter, of course. It was that or unemployment and in those days . . . well, you took what work you could get. Then, couple months later, that old man Gillroth suggested another role for Michelle on top of filing assistant, I can't remember exactly what he called it . . .'

'Border Guard?' Marion provided.

Helena raised an eyebrow. 'Yeah, that's it. Border Guard.' She grimaced. 'But even so, seeing all her friends training to be Inquirers while she filed papers ate away at her. And I think she wanted to even out the field, if you know what I mean. She made it her life's work to get her colleagues in trouble, to point out where they'd gone wrong. No one could deny she was good at that at least. Somehow, she always managed to be in the right place at the right time. Or wrong place, wrong time you could say. She knew the layout of the agency better than anyone. She—' Helena paused, distracted. The vein in her forehead pulsated madly. She rubbed it absently. Marion wondered if she knew about the map White had once owned.

'Anyway, you said you wanted to know about the safe?' Helena went on, her face now relaxed a fraction. 'I sold one to Edgar seven years ago, yes. But that's all I can say. Anything more goes against the—'

'Safe Keepers' Oath?' Marion supplied. 'I know. I also know you've already broken that oath.' She tensed her shoulders as she waited for the reaction.

Helena studied her. 'Bal told you that, eh?' Her face reddened but at last she appeared to reach a decision and nodded to herself. 'Clockwork safes are something only a certain type of person would buy. Spies, governments, lawyers. People with secrets they don't trust even themselves to keep. I liked Edgar, I did. But I always knew there was something not quite right about him. There was a sickness in there.' She jabbed a knobbly, arthritic finger at the left side of her chest.

'The day he came to me and asked for the safe, he was in a rush,' Helena recalled, 'and very nervous. He wasn't worried about the price, said his parents had died a while back and left him a bit of money. Hardly anything but enough to pay for the safe. I explained to him how it worked and that he'd have to make sure he was around to open it at the exact right time. I asked if he had a secure location for it: you can't just leave a clockwork safe lying on your dining room table, you see. He said of course, what safer place is there than the agency Lock Room.' She raised an eyebrow. 'I then asked him how long he wanted it set for.' She paused and turned around. Marion wondered if there was someone else in the back of the shop. The thought unsettled her.

Helena turned back to Marion and continued, apparently satisfied they were alone. 'He wanted it set for seven years. I'd set safes for longer, so it wasn't a shock. But I did wonder, what did he have that he'd only need in seven years? I said to him again, just to make sure he understood: "If I set it for seven years, you can only open it in seven years or whatever's inside will be destroyed." He nodded, said he knew, then he pulled it from his pocket. A little glass tube of black liquid.'

At that moment and all at once, every single clock in the shop – one hundred at least – began to chime. The chorus reverberated through the tiny shop like an earthquake. Though Helena appeared completely unconcerned by the blaring racket, Marion scrunched up her shoulders and covered her ears. The jewel-coloured windows rattled, the glass cabinet looked ready to shatter and Marion's eardrums felt ready to burst. Eventually it came to a stop. Helena cast her eyes around the shop, as if waiting for something. And then it came. One last blast as the oldest and loudest grandfather clock joined in, a minute later than the others.

Marion shook her head in an attempt to regain her senses. She pulled herself upright and took a breath before trying to remember where their conversation had left off.

'Thing is,' Helena said, resuscitating the conversation, 'I thought the vial was made of glass, but it wasn't.'

'I don't understand?'

'When he handed it to me to put in the safe, I'd never felt nothing like it before. Soft like rubber, cold like ice. It burned my skin, nearly right off.' She took a stifled breath. 'Edgar laughed, I remember that very well. He laughed at how shocked I was. Then he said not to worry, said it couldn't do much harm *yet*.'

'Yet?' Marion said, thinking out loud. 'Did he explain what he meant by that?'

'Well, no. Not exactly, but he did say something about it being a formula, something that had been attempted during the war, something Miss Brickett's had been keeping a secret. I didn't really know what he meant by that but the whole thing gave me the chills. Not just what he said, but the way he said it. Almost as if he was trying to scare me.' She moved off across to the other side of the shop, opened the glass cabinet and removed one particularly decrepit-looking wristwatch. She sat down at her workbench and proceeded to mend it as if Marion were no longer there.

But Marion herself had slipped into a state of thoughtful absence. She had dared to assume that the awful substance she'd seen Swindlehurst remove from the safe had been the missing component of the clockwork bomb, the one piece of the puzzle she hadn't found – the alchemic explosive. Fifteen times more powerful than dynamite, an acid that burns, singes, destroys.

'Like I said, I don't know what it was,' Helena said. 'If that's what you're here for, I can't help you.'

'But you must have known. You sent a letter to Michelle White the night the safe was to be opened, didn't you?'

Helena looked up. 'Who says I did?'

'Michelle is dead. She was murdered the night you sent that letter.'

Helena went pale. She did not, however, look surprised. 'You think Edgar did it?'

'I know he did. The stuff he locked in that safe, I think it's part of a bomb that was designed for a covert chemical weaponry project in 1943. Do you know anything about it? Did Swindlehurst mention anything like that?'

Helena hesitated, but only for a moment. She shook her head. 'No, of course not. I didn't know what it was. But that's why it frightened me. I'd never seen nothing like it before, maybe that's why I knew it was dangerous.' She sighed. 'It seems obvious now, looking back, but at the time I didn't realise.'

Marion waited as the old woman rearranged her thoughts, her memories.

'It was just a few weeks ago when Michelle came to me. She said she needed some advice, that I was the only one who listened, the only one who took her seriously.' She chuckled menacingly. 'I didn't, but I s'pose it only mattered that she believed it. Anyway, she said she'd lost something. Actually, she said it had been stolen. A very special map. She said she knew who'd taken it, but she didn't give a name.'

Marion tensed. She tried to relax her features, to not give anything away.

Helena continued without encouragement. 'Michelle said she was concerned because if this person – the one who'd taken the map – found the monocle needed to read it, which she kept hidden in her office, then they'd be able to *find it*, was how she put it. She didn't tell me exactly what she was afraid this person would find, just said it was dangerous. An agency secret she was supposed to protect. But the more I thought about it, the more sure I became that I already knew what it was. I'd seen it myself, seven years ago—'

'The stuff in Swindlehurst's vial?' So the secret Michelle White had been tasked with protecting had already been discovered seven years earlier. Marion wondered, of course, why Swindlehurst had gone to all the trouble of finding the laboratory and reproducing the alchemic explosive, just to hide a sample of it in the agency for seven years.

Marion refocused when Helena spoke again. 'Anyway, as soon as Michelle left I put two and two together and realised what I had to do. I had to tell her about Edgar and the clockwork safe. I made a note in my diary and decided I'd send her a letter explaining everything right before the safe was to be opened.' She drew a small hammer from her tool kit and began to tap some tiny metal part with just the corner of it. 'Course, when the day came, I had second thoughts. I knew what I was about to do might cause trouble at the agency.' She slammed the hammer onto the table and slouched back in her chair.

'But I made up my mind at last,' she went on. 'I wrote a letter addressed to Michelle, it was short but I knew it would get my point across. I said Edgar was going to open a clockwork safe that night in the Lock Room at exactly midnight. I said I didn't know what was inside, but said I suspected it might have to do with that secret she told me about, the one she was supposed to protect. I then asked that the letter be destroyed as soon as she'd read it. I didn't want no one coming around asking questions after the fact.' She glowered at Marion. 'Didn't work, obviously. I knew Michelle worked night duties in the Filing Department and that she'd get the letter. It seemed like a good plan, at the time.' Her hand began to tremble. She slipped it into her apron pocket and looked up. 'I thought there was a chance it would put her in danger but . . . I didn't know what else to do.'

There was a short, sharp silence, interrupted only by the ticking of unsynchronised clocks.

'Edgar has taken the vial and disappeared,' Marion went on. 'We really need to find him. Do you have any idea where he might have gone?'

Helena picked up the hammer once more. It almost seemed as if she were doing so in defence. An anxious look came over her. It was as if she'd just realised she'd said too much. 'I don't know nothing about that.'

The lights in the shop appeared to have darkened, the air cooled. It had become claustrophobic. Marion heard something outside in the street, like footsteps. Suddenly she wished she hadn't come to the shop alone, or at least she wished she'd told someone where she was going. She looked up at one of the clocks on the wall. It was already seven thirty. 'Please, Helena. I need your help.'

Helena moved over to the shop door and slid three large bolts into place. 'It's no good being afraid now,' she said, 'it's too late.' She turned her back to the shop door. There was a single knock.

Marion jumped about a foot in the air. But Helena did not move an inch. The person outside the door then moved off and across the window, their figure a silhouette behind the jewelled glass. Helena turned off the shop light. 'There's a way out the back,' she said, 'come on.'

Marion could only just make out the movement of Helena's plump figure through the darkness. 'What did you mean?' she asked anxiously as she followed the shadow towards the back of the shop. 'Too late for what?'

They reached a second door, made of steel and secured with five large padlocks. Helena produced a torch from her apron pocket and then a ring of keys. Desperately slowly, she began to unlock each padlock in turn. 'You shouldn't have got involved, you shouldn't have come here.' The second lock clicked open, the third, the fourth, the fifth. Helena turned the handle and pushed the door open into the street that ran behind the shop. She all but kicked Marion outside. 'Do not come back here. Not ever.'

'Wait, please—' Marion stammered but was cut short as Helena slammed the door shut in her face.

The small alleyway behind the shop was littered with rubbish bins and smelled of urine. The night had brought with it an icy breeze that did not quite suit the time of year. She turned to where the alleyway wound around the left wall of the shop. She was certain someone was standing on the verge, just beyond the light of the nearest streetlamp. There was a crunch of gravel, the swoosh of a coat and then . . .

'Lane!' Kenny said, stepping quickly into the light. 'Thank blazes it's you.'

'For goodness sake. Why were you creeping around like that?'

'I could ask you the same thing,' he said, looking left and right over his shoulder.

'What are you doing here?'

Kenny shoved his hand inside his coat pocket and removed a small brass compass. He flipped it open.

In the darkness of the quiet street, the compass's green light glowed more brightly than ever.

'*He's here*,' Kenny whispered.

21

House of Horror

Agleam in the starless night, the compass light burned with certainty: Swindlehurst was close.

When aligned, the needle pointed north-east: back up the street from where Kenny had come.

'He must be right around the corner,' Kenny breathed.

Marion turned to the lamp which stood on the street corner. It was useless and dim, spilling a pool of faint yellow light that extended less than a yard from its base. Even though the street was quiet and few cars or pedestrians traversed it, the low drum of city noise was everywhere.

Marion and Kenny edged forward.

'Have anything on you to restrain him?' she asked urgently as they approached the lamp.

'Didn't have time to fetch anything. I was in the bookshop when the indicator switched on and didn't want to risk going down to Gadgetry, in case he stepped out of range again.'

They'd arrived at the lamp. Marion peered around the corner and into the street that ran past the front of Helena's shop. All was still beyond the glistening jewel windows. She considered whether Swindlehurst was under the disguise of the strange mist, or if instead he'd make do with the cover of night.

A cool breeze touched her skin. She felt herself becoming lethargic, unbalanced, unfocused. Or was it just her imagination?

'Shit,' Kenny said, showing Marion the compass. She blinked, drawing her attention to the device. The green light flickered then dimmed, and just a few yards from where they were standing, a faint shadow drifted down the street, sometimes obviously a human being, sometimes more like a cloud of smog. Swindlehurst was under the cover of the Grey Eagle. And he was moving.

They followed him nearly three miles across town, finally coming to a stop in Turnchapel Mews, Clapham. Along the way, Marion tried to explain what Helena had told her. Kenny's reaction was one of growing unease, fuelled by the realisation that what had started out as a murder investigation was now so much more.

'I think he's going to sell it,' she said, airing a theory she'd recently formulated.

'The stuff in the vial?'

'Yes.' Her voice was sharp and heavy.

Kenny appeared lost in thought for a time. 'I bet it's the Russians. I'd damn well put money on it.'

'It doesn't really matter though, does it?' she said, breathing hard, her lungs feeling heavy. 'The fact that it exists, that he's managed to produce it is bad enough.' She stopped as a rush of terror, not just for Frank and his future but for something deeper, evil, malignant, swelled inside her. 'Swindlehurst produced the explosive and reconstructed the bomb right under the agency's watch.' She was thinking out loud, saying the words as they were formulating in her mind. And she did not attempt to soften any of it.

Kenny's breathing ceased for just a moment. His eyes focused on her. He understood, too. This was no longer just about clearing Frank's name, or bringing Michelle White's murderer to justice. The weapon had been produced within the walls of Miss Brickett's. Everyone who worked at the agency would be partially responsible – morally, if not legally – for whatever awful plan Swindlehurst was about to implement.

'We have to apprehend him. Either he's about to skip the country or hand the vial over to someone,' Marion said in conclusion as they arrived outside an old two-storey manor house. Swindlehurst's disguise had long since worn off, and they'd been able to watch him closely as he disappeared through the front gate of the fourth house on Turnchapel Mews. He, they hoped, had not seem them.

The house in question was older than any of its neighbours with a dilapidated roof and crumbling walls. It was now well into the evening and perfectly dark as the three-quarter moon crept behind a thick blanket of clouds. The air was cold and through the manor's many windows, a single lamp blazed.

Kenny removed a drawstring bag from under his coat. He untied it and peered inside. 'This is all I have, besides the compass.' He pulled out a skeleton key and handed it to Marion. She slipped it into her coat pocket. 'As I said, I didn't get a chance to grab much. We should go back to the agency and get some—'

'No,' Marion said immediately. 'We have no idea how long he's going to stay here. We can't risk it.'

'But we don't know who else is in there.' He pointed at the house and, as if in reply, another light flicked on in a second-floor window. 'I could handle Swindlehurst if he's alone, maybe.'

'I'm planning to come with you, you realise that?'

Kenny snorted. 'With all due respect, Lane, you're about the size of Swindlehurst's left leg.'

'It's not only size and strength that counts. I have my ways.'

'No.' Kenny shook his head. 'This is a bad idea. Swindlehurst is capable of murder and you just told me he's carrying around some acid that can burn through flesh. Jesus, Lane.' He ran his fingers through his hair in frustration.

'Fine, I've got a better idea,' she said, trying to keep her voice from rising. 'You go back to the agency for help and I'll wait here with the compass. If Swindlehurst leaves before you get back, I'll follow him. I'll leave you a note with the general direction and time we left.'

Kenny stared blankly at her. 'You can't be serious? It could take me hours to get back to the agency and convince anyone to come with me. Nancy isn't even back yet and most of the other employees are probably still recovering from last night.'

'Well, you'll just have to do your best.'

Kenny shook his head. 'Why don't you go back to the agency for help and I'll stay here?'

'Because I'm better at reading the compass and . . . this was my idea.' The truth was that Marion didn't trust Kenny as much as she trusted herself. Not because she thought he was some kind of double agent who might turn against her, as Bill still seemed to think, but rather because she knew he just wasn't as invested in Swindlehurst's capture as she was. She had more to lose.

They stared at each other. A silent battle of wills. The longer it went on, the more nervous Marion became. A cold shiver erupted in her core, spreading swiftly through her chest, her limbs, smothering her breath. Every second they waited outside the house, every moment they allowed Swindlehurst to further implement his plan – whatever it was – their chances of stopping him diminished.

'Fine,' Kenny said at last, defeated. 'But stay right here and don't do anything reckless.'

'I'm the least reckless person you'll ever meet.' Or she had been until a few days ago.

Kenny eyed her suspiciously. Had he met her several weeks ago, he would have agreed wholeheartedly with such a statement. 'Sure you'll be okay?'

'Just hurry,' she said as Kenny relented and disappeared down the street and out of sight.

For a moment Marion did nothing but stare at the dark house, her limbs heavy and weak. She pushed all thoughts of regret and self-doubt from her mind before they consumed her and stepped up to the large steel gates – two towering walls of solid black metal. Through the slit in the centre, she could just make out a narrow gravel path lined with overgrown and unshapely hedges that led to a short staircase and finally to the manor's front door.

The establishment appeared deserted, left to endure the decay of time and weather. She shivered. The grey light of the moon was beginning to creep out from behind the clouds. She stepped back further into the street and looked up at the two windows on the second floor, through which a warm light still shone. Through one, she noticed a tall, wide shadow move.

Swindlehurst, no doubt.

But there was someone else with him. A shorter figure, narrow shoulders and slumped posture. Marion's eyes burned as she strained to make out who the second figure was. Then the window cracked open and they leaned out. Marion dashed closer to the manor house wall.

She heard the window slam, then looked down at the brass compass. The green light burned as brightly as ever for five minutes. Then it died. Not slowly, fading as it would with distance, but suddenly and completely. She cursed. Swindlehurst must have found, removed and destroyed the Vagor Stone. It was bound to happen eventually, she supposed they were lucky it had taken him this long to realise he was being tailed.

265

She looked up at the second floor; the lights inside were extinguished. If she waited for Kenny to return, she risked Swindlehurst handing over the vial or disappearing through a back door. If either happened, all she'd achieved up until this point might be for nothing.

She now had no choice.

She removed the skeleton key from her pocket, then paused, her hands shaking, her limbs ice cold. Some invisible force pressed on her shoulders and every movement she made seemed sluggish, as if held back by the resistance of it.

She inserted the pointed edge of the skeleton key into the gate padlock. It twisted and twirled around itself until the lock clicked open. She slipped the gadget into her coat pocket, unhinged the chain that held the gate together and stepped back as it groaned and split apart. She hurried up the path just as the moonlight began to return, dangerously illuminating her in the lifting darkness.

Marion pulled her coat belt tighter around her waist as she reached the manor's front door. Curiously, the door stood slightly ajar. She pushed it further open, stepped into the draughty foyer and came to a halt at the bottom of a rickety wooden staircase. Several of the stairwell's steps had succumbed to rot and were caved in. Curtains of silvery cobwebs hung from the ceiling and the glass of a large bay window nearby was shattered.

She needed to make sure Swindlehurst was still in the house. It was the whole reason she'd come inside. And yet . . . the thought of encountering him, especially now she knew all he was capable of, terrified her. She looked up at the landing above the staircase, from which she could hear the low bustle of voices. Swindlehurst and the second man, she assumed.

A door opened in the corridor that led off from the landing. Marion launched herself into a small space under the staircase. The wooden slats above her head creaked as two pairs of feet came down the staircase.

'When will she arrive?' asked a voice that was certainly Swindlehurst's.

'Within the hour,' said the second voice, a thin rasp-like sound. There was a stilted pause. 'You're sure this is the best way? It's not too late to change the plan.'

'It *is* too late. Everything is set in motion.'

The hum of a car engine came from the street.

'Ah,' said the man with the rasping voice. 'Company at last.'

A series of footsteps entered the foyer; a pair of boots followed by the muted protests of someone who appeared to be gagged. Swindlehurst and the other man made their way down the staircase to meet the new arrivals. There was an exchange of greetings. No names were given.

'Any complications?' Swindlehurst asked.

'None.'

The muffled voice of whoever was gagged became louder.

'For Christ's sake, shut her up!' Swindlehurst commanded.

There was a thump and then silence. Swindlehurst breathed. 'I'm sure this will be a simple exchange, but in the event that things get out of hand . . .' He sighed, as if regretting something he was yet to do. 'No witnesses. Am I clear?'

There was a grunt in reply.

'Good,' Swindlehurst said. 'Take her to the basement. Not you . . . wait outside by the gate.'

'Sir?'

Swindlehurst's voice changed in tone, becoming heavier, bolder. 'I'm afraid I may have a tail. If you see anyone hanging around outside, deal with them.'

Marion forced herself to breathe. In – out. In – out. Softly, carefully, silently. One. Two. Three. She waited until Swindlehurst and the men had moved off from the foyer.

Though in her state of terror, she wasn't sure in which direction they'd gone. She pulled her knees towards her as a tremor, stronger and more vicious than before, rippled through her body.

Hurry, Kenny. Please hurry. Bring help.

As she waited, a soft rain began to fall, pattering against the windows and ceiling. The house shifted and groaned in the wind. The smell of rot was all around her. Or perhaps it was just her imagination.

Her mind ticked on furiously in the silence. She replayed everything she'd discovered since Michelle White's death, all the pieces coming together to form a looming, ominous picture. She stared at her watch as the minutes passed.

Please hurry, Kenny. Hurry.

Eventually she decided she had to move. Swindlehurst had not reappeared, nor had any of his men. She couldn't risk the chance that they might leave the house without her knowing. She pulled herself upright. Her legs were weak, cold, numb. She stood for a moment and listened. Rain and wind, the low moan of the old house, the distant drone of cars.

No voices. No footsteps.

She crossed the foyer to the room on the left.

It was wide and open with a high ceiling. Paint peeled from the walls and picture frames hung loosely from exposed plaster. She stopped and listened.

Two sounds came, one after the other.

A door clicked closed somewhere to her left. A pause, followed by a flesh-clawing scream that radiated from what must have been a basement beneath her feet. The sound was animalistic. Shrill, tearing, unbearable.

For a moment Marion was unable to move. Trapped in her body, the terrified prey waiting to be taken.

The scream came again, worse this time.

She turned to a steel door, nestled in the wall to her left. The scream was coming from just beyond. She stepped forward and pressed her ear to the cold metal.

'. . . clean up this mess!' said Swindlehurst.

In the background, a woman was moaning in drawn-out notes.

There was a scraping of furniture and a muffled yelp.

'Get up!'

'Please . . . no . . . let me go . . . please,' the woman begged. 'Cut it off, please . . . just cut it off.'

There was a loud thump. The moaning ceased immediately and was replaced by something that sounded very much like a body being dragged across the floor.

Footsteps were coming towards the door. Marion looked around her – there was nowhere to hide and no chance she could run across the foyer and back under the staircase in time. She flattened herself against the wall. The door swung open in front of her.

She closed her eyes and listened to the soft, careful shuffle as a pair of feet moved closer towards her. She cursed her stupidity, her curiosity and everything else that had got her into this mess.

The door swung back.

The man in front of her was not Swindlehurst but rather a tall, brute-like figure with a narrow and sunken face, dull eyes and thin pale lips.

For a split second, the man was caught off guard, shocked by the sight of her.

Marion took her chance. She lurched forwards, flinging her right elbow into the assailant's stomach and her left foot into his knee. He buckled over and clutched his stomach, gasping for air.

She sped past and tore back towards the foyer, then skidded to a halt. The front door was secured with three thick bolts and padlocked. Even if she managed to open it, Swindlehurst had eyes just near the gate – the other man who'd been inside the house.

She hesitated, her body flooded with adrenaline. The man she'd winded was on his feet and coming towards her. She sped up the staircase, three steps at a time. Thunderous footsteps followed her. He might have been shouting, commanding her to stop. She was far too on edge to be sure, delirious with fear.

The rotten slats creaked under her, some giving way as she sped upwards. She slipped. Her boot crashed through a decayed stair. Splinters plunged into her leg. She didn't feel a thing, ripping herself free and barrelling onwards, upwards, away.

She could feel the breath of the man behind her, hear the crash of his footsteps.

She reached the landing just as Swindlehurst emerged from a door on her right; how he'd got there from the basement she didn't know. They collided and Marion was knocked onto her back, her head crashing into the hardwood floor. A sharp, lightning-like pain travelled into her skull.

Swindlehurst's accomplice brought his right boot down onto her elbow, pinning her to the floor. She yelped as he dug his heel into her flesh.

Marion placed her right hand between her throbbing skull and the floor. Swindlehurst stepped over her.

'I thought so,' he sighed. Though dressed just the same as he always was when on duty at Miss Brickett's – neat, well-tailored, sharp – Swindlehurst's ordered and collected features were now in disarray. His normally unexpressive eyes gleamed.

Marion struggled against the accomplice's hold. He was crouched beside her, his right forearm pressing down on her throat with such force that she was sure her windpipe was about to break.

She gasped for breath.

'Not so hard, you idiot!' Swindlehurst snapped.

The accomplice loosened his hold.

Marion heaved, her lungs expanding so wildly it felt as if they might burst.

Swindlehurst shoved the accomplice to the side, then lifted Marion into a seated position, pushing her back up against the corridor wall. He unbuttoned her coat and threw it off her shoulders. 'Check it,' he ordered.

The accomplice rummaged through her coat, groping every pocket, every seam. He pulled out the skeleton key, examining it with interest and confusion. 'Sir?'

Swindlehurst was unconcerned as he looked at the gadget. 'Nothing else?'

'Nothing, sir.'

Swindlehurst turned back to Marion. He pressed his hands against her chest, then her stomach, her legs – feeling, searching, invading. He tore apart the top of her blouse, exposing her bra. She recoiled. The heat of his breath on her neck turned her stomach. Again, he ran his fingers down her chest, pausing as he came to a button slightly different from the rest, near the collar of her blouse. He ripped the bug from its anchor and traced the thread-like wire to where it connected to a minuscule battery pack attached to her skirt belt. He tore both wire and battery from her body and threw them against the wall.

He did not search her further.

When at last he spoke, it was in a seething whisper, so visceral she could feel it amplify around her. 'Idiot girl. Did you think I wouldn't check you for wires?' His face was twisted in a smug expression. He turned to his accomplice. 'Take her to the basement. Quickly.'

Despite Marion's attempts to stop him, the brutish accomplice managed to drag her down the stairs and into the basement without much effort. They entered a cold, damp and dimly lit room – the place from where the screams had come. She was thrown onto the concrete floor face first. The taste of warm copper filled her mouth as blood trickled from her lips.

Marion pulled herself upright as the man left the room and locked the door behind him. She looked around. There was a gated staircase on the other side, presumably leading to the first floor – where Swindlehurst had apprehended her. At the base of the staircase she saw a shape, a person.

'Who's there?'

Marion moved closer, realising the shape was the old woman from the clockwork shop, splayed out on the floor. Her eyes were swollen and red, her grey hair plastered to her face. Her lips were cracked and bloody, but worst of all was the smell: sickly sweet, burned. The woman, gingerly and as if it cost her great energy, pointed to her leg. Marion drew up Helena's dress. The sight that met her eyes caused her to fall back on her hands.

Helena's right ankle had melted away. Flesh and fat and muscle singed to nothing but a dripping mess, only bone and strings of sinew remained. Marion covered her mouth as a wave of nausea came over her. Helena gripped her arm, her fingernails pressing into Marion's flesh.

'Please . . . help . . .' she groaned.

Marion mustered her strength. 'It's okay,' she said tenderly, gripping Helena's hand, 'help is on the way. It's okay, just breathe.' She repeated the words, over and over.

Helena closed her eyes and let her head fall back on the concrete.

What remained of Helena's foot looked as if it were disappearing before her eyes. In fact, now that the full power of her senses had returned, Marion could hear the soft sizzle of flesh. With a horrid flash of disgust, she realised it was still burning, melting, dissolving.

'Helena, look at me,' Marion pleaded, frightened that if the old woman did not open her eyes then, she never would again.

Helena moaned and writhed. Tears poured down her face.

'What happened? Is this from the stuff in the vial?' Marion asked, though she feared she already knew.

Helena nodded. She began to mumble half-formed words. 'Devil's Blood . . . Devil's Blood . . . he found me, he came to the shop . . . he found me . . .' She trailed off as her breathing became more laboured.

The sound and smell of sizzling flesh. Helena was solidly white, drained of every last ounce of resolve. The groaning and silent pleas for it to stop continued. Marion tried everything to ease Helena's pain, but no matter what position she placed her in, or what she attempted to do to her disappearing limb, nothing seemed to help. She felt not only desperate and afraid, but guilty. Had Swindlehurst been outside Helena's shop when Marion arrived there? Had he heard all the vile truths she'd told about him? Is that why he'd brought her here, to suffer for her indiscretion?

Finally, the door of their dark prison sprung open. The brutish man was back, a pistol in his right hand.

Helena gripped Marion's forearm as he approached. She began to mumble, an incoherent string of pleas.

Marion stood up as the man raised and aimed his pistol. But before she could do anything to stop it, he'd fired a single shot into Helena's skull. Marion's body jerked involuntarily as she turned to Helena's limp form, a lake of dark viscous red leaking from beneath her head.

'It was the kindest end,' the man said, sliding his pistol into his belt. 'She would have begged for it before long.' He surveyed Marion for some time, as if he might say something further, then thought better of it. He took a step towards her. She did not back away, paralysed with shock. He slammed the butt of his pistol against her left temple.

22

The Devil's Blood

'Good, she's awake. Now let's get on with it.'

Marion's eyes flickered open as her consciousness returned. She'd been moved from the basement to another room and seated against a wall. Her wrists were bound together in front of her, coarse rope cutting into her flesh. When her senses fully returned and her mind cleared, she realised she was sitting in the corner of what appeared to be a boardroom. It smelled of smoke and urine and was furnished only with a large oval table and several chairs.

Seated around the table were Swindlehurst, his brutish helper and Nancy Brickett.

Marion's intake of breath was audible.

Nancy looked at her from across the room, though not a single muscle in her face betrayed her emotions. She nodded subtly, as if conveying something Marion alone was supposed to understand. She didn't, though. What was Nancy doing here? Where was Kenny? Why was Marion tied up and Swindlehurst free?

Nancy turned her attention to Swindlehurst. 'Well, Edgar?'

Swindlehurst's posture stiffened and lengthened, as if he were rising to some unspoken challenge. He pulled a large briefcase from the floor, opening it on the table. From inside he removed a pair of heavy duty gloves. He put on the gloves, then used them to extract a small black vial. He held it aloft, a trophy. 'The Devil's Blood,' he said proudly. 'As I'm sure you know, Nancy, the Devil's Blood is a mixture of gunpowder and an extremely powerful alchemical erosive. When exposed to flame, the substance will produce an explosion far more devastating than dynamite.' He paused for effect, then returned the vial to the briefcase and removed his gloves.

Swindlehurst looked as if he might continue, but Nancy cut him off before he could. 'What are we doing here, Edgar?'

Swindlehurst smirked. 'Isn't that obvious? I'm blackmailing you.'

Marion tried to concentrate on what she was hearing, to make some sense of what was going on, but her head thumped relentlessly. Her thoughts were dulled and useless.

'Perhaps I should provide you with a little context first, just to make it clear that my intention is simply to claim – how should I put it? – *compensation*.' Swindlehurst's tone was calm and controlled. It was the most terrifying thing Marion had ever witnessed. 'Don't worry, I'm in as much of a rush as you,' he added as Nancy breathed impatiently, 'so I'll make this as brief as I can. First, I'd like to take you back to an incident that happened eight years ago. Tell me, Nancy, do you remember the apprentice Ned Asbrey?'

'Of course I remember him.'

Swindlehurst nodded. 'Yes, yes, I thought you might.'

Marion sensed a stifling tension accumulate in the atmosphere. In a way she suspected her presence was mostly inconsequential, something to be ignored. Whatever was going on, it was between Nancy and Swindlehurst alone.

'One evening in winter,' Swindlehurst continued, 'Asbrey and I were doing what we did nearly every evening – having a drink at the library bar. But as it always was for Asbrey, one drink turned into many and by the early hours I'd had enough. I left Asbrey and went home. It was only much later the following day I realised he hadn't turned up for any of his shifts. No one had seen him since the previous night and most assumed he'd simply taken leave. But I knew something was off.

'You see, a few months before, Asbrey told me he'd found something in Professor Gillroth's office, something that suggested Miss Brickett's was harbouring a secret down in the restricted tunnels beyond the Border. I never asked him to explain further, in fact I still don't know what it was he found.'

Marion shifted uncomfortably.

'To be honest I hardly ever paid attention to Asbrey's ramblings, of which there were many. But that night in the library bar, the night he disappeared, he spoke of this *secret* again. He said he was going to investigate, *to look for it*. And asked if I'd go with him. I brushed him off. I wasn't interested in his wild conspiracy theories. But the following day, as soon as I realised he'd disappeared, I knew it could mean only one thing. And I'm sure you can guess what happened next, Nancy: Asbrey found the thing you'd been hiding from all of us.' He paused, as if to allow the words to settle. 'But then he realised the trouble he was in. He was afraid, uncertain whom to trust. If he suddenly reappeared, he'd have to provide an account of where he'd been. Of course he could lie and say he'd been on leave, say nothing about what he'd discovered. But Asbrey was a righteous fool. He saw it as his responsibility to speak up.

'I must be honest, when he met me in the common room the next day, well . . . I thought I'd seen an apparition. At first he was unable to speak, from shock and delirium, I suppose. But at last I managed to calm him down, gave him some water and food. And then he began to explain, to tell me everything all at once. He took me down to the laboratory, even. I couldn't believe my eyes. Nancy, our founder and head, hiding a chemical weaponry experiment beneath our very feet, around the corner from where we were training to solve crimes for the greater good? I was so shocked, in fact, that I didn't want anything to do with it. I just wanted to become an Inquirer. I didn't want anything to get in my way. I told Asbrey that whatever he planned to do next, he'd have to do it alone.'

Swindlehurst's features suddenly looked a shade less controlled and ordered. He swallowed nervously and continued. 'But Asbrey was insistent. He told me he was going to approach the High Council the following day and ask for an explanation about what he'd found. I was terrified. For him, for myself. I knew it would get us fired, or worse. If the agency was keeping a secret like that, there was bound to be a good reason for it. I tried to talk him out of saying anything, tried to get him to forget what he'd seen. But it was no use.' He wrung his hands together, his entire body rigid.

There was a sharp intake of breath from Nancy as something dawned on her. 'You killed him?'

'No, *no*!' Colour rose up Swindlehurst's neck, blood flushing to his face. 'It was an accident. We were arguing about what to do. I got angrier and angrier . . .' As if reliving the fury, Swindlehurst slammed his hands on the table. 'I pushed him against the wall, I was just trying to shake some sense into him but—' He spoke more rapidly now, and began to stammer. 'The wall was – there was a sharp rock – I didn't – I didn't know. He was so much weaker than me – he hit his head.' He stopped. There was a long silence, during which he seemed to regain some of his composure. But it was Nancy who spoke next.

'It was you, then, who started the rumour. You placed Ned's bag outside White's office to make it look like he'd crossed the Border and disappeared?'

'And aren't you grateful I did? I saved the agency, didn't I? I stopped Asbrey from exposing your little secret and made all your problems go away.'

Nancy raised an eyebrow. 'If that were so, we wouldn't be sitting here, Edgar.'

Swindlehurst seethed. 'No, you're wrong. I never had any intention of doing anything more. I hid Asbrey's body in the tunnels, closed the door to the laboratory and that was it. If anyone found the body it would look like an accident, like he'd got lost down there and tripped, perhaps.

'But then I saw how you dealt with Ned's family, the bribery and lies. It was the first time I'd properly considered the hold you had over all of us. All those documents you'd made us sign in the beginning, tethering us to the agency for the rest of our lives. I wasn't worried about Asbrey's death being linked to me. How could it be? And I wasn't worried about you ever bribing or coercing my family, since I had none. But I knew I needed my own little insurance policy, just in case. So I went back down to the cellar and into the tunnel beyond. Everything was still there – vials, formulas, diagrams. I took some papers, documents that proved the experiment had taken place in '43. But then I thought, is this enough to use as leverage? Does it really prove the agency had anything to do with the experiment? No. I decided I needed something more viable, more tangible, something that would make it look like the agency was producing chemical weapons illegally. So I went back to the laboratory a third time. But this time I went to learn. To *understand*.

'After much research I discovered there was a timing problem with the initial design. You see, the explosive had been concocted almost perfectly by 1944, albeit with a few mishaps here and there. They'd miscalculated the amount of time the alchemical explosive needed to mature before it was ready. It was a disaster for the operation, of course. The bomb was supposed to be ready within months but actually it would take more than a decade to complete. By which time, of course, the war would surely be over.

'So there wasn't much left for me to do. A few simple calculations to see how much longer the explosive needed to mature – seven years, as it turned out – and that was it. Of course, technically it meant that I'd have to wait at least seven years before I could use the vial as leverage, but I decided that was fine. As I said, it was a long-term insurance policy, not something I was ever hoping to use anyway.'

Nancy stared at him, her glare unrelenting and for a while the two appeared engaged in a silent battle of wills.

Marion, on the other hand, was growing more anxious by the minute. Her head throbbed, her back ached, the rope ensnaring her wrists stung as it dug into her flesh. She closed her eyes and breathed. One, two, three. She reminded herself of the reason she was entangled in this standoff in the first place. *Frank*. She saw his face, his soft eyes. She felt his hand on her shoulder, that gentle assurance that was always there when she needed it.

Subtly, she lifted her bound hands to her chest. She stretched her fingers under her bra, feeling for the cold metal against her skin. It was still there, still in place.

She looked at Swindlehurst, he and Nancy were talking again, arguing about something she didn't follow. She'd have to interrupt. 'Why did you kill Michelle?'

Swindlehurst paused mid-sentence.

'It's obvious you did,' she added, her voice stilted, fractured. She spoke with caution, saying only what was necessary, because

279

while she knew exactly how Swindlehurst had bypassed the camera above the Lock Room gate, she hadn't yet decided whether this was a revelation she should admit in front of Nancy. After all, Marion's journey to the discovery of Operation Grey Eagle had led her to break a multitude of agency regulations.

Swindlehurst frowned as he turned to face her. He didn't look afraid, or even annoyed. His expression was impassive, unconcerned. 'She was a spanner in the works, so to speak. Much like you, Miss Lane.'

Breathe. One, two, three.

'You stabbed her with her own Herald Stethoscope. Why?' Marion pursued, her voice rising.

'What else could I have done!' he spat. 'I didn't intend to hurt anyone. I didn't even have a weapon!'

Marion was thinking quickly, going out on a limb. Previously, she'd been too consumed with finding out who'd killed Michelle to pay much attention to the *way* she was killed. But now that she came to think of it, she was pretty certain Swindlehurst's use of the Herald Stethoscope – *the Snitch* – had been a ruse. 'You recognised an opportunity, though, didn't you? A chance to complicate the crime, distract the council?' She paused for a moment, watching Swindlehurst's reaction. He shifted in his seat, anxious, unnerved, furious. She was right, then. 'Yes, you didn't have a weapon and you had to act fast. Michelle had seen you. She wasn't going to let you get away with it. And of course you knew she was carrying her stethoscope with her, she always did. If you had to kill her, what better way than silenced forever by the gadget she'd used to expose so many of her colleagues? You knew the way you'd killed her would widen the pool of suspects so much that you'd be lost among them.'

Swindlehurst placed his hands on the table, wringing them together madly. When he spoke, his words were strained, hollow. He was beginning to unravel. 'I had no choice. *No choice!*' He breathed, closed his eyes. Silence ensued. 'I told you. I wasn't going to use it, the vial. I never wanted to.' He was addressing Nancy now. 'I completed my apprenticeship and was promoted to Head of Intelligence. Things were going well and I thought I might leave the vial in the safe forever. Forget about it. Move on. That's what I wanted.' He gripped the edge of the table. 'But then it began, a slow and subtle demotion. You started to ignore me, disregard my opinions, disrespect my position. And the final blow last year . . .' he inhaled sharply, it sounded like a hiss. 'You put Rakes in my position as head of the department and you made me work under her, a goddamn immigrant with half my experience? Jesus Christ, Nancy! Did you think I'd just accept that?' Again, he paused to calm himself before continuing. 'But I'm not here to rehash the past. I simply want to move on with my life, start again. Of course, I'll need your help with that, won't I?' Nancy said nothing so Swindlehurst turned to Marion. 'You'll understand one day, Miss Lane. You'll come to realise what it's really like to be under Nancy's employ, her *rule*. You'll wake up one day and think – *I want a change.* I want to live a life free of secrets. I want to come home from work and share the details of my day with family, friends. And eventually the urge to leave those dammed sunless corridors will become so overwhelming you just can't ignore it any longer.'

Marion cringed under Swindlehurst's watch. But perhaps part of what was making her so uncomfortable was that, even if by just a fraction, she understood.

'But then you'll remember. You can't just walk away, not really.' He turned back to Nancy. 'How can we get another job when we have no record of work experience? No references? No skills we're able to account for. And of course no savings, because you pay us such a pittance.'

'That is nonsense, Edgar. I'd gladly have assisted you in finding a new job, if only you'd asked.'

Swindlehurst laughed. 'Really? Maybe if I'd been someone else. An apprentice, or a skivvy who cleaned the kitchens or maintained the corridors. But I was Head of Intelligence. I'd seen it all – all the times we'd blindsided the police, interfered with their investigations. Do you remember, Nancy, August last year? I came to you, told you I wanted to resign, that I'd found a position I was interested in at a private investigations agency in Glasgow. What happened then?'

'For heaven's sake, Edgar. I've told you countless times I had nothing to do with that.'

Swindlehurst looked at Marion. 'You might not believe it, Miss Lane, but even after my demotion from Head of Intelligence, all I wanted was to resign, to leave peacefully. I felt stifled in my career at Miss Brickett's and I wanted a change. I explained this to Nancy and she seemed disappointed, though not particularly against the idea. But then I received a letter from my future employers in Glasgow. They'd suddenly realised I was not mentally fit to be a private detective. Some obscure reason relating to my wartime records as an operations manager. I'd shown signs of "mental instability with manic tendencies".' He turned back to Nancy. 'Now how on earth did they get hold of those private records?'

Marion watched as the expression on Nancy's face slowly shifted from collection and control to agitation. She didn't know what to think. Was Swindlehurst telling the truth? Was it really possible that Nancy had gone to such lengths to prevent him from leaving Miss Brickett's? Dread settled in her stomach as she considered the implications of the accusation.

'I knew then, I was trapped. I'd never get another job, nothing worth my time at least,' Swindlehurst said. 'So I had no choice but to wait a few more months and then use my insurance policy.' He glanced at the vial. 'How about we call this a severance package.'

Nancy spoke without hesitation or acknowledgement. 'How much?'

'Seven hundred thousand.'

'Don't be ridiculous. I haven't got anything near that amount at my disposal.'

'Then you'll sit there and watch as I post this vial, along with a collection of incriminating documents, to MI5. I'm sure they'll be quite interested in a covert chemical weapons operation going on right beneath their feet.' His voice raised several octaves.

'Don't be a fool, Edgar. If you did that, you'd be just as implicated as the rest of us.'

Swindlehurst looked unconcerned. 'Yes, perhaps I would. Except, you're forgetting something – I've got nothing left to lose. I can't remain at Miss Brickett's, not after the unfortunate complication of Michelle's demise. Someone would have figured out the truth soon enough.' He passed a swift glance at Marion. It made her shudder. 'I am disappearing, changing my name and starting anew, with or without your help. I'll be long gone by the time MI5 come knocking on the bookshop door. But if you pay me the money, I'll leave the vial with you and be on my way without further trouble. I guarantee you'll never hear from me again. I'll carry your secrets to the grave, and you will carry mine.'

For a moment, Nancy did not speak. Marion could hardly breathe, or feel her body. She could not think or formulate a plan. Her mind was numb.

A flash of impatience sparked across Swindlehurst's face. He checked his watch. 'Come, come, do we have a deal?'

'Of course we don't.' Nancy looked at him more intensely, more demandingly than Marion had ever seen her look before.

'You've obviously learned nothing about me these nine years if you believe you can coerce me so easily.'

'Oh, I think I know you rather well indeed.' Swindlehurst gestured to his accomplice.

The brutish man made his way towards Marion. He untied her wrists and lifted her to her feet. She stumbled on unsteady legs. Her eyes were glazed, her head spun. The accomplice dragged her across the room and deposited her on a chair at the table.

The faintest flicker of concern, maybe even fear, crossed Nancy's face. She turned to Swindlehurst and the flicker dissipated. 'What are you doing?'

A penetrating fear hit Marion in the chest. She writhed in her chair as Swindlehurst again put on his gloves and picked up the black vial. He uncorked it and started for Marion.

But then she noticed something through the window.

A glint of steel fluttered up through the air from the street below, it hovered for some seconds, then settled on the windowsill. She quickly averted her gaze and caught Nancy's eye. Swiftly she looked back at the window, then at her watch. Nancy followed her gaze. She understood.

'Very well, then,' Nancy said hastily, turning back to Swindlehurst without missing a beat. He now stood by Marion's side, the vial held carefully in his right hand. 'I'll organise the money this evening. Let her go, please.'

Adrenaline pumped through Marion's body. Her senses come to life, her mind firing a mile a minute. She had to be quick. They'd only have seconds to act.

From the window, an enormous explosion sounded. Despite the fact that Swindlehurst would surely have recognised the pseudo-blast, the manufactured sound of Professor Bal's Distracter, he was not immune to the shock of it. He shuddered and took a step back. The vial in his hand slipped. Marion

284

wasn't sure whether the force of it hitting the ground would cause an explosion or not, but she wasn't willing to find out.

She caught it with her bound hands in mid-air.

It tipped and, as if in slow motion, the sticky liquid fell in a perfect tear-drop from the vial and onto her left little finger. The pain was immediate. She had no choice but to release the vial. It fell to the floor, the awful liquid spilling forth. Thankfully it didn't explode. But the drop that had touched her finger caused a sensation that felt as if every nerve ending in her hand was being burned, cut in pieces and pulled apart. Her arm began to shake. Tears streamed uncontrollably from her eyes as the pain heightened. She could feel her flesh dissolving, her tendons snapping and her bones melting. She couldn't breathe or make a sound and while she could sense a storm of commotion continuing around her, she couldn't make out from whom or what.

In the background, the Distracter's echoing explosion came to a stop. Swindlehurst was no longer by her side and Nancy was no longer seated at the table, nor was Swindlehurst's accomplice.

Marion looked down at her finger. Her fingernail and a quarter more had already dissolved into nothing. A piece of sizzling flesh, scattered with something white that might have once been bone, hung from the tip. Her vision tunnelled. She collapsed and closed her eyes.

'Hey! Look at me!' Kenny had appeared from nowhere and was holding her upright. Her hands were unbound. It was either a few seconds or many hours later. 'We have to get out of here. Nicholas set a fire downstairs.' He pulled Marion to her feet and into the corridor at the top of the staircase. Plumes of smoke billowed up from below. The air was blisteringly hot.

Swindlehurst's accomplice emerged from the room next to the boardroom and started for Kenny. There was a violent scuffle, flaying arms and legs, but Marion didn't have time to get involved. Swindlehurst appeared at the top of the staircase. He stumbled forwards and swung his fist at her face, she ducked. She gripped her wrist on the side of her injured finger, as if to protect it, then lifted her elbow and slammed it into his stomach. He buckled, gasping for breath.

There was a mad rush of bodies and flailing limbs moving up and down the staircase. Marion stumbled forwards in an endorphin-induced fog. She couldn't quite comprehend what she was doing, she only knew she had to keep moving.

Unfortunately, Swindlehurst had risen once more. He lifted Marion off her feet.

She flung her legs forwards and once, twice, three times she missed. The fourth time, however, she connected with his thigh – a mighty thump. Swindlehurst groaned and loosened his grip. She scrambled away.

Swindlehurst's knee caught her in the ribs. A shot of sharp pain surged through her torso. There was no doubt he'd broken a rib. She gasped, but this just made the pain worse as her lungs expanded under the fracture, splitting it even further apart.

She looked up at him. His eyes widened. The madness in his face was terrifying; she couldn't believe how different he'd been just a few moments ago, how calm and collected. He lurched forward. It happened so quickly that Marion had no time to react. She fell backwards down the stairs, somersaulting, head over heels and coming to a stop midway down the staircase. The air here was hotter than anywhere, the smoke thicker.

Swindlehurst was already on top of her, his hands around her neck, stale breath touching her lips. She couldn't breathe. Nothing was left. Swindlehurst's fingers dug into her throat. The room was turning dark and then—

Swindlehurst flew off her as if by some invisible force. Marion brought her hands to her throat as she frantically tried to inhale through her compressed windpipe.

'Get up, UP!' Marion was pulled to her feet, she didn't know by whom until they had reached the bottom of the stairwell. 'Get out, go!' Nancy instructed.

She tried to ask where Kenny was, but no words came out. She fumbled forwards through heavy smoke and roasting heat. She didn't know where the fire was but it must have been close. She stumbled out into the open, along the driveway and out through the large black gates onto the street. It was raining again and the pavement was thick with wet gravel and scattered debris.

Only once the smoke had lifted and her eyes stopped watering, did she see what was in front of her: Mr Nicholas and Preston stood with Swindlehurst's two accomplices firmly restrained between them by three layers of Twister Rope.

Seconds later, Kenny and Nancy emerged from the house dragging Swindlehurst along with them.

'Rupert,' Nancy said, 'come with me. Dinn, follow us.' She turned to Marion. 'The police will be here shortly, we must be gone before they arrive.'

'Wait,' Marion called. She used her good hand to dig under her bra, from where she removed the small black button. She unthreaded its attached wire and the second battery hidden just beneath her arm. She presented it to Nancy. 'Proof, for the council.'

Nancy threaded the wire through her fingers in amazement. She looked up. 'Edgar was certain he'd cleared you of wires.' She inclined her head as the realisation set in. 'I see . . . two wires. Very good.'

Marion nodded, hesitant to fully acknowledge the compliment. 'I did it for Frank.'

23

The Legacy of Sir George Cavendish

The scent of wood polish and freshly brewed coffee met Marion as she stepped inside Frank's office. It was Thursday afternoon, four days since she'd been admitted to the infirmary and half an hour since her discharge.

The recovery had been a difficult one. Hardly anyone had been permitted to visit and time dragged on terribly. Because of the nature of her injury – the fact that her finger had been eaten away by an alchemic substance – Nancy had decided Marion could not be admitted to a hospital on the outside. It would raise questions the agency was unable to answer.

Throughout the passing days, Marion's vitals were monitored, her injured finger cleaned and dressed, a course of pain relief tablets prescribed and her hand and wrist examined for any further signs of dissolving flesh. Fortunately – unlike Helena – the acid had not been allowed the chance to spread.

Marion rubbed the edge of her bandaged stump – it was beginning to throb again – as she settled at Frank's desk to await his arrival. The office was untidy, much as it had been the last two times she'd been there. Boxes lay strewn across the floor, the shelves were packed with books in lofty, slap-dash piles. But unlike the times before, it appeared that things were being unpacked, rather than packed away.

'Marion,' Frank said with a smile as he appeared in the doorway. Marion stood. There was a short pause as they stared at one another across the room. Frank looked unkempt, his hair uncombed and unwashed, a moustache growing wildly on his face. His pale blue shirt was clean but creased, the top button torn from its cotton-thread anchor. He walked across the room and pulled Marion into an embrace. 'Thank you, *thank you*,' he said, as they separated and took their seats on opposite sides of the desk.

Marion's eyes stung with tears. The relief she felt was overwhelming – to be able to sit across from him, to see the familiar lines of his face. 'I'm so happy you're here. And free.'

He laughed softly. 'So am I. How has your recovery been?'

'I'm feeling better.' A half-truth at best. Though her physical state was improving daily, something deeper and less perceptible still gnawed at her conscious. It was as if a hairline fracture had formed in the structure of her life, not quite deep enough to fall apart, but there all the same, awaiting some final, shattering blow.

She wondered if perhaps the same was true for Frank. With everything that had happened, she imagined it would be nearly impossible for him to feel settled and at ease just yet. She searched for the familiar gleam in his eyes. It was still there, albeit faded somewhat.

'Nancy will be joining us shortly. She has a few things to discuss with you.' He paused to roll up his sleeves. 'But before she gets here . . .' His focus turned to the old clock on the bookshelf to his left – the very same one through which Marion had watched his trial. 'You obviously know I wanted you to witness my trial with the council.'

'I presumed so, yes.'

Frank nodded. 'I'm still not certain it was fair of me but – I wanted you to find out before anybody else. And I wanted you to understand, to hear the full story. Nicholas was so set on proving my guilt, I wanted you to be able to decide for yourself before the news was released to the agency at large.'

'Why was he so against you?' Marion asked, realising it was a fact she'd never paid much attention to. Frank shrugged. 'I don't think it was anything in particular. He and White were close, I think, and he just genuinely thought I was guilty. I suppose you could hardly blame him, given the facts.' He looked again at the clock on the bookshelf, then spoke urgently. 'The problem is, Nancy doesn't know you saw any of it, and I think it's best we keep it that way.'

Marion frowned. What else was Nancy unaware of? Did she know Marion and Bill had the map? That Marion had broken into the break room? That she'd seen the cellar beneath, the laboratory?

'As far as she knows, you heard about my conviction through rumour. You were not involved in the investigation until the Circus Ball, where you witnessed Swindlehurst removing something from the Lock Room by chance. I think Professor Bal has mentioned that you visited him, which led you to visit Helena. And of course, she knows what was said between the two of you there.' He patted his chest with a small smile as a knock came at his office door. 'But let's leave it at that. The less you know the better. Do you understand?'

'What about Gillroth?' Marion asked.

'What about him?'

Marion faltered. Since her return to the agency, the memory of Gillroth's warning in his office the day after she'd witnessed Frank's trial had haunted her. In hindsight, his warnings to stay out of the investigation for her own good seemed almost prophetic.

Frank looked at her questioningly, but Marion had no more time to elaborate.

The office door swung open and Nancy stepped inside. Her normally prim and proper appearance was in disarray. Her hair lay in messy waves across her shoulders. Her clothes, which were always well-matched and pressed within an inch of their lives, had been replaced by a dull brown pencil skirt and loose white cardigan.

'Afternoon, Miss Lane.' She sat down next to Frank. Her eyes traced Marion's face, softening as she took in the bruises, the old cuts. 'I hear your recovery has gone well?'

Marion took a moment to answer. Her finger throbbed, her ribs ached. 'I think so. I'm feeling better each day.'

'I'm very happy to hear it. And you've been able to see your friends? Hobb and the others?' It sounded more like a probing query than a casual one and Marion knew this was because Nancy suspected that everything Marion had witnessed at Turnchapel Mews she'd surely relay to Bill as soon as they'd had some time alone. Which was probably quite accurate.

'Bill's visited. Briefly though,' she added, implying nothing serious had been discussed between them yet.

Nancy looked partially relieved. 'Ah . . . well.' She paused, then added, 'I'm very grateful for everything you've done. I don't believe we'd be sitting here,' she gestured to Frank, 'if not for you.'

Marion nodded subtly.

'I'm still rather in shock, to be honest. As much as Edgar and I had our differences, I never suspected he was capable of everything I now know he's done.'

Marion stirred. There was something she needed to know before anything else. 'Is it true what Swindlehurst said? About him trying to resign?'

Nancy looked instantly uncomfortable. 'Edgar's career here has been fraught with complications. He was brilliant as Head of Intelligence, in the beginning at least. He knew how to manage people, how to get the best out of everyone. But the longer he was at the top, the more tyrannical he became. He refused to accept the fact that someone might have an opinion that opposed his own. I was concerned the department would fall to pieces, and considering Intelligence is the heart of the agency, I knew the ramifications of its collapse would be widespread. Of course, I had no idea the demotion would bruise his ego so.'

Not quite the answer she was looking for. She tried again: 'But he said you interfered with his application to the agency in Glasgow. Is that true?'

'Of course not. I didn't even know he had a record of mental instability and whatever else, manic tendencies. If I had, I wouldn't have employed him in the first place.'

Marion wasn't sure she believed that but before she could say anything else, Nancy went on: 'Now, while I think you deserve further explanation on certain matters, I must warn you that due to the nature of the case, everything that is said in this office is strictly confidential.'

'Of course,' Marion said.

'That includes Mr Hobb.'

'Yes. I understand.'

'Good. Now let me begin by apologising. I realise that my absence during the past few days, at such a difficult time for the agency, may have appeared insensitive.'

Insensitive was not the word Marion would've used. Reckless or callous were better.

'I hope, however, that you will soon understand I had little choice.' She loosened her collar.

Marion didn't know what to do with her hands. They were throbbing so painfully that even touching the skin was excruciating. She decided, at last, to place them palm down on the cool mahogany desk.

'I hired Mr Hugo after I realised the trouble Frank was in and how the council believed him to be guilty. I knew I needed an outsider to delve deeper into the investigation than I could at the time. Of course, it was a risk hiring someone so abruptly, even if I trusted him. Which is why I gave Hugo very little background on the case and instead of allowing him free rein with the investigation, I instructed him step by step, asking him to complete task after task without much understanding as to why. After Frank's trial, I asked him to—'

Again she hesitated. Marion knew what she'd asked Hugo to do after the trial: she asked him to find the map. But because Swindlehurst had never actually mentioned the strange parchment in front of her, perhaps it was a topic Nancy hoped to skirt over. Which suited Marion rather perfectly. 'Well it doesn't matter, the point is that Hugo uncovered something even I hadn't known existed – the cellar beneath the break room, the one Edgar mentioned connects to the tunnels beyond the Border and to the laboratory. Mr Hugo found some very interesting evidence down there, I won't go into the details now, but it explains how Edgar slipped past the camera. And several other things.'

Marion wondered how Nancy thought Kenny had found the cellar without the map, since it would have been nearly impossible to locate, had one not known it was there.

'I'd have preferred you not to have heard all that Edgar said,' Nancy added, 'about what was inside that room. But I suppose it's too late for that now.' She leaned back in her chair, not with an air of relaxation but rather exhaustion and defeat. 'I suppose it won't surprise you now to learn that Miss Brickett's has a history that extends far beyond the agency's initiation in 1948. It might, however, surprise you to know that it was Henry Gillroth, not me, who first walked these corridors.'

Marion's heart rapped a little faster.

'Henry and I worked together during the war. And while we went our separate ways after '45, we remained in close contact. One day, I received a letter from Henry – he'd heard I'd been considering opening my own detective agency but had been struggling to find the perfect address. All true, of course. Real estate was not particularly easy to come by after the war. But as always, Henry had a solution. He said that if I were willing to stretch my horizons somewhat, he might have just the perfect venue. A place that had been left to him through a series of rather inauspicious events.' She paused for a moment to stare into the abyss. 'He took me down through the bookshop trapdoor, into the tunnels and onwards for miles. He explained then that the labyrinth's foundations were old, originally a haven for a group of alchemists that had been exiled by the church for meddling with all sorts of strange concoctions, practising what was believed to be sorcery at the time, the devil's work. Which I suppose is quite apt, all things considered.'

The alchemic explosive, Marion presumed. She looked at her hand and felt the deep throb of the Devil's Blood.

'As they are today, the upper floors – those above the stone staircase – were well constructed and grand when I first encountered them. Henry explained they were once intended to be used as upper-class bunkers during the war, a place officials and dignitaries would not only be able to escape the raids in, but live with a certain degree of comfort.'

'Intended? Meaning they weren't used?'

'No, it was only ever a facade – a cover story should anyone ever find the entrance through the bookshop. They'd arrive in the Grand Corridor and see nothing but gleaming floors and well-furnished chambers. But no dignitary has ever set foot inside these walls.' She paused to inhale deeply. 'I must admit my own ignorance and foolishness in the acquisition of Miss Brickett's. I was overwhelmed by the opportunity presented to me – the chance to start a detective agency without the hinderances of legislation and public intrusion, all of which came with opening such an enterprise above ground. Which was why I chose to overlook the catch, the real reason the property existed in the first place.

'After Henry had taken me on a tour through the upper floors, we made our way down the long stone staircase. And although he showed me the entrance to the twisted corridors further on, we did not pass through them. I could see he was reluctant to reveal what lay beyond, the tale of how he'd come to uncover the labyrinth. But in the end, the burden of concealing such a truth was too much. To be quite honest, I sometimes wish he hadn't elaborated at all. Ignorance is bliss, as they say.'

Marion had to agree. She would certainly have chosen to be kept in the dark about Operation Grey Eagle, had it not been the key to clearing Frank's name.

'Shortly after the start of the war,' Nancy went on, 'the labyrinth fell into the hands of a man by the name of Sir George Cavendish, a field marshal for the British Army with a particular and rather obscure fascination with the outer bounds of chemistry and, as it turned out, alchemy. No one is certain how Cavendish uncovered the labyrinth's existence. Perhaps through his extensive research in alchemy he uncovered some reference to the group of alchemists who'd been exiled here centuries ago. Indeed, I believe it was these alchemists who first created the formula for Devil's Blood, at least in part.

'What is certain, however, is that Cavendish was an ambitious man, and brilliantly creative. Much of his early career was spent overseeing operations at Porton Down, especially those involving chemical weaponry testing and production.

I'm not sure what exactly he did there, perhaps he was an advisor of some sort, or something more frivolous. But soon he became distracted, consumed by rumours that the Nazis were producing and testing nerve gas in the concentration camps and that soon enough they'd deploy such measures on the front lines. He believed the British were lagging dangerously behind and that if a full-scale chemical war broke out, the Germans would defeat us in days.

'He began to push countless petitions at Churchill and the War Cabinet, urging them to implement stronger research programmes, provide more funding for his projects at Porton Down. But the government was against the idea, though perhaps not Churchill personally, as the use of chemical and biological weapons had already been outlawed by the Geneva Protocol. There was little point in extensive research on weapons Britain was not allowed to use in actual warfare.

'But Cavendish was not a man who could be dissuaded by laws and treaties. He continued his crusade on the sidelines, in private. Unbeknownst to the Prime Minister or the War Cabinet, Cavendish commissioned a small team of engineers, military personal, experts, consultants and labourers to join him in a covert project known as Operation Grey Eagle. All together I believe there were close to thirty of them – one of whom was Henry Gillroth, recruited mostly for his experience in managing the engineers at other facilities, but also for his particular knowledge in subterranean construction. All members of the operation were assured that everything they did, while highly classified, was completely legal, utterly above board. As I've just explained however, that was not even close to the truth.

'As Edgar enlightened us, Cavendish's project was a disaster in the end. He was ashamed by the failure and I believe he was desperate to erase the whole operation from history. Not only had he commissioned a team under false pretences, putting their lives at risk, dabbling in things he did not understand, but he had nothing to show for it. Fortunately for him, the only people who knew anything about the project were the handful he'd hired to work on it.

'I'm not entirely certain how what happened next came to be, or who was to blame for it, but one by one the members of the project began to die. While navigating the tunnels beyond the Border had been laborious and unnerving before, it had never been dangerous. But then the walls began to shift, trapdoors in the floors to open up. Doors would appear where once there'd been open space. Sections of tunnel would flood without warning. Soon nearly every member of the team was either dead or missing. Personally, I believe it was Cavendish himself who set off the traps, though I'll never be certain if this is true, or know how he did it. He fled to South America shortly after the war and hasn't been seen since. The only other person known to have survived the operation was—'

'Gillroth?' Marion guessed.

Nancy looked reluctant to acknowledge the fact. 'Henry and I both made a choice, all those years ago. Either we disclosed the operation to MI5 and forfeited the opportunity to open a private detective agency in its place, or we finally put the tunnels to good use and in doing so hoped to erase the past. Once we'd chosen the latter, of course, there would be no going back. In choosing to conceal the past, we'd forever be responsible for ensuring Operation Grey Eagle remained entombed. You may struggle to believe this, Miss Lane, but I never knew the details of the operation. Only that it was a chemical weaponry experiment that dabbled in alchemy.'

Marion looked at Frank, trying to judge his expression. She wondered if he accepted Nancy's explanation, and how much of it he'd already known. But his face was difficult to read. She turned away, considering for a moment how Gillroth had managed to escape the tunnels while all his colleagues had perished. But then she remembered what Swindlehurst had all but confirmed at Turnchapel Mews: Gillroth had been the original owner of the map.

Nancy stirred. Perhaps she saw the realisation on Marion's face.

There was silence for a moment. Marion considered pressing Nancy on the details of Gillroth's role in Operation Grey Eagle. But a more urgent question came to her instead. 'Where were you all this time?'

She sighed, as if this were a challenging question to answer. 'Mr Hugo discovered the cellar beneath the break room and tried to contact me immediately. Unfortunately, I was incapacitated at the time. Three days after I was forced to send Frank before the High Council, I received an anonymous letter. I knew immediately it had been sent by an agency employee because it threatened to expose the circumstances of Michelle White's death to the police should I not agree to a list of demands, soon to be made.'

'You had no idea who'd sent it?'

'Not then. But when I arrived at the time and place arranged – all the way in Dublin, I might add – no one was there. I realise now that this was all just a ploy to distract me, for Edgar to ensure I was out of the agency long enough for him to implement the full extent of this plan.'

'Which he did,' Marion said, indignation evident in her voice.

'Yes, for a while—'

Marion cut her off. 'Why didn't you at least tell someone where you were?'

Nancy pursed her lips, clearly put out by Marion's brazen inquisition. 'Because, Miss Lane, I was uncertain of whom to trust. I did, however, keep an eye on the agency from

298

a distance, convinced that soon enough the sender of the letter would reveal themselves, even if by accident. Which is exactly what happened. Around the time of Frank's trial, Edgar suggested to the High Council the idea of the Circus Ball as a way to raise morale for the agency. I paid little attention to it then, I thought it was a good idea, albeit a little extravagant. But while I was in Dublin, that Thursday evening before the ball, I wondered if part of the reason I'd been sent on a wild goose chase was because of the ball. Was someone trying to distract me from what was going on with the organisation of the event? Fortunately, Professor Bal had already realised there was something off with the whole thing and told Mr Hugo to keep an eye on Edgar until I returned.'

'But after the ball and everything that happened,' Marion said, her voice raw and tired, 'you still stayed away?'

'That was not my choice. The morning after the ball I received another letter. This time it was signed by Edgar. Obviously, he realised there was no longer any need to remain anonymous. He gave me the address of the house in Turnchapel Mews and told me to meet him there that evening, alone.' She finished on a sigh. 'Perhaps I should have taken someone with me, or prepared myself more, but I was convinced I could handle Edgar alone. As I said, I greatly underestimated the extent of his malice. Had you not been there, Miss Lane, things would've turned out very differently indeed.'

'Did you use the recording from the wire I was wearing? In Swindlehurst's trial, I mean?' Although she hadn't been told the details of Swindlehurst's fate, or that of his accomplices, she knew he'd been convicted by the High Council of White's murder. It was a conclusion she'd hoped would satisfy her, and in some ways it had. The case was closed, Frank was off the hook. But still a sense of unease remained, the cause of which she couldn't quite identify.

'Most of it,' Nancy said. 'It caused a stir, as you can imagine, since up until that point none of the High Council knew about Operation Grey Eagle. Like everyone outside this room, other than Henry and Edgar – and to an extent, Miss White – they believed the tunnels beyond the Border were simply off-limits on account of their hazardous nature. I'd preferred for it to have remained that way, but here we are.'

Marion wondered how the council had felt about the secret Nancy and Gillroth had been keeping from them. She also wondered what ramifications the release of this secret would have on the running of the agency. Because now, by Marion's count (excluding herself, Bill and Kenny), there were four more people at Miss Brickett's who knew the truth – Spragg, Simpkins, Nicholas and Frank. Four more hearts to bear the weight of Sir Cavendish's legacy.

The notion led to a question, one Marion hadn't thought to ask until then. 'Why didn't you just clear out the laboratory when you opened the agency?' Her tone was accusatory, but she didn't care. 'If you really wanted to wipe the history books of Operation Grey Eagle, you could have removed the evidence quite easily.'

'I didn't think it was necessary, or possible. I'd never been beyond the Border myself, never seen the laboratory, never heard of the slipway that connects to the cellar. Gillroth gave Michelle the position of Border Guard mostly because he believed she needed to feel important, useful. He asked her to inform us if anyone crossed the Border but really the role was redundant, as the laboratory was hidden within miles of impassable tunnels.' She added, a little more carefully, 'That is what Gillroth promised me, anyway.' There was a subtext here, Marion realised, something Nancy couldn't quite admit: there were things Gillroth had kept secret, even from her.

'But I have now,' she went on, 'in case you're wondering. The tunnel that connects to the cellar has been sealed off. There's no way anyone could reach the laboratory now.'

There was a long pause. Frank looked uncomfortable and agitated, as if too much had been said and the weight of it was pressing on his nerves.

Eventually Nancy wandered across the office to the bookshelf. She caressed the fracture-lined vase Marion had seen on her last visit. 'I think that perhaps we have said all there is to say for the time being.' She walked over to Marion's chair and placed a cold hand on her shoulder. 'And again, thank you.'

'Are you going to tell David about his stepbrother?' Marion asked, as Nancy turned for the door. She wasn't sure if Nancy would be surprised that she knew the link between Asbrey and David, but it was hardly something she could be reprimanded for, after everything.

Nancy surveyed her with suspicion, then spoke: 'We told David when we hired him that Ned disappeared one evening and that was all we knew. It was the truth then.'

'But it's not the truth now. The least you could do is tell him his stepbrother is dead.'

'Miss Lane,' Nancy interrupted, her tone now less understanding, more severe. 'I have tried to explain as best I can the need for discretion in such matters. David has always assumed his stepbrother died in the tunnels, what use is there in confirming the fact? And what Asbrey discovered is of no significance to David. The agency's future and all our lives depend on Operation Grey Eagle remaining a secret. The fewer people who are aware of the full truth, the better. I've already told far more people than I'd ever hoped to. But that is where it ends. No more. Am I clear?'

Marion looked at Frank. He nodded subtly. 'Yes, of course.'

'Good.' She smiled briefly and turned to leave.

Marion felt as if the ground was shifting beneath her. All her hopes about what she'd accomplish as an Inquirer, all the good Miss Brickett's was doing for the people of London, it all seemed less altruistic knowing the foundation on which the agency was based. It made Marion question her own blind loyalty and wonder what other secrets Nancy kept from her staff.

Marion waited until the door closed before turning back to Frank. There was something else she needed to know.

'You can ask me anything,' Frank said, perhaps sensing her unease.

'What has the agency done with Swindlehurst and the others from Turnchapel Mews? Are they going to be sent to the Holding Chambers?'

It took Frank an uncomfortably long time to answer and when he did, the words came out in something of a whisper, as if he were hoping not to say them at all. 'They'll be sent there, yes.'

'So they're real, then.'

Frank paled as he ran his fingers through his hair. 'I'm afraid so. It's difficult to explain the intricacies of the laws that govern a place like this. With all its secrets. I didn't know anything about Operation Grey Eagle until a few days ago, for example. And I don't know much else about the Holding Chambers, either.' His tone deepened. 'I'd advise against asking Nancy about them. As I said to you earlier, the less you know about everything the better.'

He got up and poured them each a drink, whisky this time. He paced the office silently as Marion gazed at the globe spinning on the desk, many uncomfortable feelings rising up inside her.

'There is something I've been meaning to tell you.' He was trying to keep his features calm, but he wasn't doing a very good job. He almost looked as if he might cry. 'When I was in the Lock Room the night of Michelle's murder, standing over her while she choked on her own blood, I knew things at the agency were going to take a turn for the worse. I feared what it would mean for all of us, but especially you.

'I didn't understand it; to be honest, for a moment I even wondered if I had entered some sort of crazed trance during which I'd killed Michelle without realising it. I was afraid. Confused. I thought about what would happen if I was convicted of the murder and sent away. Not only did I wonder how you'd cope with the news, but I feared what danger you'd be in from the real murderer.' He finished his whisky and sat down.

'It was me, Marion. I bought the house from your grand-mother. Those were the papers I brought for her to sign.'

Marion stared at him.

'I had intended to for a while, as soon as Dolores put it on the market in fact. But time got away from me. Then, after Michelle's murder, I knew I couldn't wait any longer. I wouldn't have the chance if I was sent away.'

Marion forced herself to breathe. 'I don't understand.'

Frank lowered his gaze. He looked ashamed, regretful. 'The house. I wanted to give it to you. But,' he took a breath and started again. 'I made a promise to your mother once. If anything happened to her, I'd step in, look after you when you needed it. Not just emotionally, financially too. That's why I offered you a position at the agency in the first place. I knew your job with Felix at the garage had ended and that if another opportunity was not presented to you swiftly, you'd allow your grandmother to marry you off. That was not the life your mother would've wished for you.

'But after the night of the murder, I reconsidered everything. I still wanted to buy the house, and Dolores and I looked over the paperwork and came to an agreement on the price.

She told me she was planning a move to America and would prefer you to come along with her. Had it been any other day, I'd have been against the idea. But with everything at the agency hanging by a thread, I thought perhaps Dolores was right for once.

'That's why I agreed to allow Dolores the chance to speak to you first, to offer you the opportunity to move with her. I hated the idea of keeping the truth of the sale from you but Dolores insisted that if you heard I'd placed the house in your name, you'd never even consider her offer.' He reached over the desk to hold her hand. 'I planned to tell you the house was yours the Monday after the Induction Ceremony. I knew I wouldn't be able to see you at my office but I thought maybe I could slip back after the trial . . . of course that turned out to be impossible.'

A bitterness welled up inside Marion to the point where she could no longer contain it. She didn't know if the feeling was directed at Frank, her grandmother or the situation in general. She tossed the entire glass of whisky down her throat.

'I know,' he said, 'and I'm sorry. I really was just doing what I thought was best for you. So was Dolores. I suppose we were both foolish to think you'd have left anyway.'

Marion closed her eyes for a moment. She was frustrated with Frank for not telling her the truth, and yet she found it impossible to hold any anger towards him, not after everything he'd done. 'Yes, you were. Thank you, for buying the house. For trying to protect me. But I'm an adult, Frank. I want to make my own decisions about things.'

Frank pressed his hand more firmly into hers. 'You're right, of course. But the house is still yours, as I promised. If you'd like to move back in, I will assist with the practicalities.'

Marion smiled irresolutely, a mix of emotions brewing inside her. She was grateful, shocked, relieved. Frank had lied to her, something she thought – *hoped* – him incapable of. But he had done so with the best intentions and now 16 Willow Street was hers again, after everything. She wouldn't go back to live there now, she thought, but knowing she had the option was comforting. Swindlehurst had been right about one thing: the sunless corridors of Miss Brickett's could be stifling.

24

The Reunion

Marion stepped into her room in the staff quarters for the first time since her return to the agency. Everything was exactly as she'd left it: the notepad she'd used to explain the details of the clockwork bomb on her bedside table, Kenny's cigarette butts in an ashtray by the wash basin, the gown from the night of the Circus Ball a crumpled mess on the floor.

It was really just a blink in time since she'd been there last. But of course it all felt so different now.

She hung up the torn dress, emptied the ashtray and pulled out a wooden box from under her bed. Inside was a roll of parchment, a monocle and a small crystal vial, wrapped in silk. She removed the map, then lay on the bed and stared vacantly at the old stone ceiling above her, gaunt grey and lined with cracks. Her fingers caressed the parchment, the frayed edges, the shallow furrows of its surface. Her thoughts wandered: to Michelle White and Helena Jansen, the violent conclusion to their lives. Their families, whoever they were, would never know the truth, never find closure.

A leaden sense of unease weighed down on her as she recalled all the secrets she was now forced to keep – Ned Asbrey's death, the extent of Swindlehust's treachery, Michelle White's final moments. And of course, what really lay beyond the Border. She flinched as she looked at her mutilated finger and felt the deep throb in what was left of it. Another lie she'd have to tell.

There was a knock at the door. Quickly, she slipped the parchment into the box and placed it back under her bed.

'Come in.'

Kenny entered. It was the first time they'd seen each other since leaving Turnchapel Mews. As always, he was a vibrant flash of colour against the dullness. He smiled and more than ever it seemed to illuminate his face. Marion felt a hint of warmth return to her body. She smiled back, a knee-jerk reaction.

'Blazes, Lane,' he frowned jovially at her, then at the room. 'This place is a mess. You feeling all right?' He settled next to her, slouching against the headboard, his legs stretched out lazily in front of him.

'Getting there,' she said, pulling her blouse sleeve over her injured hand. The bed was so narrow that her thigh touched his, firm and warm. She didn't mind. 'You look well, though. And the hair's back to normal,' she teased, glancing at his thicket of golden locks, slicked back to reveal a perfect side parting.

He gave her a one-sided grin. 'Thanks. You've no idea the effort it takes.'

'Oh, I believe it.' She recalled the array of grooming products she'd seen in his room.

He looked at her covered hand. 'And what's that about? You're not going to try and pretend you've still got ten fingers?'

'Not sure how I'm supposed to explain it to anyone.'

'Well they all know you helped Nancy apprehend Swindlehurst, just say it caught a bullet or something.'

Marion shrugged a dismissive reply. She didn't want to think about Swindlehurst, or even hear his name spoken out loud. Not here in the comfort of her room.

'Listen, I wanted to apologise for my delay in getting back to the house in Clapham. I tried to gather help at the agency as quickly as I could but—'

Marion cut him off. 'It's fine. You did what you could. The Distracter was brilliant, it saved us actually. And just in time, too.'

'It was all I could think of to create a diversion while I slipped past the guard outside.' He shook his head.

She put her hand behind her back. She really wanted to talk about something else. 'And the next step for you? Are you staying?' She tensed, waiting for his reply, hoping.

He grinned, as if he knew what she wanted to hear. 'Yeah, I am. Though I think it's more because Nancy doesn't want me to leave now, not with everything I know.'

Marion's stomach turned. A mix of relief and apprehension at Kenny's permanent assignment at Miss Brickett's. She knew he'd endured a similar meeting with Nancy and Frank just before her own. She presumed that meant he now knew everything she did. Another reluctant addition to Nancy's circle of trust. 'Right, probably not.' She touched his arm, removing her hand a second later than she'd intended. 'But I'm happy you're staying.'

Kenny pulled out a cigarette, slipped it between his lips and lit up.

'And I wanted to say thank you, by the way,' she added.

'For?'

'Not telling Nancy anything about the map, or my trip into the laboratory.'

'You're welcome.' He exhaled a trail of smoke. 'Though I'll tell you, it was just luck I didn't have to.'

'What do you mean?'

He looked at her, the cigarette loose between his lips. 'Well, I tried to contact Nancy the night before the Circus Ball, but

308

no one knew where she was. If I had got hold of her then, I'd have had to mention you were involved, there wouldn't have been another way to play it. I doubt she would've believed I found the cellar without the map. Luckily, by the time I reached her, the whole thing was over. I decided to alter the truth a little.'

'How?'

'I just said I'd been following Swindlehurst since the night of the Circus Ball, just as Bal had instructed me to do. And before he went to remove the safe from the Lock Room, he entered the cellar to clean out his things. In other words, I followed him there, didn't need the map at all.'

'Oh,' Marion said, her mind lagging and exhausted.

'But listen, Lane,' his tone was earnest and he angled his body so that he was now facing her head on. 'That map is trouble. It needs to go.'

'I know.'

'So? Where is it?'

'Bill has it.' She didn't want to lie, but something inside her recoiled at the thought of Kenny taking the map, of getting rid of it.

A look of annoyance crossed Kenny's face. 'And?'

'*And?*'

'What are you planning to do with it?'

'Destroy it probably. I don't know yet.' Another lie.

He looked unsatisfied. 'Well, you can discuss it with Hobb tonight. I'm not interested in covering for the two of you again—'

'Tonight?' Marion said, ignoring the latter part of Kenny's sentence. She'd been desperate to see everyone again, but by the time she'd been released from the infirmary and finished her meeting at Frank's office, it was long past working hours and she assumed they'd all gone home.

Kenny looked confused for a moment. 'Oh, I thought they told you. Maybe it was supposed to be a surprise.'

'Well you've ruined it now, so go on.'

'Bill and Jessica have organised a "welcome home, get well soon, happy you're back" thing. Happening in the common room in a few.'

'Really?' She smiled, a surge of relief flooding through her, rooted in the knowledge that seeing everyone again might reignite the sense of normality she so craved.

'Maybe you can introduce me to the others, properly?'

'Worried they won't like you?' she teased.

'No, because that's impossible.' He laughed, put out his cigarette and got to his feet. 'Anyway, ready for a drink?'

'A bottle, actually.' They left her room together and crossed the corridor into the common room.

Jessica and Maud greeted them at the door. Marion led the introductions, ignoring the look of fascination on Jessica's face as she looked from Marion to Kenny and back again – interpreting, analysing. She would be wondering why they'd arrived together, most likely, and if there was anything more than professionalism between them. In fact, Marion had been wondering the same of late.

'I can't believe what happened,' Jessica said a little while after, thankfully choosing to refocus her attention on Marion alone. 'I can't believe it was Edgar in the end . . . and the Circus Ball.'

'We were all out cold from the drugs, you know,' Maud cut in.

'You'd have been out cold anyway,' Jessica replied.

'What's that supposed to mean?' Maud frowned, then continued without waiting for a reply. 'Anyway, we're glad you're back. And alive.' She looked at Marion's left hand and for a while seemed to be deciding whether to ask what had happened. Fortunately, she didn't.

The group was joined by Amanda, who greeted Marion with only slightly more enthusiasm than usual. She then moved off to the central table, where several second years had set up a game of rummy and a line of drinks. The other four remained behind: Maud and Kenny exchanging jokes as naturally as if they'd known each other for years, Marion and Jessica catching up on news. The fling with Roger from maintenance was over (Jessica seemed more relieved than upset at this), Preston was off sick with the flu, John Perry had been assigned the position of full-time Filing Assistant (much to his dismay), Amanda hadn't received any further promotions and Rakes had taken over the position of Special Case Officer from Swindlehurst in addition to retaining her role as head of the Intelligence Department.

'. . . speaking of,' Rakes chimed in, materialising at Marion's side. 'Evening.' She nodded at Jessica then turned back to Marion. 'Mind if I have a word?' She pulled a file from her briefcase once Jessica had taken her leave. 'Bleeding obvious now, isn't it?'

Marion looked at the file labelled *SI 0087. The Scorch*.

'Bloody Swindlehurst,' Rakes elaborated. 'He was never against freezing operations at Intelligence because he cared about this case. He just didn't want the Inquirers to focus their attention on White's murder instead.' She sighed. 'Anyway, as you've obviously heard, I've currently got quite a lot going on and I thought you might be interested in helping me out.' She handed Marion the file. 'Since you've recently demonstrated a particular knack for tricky investigations. Would you be interested in coming on board again?'

Marion's chest swelled. Reassignment to the Scorch case was exactly the sort of thing she needed, a distraction from her thoughts, a pathway back into the comfortable reality she'd been forced to abandon the last few weeks. 'Really?'

311

'Can't think of anyone better suited.' Rakes extended her hand and they shook. 'Well done, Lane. On everything.' She looked past Marion and towards the fireplace, where Bill had just arrived with a bottle of wine. He caught Marion's eye and waved her over. 'You're in demand tonight, better leave you to it. I'll see you in my office Monday morning.'

'I've been reassigned to the Scorch case,' Marion said to Bill after they'd hugged and greeted. She sat down on the couch beside him. 'Can you believe it?'

'Of course I can.' He poured them each a glass of wine. 'I'm sure Amanda will be disappointed to hear it.'

They laughed.

'How was your meeting with Nancy and Frank, by the way?' Bill asked a while later.

Marion inhaled deeply. There was a lot she and Bill still had to discuss – her recent acquisition of 16 Willow Street, the contents of the wooden box under her bed and what they were going to do with it. But most importantly, everything Nancy had told her not to repeat. It wasn't much of a decision really, whether to tell him or not. Of course she would.

'It was interesting,' she said. 'I'll tell you everything, so long as you're sure you really want to know?'

'Course I do,' he said without hesitation. 'But, maybe not tonight. There's a time and place, as they say. I'm just so happy you're back, Mari.' He squeezed her hand, then looked across the room to where Kenny was standing, still rubbing his eyes in glee at whatever Maud was saying. He released her hand. 'Your new friend seems to be fitting in.'

Marion watched Bill's features stiffen, his eyes narrow. 'Go on,' she said tersely, 'get it off your chest.'

Bill turned to her, slighted. 'He's just so . . .' He seemed to take a while to choose the right word, or at least the most polite version of the right word. '*Loud.*'

Marion hooked her arm through his, pulling him towards her. 'Oh come on. I think the two of you will be sharing a bottle of Scotch in a few months.' She really hoped she was right. 'Just give him a chance.'

Bill rolled his eyes and threw back the last of his wine. 'Right.' He mumbled something under his breath but Marion wasn't listening.

Her focus had drifted to the other side of the common room, to a lone armchair where David sat, a pint resting on his knee and below it a dirty plaster cast. She drew a breath as they caught each other's eye. 'Excuse me for a moment.'

Bill frowned, then looked at David. He opened his mouth, as if to discourage her from whatever she was about to do, but changed his mind. He obviously wasn't interested in reconciling with David, but perhaps he realised it was something Marion needed to do. 'Go on, then.'

She made her way across the room and kneeled down beside David's chair. 'Evening.'

He said nothing, utterly uninterested.

'How's the leg?'

He finished his pint and set the empty tankard down on the floor, then picked up the crutch that lay next to it. 'It's bloody painful, thanks for asking. I still can't walk properly.'

Marion sighed. 'Listen, David. There's something I need to tell you. About your stepbrother.'

At this, he turned to face her. His blunt features twisted, the smallest show of surprise. She knew she couldn't tell him everything, but at the very least she felt he deserved to know how his stepbrother had died. 'As you probably know, I became involved in the White murder case,' she began. He looked away again as she spoke. 'And there's something Swindlehurst told me that I think you ought to know.' She waited for a moment, preparing for the significance of what she was about to say. David caught her eye, prompting her to continue. She told him then, as delicately as she could, that Swindlehurst and Ned had had a disagreement the night he disappeared about something Ned suspected lay across the Border and what they should do about it. 'There was a scuffle,' she said, trying to insert as much truth into the story as she dared, 'Swindlehurst shoved Ned up against the wall, harder than he intended I think. Ned hit his head against a sharp rock.'

David paled, his lips parted in shock. 'Swindlehurst? I'd heard they were friends but . . .' he trailed off.

Marion took his hand. He flinched but didn't pull away. 'Swindlehurst was devastated by it, I really think that. But he was a coward too. He didn't want to face the consequences. That's why he started the rumour about Ned crossing the Border and he planted Ned's bag outside White's office to make it looked like he'd disappeared down there. I'm so sorry, David. I really am.'

David stared blankly into the distance, unmoving, his eyes slowly filling with tears. Marion pressed her hand more tightly into his. Witnessing his devastation was more painful than she'd imagined. Perhaps because she'd previously thought him incapable of such emotions.

He turned to Marion, wiped his eyes on the back of his sleeve. 'The last time I saw him we had an argument, something petty. I can't even remember what about, but I told him what a useless git he was. I'll never be able to apologise for that.'

'I'm so sorry,' she repeated, her voice wavering.

David said nothing more for a while, his features unmoved. Then he seemed to gather himself, to remember where he was and with whom he was speaking. His mouth twisted into an unpleasant expression – something between a leer and a scowl. He got up, steadying himself with the crutch. 'I suppose you're not able to tell me anything else? What Ned thought was down there in the tunnels? Where Swindlehurst is now?'

'David, I don't—'

He held up a hand to silence her. 'It's okay. I understand. Thanks anyway.' He threw his bag over his shoulder, nodded and limped away.

Marion sighed and made her way back to Bill, now seated at the central table with everyone else, halfway through a spirited game of rummy. She felt a stab of compassion for David, the fractured truth he'd have to come to terms with. But he wasn't the only one. She took a large swig of wine and closed her eyes for a fleeting moment, allowing the alcohol to filter through her system, still her thoughts. And amid the warmth of the crackling fire, surrounded by the laughter of her colleagues and friends, it was surprisingly easy to believe that despite the awful start to her first year at Miss Brickett's, everything was going to be okay now.

She raised a glass to toast the table. They turned to look at her. 'To new beginnings.'

'*To new beginnings,*' the group chimed in reply.

Edgar Swindlehurst was blindfolded and gagged as he stepped onto a steel platform somewhere within the grim bowels of the earth. The platform shifted under his weight. He righted himself, sweaty fingers catching a cold metal chain in front of him. There was a ripping, grinding sound, a moment of silence and then the platform began to move.

Down, down, down.

It shuddered to a halt several seconds later, then tipped sideways, forcing Edgar to step off. He tore off his blindfold and spat out the wad of material in his mouth. But there was hardly anything to see of course, even as his eyes adjusted to the darkness. Only a shallow pool of light spilling through the hole from which he'd been lowered and the grey shadow of the platform as it was pulled upwards and away. There was a loud clang as the platform reached the ceiling and sealed the hole, and with it the last snatch of light was extinguished.

Edgar shivered as he stared into the utter blackness, trying to control the rising terror inside him. If he strained his ears, he could just make out the writhing groans of his two accomplices as they came to terms with their own private hells next door. They wouldn't last more than a week down here, neither of them. And although Edgar feared the eternal misery of the Holding Chambers as much as anyone, in a way he'd prepared for this.

He'd find a plan B. However long it took.

Acknowledgements

This book would not exist without my agent, Hayley Steed. You saw potential in what was certainly an unready manuscript and had faith in my ideas and imagination even more than I did. For that, and your eternal enthusiasm (and tolerance of my never-ending stream of panicked emails), I am so grateful.

I'm also so thankful to everyone at the Madeleine Milburn Literary Agency for their professionalism and efficiency. Special mention to the foreign rights super-team Sophie Pélissier and Liane-Louise Smith for their continuous drive to get Marion Lane translated across the globe.

I was incredibly blessed to have two British editors work with me on this book; Katie Brown, whose insight, sharp eye and editing prowess helped me brainstorm through plot holes and murky timelines and Rachel Neely, who swept in so masterfully and without any hesitation – you have both been a dream to work with.

Additional thanks the marvellous team at Trapeze/Orion, who guided me through the publication process with such proficiency. Particular thanks to project editor Clarissa Sutherland, copyeditor Ilona Jasiewicz and proofreader Fraser Crichton, as well as cartographer Mike Hall for bringing my muddled sketch of the agency map to life and Micaela Alcaino for the most glorious cover I have ever seen!

To my American editor, cheerleader and story-alchemist, Laura Brown, thank you for all the laborious hours you spent helping me shape, hone and elevate this book to a level I would never have managed alone. I'm so thrilled to have someone of your calibre in my corner.

A huge thank you to the booksellers, librarians, reviewers and bloggers who have taken the time to read and promote Marion Lane. You're my heroes!

Mom, thank you for introducing me to the world of literature and language, for teaching me how to read and write, for your early proofreads and grammar checks on this book and, most importantly, for your love and support.

Dad, you and your eccentric imagination were without doubt the inspiration for this novel's many bizarre gadgets. I will never forget the buttered-bread-cat turbine we discussed in depth all those years ago, perhaps that's where it started.

Ben, when I was imagining what particular skill set Marion Lane should have, I immediately thought of you and your love for mechanics and repair. I think it makes you both so cool.

To my dearest friends: Tarryn, Savannah, Derusha, Jade, Beverley, Carin and Natalia – my fellow apprentices in this tricky world – thank you for your undiluted encouragement, even though I'm sure you thought that suspending my chiropractic career to write a novel was probably a bit nuts.

Connie, Wildrie, Hildegard, Ric and Angie, thank you for welcoming me into your lovely family so completely and unconditionally.

Willie, you have been there through the best and worst of this writing journey and have cheered me on all the way. You never had a doubt my book would be published, even before you'd read it. Thank you. I love you.

Finally, to the majestic cities and their vibrant underworlds which inspired this tale, London and Valletta, this story is yours.

The Wartime Gadgets that
Inspired Miss Brickett's

The wondrous gadgets developed in the Workshop at *Miss Brickett's Investigations and Inquiries* are, as you might've guessed, figments of my eccentric imagination. For inspiration, I'd imagine what contraptions would be of most use to an Inquirer scouring the streets of London under heavy disguise, trailing criminals, slipping past security systems and breaking through impenetrable locks.

But dreaming up gadgets of espionage and subterfuge from scratch turned out to be more difficult than I'd initially assumed. I realised that, in order to bring these bizarre creations to life, I needed a scientific, real-world foundation for each. After some research, I discovered — much to my delight and fascination — that a plethora of peculiar spycraft tools *did* (and does) exist. Here are some of my favourites.

The Vagor Compass, *Miss Brickett's* mystical gadget capable of tracking a target fitted with a paired Vagor Stone, is loosely modelled around the Shoe Transmitter. This instrument, designed and used by the KGB in the 1960s, consisted of an inconspicuous microphone, wiring and battery, hidden in the heel of a target's shoe. The compromised footwear was planted in the enemy's hotel room by an informed maid or double agent, who was also responsible for activating the transmitter (when the time was right) by removing a small pin from the heel. The nifty contraption allowed nearby operatives, in possession of a special receiver, to eavesdrop on the target's secret conversations via transmitted radio waves. The device was a hit for the Soviets and only abandoned in the late 70s, when more sophisticated gadgets emerged.

The Shoe Transmitter, however, was by no means the KGB's only invention for collecting *Kompromat* (compromising intelligence) from the West. Indeed, the organisation developed a wide range of miniature listening devices and spy cameras, similar to the button transmitter Marion wears on her treacherous mission to Turnchapel Mews. While on assignments, KGB agents were often fitted with tiny cameras capable of taking one or two photographs. The cameras, delicate and tricky to operate, were hidden in everything from rings, bracelets, reading glasses, clothing, suitcases, cigar boxes and handbags. Even pigeons! You name it, the Soviets likely tried to hide a camera in it.

One of my absolute favourite real-life gadgets is "disappearing" or "invisible" ink, a fabulous invention that's been around — in some form or another — since the 16th century. But unlike the ease with which *Miss Brickett's* Grey Ink can be employed and read, the procedure of relaying a message in disappearing ink was arduous, complicated and oftentimes unsuccessful. During WWI, the Allies adopted the KISS methodology — "keep it simple stupid" — by using good old lemon juice which, if dried on white paper, vanished. When the message was ready to be de-coded, the paper was bathed in an iodine solution, illuminating the script. Easy, right? Not quite. The Germans, forever determined to outsmart their enemies, quickly realised that any and all lemon-scented documents likely harboured a secret message, forcing the Allies to up their game. It was the Soviets, however, who eventually developed the most advanced and effective recipe for invisible ink in the late 50s. The special gel-like substance dried instantly, leaving no imprint and rendering it completely undetectable unless placed under UV light. The invention was so brilliant that it's still in use today, though as a fanciful gizmo rather than a tool of international spycraft.

Apart from tracking suspects and passing on secret messages, the Inquirers of *Miss Brickett's* and the spies of WWII and the Cold War also required discreet methods of stalling and incapacitating their targets. Marion is unfortunate enough to face a wave of poison darts while on her secret journey through *Miss Brickett's* out-of-bounds corridors, but the real-life version of these noxious gadgets is no less terrifying. The most infamous example was the "Bulgarian Umbrella", the handle of which contained an air-powered mechanism capable of ejecting a pin-sized pellet with alarming speed. The pellets were filled with poison, most commonly ricin, which — once released into the target's bloodstream — caused a slow and painful death. The deadly umbrella was successfully used on numerous occasions (largely by the Bulgarian secret service and KGB), one of which was in the assassination of Bulgarian novelist and journalist, Georgi Markov, in London in 1978.

Credits

Orion Fiction would like to thank everyone at Orion who worked on the publication of *Marion Lane and the Midnight Murder*.

Agent
Hayley Steed

Editor
Rachel Neely

Copy-editor
Ilona Jasiewicz

Proofreader
Fraser Crichton

Editorial Management
Clarissa Sutherland
Charlie Panayiotou
Jane Hughes
Alice Davis
Claire Boyle

Audio
Paul Stark
Amber Bates

Contracts
Anne Goddard
Paul Bulos
Jake Alderson

Design
Lucie Stericker
Joanna Ridley
Nick May
Clare Sivell
Helen Ewing

Finance
Jennifer Muchan
Jasdip Nandra
Rabale Mustafa
Elizabeth Beaumont
Levancia Clarendon
Tom Costello